The Language of Trees

By Ilie Ruby

THE LANGUAGE OF TREES

The Language of Trees

ILIE RUBY

AVON

An Imprint of HarperCollins*Publishers*

This book is a work of fiction. The characters, incidents, and dialogue are drawn from the author's imagination and are not to be construed as real. Any resemblance to actual events or persons, living or dead, is entirely coincidental.

HarperCollins books may be purchased for educational, business, or sales promotional use. For information please write: Special Markets Department, HarperCollins Publishers, 10 East 53rd Street, New York, NY 10022.

FIRST AVON PAPERBACK EDITION PUBLISHED 2010.

Designed by Diahann Sturge

Library of Congress Cataloging-in-Publication Data
Ruby, Ilie.
The language of trees / Ilie Ruby.—1st Avon pbk. ed.
p. cm.
ISBN 978-0-06-189864-8 (pbk.)
1. Young women—Fiction. 2. Self-realization in women—Fiction. I. Title.
PS3618.U324L36 2010
813'.6—dc22 2009045027

10 11 12 13 14 OV/RRD 10 9 8 7 6 5 4 3 2 1

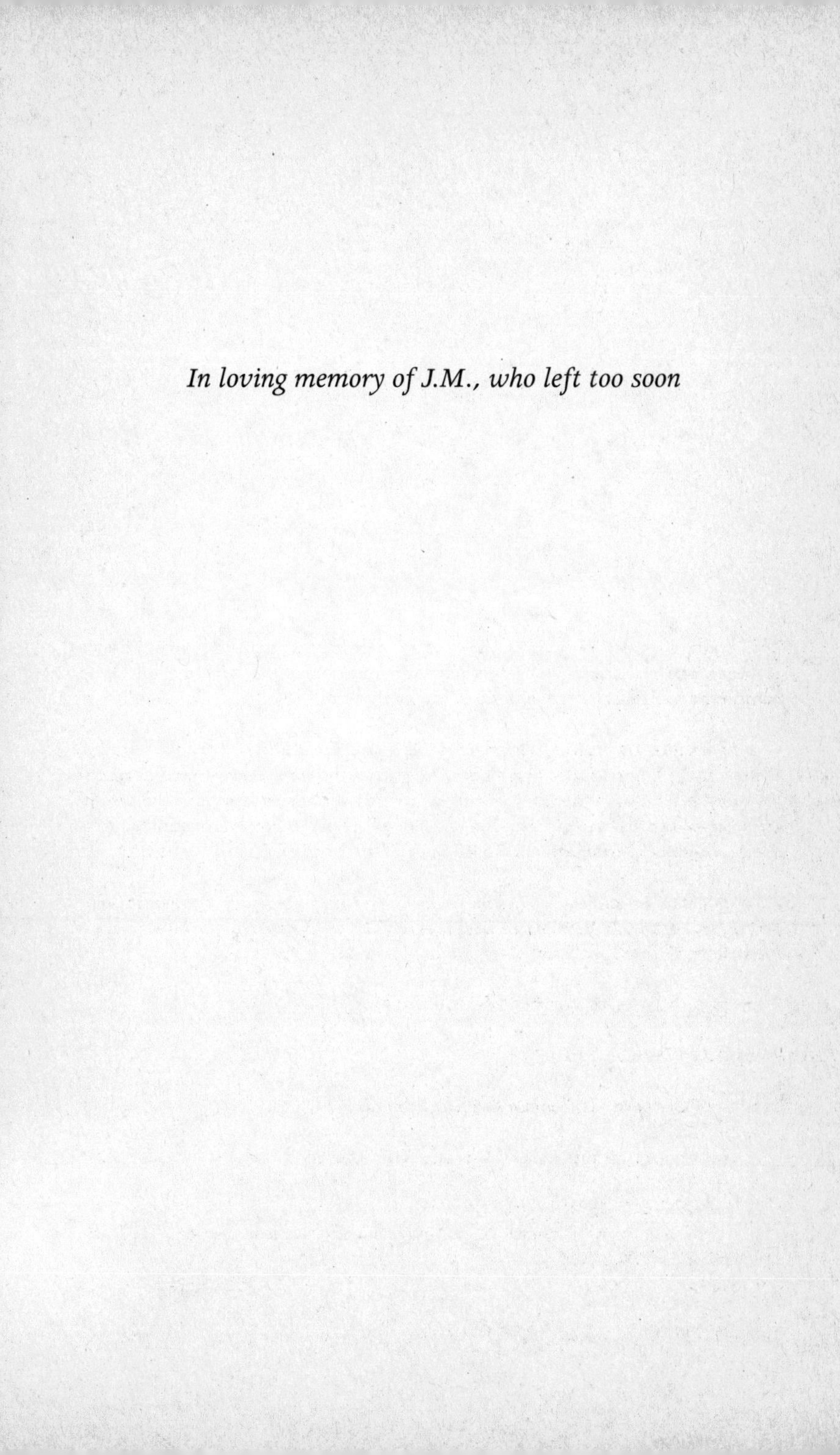

In loving memory of J.M., who left too soon

Acknowledgments

I WOULD LIKE TO thank the following people who have taught me such insightful things about writing over the years: Tony DeFusto, Dr. James Ragan, Shelly Lowenkopf, James W. Brown, the late James O'Connell, Dan Smetanka, and the community at Grub Street Writers in Boston.

MANY EYES HAVE PASSED across these pages, and I am grateful to all, but for their enduring friendship and unwavering belief in me and this book: David Flynn, James Fedolfi, Stephen Bourassa, and Jill Rosenfeld. Thanks to George V. Barden and the people of Canandaigua for verifying facts and folklore, and the good folks at Ganondagan State Historic Site for letting me explore just a little bit of their beautiful land. Thanks to Sally Wofford-Girand of Brick House Literary Agents for keeping the faith, and to Lucia Macro and her team at Avon/HarperCollins, for their vision and enthusiasm in making this a reality.

THANKS FINALLY TO MY husband, who will travel to distant lands with me and take momentous leaps to make visions come true, and to my three children, now home from Africa, for teaching me the true meaning of resiliency and second chances.

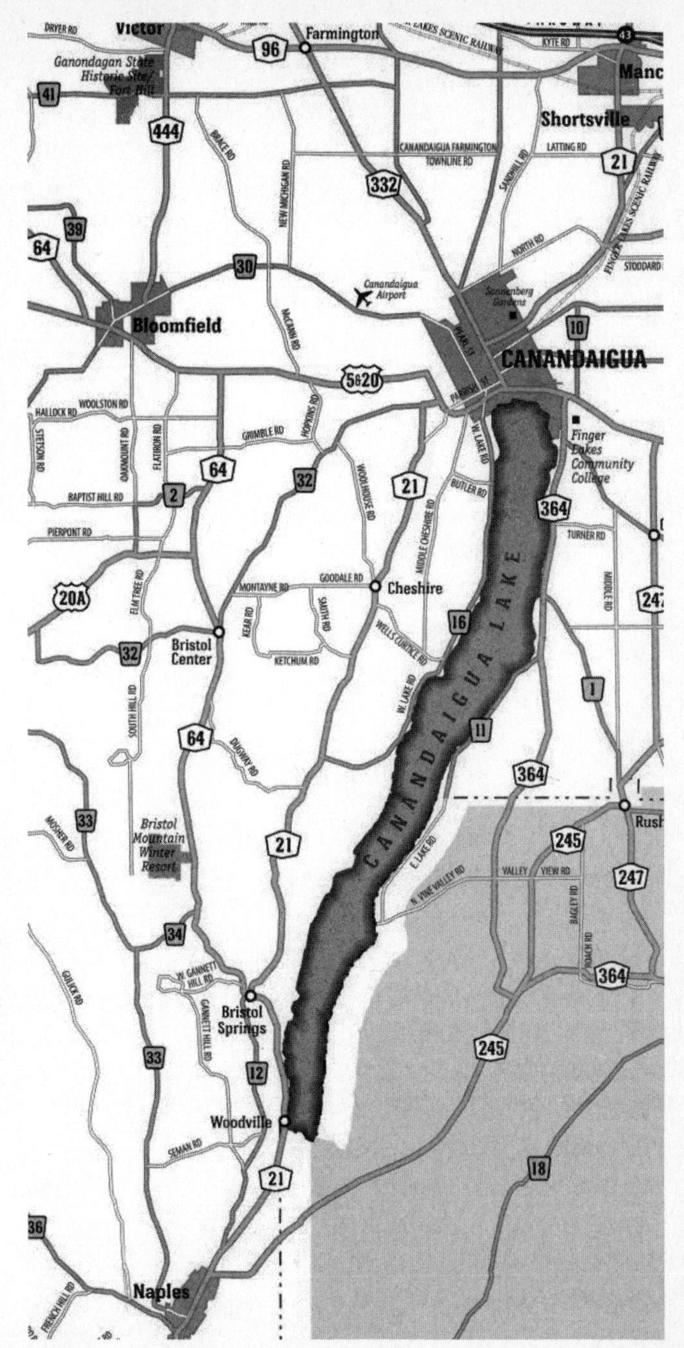

Map courtesy of www.visitfingerlakes.com

Author's Note

While every effort has been made to verify the history of Canandaigua and the volumes of Seneca folklore, this is a work of fiction. The events and characters portrayed are imaginary. Their resemblance, if any, to real-life counterparts is entirely coincidental.

Trees are the most trusting of all living creatures because they trust enough to put their roots down in one place, knowing they'll be there for life.

—AUTHOR UNKNOWN

Prologue

May 1988

The silken hair of the three children glows bone white in the moonlight as they paddle the stolen canoe out into the icy waters of Canandaigua Lake. The May wind is like a rabid wolf howling in the darkness, darting this way and that, biting at the rain as it sweeps across the surface in blustery sheets, hitting the children's flushed faces. The children know that on nights like this, the spirits of the Seneca Indians are weeping. Some are buried out on Squaw Island, a few miles away, and the children know if they put an ear close to the water's surface, they will hear the spirits calling, inviting them under.

Melanie Ellis, the eldest, sets her heavy wooden paddle down at the stern, and leans her thin body over the side of the canoe to listen for their whispers. Her long blond hair trails over the water, making large ripples. Her purple cotton dress billows up, revealing two bruised knees. Maya, just eight, jostles the boat as she pounds her fists and drums on the canoe's seat. Little Luke sits precariously on the canoe's edge, his head of blond curls tossed in the wind. Luke can withstand a thing like the foul weather, even if he is only seven, even if his body is so light, his skin so pale under the glowy moon, his sisters tease him that he looks like a ghost.

The sky becomes a deep pearl gray as the fog thickens around the coast of Squaw Island, a mystical and forbidden place that the children have only dreamed of visiting. It is the only place on earth where rare white lime deposits known as water biscuits exist. Illuminated by moonlight, they cling to its shores.

The island is too far out to swim, but not to row.

Melanie plunges the paddle into the icy water. Squinting toward the hazy distance, she can see the island encircled by feather trees brushing the sky, the edges of its shoreline vanishing into the lake. The high water level has swallowed up the land bridge that once connected it to the mainland. Long ago, the island was so large one could get lost in the trees. During a war in 1779, Seneca women and children escaped to safety across this bridge to hide in the grove of trees that covered the island. Melanie has always imagined them seeking shelter in the knees of trees and praying silently, sitting still as stone, and breathing so quietly that even the wind wouldn't notice them. Just as she, herself, has done on nights when her father drinks too much and the smartest thing to do is sneak out of the house and hide, and breathe without making a sound, and imagine that she is disappearing.

The drops of rain are coming harder now, not soft marbles that roll down her face, but drops that feel like a million needles. Everything going on at home is distant now, pushed into darkness by the clamoring rain and the scent of restless spirits.

The storm is kicking up.

Thunder wracks the sky as Melanie forces the paddle against the waves. The wind howls, rolling the water like a serpent under the canoe. The lake begins to buck and push.

The waves splash up against the sides of the boat, drenching the children in icy water. Maya and Luke have started to cry, begging her to go back. Melanie pushes her wet hair out of her eyes and glances behind her toward the Shongos' property. For a moment, unmoving, she is captivated by the sight of the Diamond Trees, the two great willows whose flickering leaves, when caught in the moonlight, create diamonds of light scattered across the water. These trees light the way for those who are lost. She quickly turns back toward the island, trying to gauge the distance ahead. She can see it out there in the mist, floating toward her.

The waves are pushing the canoe toward the island.

The heavy paddle slips from Melanie's hands, the waves wrestling it away. She crawls toward the front of the canoe, straining to retrieve it, but the paddle is quickly disappearing into the darkness. The boat is tossed aimlessly, caught halfway between the mainland and the island. The children cry out for help, their voices lost in the fog as they hold on to each other. Icy water surges up, filling the boat. Melanie must think fast. She edges toward the middle of the canoe, takes a deep breath, and plunges her hands into the numbing water to paddle. Luke reaches out for her, but she pushes him back, trying to keep the island in view. As the waves pull the boat closer, Melanie suddenly sees something: a figure moving on the island. Through the moonlit mist, her eyes can just make out the shimmering silhouette of a man so tall storm clouds rest on his shoulders. His body is so large that when he bends over with his shovel, he carries the moon on his back. He is digging furiously.

Trembling, Melanie calls out to him but her voice disappears into the crashing waves. She hears her siblings whimpering, and looks at their small bodies huddled against the seat, frozen, wide-eyed, watching her. Bracing her feet against the sides of the canoe for balance, she waves one arm at the giant as she struggles to stand. The island is closer now but the giant does not hear her. As the waves tip the canoe back and forth, she leans her weight from side to side, yelling to the giant again and again. Then there is a sudden roar of thunder followed by a whip of lightning that cracks the surface of the lake. In the flash, Melanie can see the giant more clearly, his wide face and black hair. She watches now as he throws down his shovel and picks up a large axe. Her eyes focus on the shadows as he lifts the axe into the air and down again, over and over, as though smashing the moonlight.

Maya catches the shock on her sister's face as Melanie panics, tipping the canoe, her feet slipping out from underneath her. Melanie falls, her cheek slamming against the seat, her arms and legs scraping and sliding against the cold, wet floor. Her vision blurs. And as she begins to black out, she can see Maya moving near the edge of the boat, the red of her dress darkening into the sky's gray. She can hear the sound of her name being called through the wind.

Small cries are wrestled into a deadening quiet. Rain stops. Then there is nothing but the swishing of the boat.

NEAR DAWN, THE SKY is hushed pink. Wisps of clouds rise from the chalky white shoreline of Squaw Island. Melanie is awakened by the soft scrape of white stones against the canoe's floor. Peeking out from the island's thin trees is the rusted door of an old Boy Scout cabin. Where there once was a giant, now only his imprint is left in the trees, his dark shadow clinging to the leaves and branches.

Floating in a lucent pool, Melanie trembles as she pushes herself up, despite the piercing pain that weighs her head down. She whispers Luke's name as her eyes search for him.

Melanie feels her heart quicken when she doesn't see Luke in the canoe. Only Maya, who is staring at her, her arms wrapped around herself, her dress, torn at the shoulder.

Melanie scans the horizon. On the island, she can see a shovel stuck in a pile of dirt.

A heavy curtain of mist slowly lifts off the water.

The lake still reflects each star, as though it were holding on, unwilling to let them fade.

"It's all your fault," Maya whispers, with pale eyes.

PART I

1

May 2000

At dawn, a tornado hits the Shongos' cabin window like a fist. Broken glass pierces the sky before piling up in the grasses at the foot of the two largest willows on Canandaigua Lake. Grant Shongo runs out onto his porch, imagining this as the sound of his own heart breaking. He recalls Susanna's words as she left him just over one year ago: *I love beginnings.* She had told him these words on their first date and repeated them on the night she left. There was nothing more after that but the sound of her car disappearing down the rainy street.

An amethyst sky bleeds up from the bank as he scans the homes that ring the 36-mile shoreline, the old summer cabins built from wood and cobblestone, and new lakefront mansions covered in stucco and brick, with lavish front lawns that are an unnatural shade of green, next to gleaming boats resting tentatively by their newly christened docks. It is early, he guesses. There is no working clock in his cabin and he threw out his watch when he left Rochester three weeks ago. Though he hasn't been back here in five years, he can still tell time by the color of the water, which changes from rose at dawn, to dark gray-green in the afternoon, to a rusty golden patina in the evening. It's about five o'clock in the morning, judging by the water's hue. The lake is still in motion. Its restlessness has always calmed him. He looks out at the trees, the way they seem to be pulling the dew across the uncut grass. Felled branches crisscross the lawn. The scent of destruction that tore through them last night is still in the air. The oaks are breathless.

All night, the wind kicked up glassy leaves that stuck to the porch screen like wet paper. Grant had sat on the twin-size mattress, listening as torrents twisted through the reeds, tossing skeletons of driftwood back toward land. But even the sorrowful whine of the oldest oak being ripped from its roots couldn't stop him from grabbing his knife. The cry of the splitting branches and the wind's moan didn't let up. Even the wolves' howling couldn't loosen his hands from the wooden statue he held in front of him. Although he hadn't picked up a knife in several years prior to his return to the cabin, he carved the entire night through without stopping. Even though sweat burned into his eyes, his fingers and palms chafed with wood dust, he just slicked the knife faster, carving the statue of a Seneca warrior in quick precise movements until his hands felt like claws. At thirty-three, his hands remembered the shape of the statue by heart, the warrior's wide face, long straight nose and sharp cheekbones, the head shaved for battle except for a lock of hair at the back; a cap, with one eagle feather sticking straight up in back, distinguishing it from the other Iroquois tribes. The leather breechcloth, and leggings that went from ankle up to mid-thigh to protect the legs when running through brush. A belt wrapped around the waist where a knife was kept close to the body, the pouch filled with arrows, and the thick powerful hands that held a bow. Even the physicality of carving couldn't cut his guilt away. He had thought that leaving Rochester would dull the painful memories.

Grant had stayed in the old Victorian on Park Avenue for a year after Susanna left. Rochester was a far cry from New York City, but compared to the sleepy town of Canandaigua, it was bustling. Their gentrified neighborhood was thriving and replete with distractions: trendy bars, restaurants, and sidewalk cafes, where Grant liked to sit alone for hours on Sundays reading the newspaper and grading papers, drinking shots of espresso, and losing himself in the latest educational dilemmas facing schools. There had been comfort, not loneliness, in the routine.

But once Susanna left, the emptiness had hit him hard. Their charming house only haunted him, the bright green shutters and the elegant bay windows, the garden patio that he meticulously constructed to her design, brick by brick. Even with all the noise of city life, the house held the silence of their marriage. Susanna told him she would never return, but he hadn't believed her. He had always been the one who had doubts, not her. So he waited for her in the house for a year, angry, impatient yet unwilling to leave. There were nights he thought he heard her footsteps on the patio. He'd lie still, one minute wishing it were her, and the next, praying those cries he heard were only the wind. Her leaving was right, he felt. But he did not know what to do without her.

There had been miscarriages. Three, one right after another. Susanna first blamed herself for the three souls that came and then left, each following the other to the spirit world. Their stays had been brief, but each had left an indelible mark. Their few months of life had made her a mother. And just as quickly, their passing had made her something else.

One night, he had found her kneeling in the backyard, her dark hair smeared across her cheeks with tears as she clutched the ultrasound pictures to her heart. She blamed the losses on her teenage promiscuity—how she had prayed for negative pregnancy tests back then, on her inability to complete any project, on the Camel nonfilters she occasionally snuck in the garage when he was up all night grading papers and writing lesson plans. When she could no longer bear the weight of the grief, she blamed Grant. He never truly gave her his heart, she said. He hadn't ever let her in. She had felt it throughout their four years of marriage. Their babies had, too. That's why they didn't survive, she said.

He wants to tell her she deserves none of the guilt.

If Susanna believed in fate, she'd realize that some souls know beforehand that they're going to leave, their purpose having already been fulfilled.

He would never admit that he has been skipping rocks to send messages to them through the water.

Strands of long black hair fall in his eyes as he turns the wooden statue on its side. He squeezes the knife in his fist, letting the hot metal bite at his skin, and then he watches a few drops of blood fall. Pain is a signal that he is awake and alive. It is because an uncomfortable numbness has come over him, not unlike how he imagines death to feel: one day fading into the next, the hours blurred, merging waves lost in the lake.

Time is different here: the minutes, hours, and days tracked by a set of different colors, smells, directions and strength of wind across the water. At night, Grant counts the hours by the direction of moonlight on the shifting water.

And the days, by the number of statues of Seneca warriors. Twenty-one statues fill the cabin, one carved each day since he's been back to the place of his childhood. He needs to connect to his ancestors this way, through this language of mourning, a language his father once shared with him on summer nights after Grant's mother had gone to sleep.

Grant would watch his father's skilled fingers work the knife as though it were a part of his hand, quickly carving a beaver or a bear, which would then be packed in a cardboard box and taken back to Rochester in September to be placed in a bigger box and carted up to the attic, never to be seen again. Even on nights when there was little moonlight, Ben Shongo would sit on the porch and carve these figures so easily and with such swiftness and detail that Grant believed his father had the power to see in the dark. His father had told him this was good exercise for the mind, that if he had the right attitude and focus, he wouldn't ever need to actually see the wood, that the picture he held in his mind was enough. After he had been sent to bed, Grant would hear his father out on the porch, and he knew his father was carving other things that Grant would never see. In the morning, there would be nothing but wood shavings and dust.

This morning, Grant's statues stand on the keys of the antique organ, on the mantel of the old cobblestone fireplace, and under the railing of the side porch that slants at almost 40 degrees. A few balance precariously on the arms of the rattan furniture, and on the fence posts of the abandoned garden that will soon be filled with his late mother's wild orange tiger lilies.

He knows that fighting emotion only creates dangerous pockets in the mind. Things can be brewing deep inside, unknown, until one day, the body is filled with wrenching uncontrollable sobs. Or a person can find himself racing along the highway at midnight in his sky blue Fleetwood for no apparent reason, the gas pedal pressed to the ground, hitting a patch of black ice and flipping the car before it explodes into fire, just as he had done one night when he told Susanna he was going out for a newspaper and instead totaled the car. And yet, he had escaped with only a few scratches. But the sight of the burning car left him with the distinct impression that it was better to sit in one place until he had a better handle on himself. The three children were losses for him, too.

There is nowhere else he could have gone but to the lake. Canandaigua is the place where he feels God in the trees, a place the Seneca call the Chosen Spot, where the Seneca say the earth split its seams and the ancestors emerged, a people for whom nature dwarfed all else. The willows here grow to enduring heights of one hundred feet, their narrow leaves and long branches bent toward the ground, never forgetting their home. During his boyhood summers, Grant would press his cheek against the thick, fissured bark and listen to the life rattling inside, just as it had in the years since the seedlings first tumbled down Bare Hill to settle at the shore, where their roots would one day climb over the stones to hold the shoreline in place. For years, folks in Canandaigua have called the oldest and biggest willows the Diamond Trees. They have been growing on the Shongos' property near the foot of Bare Hill for more than a century, their girth wide, the bark thick and craggy to protect from water and ice. At night the wind spun their flickering leaves, making it look like diamonds shimmering over the water. All lit up in the moonlight, folks said you could see them from every part of the lake, that they were a beacon for nighttime swimmers, sailors, and lost spirits.

It was here that Grant first tasted the thrill of diving into the cold water and discovering the large white stones, and the small spherical rocks, which contained crystals that tossed strange shapes of light after he'd break them open. He liked to pretend they had come from another world, that his Seneca ancestors had scattered the treasures of their loved ones across the water, hoping one day, they'd be found by a boy just like him.

Grant knew about the white stones, the ones geologists called *septaria*. Folks said these smooth white stones were the skulls of the Seneca people, expelled from the mouth of a snake monster that had devoured a Seneca village at the top of Bare Hill before being shot by the arrow of a little boy, and then rolling down the hill in a death struggle.

The monster is still out there, some people say, dwelling in the depths of the lake, the pet of a lonely giant that lives on Squaw Island, where no one is allowed to go.

As a child, Grant would climb one of the trails marking the snake's path to the top of Bare Hill just to feel the rough wind rushing past his face. Looking out over the gold-gray water returned him to himself, time and time again. When trying to will away the resentment over his mother's death or his confusion over his father's distance, he'd squeeze his eyes shut, trying to invoke the legendary Peace Maker, a Huron prophet who taught negotiation instead of violence to five warring tribes and united them as the Iroquois Confederacy. Still, the area continued to be filled with bloodshed. In 1687, in a battle over fur trade, French soldiers decimated the Seneca village of 4,500 people, at a place now called Ganondagan, at the north end of the lake. A period of darkness crossed the land after that. The earth there was once swollen with artifacts, but many had since been stolen from the site, including a rare silver tomahawk from the 1600s. Grant knows the spirits here don't like it. And that they still won't let go of this place.

ACROSS THE LAKE, WHAT'S left of the moonlight is turning the water a smoky lavender. Grant gets up from the porch and wipes the sweat from his forehead. Tying his long braid back with a piece of twine, he walks into the living room to check out the damage to the window.

He rubs his eyes in case he's imagining things.

Pieces of broken window glass form a perfect circle on the carpet. He's not easily shaken, not by the pull of lost spirits. But the circle of glass in the middle of his living room has him a little worried. Then, something catches his eye—one small soot print, then another, then a whole trail of tiny prints leading from the broken window to the basement door. If he were crazy he'd say these were footsteps.

Grant has tried not to think too much about the blithe spirit that has moved into his dreams each night since his arrival three weeks ago, rousting him out of bed to float over the brambles lining the lake. Grant knows who the boy is even if he won't tell anyone about it. He remembers the midnight house calls his father made to the home of a sick child named Luke Ellis. And the old dugout canoe and paddle his father had made from a birch tree, and had carelessly left out under the Diamond Trees one winter, the one the Ellis children found that rainy spring night twelve years ago, when they managed to paddle out to Squaw Island. No one will ever forget the accident, the tragic loss of the boy, and the subsequent rumors of a terrible giant that loomed from Squaw Island, hacking the moon apart with an axe.

The men dragged the lake for a month, all 15.5 miles of it, down to its 276-foot depth. The water was so cold Luke's small body didn't rise to the surface for almost a year. Then, on a particularly warm May morning, it floated right up to the shore of Squaw Island almost exactly where Luke had disappeared. The eyes a shocking moonstone blue. The golden curls uncommonly smooth, as though they had been freshly washed and combed.

Grant doesn't know why Luke Ellis has moved into his

dreams. But he doesn't mind being taken up by the little boy. He doesn't mind the company.

Night after night, the boy tugs him out the door, barely leaving him enough time to pull on a shirt. When Grant is with the boy, he can fly. Luke is weightless, floating effortlessly through the air. Together, they travel the entire lake from south to north, skipping over the creek bed that runs through the gorge of Clark's Gully, then darting in and out of two cascading waterfalls dropping over sixty feet, and down through Vine Valley. Then to the top of Bare Hill where they can see the whole lake for miles. Afterward they climb among the forgotten vineyards, where Luke likes to blow the dew off the clusters of grapes peeking out from the broken wire trellises. Sometimes they hover over the dusky blue road that leads north to town, floating in and out of old barns, half-charred from a fire that seared the woods one summer, leaving everything thirsty. Luke likes mischief, likes to race to the northern end of the lake to pull hay from stacks that dot the farmlands, to tickle the udders of cows, his blue eyes dancing as they rise above Ganondagan State Historic Site, 10 miles north of the city of Canandaigua, where a replica longhouse now stands.

With Luke leading the way, they zigzag through the city of Canandaigua, stopping at Scoops Ice Cream Stand near the marina, and then to a place on the shore, where they can see Squaw Island.

From there, they drift near the people who still long for Luke. It is because their thoughts call to him; they are sweet, like the sugar "rock" candy he used to get from the Feed & Grain. They go into the backyard of Luke's mother, Leila, where Luke likes to rest in the branches of her overgrown lilac bush, so full with blossoms in May that it dwarfs the headstone that bears his name; then across the rooftop and along the leaf-swollen gutters of her next-door neighbor, Clarisse Mellon; and finally to his sister Melanie's new apartment in town on Highland Avenue, with its fire red door and purple trim, before careening back to the place where the deep pink bloom of wild peas meets the highway. On their way back to the cabin, Luke is trying to lead Grant to O'Connell's Feed & Grain, but Grant is not ready yet. He isn't ready.

GRANT CAN STILL REMEMBER the months in Rochester after Susanna left. The weeks of bad winter storms. The darkness of dense, ceaseless snow. The three errant blackbirds, wings coated in ice, that circled above the house, landing each night on the telephone wires like glistening upside-down icicles. The wet spot on the doormat where he left his boots that never seemed to dry. He vaguely recalls digging a neighbor's car out of the driveway. Other than that, nothing. He's sure he taught his English classes at Hallandale Arts Academy, an alternative school for underachieving boys. Positive his students thought he was losing it, coming in day after day with bruisy eyes and an absentmindedness they'd whisper to be the effects of alcohol, or pot. He was a favorite teacher, but even a wry sense of humor couldn't hide his ineptitude after a while. These boys weren't the types to suffer with a teacher that just showed up to hand out, God forbid, worksheets.

Still, that's exactly what Grant had done for months, until Dean Stiles called him into his office to say he was letting him go a few months early to "get himself together." Arrangements had already been made for someone else to handle final exams even though Grant's contract was being renewed for another year.

"I deserve a lot less," Grant said, as sunlight bleared in through the shades. His fingers traced cracks in the leather arms of a chair that had supported hundreds of young boys with dignity, whether they knew it or not.

"It's time to deal with it. You've got to address this thing."

The dean removed his glasses and pointed to a paperweight in the corner of his desk. The egg-shaped crystal was a gift from the parents of a failing student named Alden James whom Grant had turned around.

"You did this," the dean said, holding the crystal in both hands. At the start of his popular ninth-grade "Not Nice Novels" class, Grant had created an entirely new curriculum for Alden, tailored to his only interest—horror. All the after-school hours of tutoring paid off. No one could believe that the gaunt-faced delinquent had scored 750 on his SATs. Grant had become a school hero, and Alden, Hallandale's greatest success story.

"You saved that kid. And others. Good teachers are worth fighting for, just like good kids," the dean said.

Sunlight rushed through the crystal and into Grant's eyes, causing them to water. He felt unable to locate an ounce of faith in his body. Grant had argued, the words shooting out with force. He felt unable to tolerate positive feedback for fear it would rip into his delicate armor. He had become more like his students than he realized.

"Look," said the dean. "You need to figure out how much of the stuff you have going on is out there, and how much is in here." The dean held his hand over his own shirt pocket. "Come August, I'll fire you if that's what you want, all right? But a few months of introspection won't kill you."

"That's easy for you to say," Grant told him as the dean walked out, leaving him alone in the leather chair.

That night Grant packed a bag and drove 35 miles down the New York State Thruway to exit 44, for the first time in five years.

* * *

IN THE LIVING ROOM, Grant eyes a patch of sunlight that has spilled all around the broken glass. He kicks apart the circle, displacing the pieces of glass. Grant grabs his mother's old gardening gloves and a plastic garbage bag. He could take off the gloves. He could clear the rough edges of the window frame with his bare hands until they are cut up and bloody. But he opens the screen door to let the air wash his face clean of these thoughts. At once, he's caught by the hiss of wind sweeping over leaves as it rushes in from the head of Canandaigua Lake.

OUTSIDE, THE EARTH IS cold and wet under his bare feet. The sun is beginning to spray hints of lacquer across the lake. Ahead, an old birch has fallen into the water. Grant steps carefully onto the smooth trunk, pacing farther and farther as though the lake were pulling him toward its center. He has always felt things in his body first, his mind taking longer to catch up. Sometimes the intensity of the feeling has propelled him into action. Other times, it has paralyzed him.

Grant can feel the soul of the old tree beneath his feet, ceaseless and forgiving, knowing it has only itself to blame, never having settled its roots deep enough into the rocky ground. He moves forward as waves crash against the breakwall, their frothing crest swelling back as the water underneath rushes forward. Does he have a right to anything more than a few moments of clarity?

If he can just get out there near the fallen tree. There, a bit farther, where the trout are dancing.

Grant is suddenly aware of the scent of a dying bonfire trickling in from up shore. He looks up. A heron is standing on the dock a few feet away, its narrow head tucked between its shoulders. Its ember eyes are motionless. This bird's meditative quiet reminds him of something he has lost. Every morning after carving, Grant walks out to the dock to join the herons in their perfect stillness. Years ago, the heron's lightning speed awed him as it speared its prey. Now it's the bird's patience that impresses him.

He glances back at the screened-in porch in the front of the cabin, which looks small and dark, with its rough graying wood, wide broken window, and slatted sunken roof that may not withstand another winter. It looks safe somehow, huddled under the trees.

He'll throw himself into fixing up the cabin. Hadn't his father rebuilt his mother's kitchen four times in the years after she died? That was the way his father dealt with loss. It was then that Grant saw how human beings needed a way to put their hands on grief, to hold it as though it were the lost loved one. Grant was twenty-three when his mother passed, and after years, he still hadn't gotten over his breakup with Echo O'Connell.

He had listened outside his parents' bedroom door to his father's muffled sobs over the loss of his mother, to the footsteps pacing back and forth, sometimes until dawn.

Each day Grant stood motionless as his father wore his grief deep into the wooden floorboards. As Grant placed his hands on the door, he could actually feel them going numb. Later, Grant would creep downstairs into his father's dark study, where light slithered through the blinds and across the shelves lined with animal carvings, and across the dust-heavy desk, circling the stethoscope, and the pencil case, which always held freshly sharpened pencils, tips up, along with one tall feather, and then around the mahogany-framed photograph of his mother smiling sideways at someone Grant had always imagined was himself, though he did not remember it. Grant sat in his father's high-backed chair, just as he had done as a child, trying to position his head so that it fit into the impression of his father's head. He would stare at his father's black doctor's bag on the floor in the corner. Then, he'd close his eyes and wait for the scene to become clearer, that of his mother waving from way out in the water, and his father's six-foot, six-inch giant frame walking toward her right into the lake until only the back of his head could be seen. Panicked, Grant had rubbed the worn velvet over the arms just as he had seen his father do after his mother became ill, to hold on to every piece of her, even the skin and the prints.

His father strongly believed the words of his Seneca ancestors. That when a man left this lifetime without repenting for his sins, the Punisher would take him in his hands and turn him into ash. Then he'd spread him into earth to do everything all over again.

Two years later, when Dr. Ben Shongo died in his sleep, they couldn't find a thing wrong with him. Even though a man of his height was prone to heart trouble, they hadn't found one medical irregularity. But even Grant knew about his father's broken heart. And he still hasn't forgiven himself for his cowardice, for not going into his father's bedroom and trying to help way back then. Too afraid of what he might have seen.

Coming back to Canandaigua is about making something new.

When he actually thinks about it, the list is manageable. Repairing the phone can wait. There's no one he wishes to talk to. But both the window and the linoleum that's peeling up from the kitchen floor are another story.

The wooden entryway is scuffed from hiking boots and could use a good sanding. Scattered embers from the fireplace have singed the yellow shag carpeting. It's not all a throwaway, though. The canary yellow walls are actually not as dismal as he'd remembered. Perhaps he'll buy a watercolor from one of those galleries in town. Maybe one with autumn trees. He could even plant tomatoes if he wanted, the kind that grow so furiously and impatiently, they'll split themselves open right on the vine.

Thankfully, there's work to be done. This is why he is about to walk to O'Connell's Feed & Grain. It's eight miles down the road but it's the best place he knows for supplies. He has to get his mind off the tracks of coal footprints now zigzagging all across the room, leading right to the basement door that has suddenly been thrown open. The spirit of Luke Ellis will get what he wanted after all.

2

ONE DAY OUT OF the year, the mayflies swarm Canandaigua Lake. Their lifespan of twenty-four hours is entirely consumed by the search for a mate. In that time, they are so frenzied, so drunk with love, that the faintest wind blows them into cobwebs and porch screens. Their sail-like wings stand perpendicular from their thin bodies as they tumble and collide, mating in the air. There are so many of them that they coat the docks, landing on everything in sight. After mating and just before dying, the females fly over the water, dropping thousands of eggs back into the lake, their children sinking to the muddy bottom.

Grant pulls up his collar to keep the flies away. He takes off, running down East Lake Road to O'Connell's Feed & Grain, halfway between the lake's north and south ends. He can see that a hazy light has begun to spill through the downed leaves, turning the water into a smooth sheet of glass. It is just a matter of a few hours before the mayflies are in their glory. The swallows are already having a feast, darting back and forth an inch above the lustrous lake.

Up on the road, the phone lines are down, but Grant's not

even angry about the inconvenience or the mess. The storm has forced him to leave the cabin for the first time in three weeks. It's time to set his eyes on another human being, if only to prove that one exists. He passes a row of identical small clapboards. Clarisse Mellon is one of the few people out. Kneeling in her garden, she waves a muddy-gloved hand. "The swarm's coming! Tough day to be out!" she calls, holding up a very large smooth white stone. He waves, wondering whether she'll actually wait until he is out of sight before she runs to a neighbor's house to spread the news of his emergence. Still, the rest of the place is fairly quiet but for the birds. All the pets in the neighborhood have been brought inside because of the mayflies.

The Feed & Grain is hedged in on either side by an eighty-foot fence of Northern red oak. Grant stops. He's near enough now to see Joseph O'Connell's shock of white hair. The old man is standing on the porch steps, scratching his ruddy face and puffing on his pipe. The chalky smoke from his tobacco curls in tendrils over the roof.

Behind him, Squeaky Loomis is seated on an old wooden soapbox, near a card table where he and Joseph usually play yukor. They do this to pass the time in grizzly to fair weather, telling stories, sharing bits of news. Joseph is a man of tradition, and the fact that men gather here to talk for hours, just as they did in the twenties, when this was the original Farmers Co-op, is thanks to him. On cold mornings, men still wake before sunrise to crowd around the potbellied stove. Embraces are still common. Grant has seen many, for this is one of the few places on earth where men will tell their secrets.

On the morning of his twelfth birthday, Grant's father brought him to O'Connell's to have coffee with the men before they put out the docks. It had been a frozen morning, but

Grant was thrilled, feeling the trill of happiness for the first time in years. The distance and rejection he felt from his father had left him with a terrible stutter that all but choked his voice. He hadn't felt comfortable anywhere on earth. But sipping that bitter black coffee had strengthened him. It meant that his father considered him a worthy human being, capable of being in this place, with these men, who seemed as much a part of this land as the trees, the memory keepers of a secret history. Grant had loved every minute of it, listening, taking it all in. They didn't care that he could hardly manage a hello. Because he was with his father, they had accepted him unconditionally as one of them. Grant sat in front of the lit stove that morning listening to Joseph talk about his missionary work in Kenya, about the Wataita people, and about the spirits of the Seneca ancestors here in Canandaigua that whispered across the lake. Years later, when Grant had come back with Susanna, there was a new ghost story—that of little Luke Ellis, who had drowned in the lake twelve years earlier. Squeaky Loomis claimed to have seen his ghost hovering in the branches of Leila Ellis's huge lilac bush when he was ambling by on his early-morning walk. He had reported that he was suddenly met by Clarisse Mellon, who lived next door and had seen Luke several times, she whispered, usually just before a rainstorm.

Joseph O'Connell is making his way down the steps, waving his cane. "For Pete's sake, boy, where have you been?" Joseph bellows. The old man is like a grandfather, a bit of a folk hero, mainly due to his belief in the goodness of the human spirit, which he'd remind anyone of in the event they forgot. Grant doesn't even need to inhale the scent of the cherry tobacco to know that Joseph's pipe is filled with it.

When Joseph embraces him, Grant's body becomes a sponge,

absorbing all the warmth it can. Why an embrace should make him feel sad, he's not sure. He's worried he won't know when to let go, or that he won't be able to.

Joseph gives Grant a customary pat on the back, a hugger's traffic signal. "Sorry," Grant whispers, letting go so Joseph can breathe again. Seeing Joseph again is completely disarming and Grant can't believe the relief he feels.

"No apologies. Just glad you're here," Joseph says, swatting at the flies with his cane. "Now come up and say hello. Folks have missed you."

"Window's broken," Grant explains to no one in particular as he follows Joseph up the steps. He finds himself staring at a spider web stretched under the porch light. It's marked with the first of its victims: A mayfly's forked tail twitches slightly, caught in the threads.

"So, the silence getting to you, finally?" Squeaky asks as he pulls his fishing hat down over his pink whiskey face, forcing tufts of white hair over his ears. He smiles quickly at Grant, and then fastens his yellowed eyes on the game of cards. The fact is he can recognize desperation on a man's face as easily as he can spot lichens on a sugar maple and it makes him uncomfortable.

"We've been wondering how you're doing," Joseph explains.

"Oh, can't complain." Grant shrugs and looks away.

He doesn't want to have to tell the story of Susanna. Anyhow, there's a good likelihood Joseph already knows enough of it. For the first time ever, Grant Shongo is thankful for gossip.

"Complaining's one of life's little pleasures." Squeaky laughs. Joseph closes his eyes and nods, as though this was the most covetous secret they share. Both complaining and remembering provide a reason for breathing. They talk about the legendary Canandaigua snake monster that was said to coil the seaweed in Canandaigua Lake. That mysterious giant on Squaw Island kept the serpent as a pet, folks said, and he buried the heads of lost swimmers in the sand until it was the serpent's feeding time.

"Pride's an enemy, boy," Joseph says, his emerald eyes splashing up, knowing Grant won't discuss his failed marriage.

Speech is difficult under the tidal wave of emotion. Grant hedges, looks down. He's lost weight. The old Syracuse University sweatshirt hangs off him in tatters. At thirty-three, it is only by the grace of good genes that his muscles have any definition at all. He could be the ramen noodles poster man. He's lived on it. He could write a jingle about the wonders of ramen noodles soup.

"You'll be okay, you hear?"

"Sure, Joe, I'm doing fine."

"You know we got a snowy owl around here now?" asks Joseph. "Come all the way from the Arctic, got lost up this way. Only seen him once up there in the trees. Real big, fat white thing. Folks say he fell in love with the snow and hasn't gone back. Thinks he's home."

"That so?" asks Grant.

"Caught up by the quiet, I imagine. But not too wise for an owl," says Squeaky, who is trying not to stare. The truth is, people have been waiting for Grant to show up for weeks, if only to have something new to report. No one wants to be that openly nosy, but any kind of change is news around here. It doesn't take much in a town where some of the men have donned the same flannel shirt every winter for twenty years. These men will tell you that at a certain age there is no need for new things. Almost always, what a man had in the beginning would've served him. The need for newness can make him wreck his life if he doesn't grow wise to it.

"Well, one thing's certain," Joseph says, cracking the silence. "There's not much left of you. Skin and bones."

Grant puts his hands in his pockets and turns away. "Your place needs painting," he says.

"Grant, folks tell me things. Remember where you are. Word travels faster than a runaway train 'round here. Now I don't pry. You know I don't have a need to. But when old friends are concerned—"

"I could paint it," Grant interrupts, looking around.

Squeaky has the feeling that he is fading off into the background. It happens naturally these days. It's a product of being old and male, of sitting in khaki gabardines for too long with aching joints, in his daughter-in-law's house, in his doctor's office, or on the peeling steps of this old porch. Everyone thinks an old man's face is a puzzle. People try to squeeze wisdom from him as though it were juice from an orange, convinced his wrinkles speak of troubles, even though this belies the way he feels. In reality, he has never felt better, his biggest worry these days, where and what he will have for his supper.

Grant looks at Joseph. "I should get that duct tape. Tornado broke the window."

"Biggest tornado in years," says Squeaky, trying to hold his attention. "Heck, now you got a reason to fix it up. You might think about renting your place after that. Scout Point's prime real estate. Property's skyrocketed. Cottages are renting for six thousand dollars a month. We'd all be rich if we'd sell. They just want to knock down what we got and build fancy mansions anyway."

The lake has become a favorite spot for boating, fishing, scuba and the best summer living. This land has always been invaluable to somebody. Humphrey Bogart spent his summers on Canandaigua Lake, along with many a wealthy landowner.

Before that, local fishermen posted their shacks along the lake. Hundreds of years before the first white settlers arrived, in the 1700s, the Seneca lived along these banks. But Grant is certain his ancestors wouldn't like the activity, even if this is now one of the most expensive lakefront properties in the nation.

"You hear about Squaw Island? Not bigger than the size of two tennis courts now. State won't maintain it anymore. Doris headed up a citizen action committee to take over its protection." Grant looks out at the lake. He can see Squaw Island in the distance, now walled off with heavy granite boulders that protect it from the wind, ice, and changing water currents from boat wakes that have altered the lake's wave patterns. The island, an eroding sandbar, had been deemed New York State's smallest state park, and was forbidden to visitors, due to its fragility. Once two acres, now it was one quarter the size.

"Don't worry, I won't ever sell," Grant says, and starts inside.

"Just like your father, zipping off like a mystery." Joseph shakes his head in the silence, puffs hard on his pipe. "You're not the only one who's had troubles. We've all been there. Every one of us has walked across the bottom of this lake, boy, at least once."

Grant stops and turns around. There are a million things Grant could say to the old man right now, but not a one would be the thought of a sane man. He could tell Joseph he has whittled twenty-one statues, one for every day he has been back at the lake. That he thought about impaling himself on the barbecue fork at least three times. And at night, well, that's the ultimate in lucid dreaming. You see, he could explain, the goddamn ghost of Luke Ellis has been taking me flying for almost a month now.

"I know what you're thinking. It's all over your face," says

Joseph. "Listen, you'll be okay. You're a good man. Don't forget it."

Grant looks down, examining the frayed cuffs of his sweatshirt. If you only knew how I have wrecked my life, he thinks.

Joseph, holding up his hand, starts to speak. "When you were this high? You'd be standing there wearing your father's coat, wearing his stethoscope around your neck, and your yellow high-water boots up to your knees. Watching me like a hawk, making sure I wasn't cheating your mother out of her groceries. You were a pain, you know. Corrected my math more times than I can count. Then, of course, you and Echo. Boy, one wrong move and I'd have tracked you down myself."

Grant startles at hearing her name. He smiles, despite himself.

"I suppose I should confess that I cheated you out of a few loaves of bread," Grant says, trying to change the subject, swatting a few more flies that get right into his face.

"I don't buy it. You didn't have the heart," Joseph tells him.

Squeaky gets up. Waving bugs away is too distracting and it's aggravating his arthritis. "Let's all go in then," Joseph suggests, but Grant doesn't hear. He's looking at the moving trees. He recalls Echo was like that, restless like the trees.

EACH SUMMER, WHEN THE Naples vineyards were thick with sweet June air that inflated the clouds for miles, Grant and Echo would bicycle through Vine Valley. They would pass crowds of sheep and dairy cattle, and the old farms where equipment had been left to rust like skeletons in the hay. Old-timers would stop work to tell them about the days when wild grape vines, bees, and rattlesnakes festered on the Valley floor, and it was common to see a neighbor covered with welts as he passed on the street, or stood in the scorching sun as he cleared the space for planting.

Inside abandoned barns, Grant and Echo climbed over reams of old carpets, amidst spider webs sagging in the heat. Echo would sift through countless antique hope chests in pursuit of the mystical crazy quilts. Within these patternless cloths, she explained, you could sense the quilter's personality. You could read her entire life in those zigzag seams, faded prints and discordant shapes, for these spoke of the secret stories, the ones the quilter never talked about but instead sewed into her memory: the scraps of shirts of the men she never thought she would fall in love with, and the hems of skirts worn by the daughters she never thought would leave her. The cloth worn over a lifetime held threads of the deepest truth, Echo said. She'd once uncovered a century-old quilt that had handprints of several family members embroidered in its center, along with the dates of their births and deaths. Echo had buried her face in the soft threadbare material, as though trying to inhale the family ancestry. Being orphaned had robbed her of her own stories.

"Feels like a different life completely," Grant says, leaning up against the railing.

"That's where you're wrong. Same life, boy. Different you," Joseph says, anxiously. Then, Joseph begins to cough. A high-pitched wheeze seers the air. He holds his side. Squeaky looks at Joseph, worried.

Grant takes Joseph's arm. "You okay?"

Joseph nods, eyes tearing, waves them away. "I'm fine, fine," he chides them as he hobbles off by himself, leaning far too heavily on his cane. Squeaky eyes Joseph nervously, reminded of his own fragility. Grant stays where he is, watches as Joseph's chest heaves with each laborious breath, and realizes he is not the only one who suffers. Left alone, Joseph composes himself.

Just then a police car pulls up in front of the store. Detective Charlie Cooke gets out, smoothing back his wet gray hair. "Need to talk to you for a minute, Joe," he calls, slamming the creaking car door a little too hard.

"Sure, Charlie, give me a minute then," Joseph calls, taking a deep breath. "Fresh coffee on the counter inside. Help yourself. I'll be right in." Charlie nods a hello at Grant and walks inside.

"Why's Charlie here? Kids still stealing from you, Joe?" Grant asks.

"No, the Ellis girl disappeared. Run off again," Squeaky interjects, hedging on the last step. "Leila's oldest, Melanie."

Joseph shoots him a look.

"Well, none of us believes it, no sir," Squeaky adds quickly. "That she's run. I mean, why would she run, now that she's staying clean? You know, being a mother and all."

"Hearsay," Joseph says. "She didn't run. I know her."

"She worked for Joe on and off for years," Squeaky tells Grant.

"Know her very well." Joseph packs his pipe. "Good-hearted, honest girl. Know Melanie like my own daughter," he adds, lighting the pipe.

Joseph stubs out a fallen ash with his sandal. He tugs at his collar, his neck damp and itching hot just as it was the day little Luke Ellis was buried. No one had seen a day as hot in May. A record heat wave in Canandaigua at 85 degrees. People packed into the church and the ones who couldn't fit inside lined up half a block out. Women in puckered nylons held crying children who pulled their own hair. Their patience was coming undone like the ribbons that fell from the long blond ponytails of the two Ellis girls, who stood on either side of Leila in long black coats, their faces moist, reddening as the service went on. Melanie's hands shook so badly she had dropped her bouquet of lilies four times that he counted, leaving tiny white petals on her shiny patent leathers. By the end of the service, she stood in a halo of white petals. But her eyes never left the casket.

"Melanie. She made the paper years ago, I remember. Harvest Queen? Long blond hair? Lives in that apartment with the bright red door and the purple trim?" Grant asks.

"Blond, black, or pink hair, who can keep track?" Joseph answers, staring out at the serpentine clouds moving in and out of the trees. "Wait a minute. How did you know about the red door?"

"Well, I mean, how can you miss it? It's bright red."

"But how did you know it was *her* door?" Joseph stares at Grant. He won't meet Joseph's eyes.

A momentary silence passes between the two as Grant picks up a broken branch and tosses it into the trees.

Joseph glances at Squeaky, then continues. "Well, she was at the top of her class, too. Quite a girl. Wasn't but a few years ago she was the town's pride and joy, riding up on that float, waving at the parade. Then, so sudden, she fell into her trouble because of that good-for-nothing boyfriend."

"Neither girl ever got over their brother's death," says Squeaky.

"But she has done a lot of work on herself since her baby was born. To be a good mother," says Joseph. "Only twenty-one years old for God's sake. Folks don't let you live anything down in this town. Always fighting their opinions. Folks just had high hopes for her, that she would redeem her family's name."

"Got a nice tattoo on her arm. Almost as nice as this one

here." Squeaky pulls up his sleeve, revealing a black heart that says "Doris."

"Who's Doris?" Grant asks.

"My first wife," Squeaky replies. "Melanie's got a bird. Says 'Luke.' " He leans in toward Grant. "The dead brother."

"Right," Grant tells him.

Joseph shakes his head. "Tears me up. You'll see a whole lot of books in there, stacked 'bout so high." Joseph holds his palm about two feet off the ground, and then notices the dark liver spots. He pulls his hand back.

"School books?" asks Grant.

"No. Self-help books. She could break your heart, the way she was trying so hard. She planned to start college next year. Kept saying her life was about healing now. She wanted to heal things in the past, with her sister, too. See, damnedest thing. She was just beginning to remember what happened the night the boy died. Said she blamed herself. That she'd been trying all these years to get the picture straight."

"She remembered seeing the giant out on Squaw Island," Squeaky says. "But she was just a kid of nine, so who knows."

"Maybe she was remembering a ghost story. I don't ask, never needed to know," says Joseph, "but she needs to know."

"Staying clean frees up all kinds of things from the mind," says Squeaky. "I mean, that's what I hear."

GRANT WAS TWENTY-ONE WHEN Luke Ellis drowned. But this is not the memory shifting through his mind. He remembers how the three Ellis children once left footprints of coal dust on the yellow shag carpeting in his cabin. How they had stood in his mother's kitchen years ago, their ice blue eyes glowing against blackened cheeks, rosebud lips quivering, clutching each other so tightly that they became one trembling mass of blond tangles, as though trying to disappear into each other. Melanie had stepped forward and told Emily Shongo that they were hunting for diamonds in the basement coal bin. She had learned in school that diamonds came from coal. She said they would collect the shiny pieces that were changing into diamonds, just before the Diamond Trees could pull them up through their roots and into their leaves. She promised that they'd only take enough to make their mother rich. Melanie spoke so clearly, her hands moved so gracefully through the air that she seemed a very adept storyteller even at the ripe old age of eight. No taller than the kitchen counter.

"Goblins, that's what my mother called them. Blond goblins," Grant remembers. "Said they were afraid of their own shadows. One minute they were explaining and the next, they took off running like cats out of a bath."

"Ah well, Leila's got her hands full now. Melanie's boy's almost two years." Joseph removes his glasses again and rubs his bloodshot eyes before taking the photo from his wallet. "Here's Lucas. Near five pounds at birth. Almost didn't make it. Get a look at those eyes, real watchful."

Grant takes the photo. From outward appearances, Melanie's past has done little to harden her. She's smiling in a black bikini top and purple shorts, kneeling in the grass and holding a toddler in red overalls. Her blond hair is swept back from one side of her face revealing dewy skin that would make her look more like an Ivory girl than a drug addict, if it weren't for the deep red scar at the corner of her left eye.

"Who's the father?" asks Grant.

"Lionel Williams," says Joseph. "Good man. Works down at the garage. Rough around the edges, you'd like him probably."

"Fixed my car last year," adds Squeaky, now seating himself on the step. "Saved me two hundred dollars."

"Christ, Melanie looks so young to go through all that," says Grant.

"Ah, not for us to judge. We can't know, can't even try to guess the Creator's plan," Joseph says, motioning toward the trees. "Who can say what they'd have done in her situation? She's stronger than she knows. I tried to tell her that every day, too."

"Was that the truth?" Grant asks.

Joseph smiles. "You ever see a tree that's dying, it's nothing but a bunch of dried-out branches? You can talk to this tree, tell it all about how its leaves are growing green and healthy. Then you sit back and watch how it changes."

Grant looks at him, interest piqued.

"You don't believe it?" Joseph says. "Well, you should have seen Melanie's face light up when I said that to her. Most beautiful thing is to see hope come back into a face. That's all she wanted. People to believe in her without wanting anything back. People don't need much else."

The sky is incandescent, like the pearly inside of a shell. An explosive cough cracks the air. Joseph doubles over. His pipe rolls across the porch. Squeaky dives toward him, helps him to a chair. "I'm fine, I'm fine," Joseph says in a low voice, but this time he'll not send help away.

Instinctively, Grant rests his hand on Joseph's back, right between the shoulder blades and waits. After a moment, he removes his hand. "You should get to a doctor, Joe. Have those lungs checked," Grant says.

"Maybe one of these days," Joseph says, stunned, staring at the crown of mayflies that have gathered around Grant's feet, their forked tails twitching. He's not sure why there is a tingling sensation between his shoulder blades. As Joseph watches the clump of live tobacco burn like a miniature smoke signal in front of them, he feels better, more alive somehow. He zips up his coat. Joseph gets up without using his cane and crosses the porch, once, then back without the slightest limp.

Shrugs make their way around the porch of the Feed & Grain. It could be the air, they ponder silently. The fresh spring air on the lake is like that. It can do things to you, can make you dizzy and throw you off balance.

"Grant, what's that you're doing?" Joseph asks.

"Sometimes dirt makes a man feel clean," Grant says, rubbing his hands in the mud. He climbs the stairs as the tobacco smoke slithers away across the floor.

"Let me have a look at those hands, boy."

Grant reluctantly holds up his right palm. Joseph touches Grant's fingertips and short square nails. The two men face off for a few seconds, Joseph's knotted fingers pushed against Grant's broad palm, thick with calluses. Just then, the sheriff emerges from the doorway, and Grant pulls his hand away.

"Hey Joe, I hate to break this up but I don't have much time. Folks are crazy today, calling right and left about these damn white stones everywhere," says Charlie Cooke, spilling his coffee into a nearby section of grass. "Tornado took them right out of the lake and dropped them all over town. Anyhow, Melanie Ellis is why I'm here, so let's get to it."

"I'm coming in, Charlie."

Grant can feel his chest muscles tighten. He doesn't have to involve himself in every ounce of trouble that comes his way. He needs to get back to the cabin, needs the cool meditative compass of the water to rein him in. He thinks about a thing like perfect timing, about how the heron takes slow deliberate steps as it scans the water for minnows or crayfish, waiting, one leg held in the most tempered expectancy. Then it tilts its head, and flash. Snags its prey. And the dance repeats.

"BEFORE YOU GO," JOSEPH says to Grant, taking out his wallet one last time. "I thought you might like to see my kiddo. The picture was taken at some fancy lunch for her work. She lives in Boston. She's got a very big job now. Copywriter, you know. It's a lot of pressure, but of course she handles it."

Despite his better judgment, Grant reaches for the photo. He smiles at the wide brown eyes ringed with soft coal.

"She still has freckles," says Joseph.

"She finally got her braces off."

It was his fault. Grant remembers that fateful bike ride to Naples a week before she turned fifteen. She hit a rock and flew right over the handlebars, landing on the pavement, blackening her left eye, breaking her nose, and knocking out her two front teeth. By her own account, she looked like "a drunken sailor after a fight—hideously awful." He knew then that he didn't deserve her because of his one despicable thought: *Now, she won't leave me.*

He had sat with her all night in the hospital, holding her hand, hardly leaving her side. Her recovery was deemed miraculous. The doctors couldn't explain how her nose had healed overnight. The bruise around her eye had disappeared by the next morning.

"She should have been more careful. Only by the grace of God that she didn't lose her sight. Well, she just gets more and more beautiful all the time," Joseph says. "She's still wearing that uniform of blue jeans and T-shirts. You remember, it was all about comfort. She hasn't changed her ways."

"She always said she'd never work in a place where she couldn't wear blue jeans and T-shirts."

"She won't change. Not for any amount of money."

When they'd met, Echo wasn't what most kids their age considered beautiful, with a tornado of long red hair, and thick pink plastic-framed glasses. But each day, he'd see her reading behind the counter at the Feed & Grain, and Grant was transfixed by the wave of her lips moving silently, forming the shapes of words. It was just fine with him that Echo rarely looked up from her book. Back then, he hardly spoke to anyone but his mother. Terrified by his father, too afraid he would be teased for his clumsy speech.

On the day of reckoning, he had stood at the counter for a good five minutes in his uniform of sandals with black socks, T-shirt and tan shorts, pretending to decide what to buy. The shelves were brimming with delicious jars of jellies, vinegars, dressings, and sauces. Horseradish and jalapeño pretzel dips, Three-oak aged balsamic vinegar, and a slew of homemade jams.

"So, I guess it's you," Echo had said, looking up, closing the book, as though Grant was a long lost friend. Her dark eyes were large, sensitive and clear. He thought her beautifully human. At twelve, she was gentle with the world but not afraid of it, a quality he lacked.

He asked for five jars of the horseradish. It was the first thing he thought of to say.

Everyone thought Grant was just being helpful, running to the store on daily errands. The significance of his every thought grew with the anticipation of sharing it with her, a piece of driftwood that had sprouted a seedling, a fistful of lake glass the color of autumn leaves, an arrowhead still razor sharp as though it had just been fashioned. When Grant would stutter trying to explain something, her hand on his shoulder eased his words. The first book he gave her was from a collection about the Appalachian mountain people. Together, they read about customs, remedies, and folkways, breathless at the timbre of each other's voice.

At each summer's beginning, he and Echo picked right up where they'd left off. One of the first things Echo shared with him was something she had read. That's when he knew.

She said she wanted to be like the trees, that she had read they were most trusting of all creatures because they put their roots down in one place, knowing they'd be there for their entire lives.

At the end of their first summer, when she said good-bye, he put his finger to her lips.

"We have no good-byes. We say, *Es'GönGëheit*. I'll see you again."

His ancestors believed you'd always see again those people who meant something to you, whether in this life or the spirit world.

During their last summer, on the night before she left for college, they had picnicked on the top of Bare Hill. He had put off college for a year to be with her as much as possible. Joseph had let him work alongside her and sleep in a room in the back of the store. He and Echo had grown closer than ever.

That night the August heat made the crickets' wings slick with fervor. They had kissed for hours on the blue flannel blanket, when suddenly Echo pulled away. He had asked her what was wrong. He could see she was afraid, but she wiped the sweat from her forehead and pulled off her T-shirt. Topless, she stared at him. She unhooked the yellow cotton bra that held her small breasts, and let it fall off her shoulders. "We don't have to do this," he said. But she moved toward him, trembling. She unzipped his shorts, touched him, first gently, then harder. He reached up. Her breasts fit perfectly in his hands. He kissed her on the forehead. He told her again that they didn't have to do this, but this time, he persisted, his mouth tracing the freckles across her chest, down to her waist and then back up to her mouth as she knelt back onto the blanket and he pressed against her. He asked her if it was too soon, if she was ready to do this. "Think about it," he told her.

"Stop thinking," she answered. "Just don't think."

He pulled her on top of him, and pushed himself into her for the first time, and he felt the force of his own energy as he never had before. As he entered her, her warm mouth coursed over his neck and he moaned, aching with the intense release, his lips parted slightly.

The grass scuttled in circles around their bodies, each blade a somber purple hue blurred in the haze of moon. In a moment the flood of emotion intoxicated him. As she hovered over him, he noticed the delicate curve of her neck, the soft tendrils of hair falling across her forehead, how her skin grew more flushed with each moment, as though she were drawing all the color out of the earth. He noticed these things with unusual clarity, the way a man notices something just before he loses it. "I think I might love you," she whispered, blurting it out fast. It was the first time either of them had said those words. Grant couldn't speak. Not because he didn't feel the same. More, because the weight of that emotion was towering, and because of the promise ring that he had been carrying in his pocket, now hidden under a heap of clothing in the grass.

When he didn't respond, Echo looked away, hurt, as though she had been slapped. His silence had spoken volumes.

Quickly, she got up. She refused to look at him as she slipped her clothing on, gathered up her blanket and basket. Then she took off running across the field. For a moment he didn't move, lying there, trying to make sense of it. When he finally caught up with her, she shrugged him off. "Tonight was a mistake," she said, pulling the blanket around her body. "I lied. I don't really love you." She waited for a reaction, tears forming in the corners of her eyes.

He stammered, grabbing for the ring. It was his mother's, though she never wore it—a gift that his father had carved from catlinite, a soft red stone flecked with tiny dots the Indians called stars. This stone contained a heart-line, a straight black hair-thick line that looked like a crack. It made the stone lucky for whoever wore it.

"You can't trust me, that's your problem," she told him. "Because of what your mother thinks of me." Echo had stared at Grant, daring him to leave her. She was drumming up as much meanness as she could muster, hatred even, he felt, as he looked into her red puffy eyes. Her tears dried an instant after they fell.

"Go ahead. I could care less. Hate me," she ordered.

"I can't," he said.

"What's wrong with you!" she cried. "We're not the same. I'm no good for you. Stop feeling sorry for me." He watched her run home, the silvery grass splintering in her wake. He did not follow her.

The next day, Joseph drove her to the bus station, where she bought a ticket and left immediately for Cornell University.

Grant dialed her number that first week at least one hundred times. He could feel her breath on the line. He could picture her staring into her bedroom mirror as he once had seen her do, searching for the defect that she felt had relegated her to a lifetime of abandonment.

He knew the loss of her parents had walled up a part of her

heart, but he wasn't so different. He wanted to remind her of something they both wanted.

"We're like the trees. Remember?"

"No, you're like them," Echo had said on the phone. "Not me."

"If I were with you right now, I could change your mind. I could take a bus. I'll be there tomorrow."

"Grant, I met someone. Please don't call me again. I won't ever love you," she whispered. There was a tinge of fear in her voice almost as though she blamed him for making her say it. He hadn't talked to her since.

"WHO CAN TELL HER anything," Joseph says, with a smile.

Grant may tell himself that it is just curiosity but both men know the truth. That just as there are some people you try to love but can't, there are those you can't stop loving no matter how hard you try. None of it has anything to do with logic.

Echo had always chided herself aloud for being too sensitive. She said that her eyes betrayed her, but this was the very thing that drew Grant to her. She could be listening to him, nodding, but her eyes would tell him she was thinking of other things. She was unable to mask anything. This had made her irresistible to him. It took him a long time to get over Echo. To move on.

Now his heart needs to settle. His fingers leave prints on the picture, but that is all he is willing to leave. He hands it back quickly. Grant manages to speak. "Duct tape?"

"Second aisle up on the left," Joseph says, slipping the picture back into the wallet. "We'll be seeing more of you now. You know, boy, I always said you had some wisdom. Not a lot, don't go getting a big head."

Grant stares at Joseph. "Well, you were sorely wrong, Joe."

"Nah, look. I don't believe it," Joseph replies. "One way or another we get a second chance."

Joseph looks vulnerable, standing there, thin, brittle, with an ache behind his eyes. And Grant has seen that look before. Grant turns and starts to walk away. He knows that some people leave their mark on you forever. As much as a man tries, there will still come a day when he picks up the phone and dials a once forgotten number, or starts to follow someone who he thinks might be her, in the grocery store, in the street, at the park. He may look everywhere for a replacement. And even when he thinks he has found one, deep down he knows that it will never feel the same.

"Patience," Joseph reminds him. "It takes a long time to become young."

"Not sure what that means," Grant says.

"You'll understand someday. All folks want to escape from their problems sometimes. Some try by praying all the time, thinking Spirit will take care of everything. But they can come to depend too much on this. The fact is that people right here on earth can do more for each other than the spirits can."

At that moment, Grant looks to the right of the Feed & Grain at a flash of sunlight streaking across the grass, reflecting off the fur of an animal hiding between two bur oak. It is pawing at the grass and digging its nose into a pile of stones as though searching for the one hidden piece of moon that has fallen from the sky. Too big to be a coyote, probably a dog or maybe even a wolf, Grant guesses. Then, in a flash, it turns and runs, disappearing into the thicket across from the building.

"I thought there were no wolves left in Canandaigua," Grant says to Joseph.

Joseph shakes his head. "There weren't for years. But I saw that big one for the first time this morning. Must mean something has changed."

Grant tries not to look at the old man, whose eyes are burning into him. He tries for a clipped good-bye, but his voice catches. After weeks of silence, the words want to sit in his throat. Maybe he is too much like his father, incapable of dealing with emotion. Throughout his marriage, he had worked hard to appear in control, hardening at the first indication of crisis. And yet, in this place, he is too much like his mother, feeling too much and letting it bleed out of him. Neither of his parents seemed to have the key to dealing with emotion. They were at different extremes and instead of bringing them closer to the middle, it ended up polarizing them. Grant has spent his whole life ricocheting between the two. He rubs his neck and turns to go, eager to escape. The flies are starting to cloud the air.

As he walks off, he thinks about how a long time ago, in this very place, he found his voice. The memory is somehow reassuring. When he reaches the end of the road, Grant turns back to see Charlie Cooke resting his hand on Joseph's shoulder as the old man wipes his eyes.

at the age of six, or that the weight of her gratitude toward him often makes her shoulders ache. Gratitude can be a burden, after all. The burden is this: the world gave her Joseph, which means she owes the world for not abandoning her. She could have just as easily been lost forever. She is never too far from that fear, even now. All these years later, Joseph is everything to her; he is like the trees, rooting all those around him.

But owing the world such a debt makes her vulnerable. Who knows when the earth might want her to pay up? It might want to take Joseph back. She is never too far from this sense of vague panic.

Ahead, sunlight glimmers in streams across the interstate as the Jeep burns off the downy clouds that gather near the edges of the lake. Joseph handed her all those years ago as she stood in front of him, hungry and aching, a carrot and a Partridge family lunch box gripped in her hands. "Well, kiddo. I'm hungry," he had said. "You like juneberry jelly sandwiches?"

Echo hadn't known whether to follow the social worker back into the cab, or to follow Joseph into the store. Her hunger made the decision for her. She had no idea what a juneberry sandwich was, but she liked how it sounded. As Echo helped Joseph slice bread and spread jelly, he said to call him Pop. She giggled. *Pop* was a funny word. It meant soda, she'd been taught. She thought she'd gone to heaven when he actually said she could try on all the jewelry he sold for the Seneca people who lived around here, and as she looked over it all, she had felt, for the first time, full, and wanting nothing. Not the silver bracelets and turquoise earrings, or the catlinite charms. She preferred, instead, to relish the feeling of being able to touch them all if she wanted. Joseph even told her she could choose one of the cornhusk dolls for her very own. Echo had taken a long time to choose her doll. Made with real animal hair, the faceless dolls were meant to teach youngsters that vanity was undesirable. The summer tourists loved them.

"But where are her eyes?" Echo had said, distressed.

"She sees from the inside," Joseph had explained.

"How did she learn it?" she had asked.

He had laughed. "She already knew. You do, too."

The doll would help keep her safe, he said. When he told her that the sky had a present for her, she looked out the window, already used to the way he talked. She can still recall how the sun looked like a huge red poppy floating on the water. Her heart had felt just like that, as though it were a flower bursting with color. Her feelings about the world had changed in a few hours just as the sky had changed in a few moments.

He'd never agree that she owes him everything, but she does. He called himself next of kin when really he was only her mother's fifth or sixth cousin. Even then, Echo knew how close she had been to being abandoned. An Orphan. The word chases her still. It's the monster hiding under the bed, the shadow lurking behind the trees. Joseph always told her that she would never be alone, that her parents were up there protecting her. At night, she tested his theory, sitting in the window in her nightgown waving at the clouds as they tumbled across the sky. She imagined her parents were up there, two watchful spirits hovering over her, molding the clouds into shapes like clay, offering clues to her questions, abating her fears. She'd close her eyes and try to conjure every memory she could: her father pulling leaves from her mother's red hair as she was digging up flower bulbs; her mother dragging plywood and two-by-fours across the yard the day Echo's father built a tree house, and that lazy Tuesday afternoon that her mother had kept her home from kindergarten because of a cough, and had read to her for what seemed like hours and how that night, all three of them had piled onto the big beanbag chair to watch the nightly news in the paneled den. Echo had watched her mother's tears fall across her freckled cheeks as the newscaster announced the death of Picasso, who had been her favorite artist.

When the memories didn't help, Echo would run and find Joseph on the porch. She'd crawl into his lap and fall asleep, comforted by the sound of his breathing, and the men's voices and the smell of their pipes. She loved their big stories and their deep laughter that sounded like wind and drums.

The fear of losing Joseph is never far from her mind, makes her want to try and stay awake for days as though she will lose track of him if she sleeps. Alone in her apartment, the impossibility of that big vague sky sweeps over her in an instant. It follows her into bed, and even the two cats lying on her stomach and perhaps a phone call to Joseph will not put her mind to rest. When the feeling is really bad and she is exhausted from nights of insomnia, she won't call, afraid she'll worry him with the sound of her voice. Only the cats know how she is shivering, trying to ground herself with her back pressed up against the wall.

She is lucky, she tells herself. It's not that she doesn't want to dwell on the loss of her parents. She simply can't. The kindest, gentlest man in the world raised her. In fact, out of all the places she could have landed, she had always thought she was the luckiest girl in the world, living above Joseph O'Connell's store.

She and the old man had made the apartment above the Feed & Grain into a cozy home. Thirsty for a drink? Right downstairs. Need an extra lightbulb? Back in a flash. She still feels her life was more extravagant here than anywhere else, even if her bedroom was never big enough for more than a cot, a lamp, and a bookshelf. She never needed much more than that.

From an early age, she had the responsibility of stocking and reordering the paperbacks on the movable rack next to the fishing lures. She probably wouldn't have fallen in love with books if she hadn't worked there to earn her tuition for college. This is a deal she and Joseph had made. She knew from early on where she was going and why.

She can't lose Joseph. Not yet.

She doesn't want to come off preachy or desperate or condescending. He won't hear it. They both know stubbornness is a family trait, and neither was good at giving things up even though they could put on a convincing show. They have at least some of the same genes, after all. Even though his cough is horrible, he won't relinquish that pipe. Could she honestly say it was so easy letting go of Stephen? He's seven years her junior. They are worlds apart, but on certain topics like the impossibility of commitment, they meet perfectly. She didn't want to get married. At thirty-two, she paid no attention to a biological clock, and was in no rush to settle down. She told herself they were having the sort of fun most people wished for, and so it was all worthwhile. At least they were honest about what they were and weren't looking for, if not about the fact that he had broken the rules and had fallen in love with her.

The beginnings of crow's-feet shoot from the corners of her wide brown eyes. Often they redden and ache from reading for eight hours straight, but Stephen tells her she is beautiful. Still, there have been days, entire months, when she has looked into the mirror and another face has stared back at her, one that resembled an old sepia photo framed in Joseph's office, a photo of a woman whose face was raked by lines beginning at the eyes and continuing downward in large deep circles, curving around the nose, mouth, and chin. When Echo was younger she'd trace the lines in the face with her finger, thinking the face was beautiful. She was never concerned with things other girls were, like perfect skin and brushing her hair fifty times on each side. Other things took up her mind: precious words, sculpted and balanced, and of course, the good health of the person she loves most in the world.

Now Echo's worn leather sandal catches the brake pedal as she slows for the tollbooth. She's trying to free herself from the seat belt, but her hair falls in her eyes and she can feel that she's holding up the entire line of cars behind her.

"Sorry, sorry," she says, handing the ticket to the guy in the booth. Why is she still apologizing? She used to apologize for everything—a woman tripping over a crack in the street, the Xerox machine eating her boss's report, the rain on a Saturday afternoon.

"Seven seventy-five," he says, craning out the window. "Like the Jeep."

She's suddenly self-conscious, wondering if he is staring because he can tell she is not wearing a bra. She turns away, locates some change at the bottom of her purse and pays him quickly.

Flying down the interstate at 85 mph, the sound of the wind beating against her half-open window is deafening. She can feel every nuance of the road. It is almost like walking barefoot. She's lost in thought about how to broach the subject of health with Joseph, whether she has a right to ask that he go see a doctor, whether it's correct to suggest that he leave Canandaigua and come to live with her in Boston. Echo knows the help is there. People on the lake love him. But she worries. Loneliness often masquerades as independence. She can hear it seeping from the hollowness of his voice, through his words on the phone.

Still, can she fault him for not believing in conventional medicine? Fifty years of living alongside the Indians in Canandaigua and watching the medicine of his old friend Two Bears, a famed Seneca healer, and before that, living among the Wataita people in Kenya, have taught him otherwise: that the greatest healer is the human spirit when it works in conjunction with the spirits of the earth: the plant spirits, the tree spirits, the spirits of the sky and moon, and the water spirits.

Joseph's beliefs reach into the deep forests of Africa. He had been studying to be a priest back then, organizing climbs up Mount Kilimanjaro. He had met his wife, Rose, during one of those climbs.

Echo thinks about their meeting far too often, and pictures the air so thick on a mountain that their footprints actually peeled off in the dirt.

Now with the dogwood tree unleashing its white petals into the air, she feels a tightening in her chest. If she didn't know better she'd say those were mayflies tumbling toward her.

If she squints hard enough, Echo can make out a blue flash of wings spreading across the wide bur oak. Despite the warm air, even while clamoring impatiently for the mayflies, certain kingfishers freeze in mid-flight, still holding an ancient memory of ice in their feathers.

Picking wildflowers, daisy and coltsfoot, can make certain feelings go away. She pulls over to the side of the road and gets out, stretching her long legs. Funny thing, she has finally embraced her body. Now that her breasts and hips are fuller and her stomach has softened, she likes her body more than ever. More so even than when she was ten years younger and fifteen pounds thinner. This is something she supposes a woman must learn over time. Who would have thought that as she got older, men would desire her more?

She scans the grassy slope. The tiger lilies are not in bloom, but there are purple thistle, chicory, and daisy, too, the blue and white clusters reminiscent of the oil painting in her boss's office. When her boss announced the number of vacation days Echo had accrued, Echo was embarrassed that she'd gone five years without a real vacation. She'd taken weekends to visit Joseph, that was all. Where had the time gone? Wasn't she once a person who'd wanted things? It's not like she hadn't been busy. But busy didn't always mean happy. Perhaps she'd tricked herself—sometimes any movement felt like progress.

She whisks through the tall grass and she cuts across the muddy slope. Though she's still 50 miles from the lake, Echo already needs to reign in her emotions. She will gather flowers for Clarisse Mellon, her old friend and neighbor. She pours over Queen Anne's lace, gathering stems in her hands, searching for the one without its center, the one missing its purple regal spot in the middle of the white petals. Ahead in the distance, just as she pulls a few daisy stems carefully from the dirt, she sees something darting among the trees, a crouching shadow, slowly crawling toward her. She freezes, careful not to challenge it by looking directly in the eyes. Her heart is pounding. The wolf turns and disappears into the trees as thunder cracks the sky, and it begins to drizzle.

She quickly throws a handful of flowers into the backseat and starts the Jeep. The sky is fickle, turning dark as rain clouds move in. The wolf is nowhere in sight as she steps on the gas. Her goal is to surprise Joseph before sundown. Before long, she reaches the edge of town, and the new Walmart store with its discount down winter jackets out on the sidewalk rack. She drives down Main Street through Canandaigua, with its wide tree-lined streets and stately mansions. She passes the Pickering Monument, a granite boulder set on the courthouse lawn and inlaid with a bronze plaque to commemorate the last general council of the Iroquois and the Canandaigua Treaty of 1794, one of the first treaties the United States entered into with the Indians, signed by George Washington, and which served as a proclamation of friendship and peace between the U.S. government and the Iroquois, a promise not to lay claim to, or disturb Indian lands. It is now a reminder of a promise unkept.

Echo thinks of the pillaged burial grounds and the stolen Indian artifacts each time she sees it.

Echo heads toward David's Barber Shop but she does not make a wish when she passes the gold dome of the town hall. All the children in town make wishes when they see it, but Echo never did. She is not a person who believes things happen because of a wish. Wishes are dangerous things. They can get lodged in a person's mind, and passed down through generations. The Tiffany lamp in the window of the Garlock house is still on, as it has been for decades, a tradition begun by the mother of a boy killed in a plane crash, and continued by every owner thereafter.

A gift shop has moved in next to the wooden fence painted in the facade of an old storefront. Then there's Pizza Hut, its signature red roof absent in the white Victorian-era shell. Echo turns off the main drag and onto East Lake Road, where the roots of hardy weeds writhe under the ground, sprouting up in potholes on the road. She passes four large lakefront houses hidden from the road by the trees. She's memorized the list of last names burned into wooden signs, nailed along the tree trunks. Kornegger, Loomis, Bray, O'Reilly.

Despite the drizzle, a brilliant orange sun emerges, flickering in streams across the highway as she speeds by. After a few minutes, Echo turns onto the old dirt road. She cannot wait to throw her arms around Joseph O'Connell, and she once again steps on the gas.

4

THE EARLY AFTERNOON DRIZZLE starts and stops as the flies swarm in smoky clouds that seem to dip and curve through the air. The Feed & Grain disappears into the distance as Grant heads home. He picks up his pace each time he passes a burial ground, taking care not to slip on the roadside gravel. To avoid the possibility of meeting anyone on the road, he takes a shortcut, running fast across the grassy slopes, and jumping across the small creek beds, taking comfort in the light rain, the soft pad of the wet grass, the slight slip of mud under his feet. He almost doesn't see what comes next. He almost runs right into it, but catches himself just in time to miss the large gray wolf dodging across his path, its fur blurring into the mist as though it were a patch of moving fog.

Grant stops to catch his breath, watching as the wolf emerges from the haze and comes closer. It's around ninety pounds, thin and angular with long legs and a thick gold-gray coat. He can tell this animal is not pure wolf. It is one of the lost hybrids of Canandaigua, reminiscent of a German shepherd with its pointed ears and long muzzle. But its head is larger than a dog's, its tail bushier, its feet longer and paws heavier. The wolf slinks away and waits under a nearby flowering dogwood tree, watchful, as though taunting him. Grant kneels, examining the tracks. The hind foot has been placed in the track left by the front. Overlapping tracks are singular to wolves, not dogs. He has not come across this in years. He remembers his father telling him that many years ago, packs of wolves were just as commonplace in Canandaigua as Indian burial grounds. The wolves acted as the protectors of the graves. When the graves began to be robbed and the artifacts disappeared, so did the wolves.

A wolf had been shot dead the night Two Bears was murdered in his cave decades ago. But only the wolf's body had been found, not Two Bears. The Seneca healer's body had disappeared. His silver tomahawk was gone. It was highly prized because of its silver cutting edge on one end and pipe on the other, symbolic of both peace and war, given to an Indian leader named Cornplanter by the Europeans during King Philip's War, in the late 1600s.

Some people believed that an archaeologist was behind Two Bears's supposed murder, but there was no proof and it never went further than suspicion. What was left behind was the bloody body of a lone gray wolf that had obviously fought its murderers to its death. A ripped bloodstained piece of cloth and a patch of human hair had been found in its teeth.

For years, every time a parking lot or a swimming pool was put in, arrowheads poked up from the dirt. Once in a blue moon, a pack of sorrowful wolves would appear quite suddenly on the excavated land, more like ghosts than living creatures, maddened, thin, and howling. Some said it was Two Bears's ghost showing his disapproval. Although the wolves disappeared, the progeny is still out there: a shaggy mix of dog and wolf with ice blue eyes and a tail that wags incessantly, a breed friendlier than it should be yet content to be strays. Trailing the roads and the sweet clover. Howling at the fog lights. Only coming out in the quiet.

RIGHT NOW, IN THE swirl of bugs, Grant hears a howl unlike anything he has ever heard before, a low dull cry of this sorrowful wolf that has been following him for the last one hundred yards. After skulking across the muddy creek, about ten feet away, it has reappeared, snarling at Grant, its fur stuck with prickers. It circles him hypnotically, baring its teeth, squinting its yellow eyes. But the loose jowls and sorrowful howl belie its ferocity. Grant stops and walks him down. The animal backs up. But Grant keeps coming despite the possible danger. Grant circles the animal, feeling momentarily victorious when the animal lies down. He edges closer, crouching. The animal does not recoil, only whimpers.

"Go home," Grant orders, as the animal begins to beg at his feet. The rain is coming down harder. Grant looks up. He can see the impatient moon already high up in the sky. The rain clouds ebb and flow across it, causing the sky to change from dark to light and back. At this time of year the weather is fickle, sunlight interrupted by light rain, which dissipates into fog. When Grant looks down, the wolf has disappeared. Grant continues his run, but he knows the animal is tracking him. "Get lost," he yells back, though he cannot see him. He can only smell the heavy scent of sweat and mud left in the air. Grant sprints down the dividing line headed for home.

Grant uses the bag of duct tape to wave the bugs out of his eyes. He picks up the pace but suddenly the animal reappears, trotting alongside him. A green Jeep whizzes by, blares its horn. Massachusetts plates. That figures. Grant has to practically dive off the road to keep from becoming roadkill. He looks around but the wolf has disappeared once more.

The wolf re-emerges, nipping at Grant's heals in the breakdown lane. Why do only the most desperate creatures want to cling to him? Susanna had said that it was his compassion. Grant thought it something far more ominous, something karmic and dark known only to the most tortured of spirits.

Grant knows he's got to get back inside the cabin soon, otherwise his clothes will be full of the tiny bugs. If Grant didn't know better, he'd say the petals of the morning glories near Hobson's Bay were folding up in self-protection. If he squints, out there in the distance it looks like there are shadows diving into the black water.

The scraggly animal is trying to lick his hands, trying to get his attention by running straight into his legs. "I can't help you," Grant says. It stares at him with its watery bloodshot eyes, and then turns around as though it disapproves. Grant watches as it bounds up the center of the road until it's little more than a gray speck on the dusky horizon.

Grant continues his run. As he makes his way to the top of a hill, he recognizes the green Jeep speeding along the highway. He notices something in the middle of the road. At first he thinks it is a boulder. As he gets closer, he knows it is the wolf. Its fur looks almost white under the hazy sky. The Jeep is speeding faster and faster toward it. The wolf does not move. "Run!" calls Grant. A horn blares. The driver of the Jeep suddenly brakes. Then he hears the screech of tires sliding across gravel and the sound of metal as the Jeep skids and crashes into an oak tree.

THE WOLF TROTS OFF toward the woods, head hung low, fading into the fog.

Grant could turn a blind eye. If he just started running, no one would ever know that he was a witness to a crash. It doesn't look like too much damage, just a fender, maybe some dents, and a new paint job. Amidst the swarm of mayflies, his eyes are fixed on the long auburn hair beginning to spill from the window. As the Jeep's broken door opens, brown leather clogs hit the ground, then the pale figure of a woman in jeans and a white T-shirt emerges. She stands, one hand resting on her forehead, the other on the door. She looks up at the sky, her pale freckled face wet with rain. Then she collapses.

As he lumbers toward the Jeep, he feels his legs moving of their own accord. The future is competing with the past, speeding through time to catch up.

He'd know her anywhere, the way she's struggling to get up, pushing her hair out of her eyes as she stares right through him into the rainy countryside. The woman reaches up and grabs the door handle of the Jeep and tries to pull herself up, but her long legs fold underneath her. Grant thinks this might be a dream, maybe just an illusion thrown in by the spirit of the little boy. More than once over the last fifteen years he has thought he saw Echo O'Connell crossing the room in a restaurant, buying groceries, driving fast with her windows down. He's been wrong each time. Now he wonders if lifelong yearnings are always fulfilled, sooner or later.

5

Clarisse Mellon, who has lived next door to the Ellis family for over twenty years, is standing at her screen door, a crowd of orange cats gathered at her feet to watch Grant Shongo jog along the side of the road.

She hasn't told anyone how she often sees the spirit of Luke Ellis crouched in the crook of Leila's lilac tree, or how many of his yellow paper airplanes appear out of nowhere, littering her gutters and landing in her open windows. She knows grief can make you see and do odd things. If people in town think Grant is crazy, locked away in his family's haunted cabin for three weeks, she knows what they'd say about her. That she is just a lonely old woman who has spent too many years watching other women get married and have families. That she is just trying to get attention. If they only knew the truth, that her solitary situation is the result of a choice she made a long time ago. A conscious choice. Clarisse might be nearly blind without her glasses with the emerald rhinestone frames, her skin might be as mottled as a potato, her fingers as knotted as ginger root, but her mind is as clear as a bell.

That is why the first thing Clarisse did when she woke up

this morning was scrub her face with extra hot water and soap until her skin shined. She has not applied lipstick, or powdered her nose. Instead her long ivory hair unravels down her back. She is wearing her white nylon jogging suit and her Michael Jordan sneakers, the ones that make her feel she could float right above the ground and get away if she had to. She is trying to free herself from all of the sticky lies. And there's a warm north wind, the kind good for truth telling.

Without the glittering costume jewelry, without the cast of hair spray, Clarisse knows she looks plain but not embarrassingly so. It is high time that she liked what is real. She has become accustomed to the liver spots—beauty marks, she calls them—which have landed on the tip of her nose and the tops of her hands. Don't both men and women eventually end up with sagging breasts and beards? She has that sense of freedom, or of wanting to be free, she's not sure which.

Leila Ellis has been a neighbor for all these years, but when a friendship is based on secrets instead of kindred spirits, how long can it last? No one should be weighted down with another woman's trouble for this long.

Clarisse knows all about the Shongos' cabin at the foot of Bare Hill. She even knows that the mischievous group of boys who live along the lake would never go inside, curious or not. The fact is that the adults around here tell ghost stories about Luke just as the children do. But the children are braver. They play truth or dare, nighttime games. They double dare each other to run and touch the Shongos' dock. Then they tear back to their houses shouting Luke's name, the wind slamming the door behind them.

SUDDENLY, CLARISSE CATCHES SIGHT of another yellow paper airplane in her window box.

It has been as strange a day as she can remember.

The dance of the mayflies occurring on the twelve-year anniversary of the little boy's death. A dozen years have passed. Clarisse hobbles across the green kitchen to the window overlooking the Ellises' backyard. She stands, eyeing the little boy's frosted tombstone half hidden under a spray of flesh-beaten lilacs. Leila had wanted him buried right in her backyard but the town ordinances wouldn't allow it. Luke had a proper burial in a cemetery, but the next day, Leila went right ahead and had another tombstone put in under the lilac tree so he would never be far from her thoughts, she had told Clarisse. Leila had held a private funeral there, only the girls and her, with the girls dressed in their long black coats, just as they had been the day before.

Since Melanie disappeared two days ago, Clarisse finds herself fixated on the tombstone. It doesn't help that Leila's lilac tree has now grown so out of control that it is bumping against her kitchen window, its blossoms, bruisy and swollen with truth. This morning when Clarisse woke up and looked in the mirror, her lips were a haunting pasty white, as though the lilac bush had sucked the color right out of her skin.

She pours herself a glass of milk and then thinks better of it. "Lactose," she says, shaking her head. She pours the milk into a bowl and a crowd of cats quickly gathers at her feet. Clarisse scoops up her orange Persian, Ella Fitzgerald, and cups her hand under the stomach, where the sixth litter of babies is waiting inside the tummy. Today, she will line the guest room closet with old green pillows, towels, and newspaper. Cool and dark, it's the mother-to-be's favorite place for birthing.

Clarisse remembers how all those years ago Grant and Echo O'Connell delivered Ella's mother to her doorstep. They had found the kittens in an old barn and delivered them right to

Clarisse. Perhaps it was her reputation for collecting things, or her soft spot for children and animals. She had indeed kept most of those kittens. Now her house is overrun with feline children and their grandchildren. Clarisse has always been a collector of things, especially items other people don't want to keep. Her kitchen backsplash is covered with decorative plates. Statues of ceramic frogs are positioned in all four corners of the kitchen. The walls, done in ochre and olive green, are covered with collectibles: old frames, antique plates, and pictures of her ancestors. Her prized green velvet couch and chairs are worn but still regal, piled so high with needlepointed pillows that there is hardly room to sit. And now, Ella Fitz is due any day. There will be no room in this place for any more collections.

Clarisse is also a collector of secrets, and this is the most troublesome part.

She would run to the phone to spread the news of Grant Shongo's emergence if the lines were working, but the storm has pulled them down and twisted them into shreds. She keeps the folklore of the many strange things that have happened in this town, and more than a handful of them she has witnessed with her own two eyes. Clarisse recalls everything that happens here as easily as she remembers the names of each of her six cats. How, in the spring of 1988, the Ellis children stole the canoe out into the icy lake.

How, two years after the tragedy, Grant's mother fell ill and never recovered. Emily Shongo would tell anyone who asked that she would never give up her cigarettes, not for anything, including her own life. They say that she knew she was dying long before she told anyone, including her doctor husband. She even paraded around town with her lit cigarette in hand as though she had a vendetta. By the time Dr. Shongo found out, it was too late for him to do anything; the cancer had progressed too far. No one challenged Emily Shongo. It was as though dying was her way of punishing someone, Clarisse has often thought.

Dr. Shongo never got over his failures. After his wife's death, he embarked on a seemingly endless project of redesigning their house. It was rumored that he was going to flatten the old cabin in Canandaigua and rebuild, and during one particular spring, a couple of fancy architects from New York City were flown in to survey the area and draw up plans. Of particular concern was the old coal bin in the basement, which leaked dirty soot that left smudges on the walls and the rugs. Dr. Shongo never settled on a plan, and closed up the place. But the details of his bereavement traveled all the way through the phone wires from Rochester. Some say, up until the tragedy of the little boy and then his wife's death, he had thought himself a god. Infallible. And this, thinks Clarisse, is a fatal ingredient in the recipe for living.

Grant inherited the troubled life, Clarisse thinks. She walks outside to her garden and imagines she can still see Grant running even though the air is thick and hazy with flies. She walks to the end of her driveway, aware of her aching knees. All morning she has been removing old broken branches, twigs, and white stones from her garden and depositing them in the woods.

She wants to shout, to say something, to tell him that solitude doesn't automatically bring serenity, just as noise and clutter don't automatically abate loneliness. Though Grant has not told anyone in town about Susanna, everyone knows about her. Three miscarriages are enough to make anyone run away—from themselves, from a loved one. Clarisse often says that word travels in the water here. Others say it is whispered in the rustling of trees. She is not the only one in this town that has secrets to keep. Everyone does. People here lock their doors at night even though this is the country and everyone is supposed to be hospitable. But too much has happened here. Even the nonbelievers question the unbelievable bad luck of some people. Leila Ellis and her three children, in particular. What can you expect, with a husband as troubled as Victor? Right now most people are talking about Melanie Ellis, who disappeared two days ago, abandoning her boyfriend Lion and their son.

Nineteen, they all agree, was too young to have a baby. Isn't that what Doris Loomis told Clarisse in the cereal aisle of Wildman's supermarket yesterday? How was it, Doris wondered aloud, that Canandaigua's former Harvest Queen had made such a mess of her young life? "Couldn't she have gotten married at least, to redeem her family's good name?" she asked Clarisse.

"Do people still do that?" Clarisse had wondered aloud.

"You're right. I suppose it was never a good name to begin with," replied Doris.

Still, nothing explains why Melanie would have left her boyfriend, Lion, and their son. She had disappeared without a trace. Without a note, or anything. Clarisse had actually stood up for the pair when most folks clicked their teeth, shook their heads, saying mixed-race relationships were doomed from the start. But Clarisse had been the Ellises' next-door neighbor for years, and this did give her somewhat of an expert opinion on the matter. Truth is, Lion wasn't the one that Clarisse was worried about. She knew Lion and she respected him. His arrival in town had coincided with her house falling apart: A leaking faucet, a washing machine on the fritz, a gutter swollen with leaves and wet paper airplanes. Lion was earnest, capable, wanting to be helpful. She hired him to do odd jobs: installing a slip-safe bar in the shower, fixing a broken window, moving her refrigerator so that she could clean behind it. Whenever she called, he arrived at a second's notice. Clarisse trusted him completely. There was an air of sincerity in his yellow-brown eyes. And Lord knows he knew how to listen. What a gift that was. Someone who wanted to listen to her stories and to her complaints. He was good company, always polite unlike most young folks, and he wouldn't leave a job unfinished. She was certain that if the romance failed it would not be due to Lion.

Lion had told her some things, too. He talked openly about his life. He had lived through five earthquakes and one of the worst riots to ever hit California. He told her about a regular guy named Rodney King who was in the wrong place at the wrong time and changed the face of Los Angeles when four police officers beat him silly because of his skin color. When they were found innocent, the riots that followed were worse than any earthquake, Lion said. He explained how the streets turned into a crazy river of people. Rocks and bottles fell from the sky. People grabbed drivers out of cars, threw televisions into liquor store windows, and took whatever they wanted. Helicopters buzzed over street fires. He could taste the anger, he said. It wasn't he who had been beaten by those cops, but he felt like he had, and even though he was in a crowd of strangers, he felt connected to all of them by that feeling.

At some point during the riot, Lion noticed that half of his arm was split open because someone had cut him. He almost fainted from the surprise of all that blood as the crowd knocked him down and trampled his body. Even still, Lion said he believed he had a lucky angel named Matrina. "It was Matrina, doing her thing," he'd often say. Clarisse didn't know where the name came from, but it comforted Lion to think this way.

Clarisse could see that Melanie was moved by his story. Melanie would sit with her sketch pad in her lap, listening closely while Lion was working and recounting his history. Occasionally, she'd get up and rub his shoulders, asking him if he was okay. He was her hero, an unassuming knight in shining armor, unknown to most people who crossed to the opposite side of the street at night when Lion walked toward them, dressed in his black sweatshirt and knit cap.

Once, Lion confessed to Clarisse how he had gotten Melanie clean. It had been the hardest thing he had ever done, sitting outside the bedroom, which he locked from the outside, listening to her scream about smoke coming out of the walls, and not being able to breathe as she pounded the door and ripped the hair from her own head. It would be the kiss of death if he went in. He had always given in to her, whatever she wanted. But not this. He loved her so much he hadn't broken.

Only after Melanie had fallen asleep had he gone in, removing the sweat-soaked blankets, washing them, and leaving them folded at the foot of the bed. He'd bring buckets of ice and a bowl of soup, praying that Matrina would see them out of this thing. Even after he was suspended without pay from his job at the garage for missing work three days in a row, he remained solid at the kitchen table.

Clarisse is not like the less sympathetic types. They cut no one any slack.

Melanie had been struggling for a while. But then she and Lion had a son. Her sudden disappearance wasn't right, didn't make sense. Trouble just follows some families, Clarisse thinks, as she walks inside and sets out a few more saucers of milk. Suddenly, that incessant tree is scratching against her kitchen window.

"Go away, Luke!" orders Clarisse, and then she thinks better of it. "Please, go away," she whispers.

As she stands at her kitchen window, she tries not to look,

but her eyes fix on the frosted gray tombstone. The smell of the flowers is so sweet it sometimes gives Clarisse a headache. It trickles in even though her windows are kept tightly shut. There are no boundaries when it comes to that family. All those years ago, little Luke's paper airplanes would soar right through her kitchen window. Once they had landed on the belly of her oldest and most patient ginger tabby that had rolled over, just moments before, stomach up like a landing strip. Clarisse could hardly keep from laughing, even after she had marched outside with the intention of reprimanding Luke Ellis.

A black bra dangled over one side of Luke's head as he sat on a milk crate, dressed in an adult's robe, in front of a handmade sign that read, "Paper airplanes for a dime!" He was intense and focused, folding the yellow legal paper, which he handed over to his sisters, Melanie and Maya, who sent the planes spiraling out into the air. Passengers waved from car windows. People on bikes slowed to watch him. Luke had always been obsessed with collecting dimes. He had just seen a movie about airplanes on television, Leila later told Clarisse, and now he'd become completely obsessed with flying.

When a strong wind kicked up, the paper airplanes took off in a million different directions, and the girls chased them down driveways four neighbors deep. What could Clarisse do when Luke asked her for eighty cents, pointing to four airplanes on her roof? It didn't matter that he had added wrong, or that he spilled purple juice all over her shoes when he hugged her after she had given him his money. Back then, she loved having the children next door. She loved the sight of him flying down the driveway later that afternoon with a large black plastic bag for a cape, his long blond curls making him look wild, a purple scarf flapping around his neck. That evening Clarisse had gone outside to hold the ladder for Leila, who was determined to remove a slew of paper airplanes from Clarisse's roof and gutters. The children looked on, remarking that the two women were as brave as superheroes.

Still, even after all these years, a paper airplane will occasionally turn up when Clarisse is trimming back her rhododendron bush, or cleaning out her garage. It always takes her breath away.

At least Melanie is harmless.

The girl has a good heart even though it appears the opposite, with her crew cut, army boots and big blue tattoo that she got years after Luke died. Clarisse would gladly take her over Maya any day. Both girls are blonds, slight in body. They are doll-like creatures with flawless porcelain skin and wide cornflower blue eyes. Both just barely clear five feet. But what they lack in height, they make up for in presence. For instance, when Maya sits under the lilac tree it tends to seize the throats of nearby blackbirds.

When Maya is on a home visit from Cheever Residential Hospital, she never leaves the yard. She will sit in front of Luke's small tombstone for hours, rocking back and forth, humming to herself, her yellow hair rippling down over her shoulders. Sporadically, she'll sashay across the grass in a faded red nightgown, supposedly unaware that either the Poland Springs delivery boy or the mailman are lingering by the fence, transfixed by her graceful dance.

Most people explain away Maya's strange behavior saying that the tragedy took its toll, but no one has suffered more than Leila. She had spent many nights crying, holding Luke in her arms when he'd wake up with an asthma attack, his throat swollen enough to stop his breathing. At any time of night, Clarisse would see Dr. Shongo's white station wagon pull up into the Ellises' driveway. The winter months were always scarier for Leila, with the black ice coating the streets and Dr. Shongo living back in Rochester, half an hour away. On unlucky nights, when Leila could not find any one of Luke's several inhalers, they would rush to Emergency at Canandaigua Hospital. Clarisse would watch Leila putting Luke into the gold Ford Bronco, and the girls, in parkas and nightgowns, following their dolls into the backseat.

Folks in town refer to Luke's accident as *the tragedy* when they speak of it. But Clarisse knows something. One has to listen to people with more than her ears.

After the accident, Clarisse had tried to help Leila make sense of the story. She held Leila's hand as tears poured from the eyes of the two hysterical little girls. Leila and Victor had a fight that night, and Old Sally, their Newfoundland, had cut loose. Melanie told the story as Maya stood beside her, fidgeting. Maya did not look up. She pulled at the rip on her dress. She picked at her nails. She knelt to scrape mud from her shoes. She looked everywhere but into Clarisse's eyes. When she finally did look up, Clarisse felt her stomach turn at the emptiness in those eyes.

Melanie's account of what had happened continued. Victor had shouted at Leila because she had burned the garlic bread. Old Sally had slipped out the back window and the children followed, chasing her through the neighborhood and through the north of Vine Valley, all the way to the Shongos' cabin. The dog knew the way for it was a familiar route. The children often sneaked into the Shongos' coal bin in the weeks before Dr. Shongo's family made their annual trip to Canandaigua to open the cabin for the season. By dark it had begun to rain. The children cornered Old Sally on the Shongos' property, smack in between the Diamond Trees. Melanie tied the dog to the trunk of one of the trees, and the children fell to the ground, breathless.

That is when they heard the Seneca spirits calling to them from Squaw Island.

The light flickering off the Diamond Trees lit up an old canoe, half hidden under an old gray tarp. They found a paddle in the dirt nearby. The children dragged the boat to the shore, Maya and Luke climbed in and Melanie pushed them out into the cold lake, jumping in as it glided and bobbed over the water. They paddled out toward Squaw Island, in the direction of the whispering spirits.

Soon the storm kicked up. Melanie said the water pulled the paddle out of her hands. When Melanie stood up to get the attention of a giant on the island, the boat started to flip. She hit her head and, in her own words, *died for a few minutes.* Luke fell into the water and Maya tried to grab him, but he couldn't hold on. Or so they said.

Today, the island is desolate and small. But Clarisse remembers how that island was teeming with people after the little boy was lost. Some of the men camped out there for weeks, swimming the mile and a half wide lake over and over, even in their dreams. The giant that Melanie saw was cursorily investigated. The rain had washed away any sign of prints or tracks. The weather had been so bad that night, the police concluded that the giant was probably just tree branches waving in the wind. Yet the story of the giant with the axe took hold and became local legend.

Everyone looked to place blame. They blamed Leila for letting the children run off. Some blamed Dr. Shongo for leaving that old canoe out on the property all winter, when he knew kids liked to play around, and that he had been too busy to take the time to put it away properly for the season. Clarisse often wondered if he blamed himself for the death of a boy he had nursed back to health again and again. Some blamed

Victor, the children's abusive father, who never treated them well, who was more interested in guns and hunting than in his children. Joseph at the Feed & Grain always said no one was to blame.

Clarisse agreed with Joseph. Some mistakes are too dreadful to be blamed. But still she never bought the girls' story.

Even though she lives next door, Clarisse won't so much as talk when Maya is outside, rocking in that hypnotic way. The girl is nearly eighteen now, but the mark on some souls never leaves.

And Clarisse can't forget what she saw all those years ago.

A few months after the tragedy, Clarisse had been looking out over the sink as she washed raspberries picked from her own backyard. Through the slats in the window blinds, she caught sight of Maya kneeling in the grass under the lilac tree, holding a basket full of paper airplanes. How beautiful the girl looked in the sunlight, her face, framed in curls, her expression, one of pure angelic tranquility. She had a pile of dolls next to her and started setting them up in a half circle. That's when Clarisse saw the tombstone, just as small and pale as though it were Luke himself, standing there in the dirt. When Clarisse looked closer, she realized that Maya was having a tea party with her dolls.

No one argues that it was morbid that Leila Ellis had wanted to bury her son right in her own backyard, especially when the ground was so packed with spirits, there may not have been room for one more.

6

IN THE EARLY AFTERNOON hours, some people claim that there are more accidents in Canandaigua than at any other time of day. The way the color of the sky merges into the color of the lake makes it all look like one huge painted watercolor. It is easy to get lost in the middle of it, to veer off track. Right now, the sky is the color of a confession, and the air so raw, it turns both the water and the road a deep shade of red. As Echo squints, fumbling for her glasses, she hears footsteps behind her. She grabs hold of the door and stands. She doesn't want to turn around and have to explain to anyone how she could have been so stupid. Why she was driving with broken wipers, and how there came to be a wolf standing right in the middle of the road. Part of the fault is the flurry of flies that tumble, cloud-like, into the windshields of cars. Part of it. She is lucky if not exhausted. Maybe she's even hallucinating. She actually thought she saw Grant Shongo jogging back there in the break-down lane. Now her car has wound up right smack in the heart of an old tree.

Echo hopes the stranger walking toward her won't want to chat. That he'll know just enough to check out her car, change a tire, and then see her on her way. Maybe he'll tell her why the wolves just returned to Canandaigua. Flickering lights are everywhere, in the trees, the water, across the road. When she focuses in on the figure coming toward her, she thinks she may have a concussion. He's thinner than she remembers. His silhouette is a silver wire. Maybe his shoulders are a bit stooped.

He's no more than ten feet away. All she can think about is the number of times she has sat at work and written his name on her stationery. If he only knew about all the daughters they've had: Virginia Shongo, Eudora Shongo, Flannery Shongo. She is certain that he's never once thought of her. Certainly he will read the humiliation in her eyes.

Grant looks at her. "Jesus," he says, his hazel eyes reflecting the color of leaves. "I can't believe this. When did you—"?

He reaches for her instinctively.

She steps back, picks up her broken glasses from the ground. Her hands are shaking, and she prays that they will stop. Look away. Look anywhere but at him, she tells herself. What if there is everything to say?

Echo heard Grant got married about five years ago, that his wife is a talented photographer. The last time Echo saw him was right before they were about to leave for college. She had been wracked with panic about leaving both him and Joseph. She had just turned seventeen and was so full of worry that she had lost five pounds in one week and her long wavy hair had curled up so tightly that tiny tendrils framed her face. And Grant hadn't responded when she told him she loved him the night they made love. He let her stand there like an idiot, naked, waiting for his answer. She had wanted to hurt him, to distance herself. She believed Grant had always held this fantasy about his parents' marriage, but Echo knew Emily Shongo was unhappy. Whenever she came into the store, her glassy eyes hardly met anyone's gaze as she joked with Joseph in a low whisper about how the sick ran their lives, and how her husband always forgot to call when he'd be home late because *somebody needed him*. What did that leave Emily but a life of waiting and patience, she always said, tapping her short, bitten nails on the counter. On occasion, she'd sit on the bench on the front porch of the store, chain-smoking for an hour or so before returning home. Echo surmised that her tired eyes meant she was suffering, and the bitten nails, that she had spent too much time waiting.

Echo has wanted to apologize to Grant Shongo for all these years. How could he have found it in his heart to call her up and offer her a ring only weeks later? How could he have been so forgiving? "Everything is different, we're too far apart," she had told him, holding the phone against her cheek in the hallway of her college dorm. "You'll meet someone and —"

"But I don't want to meet anyone else."

She was following sage advice about moving on and letting the one you loved go free. And as a rule she didn't think about forever. The loss of her parents had taught her this. She had stayed at college over the next few summers taking classes in order to avoid seeing him. Still filled with shame, she graduated a year early and moved right to Boston, the wake of that emotion directing her life even though she swore she never thought of him anymore.

Besides, she had always told him that she would probably never get married, no matter how much she loved.

"ARE YOU OKAY?" he says.

"There was a wolf," she whispers, stupidly. Oh God, she was right not to talk. She thinks about refusing to give in and call him all those years ago. All those years of wrestling with herself, as though giving in were a sign of weakness. Now she thinks giving in may be a sign of strength. Fighting yourself takes more energy out of you than you can believe, she suddenly realizes. How much natural joy has it stolen over a lifetime?

"Easy now," he says. He takes her arm, helps her to the boulder by the side of the road. She is supposed to be the unflappable one. Her friends say she is fearless. But the truth is that she's not attached to anything. Why then, has all coherent thought just emptied out of her mind?

She puts her glasses in her pocket, still caught in shock. She absently pushes the hair from her eyes. Is it that everything has been turned on its side? A wolf lounging in the road. And the white blossoms of dogwood pawing the air, choking the earth with fragrance. "Where's the wolf?"

Grant stares off into the brush. "He's long gone," he says, hopefully.

"I saw it. It was right in the middle of the road. You see it?"

"I think I might have," says Grant. "It's not a wolf, it's one of those hybrids. You missed him by a hair."

"What are you doing here?" she asks, turning to him as though she has hardly heard him. I'm dreaming this, she thinks. I must be dead.

"I'm with Animal Control," Grant says, smiling.

His face is sunburnt. His hairline ebbs a little at the corners. He still has the space between his two front teeth. She wonders if he can still whistle.

She looks up. "Really?"

"No, not really," he says. He kicks the dirt as though he were, say, eleven.

She's on emotional overload, wipes her eyes, but the tears won't stop.

Just take a deep breath, she tells herself.

He takes the bandanna from his pocket and dabs her elbow. She'd look at him but her face is on fire. His fingers softly brush her knee. "You're okay," he says. "So you here to see the old man?"

"I didn't tell him, he doesn't know."

"Surprising him, he'll love it. Look at you. You're shaking."

She tries to smile. "That's because I haven't had my usual ten cups of coffee today. Caffeine calms me down."

"How many of me do you see?" He stares at her, wiping a bit of blood from her lip where she has bitten it. He puts his hand on her cheek, letting it rest there for just a second, noticing the heat of her skin.

"Really, it's okay," she says, pulling away. With the sleeves of his faded blue flannel rolled up to his armpits, she can see his ropy muscles. There's something about his face that makes her want to look, its openness. He's somehow taller than most of the men she knows even if he is a bit hunched over. And his skin is the same. It always seemed sunburnt across his cheekbones. The eyes: Green flecked with brown, and when he looks at her with that steady focus it puts her right back there at sixteen.

The thick cover of clouds breaks apart, showing a patch of dusky sky filled with pink and yellow hues. Still, the rain falls.

"Good day to be a duck," Grant says, looking up at the sky with a shrug. And then the stupid look on his face is too much. Echo cracks a smile, lets herself laugh. Thankfully, he smiles back. Even out here in the smoky drizzle, at least for right now, the floodgates have been opened.

It's comical how long the two of them stand there, fog circling around them, their eyes shifting across the wet ground, the dusky breeze bristling a chill into the air. Of course everyone had said they were too young, that it was too much of a good thing, too fast. But now it's as though the past has been whisked away, leaving only an empty space between them. Echo will not feed it with words. Instead she lets all the fear and apprehension spread out through the trees, jolting awake the snowy owl that has positioned itself on a branch above their heads.

Echo feels her wet T-shirt clinging to her chest, and the wind is making it worse. No bra. Careless. Unprepared. She folds her arms and looks down as often as possible. She tries to envision Grant as she did that first time. But her eyes fall on his sharp cheekbones. He looks stronger, rougher. His skin is dry and sandy, like baked earth. They're older now. People change. She can feel the emotion stiffening her fingers and catching in her throat, making her clumsy and silent.

One of these days she will forgive herself.

Striking out at him was a finely honed instinct, the same troublesome aspect of her personality that showed itself whenever she felt the most vulnerable, the same part that, at six, had caused her to put her cornhusk doll on the floor of her closet. She had left the door slightly open and had sat in bed, staring at the doll, aching to hold her. Even as tears rolled down her cheeks, she had forced herself not to move, refusing to hold the doll or bring her back into bed where she had slept alongside her for the last two weeks since arriving at Joseph's. She was getting attached to Joseph and so she was teaching herself how to say good-bye, just in case.

"Pretty incredible, seeing you," he says.

"It's been fifteen years," she says.

"It's been too long."

She nods. "I'm freezing." The goose bumps prickle up on

her bare arms. The hair blowing across her face catches in her mouth. She's all of a sudden aware that she'd like a blanket and a glass of wine. "I've got to go. I think the Jeep is drivable, don't you?"

Grant picks up a stone and tosses it into the bush. A family of napping flies explodes into the air. "Let me drive you."

The wind blowing off the water is getting colder by the minute. Does it matter that they're out here getting drenched, and neither of them cares? She's remembering the four stray hybrid wolf pups they once found in an old black stove in a neighbor's barn. She and Grant had stayed for hours, worried the pup's mother wouldn't return, as the pup's needle teeth chewed their shoes and bit their fingers. As the rain lapped at the windows, the farmer stuck his head in and said it was best not to get attached, that these strays had no right to expect much from life. Echo said she wanted to adopt them. She ached to feel what a mother felt, or perhaps it was to feel loved by a mother. All that emotion. All that belonging. She would adopt them all. Joseph would let her keep them, she was sure. She would raise them, and Grant would help her. When the ice blue mother wolf with the singed beard slinked through a crack in the wall, rib thin and teats swollen, she went right to her babies. Echo ran out and jumped on her bike. Echo didn't wear her jacket on the ride home through the rain. She pedaled hard, staying ahead of Grant, her head down and her eyes open, letting the tears soak the loss from her skin.

GRANT NOTICES THE GASH in the door of the Jeep, the twisted metal bumper. Silently, Echo follows him. She gets in on the passenger's side as though they've been doing it this way forever. She doesn't think this is necessarily the best idea, sitting in a contained space with all this emotion about to blow the windows right out. She edges as far away from him as she can because there are only two things you can do with this much feeling. Run like hell or get naked.

Grant backs up the Jeep. There is the sound of wood cracking, metal tearing.

"Wake me up when it's over," she says.

He backs up a few more feet. "Give me a second, I need to check something." He hops out. From the Jeep, Echo watches Grant run his hand along the dark broad trunk. He is trying to find the face in the wood, to see the spirit in the tree. This is something he once shared with her, something he knew that his father used to do. But only those who were a part of the Senecas' secret medicine societies could do this, and Grant's father had strictly forbidden him to be part of it.

Grant tramples around the side of the Jeep, and stands in front of the exposed orange inner bark of the black oak. This man moves her. She can't argue it. There's something that links a human soul with the soul of trees, the blue herons and the wild grasses. And he's part of that chain. The fact that he knows there's a spirit deep within every single tree is something rare. Grant told her this long ago. But she might just as easily have told it to him.

GRANT IS GLAD TO get a moment to calm his pulse. He's off balance, swears he can feel her right in his belly. He breathes a sigh of relief when he touches the tree. Really he's just trying to ground himself. Three days ago, he could barely muster the will to live let alone an ounce of desire. But now he's overflowing with it.

What is she doing here? He knows that you don't return home at this age unless you're leaving a marriage, putting one of your parents in a rest home, attending a wedding or funeral.

He's remembering the old oak tree outside Echo's bedroom window above the Feed & Grain, how he used to climb it on summer nights. It's been years, but he remembers how well his hands found the knots, how his feet trusted the thick branches to hold him as he'd climb. He'd stand on the biggest branch, looking down through the leaves at the sun-scorched patches of grass under the floodlights. He can picture their last summer with amazing clarity, how he held her in his arms, her thin body pressed against his chest. Each night, they pushed their desire a little further until soon they couldn't even be in the same room without touching. Grant would walk through the front door of the Feed & Grain, and the entire line of people waiting at the cash register would turn around to see the reason for her flushed cheeks. Echo would smile at him and he'd have to walk right back out for fear someone would see that he was nothing more than a blade of grass, flattened with the slightest wind.

Grant climbs back into the Jeep. Echo is shivering. He wants to put his arms around her but that was another life. What doesn't make it any easier is that she still has the freckles spilling across her face and arms. He feels such a strong affection for her that he has to roll down the window to get some air even though it is still raining. Then he takes off his windbreaker and hands it to her. "Put this on."

"Your wife," she says, staring at the jacket in her lap. "She's a wonderful photographer. I came across some of her work a while ago in a magazine."

"How's Boston?" he says, pulling a stick of gum from his back pocket before pushing the gear into reverse. In his mind Grant is pacing the halls of a house in Rochester on a cold December morning. Susanna's guilt made her so tired she couldn't get out of bed. Yet when she left, she had run from the house without her coat, her breath forming icicles out of things she could not say. The turquoise barrette must have fallen from her hair as she pushed her bags into the trunk. He found it just yesterday.

"Cambridge," says Echo. "My house is near a pond. Has everything. Fish, ducks, geese, frogs." She smiles.

"Any good trees?"

"A huge sugar maple," she says. "Right out in front of my house. It has thick roots that buckle the concrete. In September, it's pure fire." She sits back and crosses her arms. "I can see it from practically every window. It's just the same as seeing the Diamond Trees from every part of the lake. And there's a Dairy Queen next door."

"Now that I'd like to see."

"Mmm." She fastens her seat belt, untangles her hair. They'll just keep talking about trees and ice cream and it's fine with him. He can still smell those smoldering leaves along the upper trail of Bare Hill when the Seneca leaders stand by the boulder on the Saturday of every Labor Day weekend and give thanks for peace by lighting a ceremonial fire at the summit. So began the Ring of Fire, the end-of-summer celebration in which homeowners light a bonfire or a red flare on their piece of the shore. Each year, Echo and Grant would join with the rest of Canandaigua residents, and watch the circle of light creep around the lake after dusk, signifying the end of summer and the beginning of their hiatus from each other's lives.

"BOSTON. I'VE BEEN MEANING to get there," he says.

"Autumn in New England isn't the end of something, like it is here."

"How so?"

"It's the beginning. I love beginnings."

Grant bristles at the words. He starts to say something, but then becomes quiet, just looking at her. Echo is not sure what to do, so she keeps talking.

"Oh, there's so much activity. Cambridge speeds up. Everyone is running from here to there, late for meetings and classes. People are running through Harvard yard with their books. The entire city is a campus. My office is right in Cambridge. It's not beautiful like Naples, though. There's something so fragile about this place. It's not as fragile as here," she tells him.

"Not much is."

"No," she agrees. "Maybe not."

She sighs heavily. "This is so awkward," she says. She takes a deep breath and looks over at him. "Listen, I need to get something off my chest. After your father died, I wasn't sure if it was right to send you the cards. I know you and your dad had this wall between you. But I knew you would miss him. I knew you would take it hard and I felt so terrible because I hadn't gotten in touch with you when your mom passed away. I didn't know if you wanted to hear from me. I wasn't sure I had any right to try. But I wanted you to know I cared."

The tightness in his throat makes him look away, recalling how his mother had insisted on not having a funeral, her only request that his father spread her ashes across the lake. "I guess it was easier not to call."

"How could I expect you to? After the horrible things I said. We were too young," she says, shaking her head. "God, I was terrified. I said terrible things. You hurt me. I wanted to hurt you back."

"I don't hold it against you. I never did. Anyway, you met someone else. That's it. Life happens."

"I didn't meet anyone else," she says. "I lied."

He stares at the windshield masked with wet leaves, unable

to speak. "How are you doing? Now, I mean," he says finally. He reaches around and tries to push the leaves off with his hand. The wipers won't budge.

"Oh, I'm great," she tells him. "Really super, actually. Pretty great."

"That's good. Really, that's—"

"You?"

"Yep. Great. You know, overworked. But who isn't?" This isn't a complete lie. His hands are worn. He has open blisters on his palms, but this is nothing compared to how he feels inside. Raw. Open. Obvious as hell. He has always pushed himself, he was compelled to. He could never just run one mile, it had to be a marathon. He couldn't just carve one statue; he had to fill a whole house with them. In high school, he carried a stopwatch in his back pocket everywhere he went. He'd time himself, clutching it as he raced along the upper trail of Bare Hill to the large boulder at the top, a place that marked the Senecas' annual ceremony of peace. Then he'd race down to the dock, where he'd dive into the cold lake and swim the mile and a half across. Time. He'd hit the button. The race against himself has never ended.

The Jeep stalls. "Easy on the clutch," Echo says.

"As I recall, I taught you to drive."

He starts the engine again and backs up across the dirt and out into the highway, branches scraping the hood. An acorn falls in through the window. "Two years," he says, dropping it in her lap.

"What?"

"It takes it two years to ripen."

"That's a lot of patience for a little acorn." She waits for some reaction, a smile, but he doesn't move. "It's good to see you again."

He won't answer. They drive for a while in silence. "She left me," he says finally, pushing the words out between them. "Susanna, my wife." His voice trails off as the engine sputters, sending the mayflies swirling.

"I don't know what to say," she says, her voice hushed.

"Perfect. Let's not talk then." He's thinking of the way one tiny rock can change the direction of an entire river. And how the bark of a tree grows around an injured place, becoming a knot, changing its whole landscape. He thinks about the tree she just hit, how it now holds the memory of an accident, and a reunion.

She pulls her hair back into a ponytail, and he tries not to notice the way it falls in a fan over her chest. "Wait. Don't look," she says. She opens the glove compartment and grabs something. "I told you not to look."

"I'm driving. Some of us actually think that watching the road makes us better drivers."

"Not me, I drive on intuition alone."

"How's that working for you?"

"Clearly not that well." She smiles. "You won't believe this. I've never been able to throw this out."

"You know your wipers are broken?"

She nods, opening the book.

"So, how exactly do you drive in the rain?" he asks.

"I don't actually drive. Not technically. Not that often," she shrugs. "I bike to work. The mayflies here are worse than rain anyway."

She holds up a tattered paperback. *The Foxfire Book*. The pages are still dog-eared.

"Jesus, that thing is ancient," he tells her. Reading together from this book is one of the most intimate experiences he's ever had with a woman.

"So much history here," she murmurs, staring out the window at the old boathouses lining the lake. Ancient things make her feel comfortable: a well-loved threadbare couch, and a slight wrinkle to a man's shirt, worn hardwood floors. But he doesn't hear her. "You know when a place is so filled with memories, you can't even see it for what it really is?"

He nods. Too soon, they are nearing Bare Hill. He pulls off to the side of the road, stops the Jeep, and gets out.

"What are you doing? It's another half mile to your cabin," she says, concerned.

"It'll be better if I walk from here," he says, as she gets out. She hands him back his jacket, anticipating something. A handshake. A hug.

But he's staring up at the Diamond Trees. He's imagining the old wooden swing glowing against the dark curtain sewn with lights. The frayed rope is caught in moonlight, wrapped around one of the highest branches. When he was very young, during one long winter, his father teased him about being afraid to jump from the swing, bragging about how when he was a boy on the Tonawanda Creek Reservation he could jump from branches much higher. Grant had been reluctant to climb that high, and even more so, to jump into the deep black water. His father said it was because Grant thought too hard, and too much. That a boy had to be broken of this type of negative thinking or it would ruin him when he was a man. It was a lesson.

His father listened with relief as Grant protested that he wasn't afraid to do anything, much less jump from a tree into a lake. Over that entire winter Grant dreamed of climbing the great willow, climbing to the very top, his head poking out from the canopy, looking down on his mother and father with the swing positioned underneath him, then jumping off the branch, arms outstretched before floating down into the water. In his dreams his body was weightless and the usually cold water was as warm and as welcoming as a bath. When his family arrived at the cabin the next summer, Grant jumped the first day. But the water was cold and as hard as glass when he landed. Still, he jumped all summer long, shattering it, his skin permanently stung red, his father looking on with pride.

"You sure I can't drive you home?" she asks. He turns around and she is standing behind him. The wind floods her T-shirt. He can feel her warmth even if he can't exactly see her eyes.

"Very sure," he says. "I need to walk."

"Positively sure?"

"Echo."

"Okay, give me back my book."

He turns around with the book in his hand.

"Forget it. You keep it," she tells him. "Just for a while. Maybe you'll feel like reading. In case you get the urge to make moonshine." Echo smiles. Their dark eyes meet once, and then he's pulling her close to him but only in his mind. The stillness of the water catches him.

Patience is the ability to slow down.

"Go on. You get to walk away now. And I promise I won't get angry this time," she tells him.

"Keep your eyes on the road."

"Intuition is bullshit. I agree," she says.

"Take this, it's cold out," he says, tossing her his jacket.

"You know, I'm still never dressed appropriately for the weather." She pulls the coat over her shoulders and smiles, encouraged by the conversation.

He walks away. With such weight of emotion washing over him, he no longer feels like reminiscing. When her Jeep is clear out of sight, he begins to run.

7

THE JEEP'S BROKEN BUMPER trails along the road, making a terrible racket as Echo drives into the parking lot of the Feed & Grain. This isn't exactly the sort of entrance she envisioned. She pulls up alongside a police car and her mind begins to race. Something has happened to Joseph, she is certain of it. Wouldn't that be her luck, arriving seconds too late? She dashes through the puddles, up the front steps of the store and flings open the door to see Charlie Cooke and Joseph leaning against the counter, deep in conversation. Out of breath, wet from the rain, Echo forces herself between the two men and into Joseph's arms.

"What is this? Echo!" says Joseph.

"Did something happen? Are you okay?" she cries. She squeezes Joseph tight.

"Kiddo, kiddo, kiddo, I'm fine, okay," he says, peeling her off of him. "Let me look at you. What a surprise. What are you doing here?"

"Surprising you."

"What happened to your lip, honey? You're bleeding. Let me get some ice."

"I almost hit a wolf. I hit a tree instead. I'm fine, really."

He touches her face, looks into her eyes. "Should we call a doctor, honey?"

"No, no, of course not," she tells him. "Really. What are you doing here, Charlie?" she asks, turning to face the detective, whose presence has always meant bad news.

"I'm fine, and you?" he says, with a grin.

"Sorry, Charlie," Echo says, pulling Grant's jacket tight around her. "I apologize. I saw the police car and I got worried—"

"She's worried about me," says Joseph. "And look at her with a busted lip."

"What's going on? Why are you here at Joseph's?" she asks Charlie.

"Melanie Ellis. You tell her the rest, Joe," says Charlie. "I have to be going. You know to call if you see or hear anything from Melanie, which I reckon you won't. And don't pay any mind to those white stones out back there. It's a trick by some wise-ass kids, but we'll get them."

Joseph pulls Echo close. "Honey, I am so grateful that you're home."

THAT NIGHT, ECHO WATCHES Joseph carefully as he sips the burnt coffee she has just made. She is standing behind the counter, watching him label jars of juneberry jelly. Joseph says he doesn't know how much longer he can keep up his business since the new Wildman's Grocery has opened up down the street. His store is still the only place in town where you can buy Famous Naples grape pies all year round, but he can't compete with the big guys, he tells her.

Now he's putting oranges into bags for the town's homeless couple, Dee Dee and Papa Paul.

"You sending them pies, too, Pop?"

"We sold the last two this morning," he says, scratching a note to himself on the small pad. He casually admits that he's having trouble remembering things, like ordering more Eden's black raspberry celery-seed dressing. It took top honors last year, while Steve's blueberry poppy-seed dressing and NY Dijon mustard both placed third at *Food Distribution* magazine's 1997 Superior Product Competition. He says the big guys are selling it, too. Things keep changing, getting bigger and faster. At the turn of the century there were only 160 cottages on the lake. Now, that number hovers around 1,400.

Well, nothing much matters except having good people around you, he tells her. Loving, hardworking folks are the ones who you keep around. Part of getting through life happy is keeping around the good ones and letting go of the bad ones.

"I wish you'd known her all grown up," he says, remembering Melanie was just a child when Echo left for college. "You'd have done a lot for Melanie, and I think she'd have done the same for you, too. Yes, you would have been a fine big sister. You have a lot in common, you know. You both have your books. See there," he says, pointing to the box under the counter.

She takes out the first book she sees, *Magnificent Addiction*. She reads the inscription in the front, *For Melanie. With faith, Lion.*

"Lion?" Echo asks.

"Her boyfriend. Father of her child."

"Nice name."

"He couldn't pronounce the name Lionel when he was little, Melanie said. Anyway, I just feel so helpless here," Joseph says, putting away the last of the jars. "Wish there was something I could do." He reaches up to smooth his tousled white hair.

"Try to relax." Echo touches his back, trying not to become preoccupied with his worry.

She thumbs through the pages of the book, stopping to read some of the passages underlined with red ink. Her eyes water up. In an instant, she feels like she is trespassing on Melanie's thoughts. She puts the book back.

She had bumped into Melanie once during a short visit home. Melanie had been painting the windows of the Feed & Grain for a Halloween display. She'd asked Echo about Boston and if she liked the Yankees or the Red Sox. When Echo answered Yankees, Melanie had smiled and said, "That's loyal of you." Then Melanie had gone outside to sit on the porch, giving Echo and Joseph time alone together. She seemed lost in thought, her blue eyes focused on the lake. Echo wonders if perhaps she might have said something in that brief interchange that could have made a difference to Melanie. If a few words said in passing could change a person's life.

"I remember when Two Bears disappeared, it was the same feeling, this helplessness," Joseph says, scratching his chin. "I miss the talk, you know, after all these years? Night was our time. We'd sit out here late. Two Bears and me were like two trees growing next to each other, one a willow, the other pine, both claiming the same space but needing different things from it. When the sun came up, we were always surprised because as different as we were, neither of us wore a watch. Probably the only thing we had in common."

"It's sad what happened to him."

Joseph nods. "Some folks cling hard to what they love. That's how they do it. Other folks have to walk away. Two Bears was the kind to walk away. But not until after he had fought the battle. I don't claim to understand it, but I respect his decision because I respected him. I know he had his reasons."

"What do you mean, 'walk away'? He was murdered, Pop."

Joseph starts to cough. Echo runs over and offers him a

towel. He straightens up after a moment, his eyes watering. She looks down, noticing for the first time the holes in the knees of his pants. Embarrassed, he shakes his head. "I had meant to patch them up but my hands shake too much to thread a needle," he says.

LATER THAT NIGHT, ECHO takes off her tattered blue bathrobe and lies down on the soft mattress. Unable to sleep, she is wondering how the unexpected events of the past few days could lead her back toward the man she may in fact still love. She follows the cracks in the ceiling with her eyes, trying to meditate, to let her muscles reacquaint themselves with the old mattress's dips and curves. Has she any right to be thinking about her own feelings when there is so much else going on?

Sleepless, disturbed nights like these were not uncommon when she and Grant were together. She'd lie in bed dreaming of the wreck of the *Onnalinda,* a ship that is still caught in the depths off Otetiana Point, waiting for the waves to push its bones back together. The ship took her name from a book-length poem about an Iroquois princess who fell in love with an English captain. Years ago, Echo would wake up after dreaming about the ship, only to stare at the phone. Within minutes, Grant would call. This became almost commonplace.

What is it that Joseph always says? Faith is made up of one part belief, two parts courage. Life has taught her that a gift always arrives on the heels of despair. That's just the way it has always been for her, one of the better patterns of her life. Echo shuts her eyes, only long enough to hear an ear-splitting whine outside. Is it a baby crying? There is scratching at the window. Must be that the branches of the big oak need to be cut again. Shielding her eyes from the floodlight on the roof, she opens the window.

Lit up like a ball of fire, a huge orange cat is staring at her from the crevice of a branch. Its large yellow eyes blink twice, its gaze, almost mournful, as though it is she who has been crying out for the world to hear. She reaches out her hands. The cat doesn't budge. It is content to sit and meow now, as though rousing her were its only goal. As she clicks her teeth, the wind kicks up, brushing the long white sleeveless undershirt against her nipples, making them hard under the lamplight.

"Here fat cat," she calls, shivering. The cat reminds her of the ones she once delivered to the doorstep of Clarisse Mellon. This one is so round it must be pregnant. "Come on," she calls, reaching further. She could climb out onto the branch just as she used to do when she was a teenager. Fifteen years ago impulsivity ruled her life. She wouldn't have thought twice about using the tree as a ladder. But now, she's cold and tired, and not so confident about her balance. She slowly reaches out her cupped hand, making it look as though she has some food for the cat. She has always thought the childhood trick cruel, but these are desperate times.

The cat is disgusted, and scampers down the trunk of the tree. "Nice talking to you, too," Echo whispers, pushing the window closed. She sits back in the pocket of cold air. Perhaps this will help her sleep. She closes her eyes and counts down from one hundred.

At the count of eighty-two, she gets up and grabs some photos out of her drawer. Her graduation picture. She looks squinty, her smile cuffed by thick silver braces. And then there is the hair, wild and uncombed. Her curly hair had resisted the once popular feathered hairstyle, while all the teenage girls carried round brushes in their purses as though they were arrows poisoned with love.

While other girls were practicing their flirtations during

recess, she was reading her beloved autobiographies. Echo always thought herself too awkward to have been anything but studious, absorbed in biographies like the one about Susan B. Anthony, who was put on trial right here in the Canandaigua Courthouse.

Echo closes her eyes, puts the photos underneath her pillow and presses her back to the wall. It is good to be back in her own room, close to Joseph, so close that even from up here in her bedroom, she can track his movements downstairs if she lies very still. The walls are paper thin and the floors are old and scratched. She can hear the opening and closing of cabinet doors creaking in the kitchen, then the sink faucet, and the *tick tick* of the gas stove where he is boiling water for tea. She hears him taking out the jam jar and banging the lid on the side of the sink to loosen it. Then the sound of two pieces of bread popping up from the toaster. She knows he eats his breakfast at night. She could go downstairs and join him like she used to when they would sit across from each other at the kitchen table in front of the big picture window and talk for hours as the sun rose, and in that perfect space between night and day, dark and light, she would empty herself of her fears and dreams, pour them all out to Joseph who would listen, unfailingly, hearing every word, and then tell her stories about himself that made her feel better. He was not perfect, but honest about it. He had been foolish and stupid, he told her. He had done things he wasn't proud of. And he had times when he was afraid, but he did something courageous anyway, like leaving the priesthood for a woman he met climbing Mount Kilimanjaro.

She is glad she made the decision to come home, where people let you talk at whatever time you need to and there is always an ear to listen. She has been walking around with that full feeling for too long, like her thoughts were in a locked box just waiting to be opened. She keeps everything so stored up inside her that she often walks around feeling like she might burst. It causes her to cry at little things, at unexpected moments. She thinks of the dawn rising over the reeds and then the fog dissipating over the gray lake where she and Grant used to skinny-dip at night, alongside the soaring herons that live in pairs. Echo liked to believe that the herons were their angels, their watchdogs, protecting them from intruders. They had done their job well, except for once. One night when Echo was sixteen, Grant's mother saw something in the lake, something rising off the moonlit water and she had crept across the backyard and down to the shoreline as silently as a ghost. Pale and thin, her arms looked as willowy as the reeds as she pushed her way through the foggy air toward the shoreline. Having spotted Grant and Echo in an instant, Emily stopped halfway to the shoreline, holding their gaze. Echo and Grant froze in place, treading water, staring back. Emily's mouth opened to say something but she stopped. She put her hands on her hips and stared a moment longer. Then she turned around and walked back up the yard, swinging her arms forcefully until she got to the porch, where she sat down, hands on her knees, staring out in the opposite direction of the lake and chain-smoking cigarettes until after Grant and Echo had shamefully slipped into their clothing. As they passed by, his mother didn't say a thing, which made Echo even more uncomfortable. Echo smiled quickly at Emily but Emily kept her eyes down, continuing to smoke.

Afterward, Grant swore to Echo that his mother did not hate her or label her as "loose," and he told her to forget about it. But Grant never knew that they actually had a conversation about it. More of an announcement, really. Echo had run into Emily a few nights after the incident, while Echo was closing up the Feed & Grain. Emily Shongo waited for her outside. Echo saw her walk to the gravel parking lot, set the grocery bag at her feet and light a cigarette. Echo felt it was only polite to approach her. She had no idea what she would say but she told herself she had to set things straight. She was not a harlot. She was not trying to get pregnant. It was none of that, and of course they hadn't had sex, not yet. She loved him. She would tell Emily Shongo that, and then maybe the woman would see she was honest and well-intentioned, and would welcome Echo with open arms, becoming the mother she never had.

But friendship was not Emily Shongo's goal. It never had been. Instead she put her arm around Echo's shoulders, pulled her close, and whispered, "I know that you think nothing can match the passion between you two, and that you think none of us old folks know a thing about it. But I can tell you, we've all had it. Fire like yours burns itself right out. The hotter the fire, the sooner it dies." Then, Emily Shongo gave a compassionate smile. She stubbed out her cigarette with her heel, grabbed her grocery bag and headed home. She died two years later with the same type of abruptness, her last wish: no funeral or memorial service, simply the spreading of her ashes across the lake at night.

Echo hears a plate crash to the floor. "You okay, Pop?" she calls.

"Just dropped a cup, that's all. Go back to sleep." She waits and listens to Joseph sweeping up the broken pottery. Then she hears the TV flick on and the sound of muffled voices. Soon after, she can hear his light snoring. He needs her here, she is certain. She feels empty and afraid when she thinks of how old he looks now, so much older than last time, his ashen complexion, his wrinkled face, the hands that tremble whenever he is at rest, causing him to drop cups and plates. The sounds of his

8

After watching Echo drive away, Grant races the setting sun on his way back to the cabin. His mind is cluttered with thoughts of her. His heart is racing. The air fills his lungs, cleansing them. The earth is buoyant under his heels. Ahead he can see the day's last mirage, the silver light spilling over the potholes like molten metal. These battered roads are remnants of the ice storms that do enough damage in three months to keep anyone from ever calling this a good road. An eerie self-consciousness overtakes him.

He knows he's being followed.

He slows, and then whips around. Nothing. He begins running again but after a minute, the same feeling. He spins back. *Yes.* The scraggly hybrid wolf, the one from Echo's accident. He's there watching Grant from under a dogwood tree about twenty feet back, one paw lifted as though Medusa had cast her eyes on him, still as stone.

"Go home," Grant orders, trying to harden his voice. "For God's sake," Grant says, trying his best to muster up some kind of annoyance. But who is he kidding? He's a sucker for animals. The more wounded, the better.

Slowly it limps toward him. It's an Academy Award performance.

"All right. Come."

He kneels, claps his hands together. The animal begins to prowl back and forth, confused, not quite sure what to do with the kindness. Grant whistles through his teeth, and it comes galloping forward and assaults Grant with kisses that smell like sour eggs. The wolf-like ears don't fit with the rubbery jowls spilling out of both sides of his mouth. "Hey, easy now," Grant says, running his fingers over the matted fur. He touches something that feels like raw fish, and the animal whips backward with a high-pitched yelp. Grant carefully moves the skeletal body around. A flap of skin is hanging off, exposing the pink hamburger flesh that is leaking blood. Grant takes a deep breath and looks around. He is alone. He turns his attention toward the wolf, and holds his hand about two inches above the area, feeling the waves of piercing heat lurching out. Then, an aversive energy makes him pull his hand away. The animal lies down and utters a low whine. Grant hesitates, stares at his hands, which feel as though they're immersed in warm water.

He can't remember feeling so clear.

He looks around again to make sure he is alone. And then, without any more thought, he places his hand back over the wolf's body, above the wound. He closes his eyes. He begins to sweat, feeling the heat energy that signifies pain, sensing an orange haze rising above the animal's wound like a smoke signal reverberating throughout its entire body. Grant begins sweeping his hands in the air from the front of the animal to the back, smoothing the heat that is pulsating from the animal's wound, and pulling it out into the atmosphere. The animal goes limp, closing its eyes. Grant opens his left palm up to the sky, then positions his right palm about an inch above the animal's upper back, pulling a golden light from above and down through the bloody fur, into the battered skin and flesh, to muscle, tissue, organ and moving it through the animal's body. Grant breathes deeply, concentrating, picturing the golden ball of energy and filling the animal's body with it. The animal growls, opens its eyes, and Grant pulls his hands away. It stands up and shakes off the air as though it had been swimming. Then it stretches and begins to walk, circling Grant. Grant rubs his hands in the dirt until his skin is coated with the grounding earth. He glances up at the wolf. Dodging toward him and back, taunting him with play, the wolf is as good as new. Grant checks over the wolf's body. The wound is gone.

The wolf follows Grant back to the cabin, never straying too far from his heels. Grant feels strange, invigorated, his muscles tired but strong, as though he had just run ten miles. The lake is crushed with sunlight. When the animal falls asleep on the porch, Grant notices he is thirstier than he has been in months. He walks into the living room, duct tape in hand. He feels confident about being able to put the window back together. He stares at the broken glass scattered across the soot footprints zigzagging across the yellow shag. He leans down, brushing his fingers over the coal dust.

9

LIGHT. MELANIE WAKES SUDDENLY in the darkness. It has been fifty-four hours. She has been listening to the waves lapping at the shoreline mixed with the sound of her own breathing. Nothing else. Lying face down, her wrists are tied in back. She can feel the springs of an old mattress poking against her belly. A blindfold pulls at the edges of her hair. Her head throbs in back where someone hit her. Musty air fills her nostrils. She hasn't enough energy to raise her head. Her eyes ache. She is so tired. So tired that she cannot keep herself from falling in and out of consciousness. Sleep takes her suddenly, like a huge snake, dragging her into the depths of the lake.

Pieces of coal fall from the sky like rain.

She dreams of pieces of shiny black coal and bits of broken white china softened by rocks and the waves. She and Maya are walking across the lake floor, collecting coal in the baskets they have made by pulling up their skirts. Only one of them will find the piece that will turn into a diamond.

Above, Melanie sees a crown of golden curls floating on the surface of the water. Luke's hair sways like seaweed. Melanie struggles to reach him. She tries to swim to the surface, but he floats farther and farther away. She tries to call his name but she is under water. He is leading her higher and higher, climbing through the water to the crowning yellow light at the surface.

Awake. She splashes to the surface, gasping, trembling. Light warms her legs. The heat has raised the scent of urine from the old mattress. The sour smell of her own body is almost too much.

Despite the sunlight, her teeth are chattering. Even though her hands and ankles are tied, she can make a racket by kicking her feet up and down. But she has only so much energy.

She has never been so thirsty. Hunger claws at her stomach.

She can hear the water surrounding her but she cannot taste it. Her throat is raw with unleashed screams. Her mouth is so dry, she has forgotten how to swallow. She tries to speak, but the pain is too much, she fears her vocal cords have been cut.

In the cool blue center of her mind she pictures her child.

Strange, this feeling of wanting to fight for her life. It's because of Lucas. It's because of the way his eyes hold her as she moves around the room, never letting her go. She wants to scream. Tries to lift her head, but her throat is so dry, she cannot make a sound. *I'm sorry, I'm sorry, I'm sorry,* she's screaming in her mind, hoping they will hear her: Lion, her mother, God. She's drained of fight. She wants her baby. Wants to smell him, to touch his skin. She knows she has caused this somehow, that it has to do with what is inside of her. Doubt. Guilt. Maybe the feeling that somehow she didn't deserve this life that was shaping up.

She knows that when you are weak, everything is a trigger.

The gulls cry on the rafters above her, a promise of escape. Melanie tries to move but her body isn't strong enough. After a while, she doesn't fight. She's been teaching herself how to die for some time now.

PART II

10

GRANT HASN'T WANTED TO go anywhere in three weeks. But seeing Echo has ignited a new sense of hope. He has showered and put on the only clean clothing he has: jeans and an old flannel shirt he found in the back of the closet, probably one of his father's, from the way the rolled sleeves are creased. He has fed the wolf and tied him up outside. The animal is content to sleep for hours, only looking up once in a while to make sure Grant's car is still there.

He is now intent on driving the old Cadillac down the dirt road, belting out "Freebird" at the top of his lungs. It's a reclamation. A cry of possibility. Though why there are more wild turkeys now crossing the road, Grant can't understand. The damn birds still flood the area. When he was a boy, teenagers used to shoot BBs at them from their car windows as sport. Turkey-plinking, they called it, similar to the way buffalo were once shot from moving trains. Grant always wondered why the turkeys never ran. They never learned. They were machine-like and unafraid. They simply remained easy targets as they hovered near the roadside, apparently feasting on the gravel. Even the trucks didn't scare them.

He passes the last clutch of turkeys as he drives down East Lake Road, one eye on the black glistening water. The buoys, part of the yacht club race course, are white in the moonlight. The waves are high, crested with frothing white foam. It's almost time to put the docks out, he thinks. In the next few days the shores will be busy with men hauling out huge heavy pieces of metal to fish off of and to tie their boats by.

Ahead, he can see the orange neon sign, KELLEY'S BAR, the electric swirls lighting up the row of trucks in the packed parking lot. He pulls into the lot. He hopes the place is still mellow enough to have a long conversation. He has that need to talk and it doesn't even matter to whom.

The place is packed. A far cry from the small empty dive bar with its creaky benches and weary dartboard that he and Echo used to frequent. There is hardly any empty space left at all, not on the walls taped with photos of movie stars, not on the ceiling papered with posters, *Casablanca* and *The African Queen*, not even on the beer-sticky floors. Two large pinball machines face off in two corners, one labeled "Harold," the other "Maude." Tables and chairs are scattered about. The rudder of the *Onnalinda*, the largest of the old Canandaigua boats, has been turned into a table in a corner of the room. The ship, dismantled in 1913, refused to be pulled from the lake. She broke free of her towline and her pieces drifted across the water. On East Lake Road there's a house built almost entirely from its lumber.

Grant moves through the bar. An eight-foot tropical plant with thick prehistoric-like leaves is flourishing in another corner of the room. Tied to one of its branches is a photograph signed by Mel Gibson.

"I met him once," the waitress says, cracking her gum. "He's short. Not like what you would think." She repositions the tray of drinks on her arm. "You want something?"

"Thanks, not just yet," he tells her.

"I'm Georgia, when you're ready let me know." He watches her disappear into the crowd, tray held up high above her head.

In the corner, a couple of young men are arguing, making a lot of noise. Both look drunk. Grant cuts through the crowd to the back door, which opens onto a muddy beach. Two empty picnic tables stand in the muddy sand. Grant pictures himself and Echo sitting on the tables, watching the fog encircle Squaw Island, making the trees look as though they were floating above the water. From here, you get the best view of the gulls as they spin hypnotic circles, searching in vain for fish that never come close to the island due to the lime deposits that cluster at the shore. Why do the gulls stay when there is no food? Some people understand. Others marvel at the oddity. On Saturday afternoons, once upon a time, Grant and Echo would sit out here, watching the gulls, sipping cheap Chardonnay and talking about life, as though they were an old married couple and not just two sixteen-year-olds.

Across the lake about a mile down, Grant can see the Diamond Trees, their leaves lighting up his dock.

"Shongo?" shouts Sean Kelley from behind the bar. "In the flesh?"

Grant smiles, walking over. "Hey Sean."

Sean peers at him, taking off his pilot sunglasses. "God, you look old. You are the spitting image of a guy I once knew. Long time ago."

"Yeah?" Grant smiles. "What was he like?"

"A lonely guy. You wouldn't have liked him."

"You're probably right," Grant says, looking around.

"Okay. Sit down, let me clean this off. Tell me everything. You okay? You look all right."

"Sure." Grant takes off his tan corduroy jacket. "Good. Place is busy. Love that photograph of Mel."

"Yeah, well. You gotta have a theme," Sean says, grabbing two shot glasses and a bottle of Jose Cuervo. "Business is great, through the roof. Tourists are killing the lake. But I got to make a living."

"More people. More booze, I guess."

"It's a catch-22, you know? I keep pouring drinks."

"You lost weight," Grant tells him.

Sean is sweating, his black silk shirt pulling over his belly. "Damn straight. Ah, the wife and me, we measure years in pounds now. Forty big ones," Sean says, pointing to his gut. "So how's things with you?" He pours two shots. He grabs napkins with his thick short fingers, and sets down salt and lime slices.

"Fantastic. Terrific, never better. You?" Grant says, picking up the shot. Grant knows he looks bad, what with his rumpled clothing and his sunken cheeks. He watches Sean down the shot. He does the same.

"Me," says Sean, wiping his mouth and setting the glass down. "I can't complain. Keeping the wife happy takes up most of my time. What'll it be?"

"Whatever's on tap," Grant says. The wizard bartender works magic. He's got three bottles going so fast, Grant can't even identify them.

Sean smiles, shakes the metal canister and pours a couple of new shots. "Do one of these. It's for what ails you."

"God bless," Grant says. He downs it, schnapps and rum,

something tropical he can't quite identify. They do two more shots without talking.

"So, you don't look in such bad shape," says Sean, as he cleans out a glass. "I was picturing something much worse."

"Like what?"

"Like maybe something crazy. Maybe you had a long beard and came out at night, throwing white stones at houses and scaring children. Something like that."

"What is that all about? Those rocks?"

"The wife thinks it's the spirits of the Seneca. She believes in that stuff. I told her it was the storm."

"Right," Grant replies. Who did he think he was fooling, hiding away in the cabin for the last three weeks when it seems the entire town has been waiting for him to scare children or hang himself? He could have stayed where he was, but the slight activity of Echo's accident, the remote hint of a new life, has pulled him toward her like a whirling planet. Sean sets a beer down in front of Grant. He notices Grant's blistered fingers.

"What in the hell happened to you, Shongo?"

"Fishing. Carp are real tough this year, like submarines. Yeah." Grant self-consciously shoves his hands back into his pockets. "Reeling in those big ones." They both know he's lying, that in ninth grade, he started a petition against a yearly bass tournament. It had made him less than popular with the locals.

"Fascinating," Sean says. He, like all good bartenders, is versed in the art of letting a lie dissipate into the air. "Well, the bass boats are making us crazy. Every morning, five thirty to eight A.M., zipping their lures into the docks and stealing all the fish." His fingers brush back his thinning blond hair. "The wife's gonna shave it all off tomorrow. Says that's the style for bald guys. What do you think?"

Grant rubs his eyes. The bitter liquid slides down his throat. He shakes his head. He's in no position to give anyone marital advice. "Don't know. What do you think?"

"Well, you know, I get along best by not having an opinion, especially around the wife." Sean grabs napkins and puts two more slices of lime and some salt in front of Grant. "So, when did your wife leave you?"

"A year ago. Bit more."

"Man, Shongo. Takes time, I guess."

"Yes, well coming here's been good for me."

"You know, once Kerry took off. For real. Because of that goddamn Indian snake monster story. You know what the hell I'm talking about, right? You remember how folks see that thing occasionally? It almost cost me my marriage. Kerry saw it out middle of the lake one morning. She thought it was a big beaver until the rest of its body rose up from the water. So, she runs inside, wakes me up. I laughed at her. I told her she was crazy. That's when she put on her favorite coat, grabbed her toothbrush, and walked out.

"Kerry was gone nine days, one for every year of our marriage." He holds up his fingers, counting off the years, one by one. "I was climbing the walls, ready to turn myself into snake bait. She came back, though. She couldn't stay away. Can you really blame her? I am a good-looking bastard." Sean pours another round of shots. "Here's to women everywhere. God bless them and the way they cut our hearts out."

With that, they both down the burning liquid. Grant feels his insides rebel, but he swallows hard. "That's tasting better. I should probably stop," he says, his voice hoarse. Still, the fire that's rising up in his belly is burning off all the worry from the afternoon. And he hasn't thought about either Susanna or Echo in almost forty-five minutes.

"Well," says Sean. "Thank sweet Jesus that she didn't leave you with a kid, like that poor bastard Lion Williams over there, the one yelling at the pinball. Melanie Ellis's boyfriend. Sure you heard about that situation now that you've climbed out of your cave."

The young man with the dreadlocks and the big leather jacket is shouting something at the ceiling. His eyes are big, light brown, and his face is thin with a square jaw. He has his hands in his jean pockets, which hang low on his hips exposing white boxer shorts. He's wearing big white sneakers with the laces untied, staggering around, piss drunk.

"Lion? Where's the name come from anyway?"

"Name's Lionel, I think. He says he couldn't say his own name when he was a kid. Called himself Lion and it stuck."

"At least it was his own idea," Grant says.

"Not a bad guy. Moved to town a few years ago. Came with nothing. Both he and the guy yelling at him, they both work at the Good Word Garage. They've been here all day. These are tough times."

"Who's the other guy?"

"Rory Post. Good mechanic. But Lion's better. Hey, you still like old cars? I got a white 1956 Porsche Speedster. Like the one James Dean died in. Lion and Rory spent all year restoring it."

Now Lion is trying to shake the pinball machine, and Rory is trying to body slam him away from it.

"Hey, you better cut them off."

"Georgia, do your thing," orders Sean, motioning to the waitress. "I leave it up to her. She'll let him know when he's had enough."

Grant is vaguely aware that Georgia the waitress has been

listening to the conversation, and is taking far too long to garnish her drinks. Standing in front of him, she looks about sixteen and busty, her breasts swelling in the tight, lemon yellow low-cut shirt. "Hi again." She looks up, smiling nervously at Grant.

"You messed me up!" Lion is yelling at Rory.

"What are you gonna do?" Grant asks Sean.

Sean shakes his head. "Nothing, until they break something. A bartender in Rochester just busted his spleen breaking up a fight." Sean washes out two shot glasses, holds them up. "Whatdaya say? One more?"

"Not a chance."

"For old times?" Sean says with a smile.

"Maybe later," Grant tells him. "Phone still broken downstairs?"

Sean grabs his cell phone from under the bar. He slaps it on the counter. "Would you believe? People are still shovin' bottle caps into that goddamn pay phone. Not like anyone uses it anymore anyway. I'll never understand human beings. Always got to destroy something. Hey, let me guess, you don't own a cell phone, do you?"

"Why in the hell would I?" As Grant dials, he keeps an eye on Lion. The fight is heating up. Testosterone and anger and alcohol don't mix, that much he knows from experience. "Sean," he calls. "Bartender. If you don't do something, I will."

Rory's hair is flying wildly as he tries to dodge Lion's jabs. He zips out his BB gun and points it at Lion.

"Ah, not again. Every goddamn Sunday, it's the same old thing," says Sean. "Guys come in here bloodthirsty as all hell. Goddamn obsessed with shooting turkeys. Gets 'em all riled up. Never stops." Georgia starts to make her way over, but now it's too late.

"You scared? Lion, motherfucker, let's see what you got," Rory spits.

Grant hangs up before Echo answers. "Dammit," says Sean, slapping the towel down on the counter when the gun is knocked from Rory's hand. Lion swings at Rory with his left hand. Rory ducks, but Lion comes at him with a right hook and Rory's head is knocked back. Blood streams from Rory's nose as he falls, holding his face in his hands. Lion picks up the BB gun and points it at Rory, who is on his knees. Lion holds the gun with two hands, shaking, with the barrel about an inch from Rory's face.

"Not in my face, man," sobs Rory.

"I don't care about your face," shouts Lion, staggering back a step.

Grant hops off the barstool. Sean jumps sideways over the bar but Grant has already knocked the gun from Lion's hand and lodged himself between the two.

Someone swings and clips Grant's left cheek, numbing one side of his face. Bodies are falling, arms and legs entangled. Grant can tell this is a desperate fight, not a fight over money or property. A fight fought in order to exhaust the sense of desperation, which means this fight is more dangerous. There's nothing at stake. The goal is only to hurt and get hurt. Grant manages to slip out and push Lion back into a table, holding his arms. But Rory won't quit. "Where's your goddamn junkie girlfriend now?" Rory yells, spitting his words through blood.

"Motherfucker, I'll kill you," Lion yells, nostrils flaring. Grant can feel the pull in the air between the two boys. He's using all of his strength to keep Lion back, but Lion wriggles out of his arms, scraping across the floor for the gun.

Sean jumps in and grabs Lion's collar. Grant kicks the gun aside with his foot while he gets a good grip on Rory's neck.

"It's over," Grant manages, with his mouth full of rocks. He has done this more than once. Working at Hallandale Arts has provided ample practice. And when he was younger he knew a thing or two about this kind of fighting.

"SOMEONE GET ME A Kleenex," says Rory.

"I got it," says Georgia, pulling a pack from her apron. "Allergies," she explains. Now the way Lion responds, staring at Grant with his head slightly bowed, you would think Grant had some kind of power, some kind of reputation in town. Whatever it is, it is working to Grant's advantage.

Grant knows he must tread carefully. He doesn't want to drive things to the critical point where somebody has to make a decision he'll regret, just to save face. Thankfully, Rory breaks the silence. "Man, Lion. If I didn't already owe you," he says. "Listen, whatever I said, forget it."

"You don't owe shit," Lion spits, his skin dark and glistening.

"Let him owe what he owes. It's over," Grant says.

"Let him fight, asshole," Lion yells at Grant, his once warm eyes now inky black. "Stay the fuck out of it."

Grant doesn't flinch.

"This is my goddamn bar," yells Sean, louder than Grant has ever heard him. "I call the shots."

"Nice pun," notes Grant.

"You fat shit," says Lion. "Hit me," he orders Sean. Sean lets him go.

"Zebra," Rory hisses.

Wrong move. Lion reels a punch, missing Rory by a mile. Sean grabs him again and has got Lion's hands behind his back.

"You've really lost it this time, Williams."

"My arms," Lion winces. At once, tears are streaming down Lion's face and into the neck of his torn gray sweater. It's difficult for Grant to watch this man crumble, sobbing for all to see. He wants to protect him from being seen like this, more so even than he wanted to protect him from being punched. It's even more difficult to watch given that he has a child at home. He shouldn't be baring his soul in the middle of a bar. Exposed like this.

Sean releases Lion, who drops to his knees. Rory holds his hand out to Lion. When Lion shrugs him off, Rory turns to Grant. "It's okay. He's not himself since his girlfriend split," Rory explains.

Grant keeps his eyes on Lion as he grabs the phone book from the corner and calls Leila Ellis. She answers expectantly. He doesn't want to disappoint her. He can hear her voice drop off when she realizes he's not calling about Melanie. Grant tells her he thinks it's best if Lion stays at his place. "Let Rory bring him home," Leila urges. "They have this love-hate sort of thing. It'll be fine. He has to be at the apartment in case Melanie comes home."

"He's had a couple too many. He needs to dry out."

There is silence on the line. "But he doesn't drink anymore," Leila finally manages. Grant doesn't know that the floor under Leila has just slanted backwards and she is falling off the earth. "If I could just talk to you in person," she says. She grabs hold of the counter and glances out at the lilacs waving in the breeze. The tree is almost twenty feet tall; it might just take over both her own house and Clarisse's. "He has been sober for years. He's never slipped," Leila whispers. Her hopeless tone brings Grant back to those days when she'd call in the middle of the night, pleading with Dr. Shongo to come quick because Luke was sick. Dr. Shongo would never tell his wife where he was going on these late night calls. Whenever Leila called, he would run out, saying on his way out, "People need me." Nothing else. Emily Shongo's face would grow pale and she'd storm out of the room. Grant always wondered why his father never said it was Leila who had called. Dr. Shongo always told his wife who was calling whenever anybody else called in the middle of the night.

"I'll bring Lion back in the morning, Leila."

"I guess it's better that Melanie doesn't see him like this."

"He'll be good as new."

"I put my faith in the hands of your father for a long time," she says. Grant hesitates. "I'll have to trust you, too," she says, and hangs up.

While Lion is still crying softly, muttering to himself, Grant slides him into his car. Lion calls Grant a motherfucker a few more times before passing out. One of Grant's front lights is out and he relies on the moonlight to show the way home. It is a full moon tonight. He glances out at the lake just in time to catch a glimpse of something breaking free from the net of dense fog and rising off the surface of the water and into the low clouds.

11

TWICE A YEAR, MEN who live along the lake put on their bathing suits and high water boots and wade out into the freezing water to set out the docks in front of their shorelines. This ritual—the docks go into the lake by Memorial Day and out by Labor Day—was created in response to the ferocity of bad winter weather more than anything else. The fact is that nothing can be sustained in the icy water throughout the winter, not even the metal sections of a heavy dock. And so they are taken apart each season, the individual sections dragged up from the shoreline, only to be returned again in May. Then, men can again fish off them, women can sun themselves, boats can be hoisted up to them, and children can run across the slippery surface in their wet bathing suits, inevitably sliding off and into the cold water, resurfacing in tears, and with their first real bruises.

Usually the water is so cold, so choppy, nobody in his right mind wants to do the job. It's not a thing one can do alone. Some docks require several men to drag all the sections into the water and fit each of them together. That's why being neighborly on the lake is a necessity. A person can't see a thing beneath the water, not the bone white stones under his feet, or the metallic flash of a sunfish. There's no time like the present to put the dock out, but Grant needs another man, and though Lion Williams would not be his first choice, he decides to put him to work.

LION WILLIAMS HASN'T WOKEN up with a hangover in five years, not since he stopped drinking Jack Daniels and smoking pot. But when Grant nudges him at 7 A.M., Lion is caught angry and off balance. It's not the fact that his tongue feels like leather. He welcomes the punishment. He's more worried about his girlfriend, who has now been gone for three days. To add to the feeling, he sees water when he looks out the window of the cabin. Gray water everywhere. Miles of it.

Lion knows he will die in the water. He's always known it ever since he was three and his cousin threw him into the pool at the YMCA. He sunk right to the bottom and didn't come up. That's why he's whispering to himself, trying to count down from one hundred. He is convinced that all the evil in the world ends up in the water eventually. He is already cold, and may freeze if his lungs don't explode first. He has read books on drowning. He figures if it's going to happen, he should at least know how. As soon as the body gets stiff from fear it begins to sink. After two minutes a person becomes unconscious. The heart beats for several minutes thereafter. A person might not even rise to the surface before he dies. People die while they're sinking, all swollen like those baby birds that wash up on the shore after falling out of nests from the trees that line the lake.

He needs to get back home. Lucas, he needs to see Lucas. Where the hell is his car? He peers out of the other window and into the woods, the sunlight burning into his bloodshot eyes.

"Leave me the fuck alone," he tells Grant. "You kidnapped me. And now you want me to do work for you? Are you kidding me, man? Where the hell am I?"

He swings his long legs off the bed, and rubs his stubbled chin, pushing the thin flannel blanket off of his legs and onto the faded yellow shag carpeting. "Look, I gotta find my wife," he mutters. "I gotta see my son." But Grant doesn't listen. Lion can smell bacon cooking. Grant mentions something about breakfast and Lion's car being left at the bar. Lion watches Grant lumber back into the small kitchen with its dark oak paneling. The whole house smells like grease. Grant doesn't seem to care about what is going on in Lion's world. It makes Lion want to spit.

"Make the damn bed and then I'll feed you," Grant calls in.

"I don't want your food," mutters Lion.

He really wants to hate Grant Shongo. Really wants to detest him with every aching fiber he has. Lion gets up and stands in the doorway watching Grant flip flapjacks into the air. The place is pathetic. Small, with an old brown couch and a bunch of wooden Indian statues everywhere he looks. He doesn't know why the guy's long hair bothers him.

Lion clears his throat. "Man, take me home. Or I'm gonna walk."

"Sure you know your way out of here?"

Lion looks out at the lake. He is trapped. A hostage.

Grant points to a seat at the bony oak table where elbow-worn circles mark the seating. There's a red and black woven placemat, a fork and knife to the left of a white plastic plate. Staring at his reflection in the empty plate, for a moment Lion has the feeling that the bottom has fallen out of his life. When he started smoking pot, that's how empty he felt. Empty and lost. All he could see in his future was a one-way ticket to a particularly unattractive destiny on the streets of Los Angeles for the rest of his life. He had nothing. Nothing to look forward to. Nothing to give. He couldn't feel the *Lion* inside of him. He was a nowhere person, stuck between black and white, devil and saint. He hasn't felt that way in ages, not since meeting Melanie. When he got her clean he became a hero and his destiny completely changed.

All Lion wants to do is to sting Grant for helping him. No matter what, they'll never be friends. Grant's like all the other "normies," which means he'll never know what it takes to wrestle addiction to the ground, which means he'd never understand who Lion is at the core. He doesn't tell Grant that every once in a while he answers a stranger's desperate midnight phone call. Without thinking twice, he'll haul himself out of bed and drive through the rain, the snow, to the other side of town, to the opposite end of the state, in the direction of someone else's nightmare. Hitting bottom is life or death, and it doesn't matter where you live or how much money you make. Hitting bottom is all about one thing: Truth. He's got antennae for it. Grant doesn't know how an addiction changes you, the deep oceans it sinks you to. Grant probably lives in a trance, never knowing what's wrong or even how to see inside himself. But Lion can tell Grant has bottomed out.

There are telltale signs: he sleeps on a tiny twin bed without sheets or pillows. Piles of wood shavings litter the porch. There are empty ramen noodles wrappers all over the counter. And a goddamn big gray wolf is tied to a tree outside. The damn thing looks ferocious, licking his chops and eyeing Lion like Lion is his next meal. The guy is definitely off balance.

No, addicts are the strong ones, Lion believes. Once they learn to focus their energy in another way, they can do amazing things.

But he'll just let the guy think he's so superior.

Lion tries to think about Lucas, and that brings him back.

Lucas, the miracle. How is it that this new person has become his compass? His true north.

Lucas needs him. Everybody's got to be needed.

Lucas is a beautiful child. People in the mall do a double-take to try to get a good look at him with his coffee-milk skin and light blue eyes. He's got old eyes, deep and glassy. He looks at you like he has seen it all before, Lion has tried to explain. Like Lucas just *knows*.

Lion's love has everything to do with who Lucas is, and what that love has made him. Lucas is trusting and Lion wants him to stay that way, the way Lion used to be before he hit the streets of Long Beach on the afternoon of his fourteenth birthday. He had to make it on his own. He had to learn how to talk, how to deal, how to blend in and how to stand out. He made up a whole new person, and slipped him on like a new suit.

Years later, when Lion got sober, he had to unlearn all those things. He hadn't counted on the fact that those different selves were harder to take off than to put on.

Lion won't let that fate come to Lucas. At least the boy does take after Lion in one way: he has the same long legs and spindly fingers. And he doesn't like vegetables, especially peas and cooked carrots. Lucas spits them out every time Melanie tries to disguise them as something else. Even after she bought the special Goofy bib and fork for him, even when she makes the one-eyed Grinch face, Lucas still spits out those vegetables. He can't be fooled, and Lion admires him for it.

They're night owls, all three of them. If they were birds, they'd be a family of owls living in a tree. When Lucas wakes up just before midnight, Melanie brings him into their bed, and she sings songs to him that she makes up. Lucas makes his gurgling laugh that sounds like some kind of frog so you know he's happy. Lion loves to hear Melanie whisper to him about Felf the Elf and Punchkin the Munchkin. She doesn't tell him scary stories that will make his head ache for the rest of his life whenever he finds himself alone. Lucas doesn't even care that her songs make no sense. He starts pulling at his tawny curls and kicking his little feet, and when Lion sees that bent right pinky toe moving back and forth he knows everything is perfect.

The food smells good. Lion's mouth waters, despite himself. He takes a bite, but he doesn't look up. He is thinking of Melanie. Worried. Is she eating breakfast somewhere far away? Has she just come home, expecting to surprise him, sorry, and full of kisses? He won't tell Grant that banana pancakes are Melanie's favorite, that warm bananas melting in her mouth are one of her favorite things on earth.

"HOW ARE THEY?" GRANT asks. He doesn't want to hover but he can't help it. Despite the dull memory of alcohol, he's ready. The ritual of cooking, of caring for someone other than himself, has awakened a part of him. It's true he feels somewhat anxious. The place has become a fortress, a sacred territory all his own, but the company, however belligerent, is better than the isolation. Grant could build a house today. He's already cleaned up the living room and ripped three old screens away from the porch. They're lying in a curled mess across the yard. Every so often he steals a look into the living room to make sure no coal footprints have appeared.

It's too bad Lion smells like beer and smoke. Grant would offer to wash his clothes but he doesn't want to mother him to death. He's about to suggest a shower when Lion stops chewing and looks up.

"Kind of rubbery," says Lion. "Like a tire."

Grant folds his arms across his chest and smiles. There's a sulfur spring near an old Boy Scout camp on Tichenor Point where surly campers were dunked. He and Lion might have to take a field trip there.

"What are you looking at, man? You're making me nervous," Lion says, flatly. "I hate people staring at me."

"Sorry," says Grant, looking down. He sighs, all the while keeping his eyes on the ground. Grant waits for a reaction, some sign of life from Lion. Nothing. A waiting game. A minute of silence passes.

Lion tries to hold back but he cannot stop himself. Lion is hungry after all. He hasn't eaten since early yesterday.

"You don't have to stare at the floor," says Lion, biting into the pancake. "Just don't stare at me."

"Okay, okay," says Grant. "At least you're human. I wasn't sure."

"Not really," Lion tells him, swallowing. "Not much."

"Where'd you get so tough?"

Lion keeps his eyes on his plate. "You a full-blooded Indian?"

Grant picks up his fork to spear a section of pancake. "Half. My father was Seneca, my mother was white. Why?"

"Just heard you were a full-blooded Indian."

Grant shakes his head. "No."

Lion raises an eyebrow at Grant. "You wish you were?"

"What?"

"You know. Pure."

"I've had some time to get used to it," Grant tells him. "All Indian, all white. Doesn't make you pure. Or strong."

Lion nods. "You'll say that."

"It's what I believe."

"Well, I ain't pure-blooded either. White mother. Black father. He liked banana ice cream. That's all I know about him. And he didn't like kids. He was going to college. He thought he was too smart for her. She always talked about his wristwatch. Like she was real impressed that he wore a watch. Like that meant something. But, anyone who doesn't want to know me I don't want to know," Lion says, rubbing his temples. Suddenly, the wolf attacks the glass door with his tongue, licking it with too much enthusiasm. "Holy shit, get that thing away from me!" yells Lion, jumping up from the table. The wolf has been waiting outside on the porch, ears pricked up, pacing back and forth, penitent, drooling, watching Grant and Lion through the sliding glass doors.

"He's friendly," says Grant. "He was injured. He's staying here for a while until he gets better. He's tied up, don't worry."

"Man, is your head on right?"

"Perfectly fine. Your head okay?" Grant says.

"Yeah, except my eyes are on fire," says Lion, blinking.

"Aspirin's in the cupboard. Help yourself."

Lion shakes his head. "Nah, I'm all natural, man. Can't believe you're keeping a wolf as a pet. What's his name?"

"He doesn't have a name yet. He isn't mine."

"Yeah, right," says Lion impatiently. "Listen, lost my cell phone last night. You got a phone?"

Grant ignores him. "The phone is right there. But it doesn't work. Finish eating and then you can help me set up the docks. And then I'll drive you to Kelley's to get your car."

"You're bribing me, man," says Lion. "What do you mean, the docks?"

"The boat docks. See out there," he says, motioning toward

the water. "Everyone is putting the docks out today. It's tradition." Lion peers out the window. Groups of men are gathered at the shore all along the lake, moving pieces of metal and wood.

"I ain't going outside with that goddamn wolf. And I ain't going in the water," warns Lion.

"Why not?" asks Grant.

"You got to get someone else. No way I'm going."

"Well, can you help me get started at least?"

"Damn, you don't even have a boat. Why do you need a dock?"

"Everyone needs a dock. For fishing, and other things."

"You kill fish?"

"Just hurry up and eat, Lion."

"Is this the freakin' army or what? I have my rights."

"You lost your rights when I saved your ass," says Grant.

"Nah, man, you didn't save anything." Lion scoffs. "Whatever, man. I gotta call Leila. My mother-in-law. She's probably worried. Probably been up all night, worried sick. And Melanie is probably home now. I gotta get home." Lion is the one with the sick feeling in the pit of his stomach. He knows how disappointed Leila will be to learn that he's broken his abstinence. She had been so proud of his sobriety. And it was obvious that if he wasn't clean, he wouldn't be able to keep Melanie clean. And this would make Leila worry even more. Lion thinks about how each year on his "abstinence anniversary" she has made him special cupcakes.

"I called her last night," says Grant.

Lion is looking through him, glassy eyed. "You called who?"

"Leila. I had to call her."

"But you didn't tell her, right?" Lion puts down his fork. "You didn't say—"

"That you needed to sleep it off. You just had a bit to drink. That's it."

Lion puts down his fork. "Man. Why you gotta go and do that? She's probably a crying mess right now. I didn't ask you to get in my business. She doesn't have enough to worry about? She has to worry about me, now? You just about ruined my life."

Grant shifts uncomfortably in his seat. He wouldn't be surprised if Lion gets up and flips the table upside down, a classic move, and a real show stopper. "Look, you slipped up once. It happens."

"Not to me."

"Sorry. I didn't know. I'll take you back soon. Promise."

Lion pushes a lone banana slice around the plate with his fork, and then he once again notices the wooden statues lining the perimeter. "You make all those? How many you got? Like one hundred?"

"Twenty-one." Grant points to a few fresh pieces of wood piled in the corner. "Basswood. It doesn't grow anywhere else nearly as well. I had a little time on my hands, no, a lot of time on my hands . . . so—"

Just then, the wolf paws the sliding glass door and begins to prowl back and forth on the porch. Grant goes outside and rubs its stomach. Lion watches. When Grant comes back inside, Lion seems different. "I know you didn't mean to nark on me to Leila. You just, you thought you were helping, right?" Lion says, wincing, as though the words are painful. "Just forget it."

"Thanks. I thought I was doing a good thing."

"It hard to do? Carve those statues?"

"Not if you learn the right way," says Grant.

Lion picks up his glass of orange juice and sips it. The acidic taste makes his mouth burn. "How'd you learn it?"

"From my dad. It's good for your hands. Keeps them strong." Grant had sat with the wooden sticks as a child, waiting for the spirit in the wood to seep out. First, you had to know that you were actually only the tool, only there to do what the wood asked. Only then would the shape reveal itself.

"How'd you learn to help wolves?" Lion asks.

"Got that from my dad, too," says Grant.

What Lion needs, Grant has decided, is some physical exertion, a chance to be successful at something. The wooden statues have taught Grant about this. There is nothing that pulls a man out of a slump faster than working up a sweat.

When they finish breakfast, Grant gives Lion a minute to himself. Meanwhile, he rifles through his closet for a pair of pants and some mud boots for Lion, not the kind Lion is used to, but big yellow rubber boots built for high water. Grant knows these will do little good for the job they have to do, but then wet clothes are just one more thing Lion will have to deal with. It's a risk he's willing to take.

"Come on outside," orders Grant.

He opens the door, and Lion follows him out onto the porch, making sure to edge far away from the wolf that is asleep under the porch swing.

"Man," says Lion, staring out at the two huge willows fluttering in the breeze. "I know where we are now. The Diamond Trees Melanie was always talking about. You got to be kidding me. This is where her brother died. Man, this is the haunted cabin I've always heard about. You can't keep me here," he says, glancing up at the gravel driveway. "Where's the road to town?"

"Look, it's still early. You do something for me. I'll help you."

"Help me. Help you," mutters Lion mockingly, out of the corner of his mouth. "Help you, help me." Lion's hateful thoughts are being triggered again. He shivers, recalling Melanie's stories about Luke. This was the place where it all happened, the place where someone she loved had been lost forever. Lion feels closer to her, and farther away.

"What?" asks Grant, but Lion doesn't respond. Grant goes inside and puts on his pants and boots. Minutes later, Lion is straining, stretching to get the boots on as though he were pulling on a second skin. Grant knows there's room in those boots. Lion's feet are two sizes smaller than his.

"You got a cigarette?" Lion asks, wiping his forehead dramatically, one boot in hand. "Man, I could use one before we do this."

"Never smoked," Grant says, tightening his father's boots. Lion rolls his eyes. "Smoking killed my mother. Lung cancer," Grant says in a clipped tone. "Get that other boot on."

"I don't smoke a lot," says Lion.

"Whatever. Let's go. Water's rough."

"What if it starts to rain?" asks Lion, as he looks around, eyeing the water miserably. "What's that big black cloud in the sky?"

"Rain or not, the docks go out today," says Grant, sounding like his father. They traipse silently into the garage, where the sections of dock are kept, Grant in his father's invisible footsteps, Lion close behind. Together they clean off the layers of dust and spider webs, some of which are so thick, you can practically hear them tear when the large pieces of metal and wood are pulled from their place against the wall. The spiders tumble down around their feet and scatter in every direction across the floor. Lion doesn't even balk, and this makes Grant like him more. Lion has surprised him.

"I saw a spider strung out on pot once . . . marijuana," says Lion.

"A spider?"

"Yeah. It was in a book at rehab, when I was getting clean. A bunch of photos, with all these different webs. Some on pot, mescaline, coffee. The scientists fed it to them. Like a study. You know, some webs were kind of saggy. Some lopsided. The coffee webs were the worst, loose, crooked. You should have seen it."

"What about pot?"

"All ratty. Like they forgot to make the in-between threads."

"Hmm," says Grant.

"Yeah, but I didn't like them messing up these spiders for no good reason."

Together, they drag a one-hundred-pound section of heavy metal dock down the backyard slope to the shoreline. While Lion guides and pushes, Grant lifts the section on one end so that the wheels on the other will roll down the shoreline. Grant has already estimated by the lake's low level that it will take two sections this season. As though some primal peace has taken over, he and Lion now communicate only through hand signals. Grant pointing. Lion following. For a minute, they're even in synch. Together, they drag another section into the water, with Lion dragging and Grant guiding it.

The water is rough, as Grant had predicted. It begins to rain. Lion looks up at the sky and shakes his head. He's wet and cold and resentful and can't stop thinking of Melanie and Luke. He has that vague sinking feeling that he's trapped, like he's gotten on the too-old-to-be-a-good-idea roller coaster at the old Roseland Amusement Park and the bar has just slammed down on his thighs.

"Let's go." Grant refuses to let him off the hook. A little rain never killed anybody. Grant glances up at the wolf, which is watching from the porch. Then he wades into the water near the end of the first section of dock, pliers in hand, and begins fitting the sections together. The water is cold but not as icy as he remembers. Some years, he's lost feeling in half his body. During these times, his father's cheery optimism had just about driven him nuts. Grant became thankful for the times of crisis, for that's when Ben Shongo's heavy moods always seemed to have lifted.

Grant could annoy Lion with more humor and optimism. Besides, as long as he still has feeling in his toes, they should keep going. The section is slipping. Grant moves out deeper and hangs on to the edge of the first section. He looks down at the submerged leaves caught in a breezy underwater wind. The bright lobes are the perfect size for the minnows, which are everywhere, diving for cover. Occasionally a logy carp rolls by. They're huge, between three and four feet. They come by every few minutes just to check on everything.

Grant's boots are filling up with water as he motions to Lion. The boy hesitates on the shoreline, glancing back at the wolf. "I'll stay here," yells Lion, his voice searing through the sheets of rain.

"No way!" calls Grant. "I need you. Can't get the thing to fit together myself."

"What?" The rain is coming down harder now. They can't hear each other, so there is no point in talking. The wolf gets up and begins to howl. Slowly, Lion steps out onto the first section of metal dock with trepidation. There is a foot-long gap between this section and the second. Lion stops once, looks around. Grant can't quite make out his expression through the shifting slats of water as Lion jumps onto the second section. "No!" Grant calls. "Help me push from down here." He is trying to tell Lion to get off the dock. It is not sturdy and more than likely it is slippery. For a moment, he turns back to look at the cabin, picturing himself sitting in his father's favorite chair looking out at the lake, as he used to when he'd imagine his father walking into the lake until his head and shoulders rested just above the water like turtle shells.

"I can hold it from up here," Lion calls back. "Let me do it this way!"

Grant sloshes through the muddy and rocky bottom. Standing out here, he can almost hear his father's voice through the rain, shouting instructions.

Standing on the slippery metal, Lion feels a jolt underneath him as though the earth has moved. He feels the metal sliding beneath him. Lion tries to catch himself but slips off, his yellow boots hitting the water. Lion sputters, choking, his arms flailing wildly, his body dragged down by the water-filled boots as though they were cement.

Through the hazy green water, Lion is falling into an eight-foot depth of despair. He is drowning. He always knew it would happen this way, but he didn't count on feeling everything, every minute of it. He didn't count on the feeling of suffocation, the pressure in his lungs, the reflex of gasping. The water is frozen, turning his body to ice. He opens his eyes as he swallows murky water. He can hardly see. He is shouting but his words come out in long strings of bubbles. He can hear his heartbeat. He is certain his lungs are going to burst, certain they are going to pop like two balloons. Suddenly, he sees large white skulls, or are they fish, floating up all around him. And then, just when Lion's eyes begin to close he feels the tug on one ankle and when he looks down, he sees, for a moment, a small pale face framed by blond curls peering up at him.

Though his boots are filled with water, Grant manages to slip them off and he dives toward Lion, through the cloudy water, and grabs hold of one of Lion's boots, which slips off in his hand. He manages to grab Lion's arms and drag him toward the shoreline as Lion splashes and sputters. "Don't panic!" Grant orders, but this is like telling a volcano to stop erupting once it has started.

Later, after Lion has dried off, he is sitting cross-legged on the shag carpet with a blanket over his shoulders, staring dejectedly at the wolf staring back at him from under the porch swing. It is still raining. Lion is mimicking the rain's rhythmic drumming with his fingers. He puts his palm up against the cold window and gently hits his head against the glass. The wolf gets up and comes right up to the window, trying to paw Lion's hand. Lion does not pull away. Lion bangs his head on the glass again and the wolf stares at him quizzically. Lion feels mean. Humiliated. Broken inside. "Why don't you let the wolf come inside?" asks Lion, who is convinced he has just had a near-death experience. He is wondering how it is that he has survived. Although he may have imagined it, the image of the blond-haired boy is stuck in his mind. He shivers, pulling the blanket tighter around him. His voice is caught in his throat. His sinuses are burning from the water and his ears are clogged. He feels like he might like to cry, that is how cold he is. He swallows back his tears and does his best not to look at Grant.

"It was the boots," Grant says. "I should have warned you." There's no excuse, Grant tells himself. He should have seen this coming. For years, he had helped his father with the docks, and he knew how to get boots off quick or they'd become lead weights, filling up with water. But how could he have known Lion couldn't swim? "Swimming is a good thing to learn if you live on a lake," Grant says, throwing another woolen blanket over Lion's shoulders. Lion looks like a wet dog sitting there. Bony, small. "I could teach you."

"Ha. Right." Lion still won't look at him. "Last night."

"What?" asks Grant, sitting down.

"You think you saved me, man? What were you doing there? Doing shots? I saw you."

Lion's dark eyes are tight like fists held under glass.

Grant shrugs. "Just, you know, catching up with a friend."

Lion folds his arms and turns his back to Grant. "Save it. You want to sit there all big 'cause I'm here in the middle of a disaster, but it's you, you're the one, I can see it. You sit there looking like a goddamn shipwreck, but you don't say a word about any of it."

"You can't see anything," Grant tells him. "Even if I am a goddamn shipwreck, so what."

"Ha, I knew it. You're a crazy motherfucker."

"So what if I am."

"Look, whatever. We're not even. You saw me take a fall. I was helpless, you know. Now you got power over me. So now you got to tell me something. Confess something."

"What do you think being even is going to get you?"

Lion looks hopeful. "You never did anything bad? It'll make me feel better." As the edges of clouds peel back, honeyed rays fall along the bare patches in the lawn where the oaks have made the soil so acidic, it's work to keep any grass growing. Lion writes his name on the window and won't look at Grant.

"Lion, I know how it feels—"

"You don't know shit about me."

The silence passes in a wave between them.

Lion leans in and breathes on the window, the fog refining his name. "I keep thinking about that spider language. His design shows what he feels. You know his feeling if you know his language."

"Wish it were that easy with human beings," says Grant,

noticing Lion's large bloodshot eyes, and pierced right ear with a tiny silver skull earring.

"You ever been sleeping next to someone, you're lying in the dark but you can feel they're awake, like you can feel them thinking?" asks Lion.

Grant nods.

"Sometimes at night, when I'm lying next to Mel, she covers her head with the pillow and faces the wall, but I know she's awake. It's like she wants to be swallowed up by the dark. I'll say her name but she won't answer. She pretends to be asleep. In the morning, her eyes are all red and she'll stay in the house all day wearing one of my ratty sweatshirts. And I know she's thinking about Luke." As he says this he pictures the little boy's face again. He blinks hard, trying to will it out of his mind. "She thinks that she caused it, you know? I know she's trying to figure out what happened, that it's in her subconscious or whatever. She's trying to figure out if it was her fault or if it was Maya's. Or if either of them could have saved him."

"They were just kids."

"I tell her that. She says it was her idea to get into the canoe. But she lost the paddle. She says something in the water ripped it out of her hands. Some*thing* in the water."

"She was just a kid, of course she'd think that," Grant says. "It was the waves."

"I can't make her believe that," says Lion. "I've tried. I'd do anything for her. It's scary what I would do for her. I scare myself."

Grant leans back, guarded. "I have some experience with that."

"Right," Lion scoffs.

"When my mom was dying of lung cancer. The only thing she asked for was her cigarettes."

Lion stares at Grant, silent.

"It made her happy. It was the only thing."

"Man, how did you deal with that?"

"I was broken. So was she. That Polynesian restaurant, the Aloha, on Monroe Avenue? They had a cigarette machine in back. I'd run the whole way and back, like a man on fire."

"Yeah, yeah. Your dad, he saw?"

"My father wasn't a big talker. If he saw he never said. It was like it was going to be him or me that had to do it."

"He couldn't do it. It had to be you."

"Yeah," says Grant, staring at Lion.

"You hated him," says Lion, folding his arms. "For making you do it."

"No. Only myself."

"No way, man. I would have hated him." Lion shakes his head. They are both full of guilt, but for different reasons. Guilt is a magnet for bad health, Lion thinks. People refuse to let it go even when they get mysterious addictions.

Grant runs his fingers across the carpeting. "When I was a kid, I had this crazy stutter. Could hardly say my own name. So one day before school, I'm twelve, I think. Out back on the playground. I'd always get there early enough to run around the track a few times. Some tough kids are in the bleachers, yelling, teasing me, and I don't stop running but look right at them as I pass. Then I stop. I give them the finger. I just stand there, holding my hand up. Six of them and I'm there alone. Then before I know it, they're kicking the crap out of me. . . . I wanted to get the crap kicked out of me."

"Yeah. I can see it."

"I didn't move. Didn't do a thing. You know how when you're a kid, you know you should run but you don't? You just stay in one place, daring yourself to see how long you can last?"

Lion nods. "Know all about that."

"She thanked me. My mother was lying in bed, coughing up blood. And I lit her cigarette."

"That's crazy. Damn. But it doesn't matter what you did. You were her son. You were messed up." Lion wipes away his name on the window pane.

"I couldn't look my old man in the eye after she died. I went pretty crazy."

Lion looks at Grant, his eyes filled with compassion. "Damn. But you did what you had to. Doesn't matter what anyone says. You did it because you were her son and she needed you to do it."

"Yeah." At once, they are equals, and it is better this way, just as Lion had said. A few moments pass. The rain is gone. Grant is watching the sun's rays reaching through the porch screen and into the house. Within seconds, it's so bright out, even the kingfishers look frightfully pale, their blue tufts of feathers appearing a hollow gray. The trees are now only hazy reflections of themselves in the water. Grant blinks hard. The wolf has now stretched out in the middle of the lawn, looking relaxed and incredibly big. "My mom was a pretty strong person. But she wasn't a happy person. I wish I could remember her being happy."

"Melanie sings when she's happy."

Grant smiles, grateful for the distraction. "That's great. What does she sing?"

"She turns up the radio loud. She thinks she's singing along. But she makes up her own words. It's pretty funny. She doesn't even realize she's doing it, making dinner, or painting, or whatever. I always try to hear. She gets mad when I laugh at her, though. I run out of the room sometimes I'm laughing so hard."

Grant's hands are burning. He turns them over, staring at the blistered palms.

"Go ahead," Lion says, blinking hard. "Ask it."

"It doesn't matter."

"Ask it."

"Why?"

"Say it."

"Is she at Two Bears' Cave?"

"Fuck, man. You didn't have to say it. I knew you didn't believe me."

Everyone knows Two Bears' Cave on the East Side of Loomis Hill, on the other side of the hill from the Iroquois longhouse. At one time, the Cave was a sacred healing place, revered for its power, and hidden to all but a few that had been healed there but never spoke of it. So people made up stories of magical stones and herbs and animal skulls stuck on posts, of spirits cloaked under the wings of bats that hung from the ceilings. Now the Cave, with its large fire pit and shelves carved into the walls, is littered with old bags of food, empty bottles, and used needles, a hangout for drunks and general itinerant traffic.

No one can tell just who's hiding out at the place at any given time, or when the spirit of a Seneca healer called Two Bears will appear to those in a drug-induced state. The local cops stay away, content to let the vagrants have their space. Better there, out of the way, than the marina, where they'd make real trouble. Two Bears' Cave is part of the local culture, like O'Connell's Feed & Grain or Kelley's Bar.

Two Bears had a reputation in town back when he was alive. A giant, a hermit, they say, staying mostly to himself, fiercely private. He only came into town at night to buy supplies from O'Connell's Feed & Grain. Some reported seeing him at night, treading the woody trails to gather herbs. Mostly, he just kept company with the Indians who traveled from far-off reservations seeking his cures. Not many other people had seen him, although the story was that he was seven feet tall, with hair to his waist, hands the size of cabbages, and skin pocked from the lit embers of healing ceremonies. Some people said he could hold his hands in a fire for an hour unscathed.

"What do you know about the Cave anyway?" asks Lion.

"It's not someplace I'd like to vacation. There's no point in talking anymore about it. If she's not using, she's not there."

"Wish I'd have learned," Lion confesses, "how not to hate the water."

"Look, don't be ashamed. People learn to swim at all ages."

"I didn't plan on moving to a lake. I was just, you know, a drifter, kind of lost. California's home. But I never touched the Pacific Ocean. Not even with my little toe. I know lots of people who grew up looking at the ocean but never swimming in it. But then one day I just washed up here like a piece of junk, or an old candy wrapper."

"Fear's a strange thing. It's a magnet. Sometimes you find yourself running toward what you fear most. You can't stop yourself, right? Heck, it's happened to me."

"That's what happened with your mom, right? Why she kept smoking."

"Something like that."

Lion pulls the blanket tighter around him. "Well, I know it was all meant to be, anyway, me coming here," he says, nodding. "I wouldn't have met Melanie. Wouldn't have my son."

"Drink this," Grant says, pushing a cup of coffee toward Lion. Lion takes a sip. He seems almost peaceful, as though the water has taken all the fight from him, which is probably why he has always feared it.

"Hey," says Lion. "I miss my boy bad. You ever had a kid?"

Grant shakes his head.

"'Cause I didn't see any pictures around. You ever have a wife?"

Grant stares at the faded line that is disappearing from his finger. "Yeah, not too long ago."

"Where is she?" Lion asks, repositioning the blanket. He sits cross-legged. He puts his hands in his lap.

"She left."

"Why she leave?"

"She said she didn't think I loved her enough."

"Was she right?"

"There're all kinds of love."

"Nah, man, there's only one kind of love."

On their first official date, Lion had taken Melanie on a drive through Naples. It was snowing like crazy. He didn't know about the deadly black ice, which sometimes looked like a huge crow had spread its slick wings over the road. He didn't know that some lakes never freeze over entirely because of their constant current. He hadn't paid attention to the two cars up ahead, owned by ice fishermen Squeaky Loomis and Joseph O'Connell, who, bundled in layers of down, had pulled over a mile back to wait out the storm. If he'd seen them, maybe he'd have turned around, but he was so taken with listening to her describe the colors of snow that he just kept driving, faster and faster.

When they hit black ice, his car skidded off the road into a bank. After the shock, even though she hit her head, Melanie had started to laugh. She didn't even make him feel stupid for not pumping the brakes like he was supposed to. He cleaned up her cut and got out to push the car, and she jumped out, too. He told her to get in but she took one of her gloves off and put it on his hand. And he didn't want to send her running for her life by telling her how pretty she looked and that he'd never felt luckier. He just went with it, sliding in rubbery soles and getting soaked in the snow.

Snowflakes covered her hair like a veil, like a beautiful bride who was just laughing and laughing, her eyelashes turning powder white. Then he saw it, what she meant, because when he looked up, her eyes were a color he'd heard of but never seen: ice blue. She didn't care about the cold or the wet or his ineptitude. She said she was having so much fun it was all worth it, that they were making memories. He never knew memories were something you could decide to make, rather than the results of things that just happened to you.

Grant leans back against the counter. "Look, I have time, if you need help. I mean, I could drive around. Try to find her."

"Why you want to help me so bad?"

"Why were you drunk instead of looking for Melanie?"

"I had to cool down. But you. Nah man, there's something about you that's not right. Keeping a wolf. Keeping a ghost." Lion waits, daring Grant to ask what Lion saw in the water. Lion squints at Grant, peering at him as though they are both standing in the darkness of a coal mine.

"You've got a good imagination," Grant scoffs, glancing at the living room. He gasps. Soot marks have reappeared across the carpet. "I'll take you home now," he says nervously.

"I'm making you uncomfortable, right?" Lion asks. "Answer my question. Why do you want to help me?"

"You really want to know?" Grant looks up.

Lion nods.

"Fine. Maybe I have nothing better to do," Grant says.

Lion hesitates, rubbing his head. "Okay."

"Okay?"

"All right. That's all I wanted to know. I got a plan to find her if she's not back already. I don't care if no one believes it. I know her. She's not on drugs again. She's good at being a mother. She says it's the reason she was put on earth. You believe me, right? She wouldn't do anything to hurt Lucas."

Grant pauses. "I believe you."

Lion has barely any energy left. His limbs feel like one-hundred-pound weights. "Yeah. She's probably back by now. I'm her rock and she's mine. You know what that does to you when you have to be someone's rock."

"Can't say I do," Grant tells him, remembering how Susanna's sadness had weighed him down, and how his mother's illness had torn him apart.

"Yeah," he says. "I think you do."

As Lion walks through the living room toward the front door, he notices a line of tiny black footprints leading across the room to the basement door. He won't go near that door. He needs to get the hell out of here. Waiting on the porch for Grant to get his keys, he glances at the metal sections of dock. He sees a splash of water kick up, even though there are no waves.

12

LEILA ELLIS IS EXHAUSTED from driving through the streets all night long searching for her daughter, an envelope of flyers in her lap. The gray business suit she is wearing is more than twenty years old and pulls across her breasts, bought for her only office job when she was a secretary at the construction company where she met Victor. But it is not giving her a feeling of authority as she had hoped, and the black pleather pumps are only pinching her toes, not making her feel she has command over her environment so that people will take her seriously. It has been three days since Melanie disappeared, but a mother knows when something bad has happened. For the past several months, Leila has had *the feeling,* the one that lives deep in her gut and is never wrong. A mother can sense disaster coming, smell it in the air the way that some animals will lie down before a storm. "Do you know my daughter?" Have you seen this face? You *think* so. You *may* have. *What do you mean you don't?*

This searching is taking its toll. And with all this straining to keep an eye on little Lucas in the backseat, her neck muscles ache. She knows she shouldn't complain. He is a good boy, happy to sleep most of the way, but night driving still makes her uncomfortable, a reminder of the 2-A.M. hospital runs that she used to make with Luke. Now, at sixty-one, her eyes are not what they used to be. She is not so good anymore at spotting her daughter's blond crew cut in her favorite hangouts—Eastview Mall, Blood Alley, the marina. All the wild young kids hang out at the pier with their motorcycles and cars.

Things had been going too well. Leila had almost begun to relax. Even the messy divorce from the girls' father in 1991 had been relegated to a dull ache behind her eyes. When she had finally, with Lion's help, turned the gun cabinet into a beautiful glass étagère, she knew Victor was out of her life for good. The fact was that her family had enjoyed two full years of blessings—the birth of her grandson, a new job for Lion and a new apartment with a shiny bright red door for him and Melanie. And of course, this baby reminds her more of her late son than even she can admit.

The feeling almost approached happiness.

This just wasn't the type of luck the Ellises had. They were due.

Leila knows all about her daughter's hangouts. Over the years, she has tracked her down too many times to count. But this time, it won't be so easy. She knows Melanie wouldn't leave Lucas. Still Leila is doing what the police suggest. Make a list of places Melanie has run to in the past during times of despair when the battle for her abstinence was waged and lost. It was too late to try Cheever Hospital, Melanie's last resort where she historically sought refuge with Maya whenever she was very out of sorts. But Melanie had hardly seen her sister over the last couple of years. The wall between the girls only came down during bad times.

Melanie had been happy since meeting Lion and having a baby, Leila was sure of it.

But Leila couldn't argue with what the disinterested detective told her when she called to report Melanie missing. She couldn't get in touch with Charlie Cooke. And she hated to deal with someone she didn't know. She had to listen to some stranger try to make her feel bad, telling her that this was the ninth missing persons report. The *eighth* report, she corrected him.

Send a car around, sure. Anything more? Don't count on it.

Leila knew what he did not say. Why should he waste manpower on a drug addict when there were honest people who needed help? Before hanging up, he had actually said to her, "Mrs. Ellis, the city of Canandaigua has exhausted its resources looking for your daughter. Perhaps you should let her come back on her own. She always does."

Perhaps the worst thoughts came from her own mind. Had the novelty of having a child finally worn off for Melanie? Would boredom or frustration return her to her old ways? No, Leila would not believe it. People could change. There had to be room for faith.

Since Luke's death, whenever people pass Leila on the street, they smile sympathetically or avert their eyes for what has become of her children. Leila can feel the blame and the pity. She has become a pariah—such a succession of bad luck has made people afraid to breathe the same air she does. People are superstitious; afraid the bad luck will rub off on them. Perhaps she has encouraged it with her own inability to ask for help or in the way she just backed away from her few close friends, anticipating their rejection. Leila stopped getting her hair styled at Le Chic Salon because the women sitting under the dryers routinely flashed wallet-sized pictures of their children, without so much as a question about Maya and Melanie. Instead, they talked long and loud about choosing their children's classes at Harvard and Yale, about whether International Relations was more lucrative than Microbiology. Leila had no more stomach for the game-show-hostess smiles, for sitting silently with her hands folded in her lap, for wishing people knew her children were just as smart, just as good as other children—even stronger, given what they had been through.

Some children were more heroic than others, in ways you could never know just by looking at them. What about keeping yourself calm when you're suffocating, calm enough to count to ten when your throat is swelling shut and your inhaler is missing? How about beating a life-threatening addiction, or knowing, at the age of fifteen, that you have to leave a boy you love because he has abused you, even after he has cried tears of apology, knowing he will hit you for the rest of your life? Some children are far more heroic than even their own mothers.

It seemed not too long ago that Leila could fix everything with a surprise dinner at the Aloha Polynesian restaurant. The children loved the green papier-mâché trees that grew right out of the walls. The restaurant's main attraction was a fountain that rose out of a wishing pool, throwing pink ropy lights into the air every eighteen minutes. People made wishes and threw in coins. The lights made the children rub their eyes, and the sound of the slapping water made everyone hush. The children would hold hands around the table as though in prayer, and for that one moment with Melanie, Maya, and Luke, all was perfect. When the fountain receded into the pink water, Hawaiian music flowed in from all corners of the room and conversations picked back up. Luke would spend most of the dinner running back and forth to the bamboo bridge, using up all of the precious dimes he'd saved, then begging for more, his little cheeks flushed with excitement. A few years ago, Leila had gone to the restaurant alone. She had been missing him, and when she happened to look over at the fountain she swore she saw him standing there, knee-deep in pinkish water and holding a paper airplane in one hand. The image shook her. He was looking for his own dimes, he said, because he changed his mind about some of his wishes.

Leila pulls up at a stoplight, pushes her wavy gray hair back from her face. In the rearview mirror, she watches Lucas pull a curl of his own hair, his pouty lips yawning peacefully. He's angelic, a beautiful child with bright blue eyes and a funny belly laugh, the kind that lifts the spirits of everyone in the room.

When she turns her attention forward, a sweep of yellow curls streaks across the windshield, turning it golden. "*Luke!*" she cries, tears flowing down her cheeks. She gets out of the car and looks up at the pink morning sky. *Help me find Melanie,* she pleads, shutting her eyes. *Help me, Luke.*

The car behind her is blaring its horn. She blinks several times, rubs her eyes. When she looks up again, the sky is filling with golden rivulets spilling into a lavender lake. She gets back into the car and when she steps on the gas, all she can think about is how very tired she feels.

She's driving in circles.

She's exhausted. She has double-checked every place she can think of. The city of Canandaigua is not that big, but there are acres and acres of land on the outskirts of Canandaigua proper. Forests, fields, and wild vineyards. More farms than she can count. Leila couldn't cover them all, even if she tried. Well, she shouldn't even be driving. Her body is giving up now. Only for now. She pulls up in the driveway of her blue clapboard house, wraps a sleeping Lucas in a blanket and carries him inside. His arms dangle from her clutch; his thick blond curls bounce slightly with each of her steps. When Leila opens the door, she has to push Old Sally out of the way with her foot. The dog's tail is wagging slightly. That's as excited as she gets at sixteen.

Leila gently places Lucas in his playpen. He immediately turns over on his stomach. Then she drops to her knees. The house is silent. She listens to him cooing sleepily, watches him twist the blanket around his fist. "We're going to find Mommy," she tells him. "I promise you." Then, right there in the middle of the living room, Leila curls up on the floor, a draft pricking up her skin, her back pressed against the warm chest of the dog, whose breath drags along like a freight train echoing through the empty house.

Leila remembers how isolated she felt that one February when it snowed for two weeks straight. Snowflakes the weight of silver dollars sank tree branches to the ground. She remembers looking out the window at the snowdrifts and thinking they looked like geese licking the wind. Luke would have noticed it, too. It was as if all the other birds had left the earth.

The world was silent, as it had been in the months after his death. This was a dead snow, heavy and slow, the kind of snow that stops time. Meteorologists didn't see an end in sight. The roads froze over quickly, forming opaque sheets of shark-gray ice. A snow emergency went into effect, hollowing out the streets, but the occasional screech of a car spinning into a telephone pole would wake her at night. Awake in a fright, thinking of Luke. It had been three years, but he was still very much with her.

That February, Leila had been inside so long that she looked out the window and saw only squalls of geese hunting for breadcrumbs in the road. She knew she had gotten so used to the darkness and her own imagination that she stopped turning on the lamps inside, preferring to walk the dark hallways and find her way by touch. All her other senses had become decisively clear. It was February, the cruelest month, and she was lonely and heard about someone else who was lonely. She went to great lengths to disguise her need as just being charitable, but eventually, she realized she was in too deep. Suddenly, everything had changed. The dull snore of a man in the guest room, for instance, made her feel safer than the bolt on her front door that had kept her protected for years, that had even kept out Victor since the divorce. The taste of her homemade bread, heavily packed with walnuts and raisins, was not filling enough no matter how much of it she ate. And her daughters' voices sounded so compliant and distant that she lay in bed picturing their weddings and imagining how she would say good-bye, just as she had said good-bye every night since Luke had been lost.

They called it the Blizzard of '94. The girls were in the throes of early adolescence. February vacation was already in full gear. The neighborhood kids grew sullen, feeling gypped that the snow emergency hadn't occurred during school. Temperatures loped below zero. Radiators broke. Pipes froze. Tempers flared. Even the biggest bullies in the neighborhood turned down ice hockey, preferring to stay inside and save their mothers the worry. Aside from an occasional plow denting the narrow street, Leila couldn't see anything moving outside but the blinding snowflakes. The blizzard was only a natural extension of the chaos that was going on in her house.

She and the girls had gone stir crazy, sleeping too much and never feeling quite awake. They wandered through rooms like zombies as the days blurred together. Soon, the girls could hardly look at each other without an argument. The fighting was growing worse. Leila didn't know what to do. They were like magnets, bonded one minute, violently repelled the next.

Sometimes Leila wouldn't see anything but there would be crying. Other times they hardly noticed her telling them to stop, too involved in their fight, ring-bound, hypnotized by the footsteps in and out of a circle only they could see. They fought with fists. They fought with words. Sometimes there were tears but never any voices or blood, as though the feel of their tiny fists didn't register any real pain until the death blow was given. Inside, each girl felt as though her heart was a frozen lake.

They told Leila that Luke talked to them in dreams. And sometimes Leila would overhear one of them talking back to him, when they didn't think anyone was listening.

The fact that Charlie Cooke was willing to brave the snow and come for a Valentine's Day dinner both surprised and terrified Leila. She knew he was on temporary leave from work, and she had overheard that his wife, Candice, had asked him to move out just weeks before, but as Leila cooked a turkey in haste, she half wondered whether she had lost her mind to the darkness. Her divorce was over. She hadn't thought she would ever date again. When Charlie returned her call, she had mistakenly asked him to arrive at five instead of eight, which would have given her enough time to have everything ready. And when he eagerly agreed, she was so nervous she hadn't corrected herself.

Hadn't they managed to have a perfect dinner? Charlie took the seat at the head of the table before Leila offered it, as though he had always sat there, pushing aside any images of Victor still lurking in her memory. When Charlie led them in saying grace, the girls bowed their heads without a smirk, and later impressed Leila with their pleases and thank-you-ma'ams, and soon Leila wondered if they were aliens or whether they had always spoken that way. After dinner, Leila and Charlie talked over the dishes and the girls offered to go upstairs to clean their room. Clean their room? Leila was certain she was dreaming as the girls waved and disappeared, and Charlie rolled up his sleeves to dry the dishes. She felt a little nervous, a little stunned that things between a man and a woman could feel this peaceful, for this kitchen had been the source of many of Victor's rages. But as she listened to Charlie tell her about his longtime dream of having children, she began to relax. Leila told him about her adoration of an old farmhouse that she had driven by but had never gone into that was for sale. Charlie asked her a million questions about the place, which made her deliriously stupid with hope, and neither of them noticed the snow piling up against the doorway, or the frost creeping across the windows, blocking even the tiniest shreds of light. When Charlie went to leave at 4 A.M., even the veritable detective of thirty years had to resign himself to the fact that he could not and should not open the door. And both he and Leila were secretly relieved.

For three nights, he slept in the guest room without complaint. The pillows were extra hard and the room not completely dark. But he slept deeply, better than he had in years, he said, leaving the door generously open, somehow knowing his presence was filling a deep void in the home. The girls hardly blinked the first morning when there was a man who was not their father reading the paper at the kitchen table. Leila explained about the snow emergency and the girls shrugged, and said, "Okay," as they kicked each other under the table and ate their bagels and cream cheese. They felt safer somehow. Charlie's presence had created a short cease and desist. Everything was so off, a stranger's presence normalized things. When he walked in on a fight about to brew, the girls glared at each other but turned away and separately went off to play in different rooms of the house.

During the day, he read anything he could get his hands on. Old hunting magazines of Victor's that had gotten lost at the bottom of the magazine rack, some books of poetry and Leila's *Farmers' Almanac.* Every once in a while, Charlie got up and stared out the window, muttering something about the city plows, but Leila knew it was lip service. Charlie seemed lighter, jovial even. *He wants to stay,* Leila told herself, as she and the girls made birthday cake for Melanie. He seemed relaxed, almost relieved as he sipped a beer and leaned up against the doorway with his white shirt untucked, watching them as if this whole scene was the fruit of his own life's efforts. After Melanie blew out her candles, Charlie pulled two comp movie tickets from his wallet and handed them to her. Melanie hugged him hard and quick, and he looked stunned. When Maya started to pout, he made her an origami swan out of a five-dollar bill, which made her happy. Leila's adolescent jungle was an oasis compared to his desolate motel life.

On the last night, the girls had volunteered to go to bed early. Leila was up late trying to fix the wires of the VCR, which Old Sally had plowed through yet again, the cords catching in her feet. Charlie came to her then with a question about sheets. He followed her into her bedroom and when he shut the door and put his hands on her, she forgot about who she was.

When the sun finally filtered through Leila's curtains the next morning, even in a half-dream state Leila knew two things had happened: the snow had stopped, and the man had left.

Hearing the clock tumble from the bedside table, the girls ran into the room with glowing faces. Leila had forgotten to set the alarm, somehow trying to ward off the reality of morning.

Excitedly, the girls took her hand and led her down the stairs and into the doorway. Melanie flung open the back door. They had shoveled out the entire driveway and the sidewalk.

Imprinted in the snow, two snow angels shimmered across the lawn. No, there were three, the last one smaller than the others, and off to the side.

Each was the perfect shape of a child. Each, she knew, was a careful work of art. The children noticed the smaller angel as soon as Leila did, and they argued about who had made it, both denying it. Leila's eyes watered up as she stared into the blinding whiteness so that the images would freeze their impressions inside her, filling her emptiness. She didn't say anything about the three dead blackbirds she spotted lying near the fence. Later she would bag the frozen bodies and hide them in the trash.

When Leila felt a sudden hand on her shoulder, she jumped, but it was only Clarisse Mellon wanting to share in the sight of snow angels.

As the girls ate their breakfast in silence, Leila tried not to think about Charlie. In just a few days her entire world had changed. His absence was even more palpable than his presence. The girls seemed to sense her emptiness and stayed unusually close to her, hugging her, styling her hair, trying to take up the empty space.

Wind is flooding through the pale organza curtains. The shock of cold air hits Leila's face. Old Sally raises her head and lets out a low groan before pushing her nose back into the plaid woolen blanket. "Is she back?" Lion says, startling Leila. "Mom. Did she come back?" He shuts the door behind him.

"What time is it?" Leila says, sitting up. "Oh sweetie. I must have fallen asleep. Did you find her?" Lion notices how tired she looks and his heart sinks. Leila looks curious in the gray suit. Not a suit to sleep in. Not a suit to drive all night in. The fact that it's the one thing that makes her feel like she is a part of the everyday world doesn't occur to him. All he knows is that at certain times when she turns her head just so, he catches sight of her delicate features, the small thin nose and ice blue eyes, and it makes him feel connected to Melanie.

Leila runs her fingers through Old Sally's thick black fur and peers into the dog's face. She fixes the blanket around the dog's head. "I haven't heard from Melanie. I stopped by the apartment and let myself in. I hope that's all right. Obviously, she wasn't there."

"Okay," he says. Lion tries to appear calm and lopes off into the kitchen. He grabs a piece of French bread from the bread bin and shoves it into his mouth.

"Where did you look for her?" calls Leila, smoothing out the folds of her skirt as she gets up. She doesn't want to nag him but she's growing more and more worried. "Grant Shongo called me last night."

"Don't want to talk about it," he says, pouring a glass of milk.

"Your cheek is cut, Lion. What happened with Rory?" Leila asks, gently touching his face.

Lion's cheek feels a bit sore, but not bad. "Nobody's out to get me," he says, turning away.

"That's not what I meant. I'm worried you're a danger to yourself—"

"To myself? No. I'm dealing with things in my own way. Let me deal with it. And I've been praying, okay?" he says, staring into her eyes.

"You are the only thing holding us—"

"I thought you trusted me, Mom."

She loves the way he calls her Mom, adores it. It melts her

heart. And she also knows he sweet-talks her. But it doesn't matter. She waited a long time to have children. When she married Victor at forty, having children was something she had given up on. But miraculously, within a month she was pregnant with Melanie, and Maya came soon after. Hearing the word *Mom* was the most beautiful sound Leila could have ever imagined. She had thrown herself into the role as though she had been a mother forever. She sewed corduroy jumpers for their first day of school and made dragonfly wings for Halloween costumes out of netting, duct tape, and hangers she'd collected from the cleaners. She soaked pieces of rhubarb in orange juice and baked apple-rhubarb pies from scratch, and invented bedtime stories about a family of fairies that lived in a junkyard. After Luke was born, she and the girls grew even closer. Luke was the glue of the family, the bridge between so many things that were hard to describe. He was such a glorious child, despite the asthma that evaded the pills and shots. Even when he was unable to talk, he'd reach out and take her hand, trying to calm her.

She would do it all again in a second. Seven priceless years with him had not been enough. Even if he was the focus of Maya's jealousy, her temper tantrums. Even if Maya resented the amount of attention paid to him, Leila chalked it off to normal sibling rivalry. When he died, Leila dreamed about having another son, but the opportunity had passed. She was too old. The doctor told her that her eggs had dried up. Maybe it was a blessing that a woman's body knew when to quit. Victor's drinking had become unbearable, and the way he would go outside in the backyard and shoot birds in the trees frightened them all. It was dangerous. He smelled like death, like dirt and blood and whiskey. She had slept in that scent for years. Despite a three-day stint of sobriety, when he'd repainted the kitchen a horrible hospital green without asking her, he was rarely home, which was better for everyone.

Lion is her son now. He is. It has everything to do with intention. When Melanie brought him home for the first time for one of Leila's famous lasagna dinners, he talked openly about his abstinence. Leila had breathed a sigh of relief. Some mothers would have questioned the wisdom of mixing races. Sure, the kids would undoubtedly run into prejudice. But she saw that they had something stronger between them. She liked the idea of a wayward soul that had come back to save others. To Leila, it meant he was seasoned, and he would be strong enough to deal with life's challenges, namely Melanie. He talked a little about what he had lived through in California—the earthquakes and the riots. He said he had wanted to get away to the other side of the country, to the Northeast, where America had begun, where people could start their lives over.

Leila felt that the most important reason to love Lion was that he loved her daughter. She watched his unwavering support as he listened to Melanie, not so much to her words but to what was going on underneath. He saw through Melanie's tough-girl act. He knew her vulnerabilities but he didn't exploit them. Melanie had always been self-conscious about the scar on her face, which Maya had inextricably put there when she pushed Melanie into a table during one of the girls' fights. In Lion's presence, it faded. When Melanie painted a mural on a brick wall in an alley off Main Street, Lion sat beside her for three days in the searing heat, mixing her paint for her and bringing her ice for the back of her neck after a sunburn turned it the color of red apples.

Leila's love for Lion only grew over time. His difficult past gave him an appreciation for the smallest things. Whether she fixed him a snack, reminded him to tie his sneakers, or bought him a turtleneck sweater for Christmas, he was incredibly grateful. But, he had gotten Melanie clean and he made her happy, which was no easy feat. For this, Leila would always be the one who was grateful.

She pulls the tray of lasagna from the refrigerator. The sauce is cold and the noodles are sticky, but Lion will eat anything. She spoons a heap of noodles into a bowl and drenches them in sauce. Then she puts the plate into the microwave.

"Help," says Lion, the handle of the diaper bag in his teeth, Lucas wailing in his arms. Leila rushes over and takes Lucas. She hugs him to her chest. In the delivery room, Lucas had let out a scream so loud Leila had to clasp her own hands behind her head to keep from pushing her way through the crowd to get to him. He had been whisked away, his little purple fists flailing, then cried for ten minutes in the incubator. He had looked so brave and unearthly, his skin shriveled like a raisin, his white-blond eyebrows and long lashes trembling as he punctuated his debut with several loud hiccups.

"I do trust you," Leila says. "You know that, right?"

Lion smiles. "I guess."

"If you tell me she's okay, I will believe you."

"She's okay."

"Well, I looked everywhere. I called Cheever. She did go there to see Maya, but no one saw her after—"

"Don't worry." He pops open a can of Pepsi and chugs it down as though he hasn't had a drink in a week. "I'll get her back. Today. I have a plan."

Holding Lucas in one arm, Leila sets the plate of the lasagna in front of Lion. She watches a cloud of steam climb off the plate. She pats Lucas's back and tries to relax. "If only Melanie was the way she used to be. How I miss that little girl."

"Argh," he says between mouthfuls. "That's hot."

Leila stares at him, wondering how he can be this calm. "I know it's probably hard for you to imagine there ever was a 'before.' But there was. When she was younger. Melanie was such a good girl. You know, such a little mother herself. When I was volunteering at the retirement home, Melanie always wanted to come. She'd carry her box of colored pencils and paper from table to table, doing portraits. It was all very serious. She'd ask about everything: What color do you want your hair? What kind of mouth do you want? She'd list their choices—smiling with teeth, smiling with no teeth, not smiling. I wish you—"

"You wish I what?" Lion says, pushing the plate away.

Leila puts Lucas down and kisses his head after fastening the diaper tabs. "Nothing," Leila says, her voice hoarse, her throat tightening up.

Leila sighs, looks away. She hasn't seen that girl in a long time. It's pointless to keep thinking about it.

But it was true, even if no one believes it now. Even after the girls' fights threatened to rip the roof right off of the house, Melanie would always go to Maya and apologize. What did they fight over? A few worthless pieces of coal? It was as though all the love in the world was measured by it. Leila explained a long time ago that diamonds were formed from coal over many lifetimes, a result of intense geological pressure. But the girls didn't listen when she said that they could not make the coal into diamonds by squeezing it between their hands or anything near that. They didn't listen when they snuck into the Shongos' coal bin, and would come home covered in coal dust, tracking soot footprints across the linoleum floor. Even after Luke died, they still went back to the coal bin.

Melanie once told Leila that it wasn't about the coal. It was about a time when the three children were together, when they were a triangle, the strongest shape. Perhaps Leila shouldn't have ever told them that, for without Luke, the girls felt like they were too weak to go on alone.

A little old person, Leila used to call Melanie.

She had the face of an angel and the soul of a martyr, the sort of mind that was always working. On overdrive sometimes, which caused insomnia from the time she was small, well before Luke was born. Melanie resisted sleep, refused the night with all her strength. She'd be awake into the morning, drawing or reading by the hall light. Worrying, worrying, always worrying. She'd climb down the stairs in the middle of the night to find Victor passed out with his hunting rifle by his side, and it would be Melanie who'd clean him up, drenched in his scent. In the morning, Leila would find him covered with a blanket wherever he had landed, and Melanie would be sitting at the bottom of the stairway, a glass of milk in her hand and a sketch pad laid out on the step in front of her. You could see it in her eyes, the growing wariness, the silvery circles that never went away, giving her a gaunt, unearthly beauty. The blue of her irises was not like the dark gray of her sister's. Melanie's eyes were changeable, vulnerable to every cold wind and shred of light. Every thought that trickled by would change the color, from ice blue to dove gray. Perhaps some of her sadness came from the wisdom or had the wisdom come from the sadness? Leila could never tell.

After Luke died, Melanie slowly began to close up, like a flower. Watching her daughter late at night doing her homework at the kitchen table, Leila worried about the whitish cast to her lips, the hollowness in her voice. The one-word answers when she'd asked Melanie what she was thinking. There was only one night when Melanie gave her something to go on, talking about the unfairness of hidden things, the rocky shoal out in the lake that had taken down too many boats to count, the sacred objects that could heal the sick, and all the things a person's subconscious could keep secret.

Everyone had been so consumed with what was going on at home that no one in the family realized that Melanie had grown five inches and had become beautiful, all in one summer. No one could have predicted that at fourteen she'd win Canandaigua's Harvest Queen, the youngest in the town's history. Leila thought this would change things for her, give her a sense of pride and belonging, a fresh start. But it had worked just the opposite. Melanie hadn't been prepared for the attention, or for Maya's raging jealousy. The parade, ribbon cuttings, pictures in the paper. It all seemed to wear on Melanie's already heavy shoulders, bringing her back to the time when Luke died, when there was a similar kind of scrutiny, a kind of curious and judgmental attention that made her feel sick.

Melanie ran away for the first time a month later. Leila shudders every time she pictures Melanie stumbling down an empty road on a cold October night, willing to risk everything just to visit her new boyfriend, who was staying in Albany. How lucky they were that the trucker who picked her up wasn't a nutcase, but a grandfather with three daughters. He'd dropped her off at the police station and sat with her as she called Leila to come and get her.

She made Melanie see a psychiatrist for two months. Melanie promised she wouldn't repeat the behavior. But she was lying, or maybe she really believed it would end there. Leila still thinks she could have prevented this. This and the fresh-mouthed, empty-eyed boy who Melanie had met when she was tutoring kids after school. He had reveled in taking down Canandaigua's Harvest Queen, a girl who never would have looked at him had she not felt that she deserved to be punished for her brother's death. Was she merely following in Leila's footsteps? Finding someone to punish her for never being good enough, for something unexplainable? Leila thinks about an earlier time, back when Victor tore up the lawn with his car. He had gotten out and fired his gun right into the trees. One, two, three shots that echoed through the forest and caused a flurry of blackbirds to explode into the sky. Melanie, at seven, had turned to Leila and in the most adult voice said, "You're not going to let him do that again. You're going to get us out of here. Right, Mom?"

"Yes," Leila had promised. What an act of courage for a child to ask to leave her own father, she had thought. She should have listened to Melanie then. But she was too weak.

Leila forgave Victor that night, as she would time and time again. Their happiness would be bought off with a few red carnations wrapped in a plastic grocery-store wrapper and the promise that he would change. By the time Leila finally threw Victor out once and for all, the damage had been done. The girls had already suffered from the poor judgment of their mother. Leila had already lost a son. The divorce took two years. Victor had moved away and was often out of contact. The courts gave her custody of the girls, and Victor didn't fight it. Then, he disappeared from their lives.

Later that night, after they have eaten, Leila watches Lion rocking Lucas in his arms. Leila clears her throat. She tells Lion about the time, after Luke died, when she couldn't get out of bed for weeks. How can she explain that her lungs were full of lead, and that she felt dizzy each time she stood up? She wants him to know what she did to contribute to Melanie's problem. She is not without blame. They were *her* pills first. Her doctor prescribed Adderall—in effect, speed—to give her energy during the day, and Ambien to help her sleep at night, but the pills sat in the medicine cabinet, unused. She only took them for a few months and then forgot about them. She didn't have to function. Melanie took care of the house, begging Leila to let her stay home from school day after day. Leila let herself be nursed and mothered by a nine-year-old girl for weeks, something that she now knows was wholly inappropriate.

Leila hadn't known Melanie saw her take the pills. Perhaps that is where Melanie learned about them.

"At night," Leila says, "this little creature would crawl into my bed with me and talk to me. I can still feel her hands on my face, hear her little voice whispering to me that things would be okay. Hers was the only voice I could listen to. I just couldn't bear to be alone, isn't that horrible? I let a child take care of me. But we survived. That's how I know who she is, deep down, do you see? That same little girl, she's still in there. She's always with me," Leila says, putting her hand over her heart.

"Could you hold off on the when-Melanie-was-wonderful stories?" Lion says gruffly. He doesn't want to hear it. He is convinced that Melanie is trying to punish him. These stories of a girl he never knew make him ache with loss. And he doesn't want to feel that yet.

Leila sighs. "Here, angel," she sings, touching Lucas's foot, ignoring the comment.

Lion reaches across the table. "Mom, I'm sorry. You didn't deserve that."

"Well, I don't want you saying things like that around him."

"But you don't know her like I do."

"I beg your pardon," says Leila. "I'm her mother, Lion."

Lion gets up. "You think you have to tell me about her?" He paces back and forth with the child in his arms. Lucas begins to scream. "Take him," Lion says quickly, handing her Lucas, who grabs on for dear life, coughs a few times before catching his breath.

"Here you go," Leila says. Lucas sticks his toes into the teething ring.

Lion drops his head between his knees. "Do you know how hard it is for me? Not ever knowing what she's gonna do next?"

"Sweetie," Leila says gently. "There was stress on you both. It happens when you have a child."

"So it's because of me? I can't make enough money. Yeah, I'm sick of thinking about it. I never asked for this." He gets up and slams the back door, escaping out into the backyard, where he stops in front of Luke's gravestone.

Leila calls after him. He doesn't respond, and Leila can't blame him. It's true he never asked for any of this. But who asks for half the things life gives them? Life had taught Leila the practiced art of making do.

Most of all, try not to disappoint people.

Including yourself. This is something that has taken Leila the most time to learn.

Lucas's little fists grasp the teething ring so tightly that she cannot unlock it from his grip. He's more like Lion than any of them knows.

She knows to give Lion breathing room at times like this. This is what she'd tell Melanie each time she and Lion had a fight. Men need to go into their cave. Let him work it out alone. Some problems are best handled by backing away. But now she thinks that perhaps she has backed away too much. If people in a family develop certain personality traits in order to compensate for each other, Leila hadn't known. Perhaps Melanie had become so impulsive because Leila was so immobilized. She could have prevented all this if she'd been smarter back then, if she'd been more balanced herself.

Leila kisses Lucas's forehead and puts him in his playpen.

She drops into the rocking chair, trying to let her guilt flow through her body and out the tips of her fingers. She picks up the pale green acrylic yarn and the hat and boot set she has been knitting. From her chair, she sees Lion's tall shadow cut across the lawn, back and forth. He's trying to figure out what to do.

The way the light hits the windows of Clarisse Mellon's house next door and spills into the grass between the two, it's as though Leila is sitting on the bank of a golden river. She recalls the sight of a yellow farmhouse she used to drive by on the outskirts of town. Not a new house or a large house, but an ordinary house, in front of which stood a wooden trellis hung with bundles of leathery blue grapes. If Leila closes her eyes, if she tries hard enough, she can taste their sweet juice. Even though she never got out of the car, she believed she could taste them. Leila knows about longing. If a person ever wants anything badly enough, it is quite possible to turn a wish into a memory purely through the repetition of thought, sometimes to the point of no longer wanting it at all.

"I'm sorry," says the low voice behind her. The hand on her shoulder is rocking her gently for the second time today. She looks down at the large silver diver's watch gleaming against the dark skin. She still doesn't know why he had wanted it for Christmas, when he always said how much he hated the water, but she never questioned him. She stares up at Lion as he shoves his hands deep in his pockets.

"You don't have to be sorry. I'm sorry, I shouldn't have pushed you. I should be smarter," she says.

"I love her," Lion says, his brown eyes welling with tears. "I've loved her from the minute I saw her. More than I ever thought I could love anyone. She is my whole life."

"Come here," Leila says.

Lion kneels, rests his head on her lap.

"Why are you crying?"

"You won't get it," he says, staring at the floor.

"You know better."

"I messed up my insurance," he says.

"What?"

He studies the worn slats of wood, kicks at the corner of the beige rag rug with the cornucopia emblazoned in the center. "Church. I haven't been going. I made this deal. With God. A promise."

"Oh sweetie," Leila says.

He continues. "No, listen. If I didn't miss church for a year, then everything would go good. Our relationship. The pregnancy, everything. And I had Matrina on my side, helping out."

"Now wait a minute. Going to church or not. You can't control—"

"But it worked," he says, his voice pleading. "I know it did. Lucas is proof."

"Lion—"

"You can't say everything wasn't going great. And then I go and—"

"Stop this. She'll be back," Leila says, praying the doubt doesn't come through in her voice. And that her words will hold true as she forces them into the room.

"Mom. We had a fight."

"You're overtired. You need some rest. I just put fresh sheets in the guest bedroom—"

"I told her I was splitting," he confesses.

"Oh Lion, no."

"I'd never really leave her. Just trying to scare her, I guess. It was stupid." He gets up, wipes his eyes. "I threatened her with leaving. And so she did it to me first."

Leila glances at Lucas, who is fast asleep under the blanket.

"We had a bad fight. She was yelling. She never yells. She was mad that we didn't have money, and about all the bills. She wants to take a trip to Niagara Falls. She says we need a break, that we have to get back on track. She says she wants to stay in a hotel for the weekend. That she wants to take a boat ride on the *Maid of the Mist* and get a fake picture taken of the two of us in a barrel. I tell her, you don't have to pretend because we're already going over in a barrel. Why didn't I say okay? I'd never really leave her, Mom."

"I know you wouldn't, Lion. I do know that."

Leila is trembling. She pours herself a glass of water and sits down.

"But I left the house. That's something I promised her I would never do. I broke my promise on that. An hour later I came back and she was gone. She had left Lucas all alone. I couldn't believe she'd do it. Now, all I keep thinking is, what if she does this forever? I mean, what about Lucas? I don't know what I'll do if . . ."

"If what?"

"If she comes back," he says, his face now streaked with tears.

"*When* she comes back."

"I don't know what I'll do when and if she comes back."

Leila holds her hand over her eyes to shield the sun. "You have a child now, you've got no choice but to stick—you'll do it just like I did."

"Melanie promised she would, too, and look what happened."

Lion is sitting in front of her, his face damp.

"Here's a secret, sweetie. You have become the rock of this family." She has told him this before, but she's not sure he listened. It's more of a plea now.

"But Mom, when he grows up, will he hate me? For being such a screwup, for not doing it right?"

Leila swallows hard. "Sometimes it'll feel just like hate."

"How do you know what to do? That you're saying and doing the right things?"

"Here's a secret. Nobody knows what they're doing." Leila looks at her grandson. "Melanie wouldn't leave him."

"Maybe she wanted to leave all along. Maybe she wants a different life, you know, than me."

"I don't believe that. She once told me her life started when she met you." Leila is lying, but he needs to hear that. She swallows hard, wondering if he is right, watching Lion walk over to the playpen. He is wise for not telling the police about the fight, Leila thinks. It had been hard enough to get them to send a car around. Now Leila feels in her bones that Melanie is in the worst sort of trouble. As Lion picks up Lucas, the little boy lets out a cry. Leila tries to comfort her grandson but he is inconsolable, his shattering screams echoing through the empty house.

13

LUCAS'S CRIES REACH ACROSS the cold water like white ribbons of light, winding around the tips of the blue spruce that line the lake, under the boat docks and summertime hammocks, sweeping through the flickering leaves of the Diamond Trees, which can be seen from every inch of this place, and circling back across the water to the dirt floor where Melanie is being held. When people on the shoreline hear the cries, they will shiver, commenting on how the wind sounds like a baby crying. But Melanie can recognize her own child's voice. It has been four days with no food. Melanie does not know where she is, but she knows she is near the lake. She can smell its thick muddy scent. Can hear the gulls crying overhead, blending into the sound of her son's voice. She squeezes her eyes shut, and then in her mind she is holding her baby, telling him stories about feathers and dancers and drums. She is breaking into bits of light, listening to him breathe. His heart is a pendulum that measures her life.

She tries to reach for Lucas but she has no arms. Her arms are icy wings folded inside her body. She is empty. The corners of her mouth bleed and burn with thirst so deep, even light feels wet on her skin.

Gulls circle, spread their wings. Their voices, human. Melanie's own voice, bird-like.

At times like this when the despair is this close, she feels Luke's presence surrounding her. Melanie slips in and out of darkness. Desperate times come flooding back. Times where she was this close to abstinence. Times when she failed.

Once it had been sixty-eight days. This was before Lion. She had gotten herself clean. Hard times were behind her, she was sure. Leila had gone away overnight and Maya was coming home from Cheever for the night. Maya had made great progress over the course of a year and hadn't had an episode of catatonia in two years. Melanie had seen it once, seen her sister's limbs freeze up so that Maya couldn't move, couldn't speak. But that was all supposedly in the past. She had grown out of it.

Still, Melanie would be cautious with her. She would walk on eggshells, for fear something would trigger it. But she would do what she had to, just to have her sister back. Melanie was actually looking forward to spending normal girl time together. She had rented a DVD of *Seinfeld* episodes and also the movie *Fried Green Tomatoes,* a real chick-flick. She had even bought two baskets of apples and some rhubarb so that they could bake crispy apple-rhubarb pie, Leila's favorite, from scratch.

Carefully they sliced the fruit as the warming oven made their cheeks glowy. Their speech was measured at first, saying please and thank you, being generous with their compliments. But they soon fell into easy talk about how much they loved Leila, and how much they didn't like their father, who had by this time been gone for years. It was one of the few times Melanie felt connected to her sister, close without the tight cord that seemed to shut Maya off from her. After everything she and

Maya had been through, it was only important to step over the jealousy and resentment and just forgive.

This was what it was like to have a real sister, Melanie decided, as the fruit browned in the mixture of sugar and orange juice. They began to sing along with Bruce Springsteen on the radio. Maya started dancing as she pushed a fist of dough across a cheese grater so that the golden swivels fell out into the pie tin to make an even crust, Leila's trick, and Melanie stirred the butter and crushed corn-flake topping with a wooden spoon. She wanted to let the moment carry them as far as it could, and she started singing into her spoon. Soon they were both dancing around the kitchen, pounding out a beat on the pots, on the linoleum floor, on the glass jars filled with raw macaroni pasta. Even Old Sally, usually more interested in sleep than play, got crazy and chased her tail.

When the song ended, they looked at each other, breathless. They held each other's eyes for a moment, smiling through the hesitation. So what if they were always turning over new leaves? It didn't matter.

The windows were closed, but suddenly, a rush of wind brushed their faces and the scent of lilacs permeated the air. The heavy bowl of syrupy mixture spun off the counter. Neither of the girls said what they were thinking as they watched the bowl topple across the floor. Apple and rhubarb slices stuck like big brown grubs on the linoleum. Maya looked up nervously at Melanie. "It's all your fault."

"No big deal," Melanie said. "We'll just make more. You slice this time, okay?" asked Melanie, becoming Leila as she wiped up the mess, just as she had watched Leila do so many times under Victor's impatient glare. "See, no biggie," she said, her voice chirpy, and in that moment she felt she understood her mother completely.

After, when they went upstairs to get ready for bed, they found silky spaghetti-strap nightgowns folded on their beds, each with a bar of lavender soap on top, a surprise from Leila. Maya's nightgown was a brilliant crimson, her favorite color, with tiny crystal beading at the top, which she loved. Melanie's was a pale lavender with pink ribbon and two tiny buttons. In the dim light, they undressed in front of the mirror. They had the same rosy breasts and flat stomachs. Melanie could see Maya watching her, her eyes fastening on Melanie's bird tattoo. Melanie quickly pulled her nightgown over her head and her long hair caught in a button. Maya untangled it, telling Melanie she needed a haircut. Melanie's need to feel close was so strong that she asked Maya to trim her hair, the greatest show of trust she could think of. "Just the ends, just half an inch," Melanie said.

In nightgowns and bare feet, they marched outside to sit in the crisp grass under the lilac tree near Luke's tombstone. The air was loose, the leaves unfurling white tongues into the foggy night.

Out there, with the scent of browning pie reminding her of old times and the cool wind on her neck, Melanie pushed through her apprehension and told Maya about her recent abstinence. She remembered going to see Maya at Cheever and befriending the orderly, Sebastian, who first slipped her some speed after she complained about how tired she was. Now that was all over. She would never again ask Sebastian to get her pills. She wanted to remember things clearly, she said. Everyone got to a point when it was important to remember the past.

Maya had become reticent. Tufts of blond hair fluttered through the darkness. Melanie wanted to stop her, but she couldn't speak, her throat burning with fear. Fear of what.

Triggering Maya's catatonia. Or losing the connection she felt to her.

For the rest of her life, Melanie would remember the feeling of a trapped bird in her chest as she quietly watched most of her hair blowing easily across the yard, blond strands that caught in the grass near the gravestone, lighting up the night like golden thread.

A BREEZE RIDES THE prisms of light coming through the broken slats. Melanie's breathing is faint; she is almost nonexistent.

There is water seeping under her cheek. She opens her mouth, letting the water wet her tongue. She will only drink enough to lessen the burn. Melanie has no pride. Pride is not even a question.

At once she feels her brother nearby. He is everywhere. In the light, in the stone floor. He could be perched on her shoulder, whispering in her ear. Melanie exists in a dreamlike state her mother used to call twilight, when the body is heavy and immovable and yet the mind is struck by golden lightning bolts of thought. Within this state, Melanie is flitting through the halls of memory, reliving the weeks after Luke was lost. She remembers how each night, either she or Maya woke up sobbing and ran into Leila's room, where they would find her piled under blankets, her body curled into a fist, as though she could ward off the fact that her youngest child was lost—that he was somehow safely tucked against her breast, as though her body, with its sturdy roundness, was enough of a barrier to protect him.

As the months wore on, the girls stopped going to Leila. Instead, they whispered to each other across the moonlit nights. They wouldn't say Luke's name. They called him *the baby*. They told each other that *the baby* was under the bed, in the window, on the roof. That he was everywhere. They played games and said that the baby was playing, too. That he was just invisible. When late spring came, they even snuck out to look for diamonds in the Shongos' cabin, just as they always had, with Old Sally leading the way. But they both knew they were looking for Luke. They both had been dreaming of him.

Nothing had been right since they lost him. They needed him. They needed him to bring everything back together the way it was when they were a family, their own family, somehow separate from their parents. They longed for the nights when they'd stay up late in their princess costumes, dancing in their bedroom in the milky light with Luke, their only audience. Only Luke could sing to the beetles that lived under the rocks, and only Luke could see what they saw, that the stars were very old angels, that the lilac trees were really other princesses waving in the window, and that the clouds were really children in disguise who had not yet been born but were watching to see who they liked, who was fun, and who they wanted their parents to be. They told Luke stories about children that turned to snowflakes in winter and fireflies in summer. Their little bird arms and legs would flap up and down as they giggled, jumping off their dressers onto their beds.

They had always been stronger together. Three children were a triangle, and Leila had always told them that a triangle was the strongest shape. They had grown close out of the necessity of protecting each other. There was that one cold fall morning when they had been forced to go on Victor's fishing trip to Whiskey Point. They had begged Leila to not allow them to go, but she said that would make their father sad and so they agreed. They'd followed Victor through the reeds, with him carrying only a bottle of whiskey as the girls lugged the cooler and fishing poles. Luke trailed the group, clutching a can of worms. They quietly stayed far enough back from Victor so as not to smell the whiskey or hear his singing. But they didn't see that Luke had been secretly dropping the worms, one by one, back to the earth. None of those worms deserved to die on a September morning, did they? Luke would later ask. Victor's eyes blazed when they reached the point and he discovered there were no worms left. He threatened to leave the children out there for eternity, to lock them all out of the house if they ever returned, unless they found each and every worm. But the sky was as cold as sheet metal, and although the children clawed the muddy bank for twenty minutes, they didn't come up with a single worm. Maya and Luke complained that they couldn't feel their fingers or their toes in their wet sneakers, and started to cry. Melanie marched up to Victor, who was sitting on the dock, finishing his drink. She demanded that he take them home. "Right now. Before the kids get sick," Melanie said, her feet anchored apart, her old dingy gray parka pulling under her arms. Her legs trembled, but it was okay because all the strength in her body had risen right into her chest, making her voice feel like thunder.

Victor swung his legs off the dock, his whiskey breath flaring into the cold air. "The kids . . . Who in the hell do you think you are, you little shit?" He took a final swig and tossed the bottle into the lake.

"Run!" Melanie cried. And the children ran and ran through the muddy fields with Old Sally running alongside and Victor running after them, hardly able to keep up. By the time they reached the Shongos' cabin, Victor had given up and was on his way to Kelley's Bar.

When Victor returned home that night, he yelled so loud it made the windows shake. Luke and Maya hid in the corners, whimpering. Melanie refused to cry when Victor shouted at her, and this drove him crazy, so much that he sent her to bed without dinner. Later, Leila got soap in her eyes while she did the dishes and had to go out on the front porch with a box of Kleenex, where she stayed for two hours. When Victor fell asleep in front of the TV, Luke sneaked a half-eaten rhubarb pie upstairs that Leila had put out for Old Sally. He forgot to bring her a fork but Melanie said she didn't care, that it would taste better with their hands. Maya had joined them, and as their hands and faces grew sweeter and stickier, they wholeheartedly agreed that pie tasted so much better this way. Everything was better when they were a triangle. Good things, not bad things, happened in threes. Leila said most people had it wrong.

WHEN LUKE'S BODY WAS finally found a year later, Melanie and Maya stopped reminiscing about *the baby,* and stopped playing make-believe. They still raced over the wet grass, their feet tracing old footsteps leading to the Shongos' cabin. But things were different. They fought over everything. Suddenly, there was not enough of anything for them both. Certainly there was not enough of Leila. When they lost Luke, they lost each other. He was the separation, the space they needed. Without him, they collided.

Anxiously, they foraged through the coal bin and argued over a shiny piece of coal. Who saw it first? Who had gotten the last good one? They struggled. Someone hit someone else. No one knew who had started it, but by the end, they were both bruised and crying.

"Everyone knows it was your fault," Maya said. "It was your idea to take the canoe into the lake, the whole thing was your—"

"You could have grabbed him when—"

"You stood up and made him fall."

Melanie lost control and flung herself at Maya. Maya's hands pulled at her hair, leaving tufts of blond curls scattered across the coal. They fought without sound. They fought harder than ever, and they didn't know why. Perhaps because they loved each other and they didn't know how anything would ever be the same again. If a ghost had tried to separate them, they wouldn't have felt it. Potato bugs stopped moving grains of sand. Spiders stopped in midstream. The girls walked home an hour before sunrise, muscles sore, both crying silently, pockets stuffed with shiny pieces of coal.

After Maya fell asleep, Melanie snuck into the closet, her ritual. She removed the piece of floorboard from her secret hiding place. She removed the white cloth napkin with Leila's initials on it, unfolding it over her knees, spilling the contents in front of her. There she'd sat, lap full of moonlight, holding a piece of coal, a gold button from Victor's coat, three red beads, and a silver dollar. Here was all her luck. When she turned them over in her hands as the morning light snaked in, the items sparkled, tripling her luck, meaning she and Maya would be okay. When satisfied, she put everything away and got into bed, lying awake, watching the slats of light from the blinds that crawled across the ceiling each time a car passed. This was the beginning of the insomnia that would plague her for a lifetime. Night after night, she'd lie there replaying the events of Luke's death in her mind or waiting for Victor to come home. What had happened to Luke after she had hit her head? Why couldn't she remember? Had there really been a giant on the island? Hadn't he seen her and waved, just for a second? Maya said she couldn't remember seeing anyone. Now all Melanie could do was pray for them all. If she could hold her breath before the light receded, Victor would be okay. If she did this until she heard his car pull into the driveway, followed by the rattle of his key in the lock and his heavy legs pulling his body up the stairs, her parents would be okay. If he got in safely, if she didn't have to look for him and rub a wet towel around his face to clean him up for Leila, if a radio flicked on and she heard his muffled sobs of apology, it was only then that she could sleep through the night.

Years later, when Melanie was fifteen, she would sneak into the basement of the Shongos' boarded-up cabin. She was almost a woman now, and sad, like her mother. Unlike her mother, though, whose sadness weakened her, Melanie's sadness made her willful, so full of anger that she could barely contain it. It was as though a switch had been turned on. One day, she dyed all her clothing black in the bathtub, cutting off her shirt sleeves and safety-pinning them back on. Everywhere she went she saw shadows hovering in the branches of trees. She was always cold. She never slept. She spent months wanting nothing, even after she got herself a boyfriend and started having sex. Then she wanted him, and she thought that was enough. And then she discovered pills, and she wanted them more than anything. Soon, her life became all about finding a quiet dark place to take them. The Shongos' basement was the perfect place, for she could feel Luke's presence there, and he seemed to be waiting for her. She was dreaming of him again, and this provided some comfort, despite the grief. The tombstone might be in her own backyard, but her little brother was here in the cabin—at least his spirit was. Time and time again, she would peer around corners, as though she might discover him hiding. She would say Luke's name out loud, trying to scare herself. Sometimes she would feel the cool breeze of a draft on her neck and suddenly turn around. "Luke? Luke?" she would whisper. She knew it was bad luck to say a dead person's name out loud.

The spirit might get confused, might try to come back, and not be able to find his way home.

MELANIE WHISPERS LUKE'S NAME in her mind. She can hear his voice, see his face talking to her, begging her to chase him, again and again through the underwater grasses, amidst the piles of white stones and the layers of green lake glass. He is darting in and out, trying to lead her away, farther and farther away from the place where she is now.

Suddenly, she hears floorboards creaking and footsteps coming toward her. The stench of whiskey is familiar. She tries to scream but can't. Someone is removing the blindfold. Panic races through her body. She sucks in her breath when she sees his face.

Her father, Victor.

The blue bloodshot eyes are burrowing into her, pleading, filling her with that old sense of panic mixed with guilt. He has the same pale stringy hair, the dark beard, now graying, and yellowed teeth. He sets down a box of children's cereal beside a canteen. He leans over her, talking in a low voice, cradling her face in his hands. *You have to eat, Melanie. You need your strength. Help me now the way you did before. I have waited all this time. Tell me the truth about your brother.*

PART III

of the woods near his house, and shoots a pheasant. Only to maim, not to kill. Victor does not hunt for death. He shoots only to injure, to feel life regenerate. It is an act of creation to shoot the animal and force it to heal. Causing this explosion of life fills him with power and energy. He is compelled to do this whenever the scent of lilacs overwhelms him. It is almost instinct, the way he grabs for his gun, and in the two hundred milliseconds before Victor pulls the trigger, he reminds himself that he is the king of free will.

He knows he is to blame for the death of the little boy. He'd planned on moving to Mexico after it all blew over, but he'd only gotten as far as Spencerport, just under an hour's drive northwest. On many occasions, he had tried to get farther away. But he was always trapped by the sweet smell of lilacs, which made him run for his whiskey, eventually becoming so sick he'd have to lie down with a blinding migraine. More than once, while packing his truck, his pit bull had broken free from her chain and Victor had had to go chasing her down for hours. In the last year it had gotten worse—his drinking problem had escalated and now he was chained to the courts. He had just gotten his third DWI in six years. The second DWI, a felony, had landed him in prison for a short time and then probation. The third, which he had just gotten two days ago, meant he had two motions against him: a violation of probation and a felony DWI. Bail had been posted and a court date had been set, but Victor knew this would be his end. The judge would surely sentence him to more prison time. He knew a bench warrant would be issued for his arrest if he missed his upcoming court date or was caught driving without a license. But the prospect of another stint in prison was a death sentence. He wouldn't survive it. He had nothing more to lose by leaving town.

When Victor first moved away, he had wanted to be alone,

too afraid that people would question him about his past. He found a small house in a wooded area near abandoned farmland. He has lived there quietly, hardly alive. The sky around Victor's small house is always, somehow, a deep dark yellow. It is a swampy sky, thick, with feathery plants that tangle in the branches of the tallest blue spruce. When Victor's house is dark, when the air is full with quiet, Victor sometimes hears a roar in the trees that makes him want to slip deep inside it just to lose himself in a chaos greater than his own. With the air rushing through his lungs, he wants to push out everything inside him.

There are beaten sugar maples by the highway and a pile of felled branches at the entrance of the driveway and a broken blue mailbox, with the name "Ellis" printed in block letters. No one comes to see him. He has no friends, for anyone he let in would want to know his secrets. Sometimes his house is so silent, Victor wonders if he exists only in his own imagination. Sometimes he whistles just to create a disturbance in the air, proof that he exists. Other times it is as though he lives inside a tornado whose center is always chaos. The inside of a tornado is the loudest place on earth, Victor has thought. He can feel the ruins of his old life inside him, the cadence of his ex-wife's cries after the boy died are still embedded in his memory, the faces of his two girls, the scent of everything wounded, the images of the ring-necked pheasants. Each time Victor shoots his gun, a calm lingers in the air. Each time he shoots, he crawls inside a place so swollen with absence, it's the most peace he has ever known.

He checks his guns several times each day when the silence is painful, when he is out of work and at home all day and night. When he is lost and without purpose, he touches the metal barrel and fills himself up with a sense of free will. He doesn't need to kill the pheasant like his own father did, a hunter who killed for sport. To shoot is an act of free will, Victor once told Luke, a way to harness creation.

Sometimes Victor would take Luke and Old Sally with him for a day of hunting, despite Leila's protests.

After Victor would shoot a bird, the dog would chase the scent and find the bloodstained pheasant. Luke would trail behind Victor carrying the bloody bird in his arms, and Victor would pretend he didn't know what Luke was up to. They would both pretend. Victor did the wounding so that his son could do the other thing. They had become two symbiotic figures, each of which could not exist without the other. Both engaged, consumed in this act of decimation and re-creation. It was a silent agreement and Victor never asked what had become of the bird, even though he would let the boy ride home with it in his lap, Luke's clothing bloody, stuck with errant feathers.

Luke would hold the bird in his arms, sometimes crying, and then take it out back behind the house. Sometimes Victor heard Luke sneaking out at night to find the other birds that Victor had shot.

But usually Victor went hunting alone. After he had returned, he'd see Luke glance at the gun closet, and Victor knew the boy could smell it. The scent followed Victor back from the fields, clinging to his skin and his clothing for days. On this night in May, he is remembering how Luke would try to hide his own bloodied shirts after he had rescued the downed birds, and the bits of feathers that trailed behind him as he'd run upstairs to take a bath. The scent of blood would elicit Luke's sympathy. But it only made Victor's jaw tighten and his fingers ache.

Once Victor had become so obsessed with Luke's strange ability that he followed the boy in the middle of the night. Luke had slipped on boots under the pajamas, put on Victor's hunting jacket and sneaked out the back door. Victor knew Luke couldn't see the blood but could smell it clinging to the leaves. Victor had watched the boy locate a pheasant under a small apple tree. Its body was dark, stiff, its wings frozen. Hiding behind a bush, Victor watched as Luke picked it up, wet in his arms. He thought he saw little blue lights flickering around Luke. Luke stood there, flooded in the moonlight, a flurry of blackbirds circling above him. For a few moments, Luke held the pheasant there in his arms.

Then, he opened his arms and the pheasant flew away.

Luke didn't move, not even with the rain and wind kicking up, soaking his face. Victor knew Luke sensed he was being watched. But there was something there that Victor didn't want to mess with. And as Victor snuck away, he feared the child even more.

Now Victor stands in his living room, picturing Luke playing with Old Sally, remembering the sheer elegance of it, the fluidity of play and purpose in perfect combination and how he had envied it. How Luke had seemed to float across the grass, always laughing, while Maya and Melanie stumbled and fought over their jealousies. Luke did not care whether he was judged, whether he was ugly or beautiful or stupid. Victor wondered how a child like Luke could possibly be of his own flesh and blood.

THE SCENT OF LILACS has grown stronger. Victor begins to fear the outside. He begins to fear his own dog. He watches Agnes, his pit bull, whose chain no longer seems strong enough. Victor does not leave the house for days on end. From the window, he watches the dog pacing nervously. He remembers how the dog crouched behind the tree one night last week, waiting for him to pass by, snarling. Instinct is a thing to be feared, Victor told himself. It causes unpredictable behavior. Remember why the dog is tied to the tree.

Each day the anger inside him grows. Victor still smells of everything wounded, and he cannot clean it from his skin or his clothing. He hates Leila for what she has done to him. And he tried to make her pay, even more, for the fact that he loved her. They once had a bond. Victor's skin was always cool to the touch. But Leila's was always warm. He'd put his icy cheek on her chest and give her all the cold chaos inside him. This is the only time Victor ever felt strong. There was someone for everyone, a perfect fit, he would think, in those early days of their relationship, as her hands and feet became cool and his face flushed. She'd become drunk with the cold, and he with her heat, and it made them both laugh and feel as though they were good. And then the girls came, first Melanie, then Maya. And though they were beautiful like Leila, they had inherited Victor's chaos. And in some small way he found this comforting.

He could see it in the way they cried and the way they fought. But then this third child came. This pale slip of a child who possessed no chaos, only peace. Luke's huge green eyes sparked with something Victor could not recognize.

Now, on this night in May, not even whiskey will block out the scent of lilacs. He is thinking of Luke constantly. Stacks of dimes are appearing everywhere: on the kitchen counter, on top of his alarm clock, on the dashboard of the car. It is too much. Wherever he goes he sees Luke. When he finds a yellow paper airplane floating in his bathtub, he wants to scream at the top of his lungs. He cannot stand it. He buries his face into the pillow and howls there, as loud a noise as he can make. For a moment, he is nothing more than air pulsing through the walls and the doors, through the glass windows. For a moment, Victor, gratefully, disappears.

He imagines that one day a flurry of one-winged pheasants will come for him, just as he sometimes imagines that Luke is living with him. He even makes sure the bag of Reese's peanut butter cups is well hidden, where Luke won't find it. When Victor tries to leave the house now, he rarely gets farther than the porch steps on the first try. He often goes back inside to peel an apple for Luke. He peels it in a perfect spiral, just as Luke liked. Then he grabs the peels, annoyed at himself, slams the door shut and throws the peels across the backyard.

He believes he has been living in purgatory. He believes Judgment Day is coming. He knows that on Judgment Day, whoever has blood on their hands must crawl around in the dirt until their eyes are burning and their lips are cracked. The sun will burn the whispers from their lips; the sun will bear down on their backs and their fingers will ache with sadness. They must toil until desperate and think about what they have done. In purgatory, they cannot feel anything; they have no emotion. They will not feel anything until their skin is parched, and until they have wandered everywhere looking for water, and maybe even then they will never feel anything again. They have wounded too many times. On Judgment Day the sky will become glassy and red and no one will be able to see through it, not even the birds. Not even God. Everywhere, the scent of lilacs will smother the trees and blackbirds will drop from the sky.

Tonight, Victor is aching for connection. As he puts the gun in its holster and slips on a large flannel shirt, he notices two stacks of dimes on the counter. In one sweeping gesture, he swipes them off the counter. They fall, tapping across the floor like rain. He takes out his gun, walks outside in his new black boots, and makes sure his dog's chain is strong enough where he has patched it. As Victor approaches, the dog backs away, barking like crazy. Stunned, Victor tries to soothe her, for he has had this dog for five years. Only recently has the dog turned on him. Victor reaches his hand out. Ferociously, the dog tries to attack him but the chain holds. Victor falls backward, just out of reach. The dog is still pulling on its chain, baring its teeth and growling as Victor crawls away.

He is going out for a drink. Before he leaves, Victor slaps on aftershave. He needs the comfort of a woman. As Victor drives to the bar, he can't seem to get a certain memory out of his mind. That fateful day of fishing with Luke. Victor and Luke had been far enough out on a small pier, shaded by trees, he thought, in a part of the lake where they would not disturb anyone. They were engaged in battle: Victor had been trying to show Luke how to bait the hook. He wanted Luke to follow his instructions, wanted to force him to feel it. And Luke wanted no part of it. So Victor tore the worm in half and threaded it on the hook. Luke hid his face and tried to stop him but Victor pushed him off and cast the fishing line out into the lake. Suddenly, the line jerked between Victor's fingers, a tiny pressure. He could see the flash of yellow gills in the water, a sunfish, almost two pounds, Victor gauged. At that moment, Luke began to scream, to tear at his hair, to hoot like some hyena gone mad. Victor grew angry and he yelled and cursed at Luke, but the boy just ignored him.

Victor drew his hand back, and he smacked the boy as hard as he could across the face. He felt the force of his own power.

But Luke didn't even flinch.

Eerily, the child stood more solid than ever, as though made of stone.

And Victor hated Luke in that moment, for he knew then

that his son would never understand his chaos as his daughters did. And that Luke would never forgive Victor his mistakes as he believed his daughters had. He realized in that moment that he had been punishing Leila for his own estrangement from the boy, and at the same time hoping that if the boy accepted him, it would make everything that was wrong with his family all right. But that day, he knew he had ruined any chance.

Suddenly, Luke took off running toward the forest. For a second, Victor watched the boy fading into the distance as though he were dissolving into the air. Victor, stunned, let himself exist without emotion, imagining he was not Luke's father. He just stood there, watching Luke disappear into the trees. He wondered whether he had any real feeling at all for the boy, and in that empty space he felt a fleeting sense of freedom. He could let the boy run off and perhaps they would never find him. All the burden, rejection and resentment he felt would be gone. And everything would be the way it was meant to be, almost perfect, as it had been before the boy was born. Somehow, Leila would come back to him. She would give Victor the love that she once did.

A minute later, Victor's conscience took over. He chased the boy, following his trail of downed grass into the woods. When he couldn't find him an hour later, Victor returned to the dock and drank a bottle of whiskey and thought about what to do. When the rains started, the lake became a mirror of raindrops and trees. It was hard to see. The air was filled with a kind of quiet that made it hard to speak, which is why Victor could hardly open his mouth when, three hours later, Melanie walked out from behind the trees, her long white T-shirt soaked to her thighs. Maya and Luke lagged behind her, holding hands. How had the girls found Luke? How did they know the boy was even lost? Had they been spying on them the whole day? Had they seen what Victor had done? As they walked toward him, they looked ethereal: small pale ghosts in the hazy light. Although he couldn't make out their expressions, he sensed their anger with him, just as he'd get up and open the front door because he knew Old Sally was standing on the other side of it waiting to come in.

As they approached, Melanie, taller and rosy-skinned with two blond braids that hung over her shoulders to her waist, held his entire fate in her vaporous stare. Maya looked distraught, covered in mud, her hair in tangles, unrecognizable but for the red mouth parted slightly and the knowing gaze that didn't lift. Victor worried that they had seen him hit the boy. He waved at them. They didn't wave back, and Victor knew Leila would surely go crazy if she knew. When they finally reached him, Victor noticed that all three children were covered in mud, that Melanie was without socks, that her gray sneakers were wet, the laces untied, and her legs were as full and as white as two soft clouds, the skin appearing spongy and swollen. Maya and Luke stood behind her. Victor wasn't sure he wanted to know how they found Luke. They had some connection that he would never be a part of.

Victor noticed Luke's precise measurement of Melanie's footsteps. The boy took the greatest care to place his feet directly in Melanie's path as she trudged through the mud toward him, as though the rest of the ground was hot coal. It amazed Victor how Luke could stop time. Putting peas on a fork could be broken down into innumerable steps. Getting into the shower had to be approached from a few different angles before going in, as though Luke was first negotiating with the molecules dangling in the air, then the actual rays of light. Luke delighted in all these little victories, for they were contests he would always win, having figured out how best to succeed in his own universe.

Once at the shoreline, Luke would not make eye contact with Victor. Victor tried to smile as he reached down to pat the boy's head. That is when the boy's eyes closed, his head of curls fell to one side, and his small legs buckled underneath him before his body collapsed onto the sand. Luke had fainted, as though the force of Victor's slap had finally hit him.

Victor carried Luke to the boardwalk, the first time he had touched him in years, with the girls following. Luke's lashes were caked with mud, his face soiled. Victor tried to play the good father. He bought the children Buried Treasure popsicles at the ice-cream stand, after which Luke seemed miraculously revived. The girls licked the cylindrical pink ice cream slowly, humming softly between bites. Again, Victor tried to gauge whether or not the girls had seen him hit Luke. But he was certain their minds were elsewhere, focused on drawing their tongues around the cones to dig for the illusive white eagle, the prize inside. Victor didn't know how many of the damn things he had bought the kids over the years. It hadn't made them love him.

For the car ride home, Victor grabbed a blanket from the trunk and covered Luke's legs with it, just for show. Luke had already fallen asleep. Victor adjusted the blanket and glanced quickly at Maya. She held his eyes there, knowing. She smiled softly at him, and he knew in that moment that she had seen him hit Luke. And that she would keep his secret. As he got into the car, a warm breeze settled like a soft pillow behind his neck, and he relaxed into it, leaning back into the seat. Then Maya pulled the blanket over her legs and turned her back to him. Melanie, next to him in the front seat, stared straight ahead and said, "I won't tell because you'll get arrested. But don't ever hit him again. Or I'll call 911." But by that time, Victor had already decided that he owed nothing to either of his daughters for they kept secrets from him. Victor looked at his sleeping son in the rearview mirror. The child possessed so peaceful a presence that it made Victor hurt.

TONIGHT, ON THIS LAST night in April, Victor has had one too many drinks. He is stone cold drunk, and knows he shouldn't drive home. Still, he wavers to his car, tries to get his key in the ignition and finally gets the car started. It is late and pouring rain. It is not officially hunting season but Victor has just decided that any time is hunting season when you are not in it for the kill. Someone in the bar wore lilac perfume and Victor recognized it immediately. Victor will have to scrub his skin raw to remove the scent.

Somehow he makes it home. Drunk, Victor knocks over the small desk chair and it crashes against the cabinet, almost tipping the lamp over. He sees himself in the mirror: He has the reddest skin of any man he knows. He showers more than anyone on earth, just to clean himself from the scent of everything wounded. But at least, for once, he hasn't been thinking of Luke. Not entirely. Not at first. For most of the evening Victor thought of nothing but his latest pheasant. He sat across the bar from a woman he met at the gas station, sick from the strong perfume mixed with the smell of gasoline. His wife used to say he was a terrible listener, but all he could think about was walking in the wild field and making the noise only a pheasant would hear. And then shots ringing out, watching the flap flap of the wings, how they'd fall like paper tossed into the flickering air, the surge, the upswing, how the bird would tumble then, and the air would curve around the body and swell. For a moment the bluegrass would reach up, straight into the sky, as if to catch the fall and the clouds would smother over, and everything would be united, all blurred earth and sky.

And then suddenly, when he returned to his seat after using the restroom, there was a stack of dimes behind his drink, ten dimes that he counted. He asked the bartender if he had put them there and the guy looked at him like he was crazy. Then Victor felt a bunch of dimes in his coat pocket. The air in the bar took on a chill, and the memories of Luke came flooding back. He resented the boy, maybe even hated him. But he never wanted him dead.

Victor felt even more panicked. Removing the dimes from the bar, Victor had to convince himself that this was surely a better place to be than alone in the house, deafened by his own silence, and waiting at the kitchen table for something, what, he didn't know—the flicker of the lamps, the sight of a paper airplane spiraling above the bathtub, or the scent of lilacs that repeatedly tried to smother him.

Victor knows he is being haunted. He has no patience for spirits. He never liked how the boy's large blue-green eyes would stay in his mind for days, causing him to wonder whether he could read Victor's thoughts. The boy knew that Victor had chaos inside him. Luke had had a way of showing up seconds after Victor had told a lie. He'd meet Victor's eyes, and Victor was forced to skulk away. Humiliated. Shamed.

After Victor's shower, he doesn't notice his pit bull crouched in the corner of the room, having broken its chain yet again. Victor doesn't plan to fall asleep on the twin mattress. Victor's hair is still wet, his face damp against the mattress, when he is startled by the sound of sirens. Still drunk, he opens his eyes and sees a small bloody T-shirt on the floor, and a flurry of feathers circling above it as though caught in a small tornado. Luke has finally come for him. Judgment Day is here. Cars are honking and there are shouting voices outside his window. The radio suddenly turns on. The announcer is talking about the tornado, the thunderstorms, and the vortex caused by the meeting of two winds that are blowing in opposite directions, shown on Doppler radar. Loud, spinning storms striking the earth. As Victor sits up, bleary eyed, all he can think about is the scent of lilacs in Leila's yard. He can no longer bear the guilt of that night, the death of the boy. Victor can no longer live with the secrets that tore apart his family. He has to know the truth. He knows that wherever he goes, wherever he runs away to, he won't be able to forget his mistakes. He also knows his daughters won't come near him if he just shows up. He knows they will all slam the door in his face. But Melanie had been the leader, the one who had once taken care of him. Surely she still felt something for him. If he had her on his side, the rest of them, Maya and Leila, would follow. Still, Melanie would not forgive easily, that much he remembered about her.

As soon as Victor stands he hears a low growl coming from the corner of the room. He stops. Through his bleary eyes he can see his pit bull. There's a ferocity in her eyes he's never seen. Suddenly, she lurches at him. The dog sinks her teeth into Victor's naked thigh as Victor screams so loud it rattles the windows. The stink of blood fills the air. Victor grabs for the lamp. He smashes it against the animal's head. Rolling over to the side of the bed, Victor grabs his gun. Agnes lurches at him again, this time biting into Victor's shoulder. Victor tries to wrestle himself out from underneath the animal, but with Agnes's weight it's too difficult. He shoots his dog from below, directly into its heart. Agnes's heavy skull falls on Victor's bloodstained neck, her body splayed across Victor's naked chest. She twitches slightly before letting out a sigh.

Victor, face streaked with blood, knows his dog is dead. But he fires his gun again.

15

LION KNOWS HE'S GOT to do something. Melanie has been gone for four days. He needs information. He needs a meeting, fast. Needs the help of a few of his ex-addict contacts. There's this silent bond among addicts. A first name and a common history suddenly makes them kin. They're the only people who'll issue support without judgment. But Lion won't listen as they whisper quiet words about serenity. Maybe, if he is lucky, one of them has relapsed and has recently seen Melanie. For this thought, he will pray for forgiveness.

He heads over to the basement of an elementary school near Leila's house. He arrives late for the meeting, just a few minutes after introductions. Taking a seat in the circle, he looks around, almost twenty people. He knows how to read a crowd. A bunch of old-timers. A few young punks. He can tell who's still using. He can identify meth or crack just by the look in the eyes. He nods toward a handful of faces. Smiles are exchanged. One by one, people tell their stories around the circle. Soon it's his turn. He begins to talk, but he can tell they aren't with him. He can't fool these people. They can sense when a person is not feeling what he's saying, when he's cut off from his heart.

Lion knows his mouth is forming the words. He can hear himself talking about his last fight with Melanie. But he has no feeling.

He doesn't want to revisit the million and one times he's looked deep into Melanie's eyes to check the size of her pupils. He had prayed to Matrina each time. But this miracle of normal pupils happened because of his going to church; it was his insurance, he tells the crowd. He looks up, scans the faces. A few nod. He's connecting now. People are waiting for an inspiring story. Success. Abstinence. To prove it can happen. For anyone.

But he can't lie.

"After the fight, I just lost it, stormed out," he confesses. "I get back, and I'm running up the five flights of stairs to our apartment. I'm so pissed the way she just lets Lucas cry like that—she's afraid of spoiling him. I expected to see her standing in the kitchen making Hamburger Helper.

"But she's gone. Lucas was wet in his crib, his face all pink. I got real nervous. I'm thinking, what if she relapsed. It's my first goddamn thought. That she'd do this to me, to us. And I get mad at myself, you know? My faith in her disappeared, I don't know . . ."

He looks around. A few of the young women shift in their seats. As supportive as people want to be, they can't hide the fact that a relapse scares the hell out of them.

"Then I wonder if I ever really had any faith in her. And that kills me. Because we had this bond. She had faith in me. I had faith in her. And it's what got us through. Now it's being tested again."

He tells them how he looked everywhere for Melanie. In the basement, in the laundry room, up on the roof deck. He looks around and can almost hear their silent self-talk. *It could be me. It might be. I could lose it.*

Abstinence is precarious. Yes, they understand.

They fold their hands in solidarity. Not a one takes an eye off of him. *Go on.*

"I was living in a fantasy world, pretending to think it was all good. You know, like we had this nice little family," he says, his voice trailing off. "Here I am, talking about abstinence and God. You got to get this. I just replaced one addiction with another one."

He's sure they can tell that love was his replacement.

He meets every eye in the circle. "So if any one of you has seen her . . ." he says. A woman bends down to pick up her purse. An old man checks his watch. His five minutes are up. There are nods. Empathetic smiles.

At the end of the meeting, he listens to the people clamoring around the coffee counter. An old-timer stops him. He advises Lion to go easy on himself. Stay out of judgment. Love is the train that jumps the tracks. Love is the wolf you try to keep tied up. Let go and let God. Don't leave before the miracle happens. God helps those who help . . . "Look," the old man whispers, taking his arm. "I'll say what we're all thinking. Go to Two Bears' Cave. If she's there, you'll want to know the truth."

Lion thanks the old man for his honesty and leaves. He had been avoiding Two Bears' Cave because of an agreement he and Melanie made. The people there are shells of themselves, folks that have given up on their lives. She made him swear that if he ever found out she was there, he would take Lucas and move away. He would tell Lucas that his mother was dead and never speak of her again. It was better, she thought, for Lucas to grow up without a mother than to know the truth about who and what his mother was, that his mother chose drugs over her own child.

Why not just give Melanie a couple more days? Lion wonders, as he steps out into the cool air. Pray in the meantime. Doesn't she always come back?

He can't wait this time. There is too much at stake. *Four days.*

Lion hits the streets, his boots crunching the hard gravel in the breakdown lane. He is thinking that the people who hang out at Two Bears' Cave have nothing to lose. This makes them dangerous. And who knows what state of mind Melanie is in. If Lion is going to get her out of there, he can't go alone.

16

AS DUSK SETTLES OVER Canandaigua, Echo slips on an ivory vintage blouse edged in lace, then an old pair of jeans. She pulls the towel through her hair, letting the evening light catch a few loose strawberry blond strands that she pretends she inherited from her mother.

She tells herself not to be hopeful. That the call she received from Grant at a pay phone asking her to come for dinner was just him being neighborly. She and Grant hardly know each other anymore. And she is certain he doesn't see her like that now, not as someone who might actually want to be kissed. He is far too preoccupied to notice something as inconsequential as her clothing. It's not a date, she tells herself. Just old friends having dinner.

She tries on the feather earrings that she used to wear in high school, and then takes them off. She removes the rest of her jewelry, two silver rings and a chain, as she wants to feel unadorned, plain, just herself. She slips her feet onto the wooden platforms of her worn leather clogs. She has had the same taste in clothing since she was a child. She still keeps a self-portrait from kindergarten of herself in a white peasant blouse and blue jeans. Echo stands before the mirror, her reflection backlit in the flickering candlelight, her breasts, dark and full under the cotton cloth. Her bra is just sheer enough. She fastens the pearlized buttons on her shirt, all six of which match but one. It's a superstition she read about once and hasn't been able to shake. In ancient China, during the building of a temple, architects would plan a subtle mistake in the construction, a chip in the frame or an edge left uncut, so the Gods wouldn't become jealous and destroy the whole building. Echo had learned this years ago and decided her life was too precarious to tempt the gods. So she always sewed one mismatched button onto her favorite articles of clothing.

She grabs her purse and runs downstairs. She gathers up a small bag of groceries and peeks into the living room. Joseph is sitting in his recliner facing the TV, which is on without the volume.

"You want me to turn it up?" she asks.

He turns toward her, the pillow behind his head falling onto the floor. "I just use TV for company. I was napping anyway," he says, reaching for the pillow.

Echo kneels and hands him the pillow with her free hand. "I'll be home early," she says, pushing her wet hair back from her face.

"Did you find my car keys?" he asks weakly. She tells him no, she wants to walk. "But it's bad weather. Make sure Grant drives you home. You hear? It's not the same place since you left. Look at you, you're a sight for sore eyes."

"Your eyes must be very sore." She leans over and gives him a kiss.

"Kiddo. You got so much joy around you and you can't even

see it." He shivers, and then pulls the afghan tightly over his shoulders as though it were winter.

AS THE SUN BEGINS to set, Clarisse Mellon stands on her doorstep holding a warm plate of cookies. The pungent scent of ginger winds through the air among the lilac petals.

When Clarisse sees Echo walking by her house, she waves her over. It may be the north wind that's making her feel she should confess her secrets to Echo, the daughter she might have had if only she'd been brave. Clarisse has always had trouble expressing her true feelings. If she had been courageous enough, she'd have told Joseph that she loved him a long time ago. But fear kept her quiet. She had felt too vulnerable. Now she is almost out of time. Clarisse can no longer keep the secrets locked away inside of her, just as she can no longer ignore the fact that her kitchen window sometimes opens on its own only moments after she has locked it shut, letting bundles of lilacs cascade across the sill and onto the kitchen counter. She will reveal her truths in the only way that she can. Not in words but in images. Although Clarisse's hands always ache before rain, she has spent the last few days since Melanie's disappearance molding dough into different shapes, telegraphing stories into cookies. Baking is the way of age, she tells herself. It is a way for her to capture time. And secrets.

Clarisse has both hated and loved living here in Canandaigua. She once thought that standing in her kitchen, watching everyone else's life go by, was the safest place to be. But now she knows it is just the opposite. A full life, a life where she captures her heart's desire, requires that chances be taken; that paths be forged out of the soft cocoon of loneliness. She glances at her old cat, who is rushing toward a patch of sunlight as though rushing for its last breath, the same way there are certain souls that rush back into life, if only to be held once. They only come back for that. Who would believe it? After all those miles of walking.

Clarisse picks up a cookie shaped like a pipe. She presses a fist to her cracked lips as if it were fifty years ago to the day that Joseph arrived: Generous. Charismatic. Warm. She touches her neck, fingers the absence of her locket that disappeared while she was walking through the clover dreaming of telling him how she felt. That day she lost the locket, she lost the cache of her memories. She searched for it for a week but then gave up, certain that this meant the opportunity to tell him had passed. As time went on, she knew that she couldn't steal the moment back, even if she could still feel Joseph's presence around her. As she stood here all those years, baking in the kitchen, the power of her secret has felt like the great Niagara. How many years has she spent walking around the edges of this kitchen, trying to know it as though it were Joseph's heart?

For years, Clarisse believed that some things were better left unremembered. The flush of her own skin when confronted by the man she loved. The secrets of her neighbor, Leila Ellis.

"Ginger cookies!" Clarisse calls out. She knows she must be brave. Seeing the girl awakens a feeling she is not used to, a feeling that is barely tolerable—the maternal ache. It's an emptiness born of instinct. She still feels it after all these years. As Echo approaches, Clarisse notices the broken buckle on the girl's clog—a telltale sign of a motherless daughter. You wouldn't recognize it unless you were one or you knew what to look for—these women rarely comb through their hair or iron their clothing. They carry their little-girl selves through their lives like a warning. They forget to shave their legs or mend their broken shoes. Even when they are thirty-two, they delight in running through the sprinklers at night and stealing away into the treetops to spy on the birds. They carry on in this defiance and though they don't know it, it makes certain men fall in love with them. And it makes certain childless women want to mother them. Clarisse had once been like Echo. She hadn't grown up until she, herself, was forty-two.

Clarisse leads Echo inside, instructing her to step over the cats as they walk through the living room, which is full of knickknacks covering the shelves, and the walls, collections of everything from porcelain frogs to macramé planters. There are six Gold Hummingbird Paradise lanterns out on the back porch alone.

"How about a cup of coffee? No, you'd like some tea, I bet," says Clarisse.

"Mint, if you have it. If not, regular's fine, too."

The flush in Echo's cheeks gives her a child-like air, making Clarisse feel all the more maternal, making her want for what she has missed all of these years. Echo's hair is wet. Clarisse wants to dry it for her. Cloaked in a big green army coat, Echo's eyes are red, and she's staring at Clarisse, looking somewhat confused, from under a tangled auburn mop of curls. The combination of fear and beauty is compelling. Clarisse has got to relax so she doesn't let her nerves get the best of her. She has big truths for Echo. "By the way, dear, do you know you have leaves in your hair?"

Echo reaches up distractedly. "How embarrassing," she says, without removing them.

"Here, let me get that one for you," Clarisse says, just to have a chance to smooth the girl's hair. "That's better. See? It's just a leaf." Clarisse can see that the girl is red with embarrassment. "Don't worry. It's what people call character-building."

"I've got enough character to fill a small city."

"You've got some things on your mind, maybe?"

"Always." Echo smiles quickly, looks down.

"Well, you have choices to make. How lucky you are. I hardly remember when I had choices."

Echo follows Clarisse into the kitchen, which Clarisse introduces as her "studio." Clarisse sets the plate of cookies down on the counter. She can see that Echo doesn't know where to look first. Bottles of colored sprinkles and tubes of frosting are dispersed throughout rows of cookies, which are laid out across the kitchen table. Each cookie is decorated with its own Canandaigua scene—The Diamond Trees. A cabin. A Jeep, and more, many of which Echo seems to recognize. They have been painted with colored frosting. Some have been adorned with little silver and gold balls.

"My God. You are a true artist," muses Echo.

As Clarisse reaches through the open kitchen window and pinches off mint leaves from the window box, she glances at the bushes for the yellow paper airplanes. Thankfully, nothing. "Mint for the nerves," says Clarisse, setting down a cup of hot water in front of Echo. She sprinkles the mint leaves into it.

Echo examines the trays of cookies. "Amazing details. Not a crack in the frosting."

"Egg whites. I brush them and bake them at extreme heat for thirty seconds, then let them cool, repeat, three separate times."

Just then a large orange tabby jumps up on the counter and Clarisse gently nudges him off. "Bad Ella," she chides. "You know she thinks she's people. She likes to go visiting," she says.

Echo picks up one of the cookies. "Clarisse, this is my Jeep."

"A masterpiece. Take a bite."

"I've already done enough damage to it," Echo argues. Clarisse winces, tries to hide the pain she feels in her legs. "Are you okay, Clarisse?"

"My knees are giving me trouble lately. But creativity is good for these old bones, though. Here, taste this one. Don't be shy. Go ahead."

Clarisse holds up a mayfly cookie, its wings striped with blue and yellow frosting, and shimmering with tiny silver threads. "It's good," Echo says, taking a bite. "I bet you never run out of ideas."

Clarisse holds up another. "Guess this one."

"Two Bears," says Echo. "The feathered cap and all."

"He wasn't as mysterious as people think. And yes, there are enough secrets here to keep me going for the next thirty years," says Clarisse, peering out at the lilac bush, which is starting to scratch at the window. "See, I've been thinking about starting my own business. *Cookietales,* I call them. People have always raved about my baking. I've always lacked confidence. Now I figure, why in the hell not? Oh, I hope my swearing doesn't offend you."

"I admit, I do admire a woman who can swear well," Echo assures her, and laughs.

If I had a daughter, she would be just like you, Clarisse thinks, enjoying the connection as she shuffles over to the cabinet and takes out a Tupperware container. Throughout the years, she has caught herself looking for reflections of herself everywhere. *That hair. Those eyes. My daughter would look like that, sound like that. She would say things in just that way.* "I thought you could talk to Joseph about selling them in his store. I'm giving you some samples to take to him. I'll split the profits."

"Why not ask him yourself, Clarisse? He'd say yes to you."

Clarisse is suddenly distracted by what she sees in the

window. A police car driving up to Leila's house. "Well look who it is, there goes old Charlie Cooke, coming back to break Leila's heart again. The sonofabitch wouldn't be the first. Poor Leila. A person can only take so much disappointment," says Clarisse, her voice softening. "After all this time, with this family living next door. Their turmoil has drained the life out of me. And with Melanie. Four days gone. And Maya, she never got over the little boy's death. I'm not suspicious by nature. But that little boy knew how to swim. You don't live on a lake and not learn how to swim, for God's sake."

"It was an accident. There was a storm."

"Storm or not, those kids were like fish in the water." Clarisse is shivering. "It just got cold, didn't it? Keeps happening." She closes the window. "It all goes back to Leila. She made some bad choices. Even smart women do dumb things when they're afraid of being alone. As they get older, this fear clouds their vision. They settle for less than they deserve. They get hurt. Their children, too."

Echo notices something yellow caught underneath the window frame. "Is that a paper airplane?"

Clarisse is unusually calm as she picks up the airplane and tosses it into the garbage. She can no longer deny its presence any more than her other secrets. "It's nothing," she says.

Sitting at the kitchen table, Clarisse deals out the cookies in front of Echo like playing cards. The secrets of a town can weigh on a person. These stories have to come out. The canoe. Two Bears. A silver tomahawk. A medicine bag. She can't keep it silent any more. "We could start small, just with our town. Then we'll expand into a custom cookie business. People from all over the world can send us their pictures, and we'll decorate cookies for Christmas, or birthdays. You'll do the writing, tell my stories for me. You're a writer, aren't you? You know how to tell stories?"

Echo is holding the Jeep cookie. "I refuse to write about this one on the grounds that no one will give a rat's ass about it."

"Oh, good, you swear, too," Clarisse says.

Echo smiles. "We're a lot alike, you and I. Don't you think?"

"So it seems," says Clarisse, letting herself bask in the recognition.

"What would I say about myself anyway? Do people want to read about my issues with freckles?" Echo asks.

"Ah. Lemon," Clarisse says.

"Oh, no thank you." Echo looks at her teacup.

"No, for the freckles."

"It's okay, I like them now," Echo says, self-consciously rubbing her arms.

"You know what? I do, too." Clarisse pulls another tray out of the oven. "Anyhow, I think you say a little something about what you're doing now. What you miss most about our beloved town, or who?"

"I'm flattered but I'm sure someone else is more interesting. Why would people want to read about me?"

"Gossip makes people feel a part of a place."

"Then you tell me what to write."

"A story about unrequited love. You're not the only one who's been through it." Clarisse sighs, placing her hand over her heart. "Look at where we live. This is a place where hearts are broken and buried. I think this is what the Seneca really meant when they named it, you know."

Echo looks away.

"What's the matter, dear? You look like you're about to cry. I said something wrong?"

"Oh, no, I'm fine," Echo insists. Clarisse's saucer-gray eyes grow wide, her hair, luminescent with streaks of silver. They've been a universe apart but it doesn't matter. Clarisse is overwhelmed with the closeness she now feels to the girl. She tries to listen as a mother might, with unconditional love, with patience, without judgment. She listens to Echo talk about seeing Grant again. About how Echo had fooled herself into thinking that there would be no distance between them. About how all the hurt and disappointment had come flooding back, making her say things that she regretted. Clarisse nods, thinking the girl very brave. Although the confession is painful for Echo, it makes Clarisse feel no longer so alone.

"What about you, Clarisse?" Echo asks, suddenly.

"What about me?"

"You were in love once."

"Sadly, no, it wasn't in my cards. Not at all. See, in my day, when I was young, I was a wild girl," says Clarisse, blushing. "In love with everything, you know, one of those types, had fun everywhere I went. Those days, we just danced and danced. Me, I loved the Charleston."

"You were gorgeous, I bet," says Echo.

"No. But I was what they called, 'full of personality.' And I had a good pair of legs." Echo lets out a laugh. Clarisse is startled by the sound of laughter in her house. It echoes through the hallways, filling the house.

"Well, I had many suitors, but none was the right one. None was the one I wanted." Clarisse remembers how she used to boast that she liked playing the field. In truth, she liked playing it safe. No connections meant no threat of rejection. Clarisse watches Echo winding her curls around her fingers and Clarisse thinks back to those wild days, when her own hair was so thick she could hardly get one hand around it to put it into an elastic. "There was only one for me. But, I never told him."

"Why?" asks Echo, leaning forward intently.

She doesn't tell Echo that she was afraid of not being in control, of losing herself in something, in someone. The truth is that denying it all these years hasn't worked. Her feelings of love have been just as consuming, just as overwhelming. She still lost herself, but remained as lonely as ever. "It was a long time ago. Love ruined me. I let it ruin me for years." Clarisse watches Echo's expression turn serious, almost wistful, her large brown eyes burning red as she stares at Clarisse.

Echo takes her hand, comforting her. "But what if Joseph felt the same way?"

Clarisse feels the blood rush to her face. "You knew?" She hadn't known anyone could tell. Hadn't she appeared tough enough? Hadn't she kept enough distance? "I'm so embarrassed," she whispers.

"Please, Clarisse. I've always known. I've seen the way you look at him." All this time, Echo held her secret for her, just as Clarisse had held all of Leila's. Maybe there was this natural instinct among women to keep each other's secrets, especially those that were painful, that concerned love and death.

"You knew. I don't know whether to thank you or to run and hide," says Clarisse, stumbling over her words. She feels exposed, but somehow Echo's presence makes her feel brave enough to continue. It's almost a feeling of relief, coming clean. "I guess you saw how I pined away all this time. See, he was married when we met. I couldn't do that, not with a married man. I've seen how badly that can turn out. Then, his wife died, but it wasn't right. Once, just a short time before you arrived on his doorstep, he came right out and asked me if I had feelings for him. But it had been so many years, and I knew he didn't really want me. He was just lonely, the way men are."

"What did you say when he asked you?"

"I denied it. Years go by and the more time that passes, the more things seem right just the way they are. I couldn't tell him."

"Do you regret it?" Echo asks, pushing her hair from her eyes.

"Of course. Regret is a painful thing to live with," says Clarisse. It has taken her out of so many moments. It is like a constant presence at her back, a shadow of what could have been, causing her to look over her shoulder, following her wherever she goes, never truly disappearing.

"At the time I simply could not be honest with him. I had waited and waited for that window of opportunity. I should have told him the truth about how I felt. Then I'd have no regrets. I could have played the hand I'd been given. I could have just said it and let the chips fall. I waited a long time to do it. I thought I would. Then when the window opened, I couldn't jump. I was too afraid I'd get hurt. I just let the opportunity, my life, slip away."

Echo finishes her tea and takes the cup to the sink. The talk is making her anxious. "Speaking of time, Clarisse, I'm seeing Grant tonight. He is actually cooking me dinner, if you can believe that. I've got to leave."

Clarisse is trembling. She takes Echo's face in her hands. "Listen to me. Don't let him get away again. Don't make the same mistake I did. No regrets. When a window opens, jump through it." Clarisse can feel her heart racing. She feels as though she is running after a plane that's about to take off. She can feel the words piling up inside her, pushing to get out. She's running out of time. Echo is staring at her, a concerned look on her face.

"Take my cookies. These cookies here, these are little girls," says Clarisse.

"Princesses. The silver balls on the dresses are perfect."

"Now they're grown." Clarisse looks Echo straight in the eye, daring her to ask. She knows she is so far out she can't stop now.

"The Ellis girls?" Echo asks. She points to the other cookie Clarisse is holding. "And that's the old canoe."

Clarisse's heart is fluttering and she places her hand over it.

"I've kept a secret all these years. I can't live with it any longer." Clarisse picks up a sprig of mint and drops it into her cup, glancing Echo's way. Clarisse wants this to come out right so that she only has to say it once. She wants to be rid of it. And at this point, she doesn't even care if she looks or sounds crazy. It can't be any crazier than going over and over the scene a hundred times in her mind. The relief that will come will restore her to sanity. "Maybe I could have prevented something. The Ellis children, when they were little. See, I face the house like this. I wasn't looking out the window to be nosy, I was only doing the dishes."

"Of course," says Echo, reassuringly.

Clarisse's body has begun to ache, as though releasing a secret that had long ago infused her joints. She leans against the counter, silently telling the pain to go away. "I'm not ashamed to say this. I never intentionally eavesdropped on Leila. But see, I stand at the window like this sometimes when I can't sleep. Sometimes when I wake up in the middle of the night, I come downstairs and have a glass of water and I stand right here, and I notice things."

Clusters of lilacs are batting against the window. Echo startles at the sound and looks up anxiously.

"It's okay. Let him be." Clarisse knows she can't turn back.

She knows her eyes are tearing, but she can't stop herself. "Victor was away on one of his godforsaken hunting trips—that man was a menace, if you heard the way he used to yell at Leila and tear up the front lawn with his damn car—I didn't blame Leila for what she did. I still don't. Leila was alone with two baby girls and a crazy drunk for a husband. A woman gets lonely. A woman gets angry. She does things she shouldn't when she feels all alone, trapped, and it looks like there's no way out."

"What did Leila do?" Echo asks, nervously glancing at the window, realizing that it is now open, somehow, and that a cluster of lilacs is spilling over the frame.

"I'd see a car pulling up in Leila's driveway whenever Victor was away. It was always late at night. The man would stay an hour or two, never more. Then, he'd leave in a hurry," she says. "Leila's affair lasted almost a year." Clarisse knows she is beginning to sweat. "Get me a glass of water, dear? My throat's so dry."

Calmly, Clarisse grabs hold of the lilac branch that's trying to get in. She pushes it aside. The branch flops back, and she has to push it behind the flower box and quickly shut the window.

"Clarisse," says Echo. "Here's your glass of water."

"Thank you, dear." Clarisse reaches for the water, but her hands are shaking so much that she spills it. Echo takes the glass from the old woman and wipes up the mess. "I don't know what has gotten into me. I've usually got a steady hand."

"Go on, it's okay," says Echo.

"The point is that one night Victor was on a bender. Victor and Leila were out in the backyard, fighting. And the next thing I know Victor is yelling to holy hell out there, dragging Leila by the hair." Clarisse knows she should stop but her eyes are tearing. "He punched her hard in the face, cut her cheek up. It swelled like a plum and her eye, and she fell right into that tree . . . oh . . . my," she says. Clarisse looks up, realizing that she has smashed one of the cookies with her fist. Two Bears. It is in pieces in her hand.

"My God. Poor Leila. I had no idea. Clarisse, you're shaking. You're sweating. I'm worried. Can I call someone to stay with you?" Echo asks.

"No, don't. I'll be fine."

"Why not?" demands Echo, taking out her cell phone.

"Because there's no one to call!" Clarisse cries. She turns her back to Echo. "I'm sorry. It's humiliating," she whispers, rubbing her eyes. "It's difficult. Remembering. You see, Leila came running over here. I made her some tea and gave her a bag of frozen peas to hold next to her cheek. I should have called the police that night. But she begged me not to. She stayed here for an hour. And then she wanted to go home to the girls. Victor had gone, at least we saw him go. Somehow the babies had slept through it, thank the Lord. I think he knew she was seeing someone else. That she didn't love him.

"I fell asleep for a while that night, and I woke up around dawn. I heard the strangest noise outside, and I ran to the window. Victor was staring right at me, holding my cat, Bella, so tight. Bella was just wailing for dear life." Clarisse wipes her eyes as Echo hands her the glass. "I thought my favorite cat would disappear. I knew it. I could feel Victor threatening me. Victor wasn't just a drunk. He was violent. I was afraid of him," Clarisse continues. "Do you see that after living next to them for all these years, their secrets have become mine? That lilac tree survives on secrets."

"What was he threatening you for? Because you saw him hit her?" Echo asks, getting up.

"If I had only called the police then. I could have prevented everything."

"Prevented what?"

"Luke."

"What are you saying?" Alarmed, Echo glances out the kitchen window at the tombstone in Leila Ellis's backyard.

Clarisse's eyes are deep with regret. "I have no proof, if that's what you're thinking," says Clarisse. "I know it sounds crazy. But I'm an old woman and I know what I know. I've never told anyone. Not a thing. I couldn't see it would do any good. I didn't want to cause poor Leila more pain." Clarisse grabs the side of the counter, as though she might fall. "I never told Leila what I believed. I was too afraid to press her. We weren't close, other than that night that she ran over here and I took care of her. And whenever we saw each other after that, Leila would pretend it never happened. She made it known. How could I force her to remember what was already buried? I couldn't do it. Not to that woman."

Clarisse braces her hip against the sink for support. She is holding her hands under the steaming water, unaware that the skin is reddening. Echo reaches over and turns off the water.

A hush falls over them. The two women look out over the backyard. Clarisse suddenly feels safe when Echo puts her hand on the back of her head and strokes her hair as though mothering her.

"Clarisse. Why tell me? And why now?"

"Because Melanie has disappeared. Because of all the secrets. And because of who Leila was in love with, all those years ago. Women can make bad choices. Because of it, terrible things happened."

"Who was it?" Echo wants to know. She looks worried, the

color having drained from her face when she notices that the closed window is now open again. "Clarisse?"

Clarisse is unable to speak, the familiar tightness in her chest mounting. The truth is like a thread that has wound into a tangled ball in her throat, impossible to unravel. So much time has passed, and so much emotion, she feels confused, unable to find the beginning, or the ending of the thread. She turns away, keeping the truth silent, suddenly noticing a sticky syrupy smell in the air, as lilacs come spilling through the open window.

FROM UP ON THE hill, Grant's cabin looks suspended in a chromy sky. As Echo nears the driveway, she hears the hissing waves. Before Echo reaches Grant's door, she stops several times to check that she has her keys in her purse, that she hasn't forgotten anything. Would it be better to turn around? She thinks of Clarisse and her words about regret. This is Echo's chance to make it all right with Grant. To speak her truth to him so she doesn't have to live a lifetime of looking over her shoulder at what *could have been. What might have happened. If only. If only.* She wouldn't survive a life like that. She takes a deep breath, shakes out her hair, and forces herself to knock.

In the moiré window, she looks small. She feels frivolous and fearful, not quite measuring up. She doesn't even look like a grown woman, more like a little girl, her skin damp and pale but for the freckles. What sort of woman would go anywhere with her hair still wet? Without even putting on some makeup? She hears Grant's footsteps behind the heavy wooden door.

He opens the door.

His wet hair falls over his chest. His faded jeans hang loosely on his hips. A dark green flannel shirt drapes from his hand.

Look up, she tells herself. At his face. That's right. Up.

"You look great," he says.

"I'm late."

"I'm really glad to see you." He is looking at her as though he is genuinely glad. For some reason this surprises her.

Grant looks as though he wants to lean over and kiss her on the cheek. But she could be imagining it. "To brighten your day," Echo says, quickly shoving the bag of groceries toward Grant. "I hope you still like wine. You've always been pretty consistent . . ." She lets her voice drown out. What a stupid thing to say, she chides herself.

"That's what you remember about me? That I'm consistent? Jesus." He takes the bag. "Come in, come in."

She follows him, trying to concentrate on the feel of the place. "Make yourself at home." Grant turns his back to her in the kitchen. "You can see the place hasn't changed much. Been trying to fix it up a little. A very little." He turns around, smiles.

She runs her hand over the worn tropical fabric of the rattan couch where she and Grant used to lie for hours, arms and legs entwined. Echo stands awkwardly in the middle of the room, not knowing what to do. She rummages through her purse as though it were an escape hatch, as though she could shrink down and slide right into its wide dark mouth. It looks so safe in there among the loose sticks of gum and errant dimes. Clarisse's words remain with her: *No regrets*.

"Did you lose something?" Grant calls from the kitchen, picking up an oven mitt.

"No," she says, closing her purse. "Dinner smells great. Is that barbecue?" I can do this, she thinks. Just keep smiling and asking questions.

"It's my secret recipe. Been cooking the bird for hours." As he pulls on his shirt in front of the open refrigerator, she tries to look away.

He sets a wine bottle on the kitchen table. CONGRATULATIONS GRADUATE is printed across the blue paper tablecloth in big red letters.

"What did I graduate from?" she asks. "The school of bad judgment?"

"You and me, both," he says, with a smile. "It's the only tablecloth they had. It's festive, right?"

Echo notices the wolf lying nearby, under the living-room window.

"You're not keeping a wolf in this place, are you? I could swear that is the same wolf I saw in the middle of the road," Echo says, backing up.

"He's friendly," says Grant, kneeling, rubbing the wolf's stomach. "See? Not a mean bone in his body. Come and pet him." Echo reaches out to pet the wolf's golden shaggy fur, and it rolls back and forth on its back.

Grant gets up. "So, I'm consistent, huh? Is that a good or bad thing?" He leans against the counter, and she watches as his fingers expertly weave his braid.

"Not a bad thing." She remembers the last time he asked her to braid his hair for him just before she joined him on a run. She was seventeen and believed she'd be doing it forever.

"You look pretty," he says, placing the tray on the stove. "But I probably should keep that to myself, right?"

"My hair is soaking wet." She looks down, embarrassed.

"That's a good thing," says Grant. "Anyway, storm the other night," he says, pointing to the window. "Blew out the whole sheet of glass."

"You're kidding."

"Almost slept through it. You still have insomnia?" he asks.

"I'm a lifer," she admits. "No one ever beats insomnia."

"You always slept good next to me," he says casually. "Glasses are right in here, by the way." He points to the cabinet above the sink.

She walks into the kitchen. Now that she is standing with her back to him, she closes her eyes. It's all getting to her, the barbecue cooking and the lack of sleep. She should stay away from wine. Echo opens the *Foxfire* book on the counter. " 'Moonshining as a Fine Art.' Ten bucks if you can tell me the first line."

" 'Go into the woods and find a good place,' " he says, with his head in the oven.

Music fills the cabin. Old Fleetwood Mac. The tinny guitar strums out the melodic beat of "Second Hand News." Grant is pouring barbecue sauce over the turkey, pretending that he knows what he is doing. Echo brings the glass of wine to her lips, watching him from across the table. She knows he has no idea but she'll play along.

The wolf has finagled his way under the table and every so often rests his head on Echo's knee until he gets a piece of turkey. Soon she and Grant settle into a dialogue, but she's certain she's coming off as nervous as she feels. And he seems preoccupied, too. He asks her what she remembers about him as a kid and she reminds him that he wore his sandals with black socks.

"My students would love to hear that. I'm addicted to black socks."

When she starts to laugh, he tells her that she made being together so easy. He's remembering all the little things they did for each other. How they would touch whenever they passed each other at the store, no words, but a hand loosely trailing an elbow, fingers catching, and then letting go. She's moved by the memory, but every so often she thinks about Clarisse's story about Victor. His violence. She keeps drinking.

At times the clink of silverware is an embarrassing reminder of what they don't say. When Grant asks about her life, she offers a quick remark or two. She explains a little about magazine work, albeit she can't seem to muster any level of passion, especially in lieu of the fact that he's been teaching all this time, saving the future of civilization.

"It's not easy," he tells her. "There's a lot of kid-hate to swallow. Some days are hard as hell. Most days, in fact."

"Then why stick with it?" Echo asks.

He takes a swig of wine and leans back in his chair. "I'm consistent. Don't you remember?"

She smiles. She forces herself to eat a roll. Not another glass, she tells herself. She doesn't want another scene like the one that happened last year when Stephen got her so drunk on sangria that he had to sneak into the ladies' room at Dali Restaurant and hold her hair back while she threw up.

"I must have done something pretty bad in my last life to love teaching this much. When you're in the classroom and you've been talking for an hour and their eyes are glazed over and you know they want you dead, well, then, all of a sudden, one of them will get it. Even the mean ones get excited. Doesn't even matter that they just called you a motherfucker or a shithead or an asshole. It's the look on their face that's priceless. For a split second they forget they hate you. They forget who they *think* they are. You see who they really are. There is nothing, absolutely nothing like it."

He surprises himself as the words fall convincingly from his lips. "But here's the real secret about teenagers. They've got venom for blood." He refills his glass.

"Which is why you love it."

"Exactly. More wine?"

She holds out her glass.

"I was so goddamn frustrated at that age," he says. "Impatient. Always waiting and waiting."

"For what?" she asks.

"To become one of the regular people."

"You're still waiting, no?" she says, sipping her wine.

"Still waiting. Yes, absolutely."

"They like you, after, right? I mean, after they get it."

"No. Not really. Potato?" He smiles, holds up the green ceramic bowl.

She shakes her head. What has she got to show for herself except that she's made Joseph proud? Maybe that's enough. She's been at the same company since graduating college. An ability to stay in one place is no small feat. And she likes her job all right. She tells Grant that the company offers free cappuccino every afternoon, though she doesn't know why this would impress him. Well, at least there's free parking, and in Cambridge that's nearly impossible to find.

"So that's great," he says. "That you're happy, right?"

"Yes. Absolutely happy," she says, and he smiles, looking like he buys it.

"Good. I'm glad," he says, rolling up the cuffs of his shirt. He glances at the wolf pacing back and forth in front of the glass door impatiently.

"You should name him. What about Einstein?" she says.

"Because of his brilliance."

"It fits him," she says. She finishes her wine. She knows she should slow down but won't. She will, in fact, have a little too much. She is thinking of Clarisse, of a lifetime spent standing in a kitchen, aching for the man she loves. She pours another glass of wine. She already knows she'll have to wear sunglasses all day tomorrow. The relaxation she feels after the second glass of wine is seductive, making her think that she can confess things, that she can tell him that she still never feels entirely settled, that she is haunted by the thought that she may wake up one morning and find she's floating out there lost in the universe with nothing to tether her. "It's so ridiculous," she admits.

"No, it's actually perfectly understandable," he says.

"Am I rambling? It's the wine. . . . You seem distracted. What are you thinking about?"

"Lion and Melanie. I'm fine. I like the rambling. More?"

She nods, removing her napkin from under the glass. "Sure. I'll be drunk and passed out in about five minutes, in case you're timing me."

"I lost my stopwatch. I'm not timing you."

She knows she must break the tension. "Do you remember what album we were listening to the first time you went up my shirt?"

He smiles. "Best day of my sorry old life."

"Kiss. The album *Love Gun*," she says.

"You still have that pink plastic record player, and I'm willing to bet that it's still under your bed at Joseph's."

"You think you've got me pegged."

"You're pretty consistent," he laughs. The wolf begins to whimper. They look at the scraggly mutt as though they're waiting for him to take over the conversation. "Did you say you wanted a pet?" Grant asks, getting up.

He lets the wolf outside. Then he takes two candlesticks out of the cabinet and plunks them in their holders in the center of the table. "Forgot about these," he says, lighting the candles. "It's not too late for candles, is it?"

"No. Never too late," she says, finishing her wine. "Your mom always bought candles from the store. I remember."

"She lit them every night so my dad could eat by candlelight and relax. She'd sit out there on the porch smoking her cigarettes, waiting for him. I can picture it like it was yesterday."

"Your dad always came home late."

Grant nods and finishes his glass. "I hated that he did that. Seven or eight at night, fine, but nine or ten? Come on. Something was up."

"What do you mean, something?" Echo can tell he's a little drunk, but he seems to need this and so does she. She looks out the window at the row of birch, long and slender, not at all crowded for root room. In the moonlight, the bark's white skin peeling back from the trunks looks too exposed. It makes her shiver.

"She never got upset with him, though," says Grant. "At least not to his face. She should have put her foot down."

"'Waiting and patience are a life's work,' she'd say."

"You remember that." Grant touches her hand. "He didn't see her. She was invisible to him."

"Yeah, I remember."

"She tried," he says, thinking about how every morning his mother set a table with china, silverware polished to perfection, and hand-dyed Indian fabric she had made into napkins. Every night she would set the table for three as though she expected Ben Shongo would actually be home for dinner. She ate so slowly, painfully slowly Grant had thought, hoping her husband might walk in the door any minute. And yet when Ben Shongo came home for dinner, whether it was nine or ten o'clock at night, whether he had called or not, his dinner was waiting by candlelight and Emily had gone to bed.

Ben Shongo never talked much about his upbringing, only bits of stories and legends, here and there. Grant knew that his mother had been the one to keep tradition, preserving what she could from what she had pieced together. The Seneca were a matriarchal society with a tradition of property rights for women. Their governmental acts helped inspire the founders of the feminist movement in the 1840s. She thought it important that Grant know his heritage, that he knew the strength of the women in his ancestry even if his own mother possessed little of it.

"I'm sorry for what happened all those years ago. I judged your mother. She was just being protective of you. I should have been more like Joseph. Never judging anyone. I hardly understood anything back then."

"Do you now?"

"I'm still impulsive," she smiles. "You?"

In the flicker of candlelight, Grant's eyes are glistening as he smiles. He gets up and opens the door and Einstein tramples mud across the carpet.

"I could have sworn you said you wanted a pet," he tells Echo.

Einstein leans up against Grant's legs, as though bracing him for support. Grant scratches his neck. He tells her how when his mother died, she had specifically asked to be cremated, that there be no funeral or memorial service, but how a few relatives had come to the house to pay their respects. He had overheard a relative mentioning his mother's lifelong fear of snakes. Grant had been struck with guilt, remembering all the garter snakes he had brought home as a boy. His mother had let him keep the snakes, never once mentioning her fear.

"My dad put his hand on my shoulder. He said, 'Boy, she didn't want to pass her fear on to you. It was a gift.' I had no idea what the hell he meant. I never understood the things he said. It was like he was talking to me in another language. I thought if only I were smarter, he'd respect me."

Echo reaches across the table and lets the tips of her fingers touch his. The loss of their parents has forged a new bond. Perhaps she will tell Grant right now. Perhaps she will come right out and say the truth about how she feels. It will be out there, and she won't be able to take it back. And the chips will fall. She is ready. "Where are you going?" she asks. He has gotten up and is standing in the doorway.

He lifts the portrait of Ben Shongo from behind the door. The face looks younger than Echo remembers, without the signature sideburns that almost touched the edges of his mouth. The hair is black. His skin is darker than Grant's and pocked, but the high cheekbones and strong chin are the same.

"I've never seen that painting. Where did it come from?" says Echo.

"Melanie painted it from memory. He used to make house calls for Luke. Leila would call and Dad would drop everything and drive over there."

Grant starts to clear the table. "Jesus, I can't stop thinking about Melanie."

"Joseph is a mess. Four days is a long time."

"The last time I saw her was at Luke's funeral. But I remember going on a house call with my father, back when Luke was sick." Grant had promised his father that he would be invisible during the house call, that he would be a wallflower. It was rare that he got to see his father at work. He had just wanted some time alone with him. He had stood by quietly, watching as his father eased three-year-old Luke's breathing, and then eased Leila Ellis's mind by telling her she was doing everything right. He had seen the relief on Leila's face when his father placed his hand on her shoulder. If it hadn't been for these the two little blond fairies in their rhinestone tiaras, giggling, waving at him from the doorway, everything would have been perfect. "So

I'm trying to ignore them. My dad says, 'Why don't you entertain them for a while and let us drink our tea?'"

"Who was 'us'? Your dad and Leila?" she asks.

"They were pretty close. He was over there so often because of Luke's asthma."

Echo is listening intently. "And you were a captive audience for the girls," says Echo.

"A captive, more like it. They tied me up to one of those posts, had me cornered. I'm standing in a playroom watching these little girls dancing and twirling all around me, telling me I'm the prince and asking me which one of them I want to marry. What could I say? I couldn't pick one over the other."

"So you said you'd marry both of them? How insensitive can you be?" she says, tearing off another piece of bread and throwing it at him.

"Listen. I'm dumber than I look. You should know that by now," he says. "The girls start arguing over me and the next thing I know, Maya rips off Melanie's tiara and starts an all-out war and all I can think about is how my father is going to blame me for it. Leila comes running downstairs, and both girls are crying now, and I'm like a deer in the headlights tied to this post. My dad is staring at me from the top of the stairs. Last house call I ever went on."

"Women," she says, shaking her head. "Here's the thing, we'll wreck your life if you let us. Especially when we're young and beautiful and afraid of ourselves." She thinks again of Melanie.

Grant takes a deep breath, changes the subject. He tells her about Lion falling into the lake and what came after. About the fact that he couldn't swim. "He says I saved his life. But now I've got this strange feeling that I owe him."

"You got that from your father, you know."

"What?"

"The expectation he put on his patients to get well. No one wanted to let him down." Echo sips her wine, spilling a little into her lap. She must stop now or she's not going to be able to string two words together. She is starting to get dizzy.

"Good health through intimidation. That was my dad's secret," Grant jokes, getting up. He looks at her plate. "You liked the barbecued turkey? Bet you never had it before. An old army secret."

"You were never in the army."

"I know, but I've lived alone for a while now. It was a long slow winter."

"I was craving ramen noodles soup, if you must know." She glances at him.

He smiles. "How did you—"

"You've got quite a stock there in the cabinet."

"You'll have to wait until next time. Suspense," he says, sipping the last of his drink.

"Well, I'm worried about Joseph."

"You need to take him to the doctor, Echo. I'm serious about that," Grant says, clearing off the table.

"I heard you helped him out a bit with that cough." She meets his eyes.

"No, he was just happy to see my face."

He tells Echo to relax while he finishes doing the dishes. She slips off her clogs and spills herself onto the couch. She can hardly believe she's here. Every part of her wants to wrap her arms around him. She almost thinks she has no right to feel it. The night has been too perfect, the food too good. But it's more than the food. It's the warmth that fills the space wherever he is. It's his ability to know that he won't understand everything, but he'll still try anyway. She has been away from someone like this for a long time and has forgotten about a thing like earnestness.

How it makes a person.

He is whistling through his teeth. She closes her eyes and everything starts to spin. Her stomach is comfortably full, more so than it's been in months. She rubs Einstein's head methodically with her fingers as her body relaxes into the soft cushions. She and Grant have talked about everything but her love life and his marriage. She doesn't want to know what happened, not really. Doesn't want to hear that he has cheated or hurt his wife in any way. What would she do with the knowledge anyway? People change. It happens all the time. People do things that are totally out of character. Men make bad choices, too, especially when they're desperate and afraid to be alone, when they feel like they're drowning in their own lives. They grasp at anyone or anything they think will buoy them up. They don't think about the consequences.

"Echo," Grant whispers.

"I'm awake," she says, her eyes opening. "I think I just—"

He moves her hair out of her eyes. "Don't think," he says, with a slow smile. "I defrosted these myself." He is kneeling, holding out a spoonful of whipped cream with crushed strawberries.

The whipped cream melts onto her tongue. The strawberries are the frozen kind, but nonetheless they create a nice blend of sweet and tart in her mouth. She looks into his eyes. His face is too close. His body, too.

"Good," she says.

He smiles. "I have to take you home now," he says.

"Okay," she murmurs, staring at him.

Their mouths meet. She can feel the heat between them and his hand on her shoulder. Her breasts press against his chest and she slowly begins to unbutton his shirt. He's plowing his fingers through her hair. Her fingers loosen his braid, the twine falling to the floor. Then his hands slip underneath the rim of her jeans.

"Stop," she says, out of breath. She moves over and smoothes her hair.

"I'm sorry. Jesus." He wipes his mouth, sits down next to her on the couch. Shoulder to shoulder, they stare straight ahead like strangers on a bus. It always struck her how two people could be in the heat of the moment one minute and then be talking rationally the next.

Echo gets up. "Go find Lion. Joseph is probably waiting up for me anyway." She slips her feet into the cool wooden platforms of her leather clogs, and stares at him.

"Okay. You want me to back off," he tells her, getting up. "You're afraid of me."

"As you are of me."

"But that's not stopping me now." He reaches for her.

"I can't do this with you again," she says. She gently pushes him away. This was supposed to be an easy night.

"I'll take you home," says Grant, grabbing his keys.

"Where is my sweater?" she asks. He spies it behind the couch but she is already walking toward the closet.

"It's not in there," he says, as he watches her hand turn the doorknob. "Hey don't—"

Stacked in the closet are piles of wooden statues. She turns to him, unable to keep a straight face.

"Old dinner guests," he says.

She picks up one of the statues, rubs the dust off the face, which is crosshatched with tiny lines. The moisture from her hands darkens the wood. She knows Grant's history, his belief in roots. The statue feels hot and she puts it down quickly. "You carved all of these."

Just then there's a thud on the window. Einstein barks at the noise. Grant opens the sliding glass door and Echo instinctively grabs his hand as they look down at the bird lying on the wet grass.

"Its wing," Echo says, as she kneels. As rain mists around them, the dark blue bird lies there in the floodlight, its small eyes stunned, piercing the sky as its chest rapidly pushes in and out.

"Kingfisher," says Grant, the wind blowing his hair.

"I've never seen one of those here."

"It hunts for fish." The right wing is sticking out awkwardly.

"It's going to die."

"Could you get me a glass of water?" Grant asks, gently petting the bill.

When she returns with the glass, the bird is walking in a circle in front of him. Grant wipes his muddy hands on his jeans.

"What did you do?" Echo asks. The wing looks fine now. Not a trace of anything. The bird is hopping across the grass on its short stubby legs and fluttering its wings. "You did something. You healed it."

Grant stares at her. The Diamond Trees are swaying in the storm, throwing light on Grant's back as he turns and walks inside to wash his hands.

"Please take me home now," she says, when he returns.

"Fine," he tells her. "Don't ask me about the bird."

As she gets into his car, she is holding a million questions about carved Indians, about marriages that work and fail, about trees that root a person to a place, and about a man who can make a bird fly after its wing has been broken. About a lake that pulls a person back toward their fate no matter how hard they resist it.

"All this time, you never called," she says, abruptly.

"You think I didn't want to? You think I didn't dream of you every goddamn night?"

"You would have called," she says, "if you wanted to."

"You told me not to call until I figured myself out. You deserved better than what I was prepared to give."

There are so many ways Echo could answer him, but she knows she invited something she may not have been ready for. He's not the only one who has had to deal with the heartbreak of their relationship. He moved on and actually got married. She's the one who's been searching for him in the eyes of strangers ever since.

"You still haven't figured yourself out."

"That's why I never called," he says.

They ride back to her house the rest of the way without speaking, him tapping his fingers annoyingly on the steering wheel of the old Fleetwood. Echo lets her eyes fall from his profile to his chest to his hands. She stretches her neck, feeling the strain between her shoulders. The Fleetwood turns the corner and they can see the Feed & Grain.

As they pull up, the headlights settle on a man on the porch in a big leather jacket, with a head full of dreadlocks that reach to his shoulders.

"That's the guy I told you about, Lion Williams," Grant says, opening his door.

"Hey Grant," Lion calls out, his voice thin and embarrassed. He gets up slowly, as though he knows he is a striking figure out here at night. "Hey," he waves, quickly looking back and forth between Grant and Echo. "I've been waiting for you. Need to talk to you and Joseph said you'd be back *early*. Joe's getting a birch beer. He's telling stories about Africa."

"Lion Williams, Echo O'Connell," says Grant. Echo smiles at Lion.

"I've heard a lot about you," says Echo. "All good."

Lion nods, then turns to Grant. "Wondering if you could take a ride."

Echo knows they are going to look for Melanie. And she is worried. But she forces herself to walk away from him. Tonight, she'll read until her eyes ache so badly she has to turn off the light. Then she will toss and turn for hours until her sheets are hot and she has to sleep on top of them. In her sleep, she'll be telling Grant everything. By morning her throat will ache so fiercely that she'll only be able to whisper.

17

MELANIE HAS BEEN GONE for four days. If she has truly left Lion for good, he is going to make her say it to his face. If she's in trouble, he has got to find her. More than likely it's both. Lion Williams has been sitting out on the porch of the Feed & Grain in the middle of the night for no reason other than because he knows he needs to trust someone now. Someone has to watch his back, because if he's going to wrestle Melanie out of Two Bears' Cave, he can't go alone, especially if he's going to drag her, kicking and screaming. He's not a fool. He'll ask for help when he needs it.

"What's going on, Lion?" asks Grant, watching Echo as she closes the door behind her. To Lion, Grant looks giant-like, unnaturally tall and broad-shouldered in the silhouette of the headlights. This could work to Lion's advantage. Lion feels better here on dry land where there is no chance of humiliating yourself, of dying a slow death by drowning and being saved by someone who's so perfect it makes you want to drown out of sheer rebellion.

"She looks nice," says Lion. "You love her?"

"Why?"

"Because you look all messed up."

"No," says Grant, dismissively. "She's just an old friend."

"Okay, be that way."

"You need something. What is it?" Grant asks, slightly agitated.

"You offered the other day." Lion's voice thins into a whisper. "You made an offer. Said if I ever needed help—"

"Absolutely."

"I know where Melanie is."

Grant looks at him, surprised. "Thank God, Lion. Where is she?"

Lion backs up. "No questions. Not yet. I only want you to sit in the car, just in case something happens to me when I go in to get her. I don't want you doing anything. Just sit there and wait, and do what I tell you to do. Leave your car here. Don't ask any questions."

Grant agrees, hands in pockets. He's feeling the alcohol in his body. The buzz has become a dull throb. Somehow the events of the evening are dissipating. In the distance a snowy owl calls out through the spray of stars. There are flickering shapes in the water.

"You're scaring me, Lion," says Grant.

"Why?"

"Because you look scared."

"Hell no. I held up a 7-Eleven once. Los Angeles riots," says Lion.

The screen door flies open. "Am I interrupting?" Joseph asks, a beer in both hands. "Yours, Lion. Here's one for you, too, Grant. Did I miss something? You two look like you're conspiring."

Lion eyes Grant nervously.

Grant shifts his weight, leans on the railing.

A cold wind falls across the porch. Lion looks up. He can just barely see the sky and the cloud of blackbirds that are settling nervously in the trees. Lion can't take his eyes off them.

"Where are you going, boys?"

"To get Melanie," says Grant.

"Let me get my coat," says Joseph. "Where is she?"

Lion keeps silent, staring at Grant defiantly. He knows Joseph's eyes are on him.

"What's going on?" Echo asks, at the screen door.

"Two Bears' Cave," whispers Lion.

"She's not there, Grant. Lion. No," Joseph says, grabbing the railing, his face reddening, sweat beginning to bead up on his upper lip. Echo comes outside and stands next to him, taking his arm.

"Just come inside, Pop," she tells him, putting her head on his shoulder.

"Don't let them go," he says, but Echo leads him back inside. "The spirits, they're restless there. Some alive. Some not."

As Grant and Lion peel out of the driveway, they don't know that Joseph is watching them from the window, and that a huge weight has suddenly crushed his heart, causing his left arm to go numb, causing him to drop his pipe.

LION DOESN'T WANT TO have to owe Grant his life but he has that feeling already. It will take two lifetimes to repay him.

"I'm calling Charlie Cooke," Grant tells him. "Give me your cell phone."

"No cops. You don't want to do it my way, then get out . . ."

"Reverse psychology? You think you can use that on me? I'm a teacher. We invented it."

Lion doesn't flinch. "Whatever, man. You in or what?"

Grant nods. "You scared?" Grant rolls down the window of Leila's beat-up Bronco and lets the breeze cool his face.

"Maybe you are." Lion readjusts the rearview mirror. The acid is starting to burn his gut.

"Scared, no," Grant says. "Stupid, yes."

Lion stares straight ahead, hunching over the steering wheel. He tries to smile. He hopes Grant doesn't notice that his knuckles have gone white on the wheel.

The stars are whipping by, streaking the windows with light. What am I doing to the guy? Who knows what kind of state Melanie will be in? Lion wonders. Still if Grant didn't want to come, he wouldn't have agreed. It doesn't matter where I'm taking him, Lion tells himself. Grant wants to do this. Even if new stories circulate all the time about the spirit of Two Bears wreaking havoc to frighten people out of his Cave. Right now Lion could swear the bats are following them. Or it could be the fog. He'll just keep driving. He won't look in the rearview mirror.

"So you held up a 7-Eleven. Congratulations. You cleaned them out of Twizzlers and Coke, I hope?"

"Make all the jokes you want. It was cold hard cash. I had a gun. Well, it looked like a gun, but it was a Pepsi bottle. You know like this," Lion says, pointing his finger in the pocket of his leather coat. "You know who Rodney King is?"

"Sure, I remember the riots, 1992," says Grant. "I used to own a television. Why, did you know him?"

"I didn't have to. See, the guy, he changed my life. Just by getting beat. I wasn't scared at all. People going crazy. Like war, man. All I wanted was some Genesee beer. Nothing you ever probably drank. Ha. Everyone said Why Genesee? Why not good beer? You can have whatever you want today. Today's like Christmas. But, I like Genesee, and didn't see why I should like something else just because it was free."

"Why are you telling me this?"

"Because."

"You didn't take the beer or the cash."

"What? You think I'm lying?"

"You're honest. That's why you didn't take anything."

"I would have. If I hadn't gotten cut," Lion professes. He steers with his knees and pulls up his shirtsleeve and shows Grant the five-inch pink scar across his tricep.

"Painful?"

"Not so much," Lion says, pulling his sleeve back down. Lion lets the car begin to veer off the road.

"Jesus." Grant grabs the wheel. "Keep your goddamn hands on the wheel." Grant wipes his forehead with his sleeve. "And I thought you said Melanie wasn't using—"

"Don't ask me to say it again."

"Okay, kid. Okay."

They drive the three miles to Two Bears' Cave, through back dirt streets so dark it is a miracle that even headlights can light the way. At times tree branches scratch the windshield, and Grant questions whether they are going the right way. Still, the path is slightly worn with downed grass. Others have been here recently.

Lion parks under a sumac tree. He stares at the thick black forest; all the while clumps of red berries are dropping onto the window. The grass is wet with fog but the sky is dry, a sandpaper gray. Cattle clouds trot off behind the leaves, which are flapping in the wind. Above, a dark flock of birds is settling in the branches.

Lion grabs the flashlight and points it at the windshield.

Grant notices the tiny drops of sweat on Lion's forehead. The events of the night are obscured by the darkness. And if ever there was a night when the Flying Heads were going to race through the trees, this would be it. Grant tells Lion about the Seneca legend, which parents on the reservation would tell their children to scare them into coming home on time at night. Yet now the tale is somehow more his.

"Once a spirit monster—all head, no body, with bear claws—swooped down and tried to devour a brave woman as she walked through the forest. Long hair trailing behind it, it chased the woman to her lodge. It peered down the smoke hole and saw the brave woman popping a lit coal into her mouth. The monster, thinking fire was good to eat, gorged up all the hot coals."

"What happened?" Lion asks.

"Got hot-mouth, flew away screaming. Never bothered the village after."

"I'm not eating fire," says Lion.

"I'm goin' in first."

"No way. This is my game. My rules."

Grant opens the door anyway. Lion twists in his seat, looking for what has fallen from his coat pocket. He grabs the flip-open locking knives. Opens one and runs his finger across the blade.

"What do you think you're doing with that?"

"In case I need it. Got one for you, too. Just bought them new." Lion grabs the other knife and sets both on the dashboard.

"I'm not taking that thing."

"Man, I'm in charge." Lion spits out the window. He wipes his mouth on his sleeve and looks at Grant. The place is overrun with bundles of blood-red sumac. The wind pulls the juice across the windshield. "That's bad poison," Lion says, handing Grant the knife. "Those red berries."

"Not this type. My mother used to boil it for tea. Good for the body."

Grant takes the knife, turns it over in his hands, and hands it back. He doesn't like how comfortable he feels holding it. "I got your back, okay?"

"Let's go," says Lion, getting out of the car.

Three high-pitched chirps pierce the air. Grant points the flashlight into the darkness. The bat flaps its wings, dips in front of the car before toggling up the branches of a locust tree.

"Down," Lion whispers, motioning to the flashlight in Grant's hand. Grant does what the kid says and points it at the dirt.

An uneasy wind rustles the tall grass as Grant begins to walk. He cuts through the woods looking for the Cave, praying he remembers. He tells Lion to listen for the bats. Lion is following, watching the stars through the canopy. As they make their way across the trail, thorny bushes scratch at their arms, pull on their clothing as if trying to hold them back. They can hear the flap of bat wings and the high-pitched squeaks, now suddenly closer. Every so often Lion ducks when a low-flying bat veers near his head. The moon looks like old sheet metal, partly obscured by clouds. The smell of dirt and burning wood is pungent.

"She's in the Cave. She must have lit a fire. Smell the smoke." Lion stops suddenly, staring at the trail of amethyst smoke rising out from the mouth of the Cave. Tall slim locust trees cradle the entrance. The trees stand as poised as ballet dancers, their long arms gracefully bent, their trunks lengthening in gentle curves, revealing stretched white bellies.

Lion can just make out an abandoned red bike up there in the distance. And a rusted van turned on its side. Grant had better be following as they cut through the grass toward the Cave.

Lion is imagining what he'll say to her after he gets Melanie home. He'll be a lot stronger with her, that's for sure. He's not playing around. A relapse is always worse than what preceded it. He's seen it. When an addiction has been quiet for a time, it gathers up all the evil like some kind of magnet inside the brain. And if you give in, even years later when you think you can handle it, you had better be prepared for the devil to run wild inside you.

No. No more pushover. Lion's tired of all of it.

This is the last time. The last time he's going to lose her.

He'll threaten not to take Melanie back until she's checked into rehab, nine weeks of inpatient care and follow-up visits after that. They've spent enough time living on the edge. He doesn't even care that she'll never be Miss Homemaker. She'll just keep making the same dinners for the rest of their lives: spaghetti, Hamburger Helper, franks and beans. All his life he's lived on the edge of everything and now, what he really hankers for? A safe little life and the white picket fence he's always heard of. The same one he had once scoffed at.

But she's got her own groove. Her own style.

She does things her own crazy way, and yet he feels lucky every day.

Once he came home from work to find the entire apartment filled with candles. It wasn't his birthday, or even an anniversary. Melanie said she had just felt like celebrating the fact that she was so in love with him. So why waste it? The huge chocolate cake, his favorite, she had made herself. In the thick chocolate frosting, an inch thick, she put seventy tiny candles to represent the number of years she *wanted* to spend with him. She had layered the bathtub water with silver stars, and papered the floor with them, too. He found her soaking in the claw-foot tub when he got home from work. And he had felt like a king, standing on all of that silver universe.

When they reach the mouth of the Cave, there is a howling that Grant now recognizes as the hybrid wolves returned to Canandaigua. To Grant, this is a sign that the whole thing with Lion is a bad idea, but his mind and body aren't connected, because his feet are still moving forward. About thirty feet up, he thinks, pointing his flashlight around the lip of the Cave, illuminating the thin line of smoke coming from a small fire pit, the graffiti covering the walls, the wrinkled bags of potato chips and some old needles. Grant kicks a few empty beer bottles out of the way. This angers him, seeing what has been done to this place, once the home of a medicine man, a place so sacred that few ever saw it when Two Bears was living here. After all this is over, Grant will contact the town's officials and organize a cleanup. He'll get this designated as a protected site, just as Squaw Island has been.

The air inside the Cave is dank, musty. Without a word, Lion takes the flashlight from Grant and walks carefully across the Cave toward the fire pit, which is filled with a pile of old wooden statues, half charred and smoking. Grant follows. Though the wood is still hot, Grant picks up one of the carvings and turns it over in his hands. It looks like a bear. A strangely shaped piece of wood is lying to the left of the fire pit, one that is covered with layers of mud and has not been used for firewood. Grant nicks off some of the mud with his fingers. The mud falls away, revealing the shape of a Seneca warrior, with its wide-planed face and the feathered cap. There is a pile of similar-shaped carved logs against the far end of the Cave wall.

Lion shines the flashlight across the Cave. He can make out the edges of things, woven baskets and hollowed-out gourds. Shelves of all different sizes are carved into the Cave wall. Grant spies something glistening in the dirt. He reaches into a pile of ash and comes up with a fistful of arrowheads. Silently, he lets the dirt fall through his fingers. Then, there is a howling from the mouth of the Cave. One. Maybe two. No, three shadows fall across the entrance.

Hedging at the mouth of the Cave, three wolves stand in the darkness, maddened and thin. Their powerful muscles are rippling in the moonlight, forming a white silhouette against the black night. Their yellow eyes are glistening, fixed on Grant. They snarl and paw at the ground, baring their teeth. "Holy shit," whispers Lion.

"Turn the light off," orders Grant.

Grant walks toward them. They bark and glare at him but he keeps walking. When he is about six feet from them, Grant shouts something Lion doesn't understand. Then the wolves turn and run off into the dark field.

"What did you say?" asks Lion, turning his flashlight back on.

"I told them how to go back to where they came from."

Lion shines the light on Grant's face. He keeps it there, letting Grant squint and then cover his eyes. Then he shifts the light across the cave. "Over there!" he cries. "It's Melanie. Her hair. I can see it," whispers Lion, shining the light on a little enclave where an orange sleeping bag is bunched against the wall. Tufts of blond hair stick out.

"Are you sure?" asks Grant.

"Definitely. It's her." Lion holds up the four-inch blade and pushes his finger onto the tip, watching the drops of blood beading up.

Grant needs to gain some focus. Needs to clear his mind and focus on what he is here for: Melanie. He is trying to remember her face. He recalls the picture Joseph showed him. His eyes follow the beam of light across the dirt floor. Beaver skins are stacked in the corner near a pile of old woven blankets. A large metal pot sits next to one. Lion spies something else glistening in the dust. A silver ankle bracelet. He picks it up.

"Is it hers?" asks Grant.

"It's hers," says Lion.

Walking toward the orange sleeping bag, Lion calls Melanie's name. He runs over to the orange sleeping bag, tugs the corner of it. "Melanie. Mel, it's me."

A groan rises and he jumps back. An empty bottle of Southern Comfort rolls toward his feet.

Dee Dee, one half of the town's homeless couple, sits up. She licks her lips and the sweet permutation of alcohol fills the musty air. "You got a cigarette?"

Lion frowns. She elbows the bundle next to her. Papa Paul lets out a fierce growl and blinks in the offending haze of the light. Confused, he stares at them. "Gentlemen, is this a board meeting?" he says, his pale gray eyes sunken into folds of turtle-like skin. He rolls back over, burying his face in Dee Dee's armpit. When a bat crosses the Cave, Dee Dee covers them both with the sleeping bag.

Lion stands defiantly at their feet.

He twists away when Grant puts his hand on his shoulder. "Get the fuck off of me, man."

"Hey, Lion. Keep it together," Grant says, although Lion is already making his way out.

Lion walks out into the cool grass. A light breeze shifts through the trees, but Lion is too angry to be cold. "We'll look again tomorrow," Grant says, catching up, but he is wondering if Melanie has been able to change. If it is possible, really, for anyone to change.

Lion stares at him, his cheeks drawing quick breaths in and out, as though he has heard Grant's thoughts.

Lion turns around and cuts across the grassy lawn, where he kicks the rusted red bike, sending the wheel spinning. Then he takes off running.

The kid can really fly. Grant starts to chase him. He has the feeling of being watched.

"Go home!" Lion calls back through the night.

Grant can hardly see the boy now.

"Stay away from me!" Lion yells, almost completely swallowed into darkness. The moon sloughs off the clouds and brightens. For a second, it looks as if Lion is running right into the sky.

18

SINCE THE MOMENT GRANT Shongo dropped her off, Echo's mind has been racing. Lying in bed, she has been listening to Joseph's ripping cough and thinking of blackbirds. She is picturing blackbirds so confused by all the secrets spinning in the air, caught in the currents, that they fly in circles, crashing into the windows, breaking their wings, then falling in droves from the sky, symbols of all the hearts that have been shattered. Leila Ellis. Her one bad choice was like a stone thrown into the lake, creating ripples that go on for miles, touching so many lives. And Clarisse Mellon. Standing in that kitchen for years, aching to wrap herself in Joseph's arms. And Echo. Is she any better? Still afraid of her love for Grant Shongo. But mostly, Echo is worried about losing Joseph. Suddenly, she pictures Grant in his backyard, his muddy hands placed around the bird with the broken wing, and the bird's glazed eyes staring up at him, waiting.

She feels desperate. Restless. Every so often she runs to her bedroom window to make sure Grant's car is still outside where he has left it.

Near dawn, she and Joseph find each other in the kitchen.

He is sitting on a stool, wrapped in his green flannel bathrobe, reading *Food Distribution* magazine. But he is as far away as Africa, with that distant look in his eyes. He isn't handling the stress. In the silence, they take turns making pots of coffee. "Do you want more coffee? I'll make more. Even I can't drink this," she tells him. He hardly hears her. He begins to cough. A deep ripping cough that makes her shiver. He doubles over, leaning on the counter. She runs over to him. He is sitting there, his shoulders caved. "I'm okay. My arm is a little stiff," he says hoarsely. But she can no longer stand by and do nothing.

"Will you look at this? Old man hands, you see? They shake all the time." Joseph has a bad feeling about Melanie, he says finally. He wonders out loud if she has been found yet.

Echo puts her arms around him and rests her head on his shoulder. "Now your hands aren't shaking," she says, holding Joseph close. She closes her eyes. "Let me just hug you, okay?" She inhales his scent, aftershave and the damp sweat of age. As she hugs him, all she can feel are bones, his collarbones pressing into her neck, the curve of his spine, the shudder of his rib cage each time he coughs. It feels as though he could break if she squeezes too hard.

Joseph pats her back. "Only you, kiddo, could ever calm my mind."

"That's why we need each other," says Echo, not letting go. "That cough. It scares me. I want you to see a doctor."

He lets go of her and walks away. "It's just age, honey," he says, staring out the porch window. "It crept up on me. You know, one day, I looked down and saw a pair of old hands and I thought, whose hands are these? I'd do more from above," he says, pointing up.

Echo shoots him a look. She feels the rip of fear inside her. She walks over to the counter and she stares out the window, noticing how the grass, drenched with dew, looks like white clouds. "I hear that as a threat," she tells him.

"I'm sorry. I don't mean it that way," says Joseph.

"But you always said people on earth could do more for each other than a spirit could. A spirit can't comfort you or put its arms around you late at night. A spirit can't share in your happiness or cry with you when you're sad. It can't love you so much that it makes you feel you belong somewhere. To someone."

Joseph wipes his eyes with his sleeve. "I've been here a long time and I'm not sticking around forever. Listen, kiddo. I'm getting restless. I'm a traveler at heart. Always have been."

She has never heard him talk like this before. And yet, here they are. The scene she'd run from her whole life is unraveling in front of her. She'd always imagined that something would happen to him, that his death would come suddenly, just like her parents' deaths had. A car crash. A heart attack. Brain aneurysm. She's thought of every possible catastrophe, played out every scenario. But never this one. Never that he'd be waiting for it, anticipating it, longing for it. She feels betrayed, remembering that night all those years ago when she put her cornhusk doll in the closet. How she lay there, forcing herself to withstand the ache, teaching herself how to say good-bye. She finally understands. It was for this very moment. All the distancing she had done with men was to prepare her for this. "You have to let me take you to the doctor."

"No doctors. Honey," Joseph says, taking her face in his hands. "I've lived a long full life. I'm ready. You must respect my choice."

Echo is panicking. "Pop, you saved my life. Please let me do something."

"And you saved my life. You never knew that. But you did. I

never told you. I tried to be careful not to make you responsible for me."

She wipes her eyes. "I can't just stand by and watch this happen to you. I love you more than anything."

Joseph turns to her. "You have already done everything you were supposed to do for me, a million times over. Given me purpose. Given my life direction. A reason to be. Before you came along I was lost. I'm only here because of you."

She is sobbing. She is losing him. He is saying good-bye, and talking about it as though she is supposed to just let it happen. They are talking about how he is going to abandon her, leaving her an orphan once more. "It's not okay. I don't understand. Not one part of this." She puts another pot on the stove so that he can't see her burning eyes. All is silent but for the slight buzzing of the refrigerator. She can't give up on him yet. All feeling in her body is concentrated in her heart. She shudders, bracing uncontrollable sobs. "Once I lose you, I'll be alone," she confesses. He takes her hands.

"You have Grant now," Joseph says. She knows he is trying to distract her when he tells her that Grant shouldn't be going to the Cave. That nothing good will come of that place.

"Things are so hard with him. I don't understand him. I found all these statues he'd carved, that he'd hidden in the closet. Then a bird flew right into the window. One minute it had a broken wing. I walked away and when I came back it was fine. I just wanted to leave. To get away."

"What did you see, honey?"

"Nothing. I came back and the bird flew away. Grant did something. He healed it. I don't know how." She takes his hand. "But I love him, Pop. I just don't think it can work."

Joseph turns away and walks to the screen door. Echo

watches him wait there, thinking. She pours another cup of coffee. Her hands are shaking so badly, she can hardly hold the cup.

He turns back to face her. "Let me see your eyes, honey."

She stares at him a moment, and her eyes well up again.

"There is something you need to know. In a box underneath my bed. Some money and my will. I want you to take care of the store."

No, no, I can't hear this, she thinks. "Let's get you to bed."

"No, I want to be outside. I want to see the trees," he says. "I need to tell you a story. Things I want you to tell Grant. Promise me you will do this? I'm telling you this because the two of you belong together, and I can't rest until I know that this will be as it should. I don't want you to be alone, honey. I think the story will help him."

"I promise." She follows him outside onto the porch. She picks up a wool blanket and places it over his shoulders and they sit, shoulder to shoulder on the bench, looking out at the trees shuddering with morning winds. They don't talk. She waits, and rests her head on his shoulder. They stay like that for about five minutes before Joseph tells her he is cold.

Finally Joseph clears his throat. "I hope this will make Grant see things clearly, what I'm about to tell you."

"Tell me," she whispers, afraid. "No more secrets."

"It began a long time ago. A young man came through these parts in a white VW bus. Darn bus made such a rattle, you couldn't believe it ran. This man was Seneca. Called Two Bears. Now and again, he'd come in here to buy things from me, tobacco, mostly. Only came around at night. He was only a young man of eighteen.

"He wasn't a big talker. But he wanted to help people. He was good with wood, liked to build things. But his real gift was healing. Of course he was just calling the spirits, he said. They were doing the healing. He'd cool a fever, make arthritis better, you just ask Squeaky Loomis. He's got a story for you. Soon word around town was that there was a healer living in that big old cave on Loomis Hill. But most of the people he helped were Indians. I visited him a few times, watching him grinding his leaves, smoking his pipe. I would go so far as to call him my friend. He'd come here late at night, too. One time, he let me follow him along the trails out near the hills, up near Grant's cabin. He'd leave a piece of turquoise, a shell, something as thanks wherever he took a plant." Joseph takes a sip of coffee. "Ah, my arm." Joseph winces.

She takes the cup from him so he doesn't have to hold anything.

"Just a little stiff, that's all. Anyway, his hands." Joseph holds his hand up and points across the palm. "He was a big man. Tall. So tall that it looked like the clouds rested on his shoulders. Even though he worked with fire and wood all his life, his hands were soft. Most amazing thing, no cracks in the skin, no calluses, nothing. Never lost his sensitivity, you know? Never lost a human being, either, even the stubborn ones wanting to hold on to their illness."

Echo, listening silently, takes Joseph's hand.

"One day a couple arrived with their daughter, traveled all the way from Niagara Falls to see him. The daughter wouldn't eat, was too sick. Her people said her heart was black."

Suddenly, a flurry of blackbirds erupts in the trees, creating a loud twitter. "Do you hear those birds out there?" asks Echo. "They're going crazy."

"They feel the spirits. Don't pay them attention and they'll be quiet. Anyhow, my friend wouldn't believe he could fail, that his spirits could fail. Didn't believe that sometimes you can't fight the river. That the river is bigger than you. But he took that girl into his cave. Sat with that girl for six days, lighting his fires, grinding his herbs. A few mornings I woke up early and came out here on the porch. I swear I could hear his voice through the trees, saying sacred prayers. He was tangling with the spirits in there. Squeaky Loomis and me had to pull him out of the cave, and the body of the girl. Could hardly tell which one was alive. She was gone. It was a hard lesson. Two Bears had never lost anyone before.

"He couldn't take the failure. He turned his back on the native medicine, lost faith in the spirits, in his tradition. Disappeared. People said it was because of the fight over land at Loomis Hill. But they didn't know it was because when he lost that child, he lost his faith. He moved away. Changed his name. Cut off his long hair. He tried to forget all he knew. But he didn't give up. He was determined to find another way to heal. He became a doctor of Western medicine. A great doctor in this area. He took a wife and he had a son. But he looked different. He fulfilled the prophecy of his name, Two Bears. He lived two lives. No one knew who he had been."

"I know," says Echo. She gets up and walks to the railing. She looks out at the shadows climbing from the trees. She is putting it all together. "Ben Shongo," she whispers, as all of these strange things about Grant start to make sense to her. The time that he sat with her after her bike accident and her face healed. Just last night with the bird.

"It was many years later," continues Joseph. "I wouldn't have said it was the same man. Even the look in his eyes was different. We never talked about the past. Actually, only once. He asked me never to tell Grant. I had to respect it."

Echo can't believe what Joseph is telling her. "Why wouldn't he tell his own son? If he was such a great doctor, why couldn't he help his own wife?" She is confused, agitated. She is thinking about how Grant suffered under the discipline of his father, the rejection he felt. Ben Shongo had too many secrets. She is thinking about Emily Shongo sitting on the porch smoking, imagining the loneliness that woman felt. Everything in her life added up to waiting and patience. How much did Emily know? She wonders. Maybe she was punishing him. Maybe she had given up and the illness was all she had. "Do you think Emily didn't want his help?" she says.

"Don't know for sure. I think of it like this. Illness is like a knot in a tree. How can you just go ripping out that knot? The tree could die. You take away the sickness, you have to fill the hole with something else. You see? But some people are afraid of emptiness.

She thinks about if this knowledge will change Grant. How knowing who he is will make him different. How it will affect him once he knows who his father is.

She wonders if knowing this will hurt him. If this will make him angry at his father, make things worse. Or whether it will release him from all that has kept him walled off from her.

Echo is finally getting answers to her questions about what she has seen all these years. She feels overwhelmed. Tired. Her eyes burn. She wonders how she is going to bring this up to Grant.

"Grant and the birds, Pop? Does this mean that what I thought I saw was real?"

"Honey. This is a sacred place. Certain people can do things." The birds twitter around them. She can smell lilacs in the air. She leans back against the railing. Joseph gets up, holding his arms a few inches from his sides. For a second, the blackbirds that have gathered in the nearby trees stop singing. The waves stop lapping at the shoreline and for a moment, there is quiet. "Picture it, honey," Joseph says, his head tilted back. All lit up in the lamplight, Joseph closes his eyes. "Birds are easy. They don't see illness. They don't know about limits. They assume the currents will carry them. They trust. They jump. They fly. In human terms, it's called blind faith. Blind faith makes you see the world as complete perfection. They're one of the few living creatures that can see the world in this way." She looks up at the sky, noticing the temperature change. "And that, my dear, is why they can fly."

Echo can feel the heat from the feathers, from all the blackbirds swirling around in the sky. The air takes on the smell of lilac and burning wood. A strange sensation comes over her. The warmth in the air is cradling her. And although she is facing the thing she fears most, her heartbeat has calmed. She feels at peace. She is still afraid, but her limbs are relaxed, heavy. As the sun's rays reflect off the windows and scatter across the porch, she notices Joseph's expression. He looks at peace, too. And for a moment, she could swear his feet aren't touching the ground.

A FEW MINUTES LATER, sitting on the porch bench, she tightens her arms around him to still his cough. The sun is high in the air, rising off the tips of the Diamond Trees. "Well, look at that sun," Joseph says, staring at the pink glow gliding across the tips of the trees. "You have to respect a God that can make that happen." She kisses him on the cheek. When he turns to her, she can see the haziness in his stare, the pale yellow dinge across the whites of his eyes. "Honey, I worry you give up too easily. You're afraid that there's not enough love for you. But love is the one thing we never empty out of."

"Love has never made me feel particularly good."

He chuckles. "Love isn't tested by how good it makes you feel. It's tested by whether you are brave enough to feel every part of it."

Three women: Leila. Emily. Clarisse. Their words run through her mind. "Do you have any regrets, Pop?"

"Well, one. Wish I could remember jokes," he says. She smiles and pulls him close. "Always wanted to be one of those guys who could just pull a joke from memory and make people laugh."

"Is that all?" she asks, softly.

"Maybe a few other things that I'll keep to myself, okay?"

She nods. She understands. Grateful, she finally understands.

"Now help me go in and put my feet up," he says, weakly. As he is getting up, he turns to her. "Honey, is fear holding you back, fear of having something precious taken away?"

"Like what's happening with you now?" she asks, trembling. Tears stream down her cheeks. He leans down and wipes her tears away with his hand and she closes her eyes, trying to memorize the warmth of his hand on her face.

"Don't cry, kiddo. You'll always be okay. When you get older, you'll look back and you see everything happened in the right time. You gain a faith that things are as they're supposed to be. You can't imagine how much this helps your life."

"I don't know what to do next," she tells him.

"Some foreign countries you know you have to visit, right? And some of them you're just content to look at the pictures. You find your country, honey. And then you pack up and buy a one-way ticket."

"Which is the right country?" she asks, as she starts weeping again.

"The one that feels like home. The one that always has."

These words strike right to the heart and she can't stop the tears. She grabs him and holds on to him, and she knows there's nothing she can do. "Most people deserve a second chance, even you," he whispers. Through her tears, Echo glances at the Diamond Trees a few miles away.

19

LEILA DOESN'T CARE THAT she's already called everyone she knows. She's got less self-control now. Melanie has been gone for five days.

People are compassionate, they'll do their best to listen, to offer sympathies, but they've got their own lives. After they hang up, her life will just be a story. They'll grope for the snooze button on the clock radio, or they'll make love in a state of half wake with her words drifting sadly through the air. What about her? She's left with the silence. Even imaginary discussions she has with herself about the tarnished spots that crawl across her copper pots won't distract her. For a while, she'll try and focus on the fraying edges of the yellow gingham curtains she so painstakingly put together way back when she believed that the success of her marriage depended on whether she could sew a straight seam or boil a slab of corned beef to perfection, so that the meat just fell apart when touched with a fork.

She knows just how bad it is when the old fleeting urge to see Victor sweeps over her. She runs to the sink, overwhelmed by the fact that her emotions can distort reality in such a way, making him seem sympathetic, even comforting. She refocuses on a few terrifying memories, thankfully recalling them with amazing clarity. Every night for months after Luke died, Melanie spilled her milk, and every time, Victor would become so enraged, he'd slam his fist on the table as the white rivulets spilled into the grooves of the green linoleum tiles. Melanie was determined to overcome the shame, though. Night after night, Leila would sit in angst throughout each dinner, praying for the milk to spill just so it would be over. No sooner had Victor gotten used to it than Melanie stopped spilling. Strange how things in a family were synchronized that way, a seesaw of spilled milk and fists.

When Leila splashes water on her face, the urge to see Victor subsides.

It's 6 A.M. and Lucas hasn't stopped crying in almost twenty-four hours. Even though the doctor has told Leila "teething causes fever" is a wives' tale, she's sure he's sick because his molars are breaking through a swollen gum. Leila won't resort to baby Tylenol, but she wishes she could stop the pain, especially when he just stares at her with pleading eyes, like he knows it isn't fair and it's somehow her fault. One thing is certain, though. Leila remembers how to distract a little boy. She could try to make him laugh the way she did with her own son, cradle him in her arms and rub her nose against his, or put him in a bath and show him how to splash the water so that it rains down around him. But Lucas has a certain need to assert his independence. He doesn't seem to want any of Leila's kisses right now. Just squirms to get away. She wishes she could make him understand. This is just the beginning of the things to accept because there is no other choice. Even a little tooth is part of a cycle as predictable as the onslaught of the mayflies.

The house feels distant, like an island. Leila can't just sit here, comatose, waiting for the phone to ring. Lucas's cries are the only thing keeping her going. She's got to respond to him.

Where is Lion? Were those his footsteps last night? She heard him walking around downstairs, but she'd been too tired to move, even to lift her head. He'd left dirty dishes for her to clean when she woke up, which was unlike him. He'd eaten all the leftovers from the refrigerator and left the dirty plates and silverware everywhere, caked with food. Not just the lasagna but a week-old piece of pie and a container of pork and chicken fried rice from the Aloha restaurant. Lion didn't even like that food. And now there's more than three hundred dollars missing from her money box. She had gone to the bank, just in case she had to get Melanie out of a dangerous situation. Of course, he wouldn't steal from her, would he? She'd willingly give him as much as he wanted. She can't believe he'd just go and do something like this, especially when she's entrusted him with so much already. Maybe she's not thinking clearly.

For the last few days, she has had that eerie feeling of being watched. So often now, while standing in the kitchen, goose bumps prickle up on her arms and the hair on the back of her neck stands up. Someone has tracked mud all over her kitchen floor. Sometimes she even thinks she smells whiskey, even though she doesn't keep it in the house.

A thin trickle of saliva dribbles down Lucas's chin and Leila dabs it away with a cool cloth. She catches the white flash of his toothy smile.

It's just about the most beautiful thing she has ever seen, even more enchanting than the flash of white wings near the pier, and the sound of sun-bleached clamshells that litter the trees. It's the gulls' dance, a select tribe of gulls who pick up the unbreakable shells in their beaks and carry them into their nests. When a wind brushes by, or the nest is shaken, the shells rain from the sky and fall through the leaves. Up and back, the gulls swirl after the shells, drawing eights in the air.

Unlike their cousins who fatten on French fries before flying south, these graceful dancers are so entranced by their own movements that they will never leave, toughing out the coldest winters. Leila has seen this with her own eyes. After her three nights in February with Charlie Cooke, and then not hearing from him all winter, she finally contacted him. It was May by this time. And she needed an explanation. She had sat with Charlie on the granite boulder, waiting for him to tell her there was no future for the two of them, his heavy black police umbrella held over their heads as falling shells battered the taut nylon. If Leila hadn't known the difference between hail and a shell, she might have agreed with Charlie when he said distractedly what was raining down around them.

Although she's not the sort of woman to see things this way, to demand any kind of payback, her fingers dial his number after all these years in the very sort of way that her car just naturally seems to drive itself back from O'Connell's store once a week, often leaving her wondering whether she saw anyone on the way and forgot to wave.

Didn't Charlie Cooke want her once?

He hadn't just lusted after her. He had wanted to marry her. Why did he have to talk of how they were going to leave Canandaigua and move into that old farmhouse she loved? Why had he asked her to describe in detail a house she had driven by countless times, certain that if she could just live there, her life and her children would blossom like those huge roses that clung to the fence? What about the son or daughter he'd always wanted? Candice had had an emergency hysterectomy years ago and Charlie always regretted not having the chance to be a father. Leila had been thrilled with the possibility of giving that to him. She would have had eight more children if he'd wanted.

"Sorry to bother you," Leila says when he answers.

"Morning, Leila." She presses her nail into her palm to keep the tears at bay. His tone stings. She's always believed you could tell how a man feels about a woman by the way he says her name. *Leila,* Charlie used to say with reverence. *My-wife-Candice,* he'd say stiffly, and you could hear the tightening in his throat. Never just Candice. Always *My-wife*. It had sounded sinister, even. It had never occurred to Leila that one day he'd say her own name this way, with the same sort of contained belligerence. She's reminded of those painful dialogues she'd once written out between her and Candice, just to free her thoughts. She'd never spoken them though, just waited till the urge had left. And it always had.

"We caught an archaeologist that's been selling artifacts," Charlie says.

"I don't care. What I care about is Melanie." In the middle of her own kitchen, Leila covers her mouth with her hand. A flash of heat rises up inside her, making the iron-shaped birthmark blaze.

She's thinking about fistfuls of dirt and beads, and how once, a very long time ago, her girls had emptied their pockets across her linoleum floor, their dirt-stained hands letting go of the blue, red, and white glass seed beads, and a few beads of brass. Maya and Melanie had unknowingly unearthed one of the unfound burial sites, and had presented Leila with a catlinite pendant. They knew she wouldn't keep it but they wanted the feeling of giving it to her anyway. Catlinite dust was cherished for its healing properties, but that's not why they sprinkled it over Luke's grave when Leila wasn't looking. They simply thought he'd like the colors. When Leila drove them to the police station the next day, the girls had offered the precious findings to Charlie Cooke without an argument. That was when Leila first found Charlie.

"I'm coming over," he says, and hangs up.

She tries to picture Charlie standing here, but her reflection in the mirrored toaster oven catches her off guard, the chalky skin stretched tightly over her cheekbones. Despite all the rain, everything is drying up. Her skin actually flakes when she touches it. With the phone held under her chin, she reaches for the hand cream on the windowsill. Then she pours it in a line down each arm. Sweat mixes into the lotion as she massages her elbows and wrists, then her neck. The touch of her own hand feels so soothing, it's almost painful.

Leila opens the kitchen window to let his words filter out into the air. She replaces the phone in the receiver.

Leila folds back the living-room curtain and ties it on its clip. She's got to do something. She pulls out her cleaning supplies from underneath the sink and immediately goes to work on the windows. She welcomes the ache in her body, the small fist of her lower back relaxing as she pulls a sheet of newspaper in long strokes over the panes so that fibers aren't left on the glass.

Company always makes her feel better. How she longs to have a normal conversation.

Leila runs upstairs to slip on her favorite purple-flowered dress. How desperate she feels, having just agreed to let Charlie Cooke come over. When Leila comes back downstairs, all dressed and ready, Lucas is finally asleep. Leila cleans up the mess of crumbs underneath his high chair and turns on the stove. She takes out some bacon and sets the pan on the burner. Then she snips off the ends of each strip so the bacon won't curl up. She's always believed that the smell of bacon cooking is the quickest way to bring warmth into a home, and she needs that feeling now, to show Charlie what he has missed.

"That thing still alive?" Detective Charlie Cooke asks Leila as he bends down to stroke the tuft of gray fur on Old Sally's neck, the only place where the fur is still thick. He has not seen the dog since he stayed with Leila six years ago during a temporary split from Candice over that terrible February winter. Though he is far from those days now, often he wonders what would have happened if the snow had never melted or if Candice hadn't asked him to come back.

Judging by Old Sally's appearance, it may as well have been decades ago. But Leila looks the same. For a moment Charlie lets himself admire her soft blue eyes and strong arms wiping invisible crumbs from the counter. He has never forgiven himself for hurting her. Maybe he even loved her. But a few days were hardly enough time to replace a twenty-year marriage. He couldn't have known things with Candice would only get worse, or that he would be forever confounded by his own refusal to leave her. He'll always think of Leila as his other life, though. And he'll live it alongside his own. He'll spend his days fantasizing about blinding snowfalls, and walking the halls of a house that he's only ever heard about from Leila. He'll picture himself bringing her French toast in bed, or pruning roses that hold the fragrance of wine in their petals. The guilt he feels is nothing compared to the regret. And no matter how much he tries to drown himself in his work, he carries with him the feeling of owing someone a favor.

He had heard about Leila's previous call to the police station. Charlie has some new ideas, and that's why he has stopped by on his off hours when he knows damn well that Melanie will most likely show up in a few days, just as apologetic as always, and bound for the nearest N.A. meeting.

He clears his throat. "That lilac bush is pretty unbelievable."

"It thrives on neglect," Leila says, glaring at him. "Some things actually do. Unfortunately, people don't."

Charlie tries not to let her see his face redden. He opens his notepad. "So, let's talk about this. I've already been by Joseph's. I thought she'd have been home by now, but—"

"Shh, I just put Lucas down," says Leila, closing the living-room doors. She pours him a cup of tea and sets it on the table. "Please sit."

"Look, I don't have much time." He's eyeing the plate of bacon, but he can't get his mind focused.

"My daughter has been missing for five days!" she cries.

He picks up his cup and puts it back down. "That's why I'm here. Just calm down."

She takes a deep breath. "Let me heat that up for you," she says, reaching for the plate.

"Relax, Lei. Cold is fine."

"It will just take me a second to heat."

He holds his hand up. "No, Lei. Cold is good."

He is noticing the deep neckline of her dress, lower than she would normally wear, at least that he can remember. He glances at the small strawberry mark shaped like a hot iron. He knows it becomes inflamed when she's upset, and that's why he'll keep his eyes off it.

"I can tell you that pills are out of the question," she says.

"Let's look at this logically. How many times she run, I mean total?" He picks up a strip of bacon and takes a bite.

"A baby changes a woman, Charlie. I know my daughter."

"Some women, maybe—"

"Please, Charlie, be nice."

"Look, this isn't personal. I happen to know it was eight times. Eight, Lei. She came back home on her own each and every time, that right? She's an addict. I say that without blame."

Leila pushes the hair from her eyes. "This is hard to believe, I know," she says, her voice hoarse. "But Melanie is a wonderful mother to this little boy—"

"Please," he says, holding up his hand.

As far as Charlie is concerned, maternal instinct doesn't count for much. All addicts are remarkably the same. In thirty years, Charlie has buried his share of them. He knows their patterns, their excuses and their tricks, and how they can momentarily become addicted to other things before returning to their drug of choice. Perhaps motherhood is Melanie's addiction right now. He also knows that the unbridled moods of teenage girls can make even the May weather seem predictable. He has seen Melanie's firsthand. They rode together atop the Harvest Parade float when she was fourteen. Melanie was waving to the crowd, seated right next to him without so much as looking at him. She moved so far away from him that he worried she'd fall off the edge of the seat. He thought he'd glimpsed her cheeks reddening, but he wasn't sure if it was just the wind, or a particular feeling of hatred toward him. At the end of the ride, for no apparent reason, Melanie suddenly put her head on his shoulder. The gesture was so spontaneous and full of trust that he forgot to breathe. He felt his shoulder relax and for a moment he closed his eyes, letting himself fill up with feeling that somehow all his wrong choices had been made right.

Suddenly, she pushed him away.

"What's wrong?" he asked, his voice tight as she glared at him.

"I'll never forgive you for what you did to my mother, you old shit. How do you like someone screwing with your head?" Then she jumped off the float and disappeared into the crowd.

* * *

"I KNOW SHE'S A good girl. But good girls have bad times," Charlie says.

"I know that. Don't think I don't know that." He doesn't know Leila has turned toward the window because she won't cry in front of him twice in one lifetime. She touches her neck, forcing herself to wait until the flash of heat passes. But when Charlie reaches for her, Leila suddenly clasps her hands together to keep the wall in her heart from breaking apart.

Charlie checks his watch, but his mind doesn't register the time. "I'll give you this, no one at the station has seen her for over a year, but, Lei . . ."

Leila straightens the pale curtains. "Did you know my girls used to visit your mother at the rest home? Do you know we were there every other Sunday? Where were you?"

"I wasn't a lot of places that I should have been." He glances at her and looks away.

"I suppose. Well, just about everyone said it was like Christmas when the girls walked in. Maya would tap dance for them. Isn't that something? Your mother used to call here just to make sure I'd be bringing the girls with me. Sometimes she'd call twice, three times in one day."

"I never knew. Why didn't you call me? I could have stopped her—"

"I left you messages. You never called back. I had my pride, Charlie."

He looks at her, brushes his hair back with his palm. He is starting to sweat, to feel strapped in, weighted. "Well, I'm sorry, Lei."

"Your mom loved to have Melanie draw her picture. Your mother always said she wanted a simple mouth, no teeth, just as she was. Melanie'd tell her, you don't have to smile if you don't feel like it. And your mother seemed so relieved, Charlie. Such a look of relief came over her. Isn't that something?"

"Why did you do this for my mother after what I did to you?"

Leila holds his gaze, and raises her voice. "The girls thought you were coming back. We waited for you!" she cries.

She touches her wet face with the tips of her fingers. The tears are like shards of glass like those crystal prisms Melanie bought for her once at the mall, and later hung in Leila's bedroom window to catch the sun.

He nods, but doesn't say anything. Leila doesn't know how many times he had answered Melanie's frantic calls when she had hit rock bottom. Leila would think he was doing it out of guilt. But she'd only be half right. He had tried to put the Ellis family out of his mind, but he had never felt such a sense of pride and fulfillment, sitting at their dinner table all those years ago, imagining this was his family.

That's why, a few months after the Harvest Parade, he had gone to pick Melanie up himself when the call came in about a dazed girl with long blond hair sitting by the side of Highway 90, yelling into the darkness. It was four in the morning. Her no-goodnik ex-boyfriend had pushed her out of his truck—what did the boys at the station used to call him, the "schmuck with the truck"? Instead of taking Melanie into the station, Charlie handed her a blanket from the backseat, and drove her to Denny's. She was so thin and pale. She'd slid down in the seat, wanting to hide so that people wouldn't see her, as if the whole town hadn't heard her yelling at heaven. Charlie could see she was coming down from a high. There was no paranoia or hallucinations, but maybe marijuana, he thought, by the way she ate two helpings of eggs Benedict and a plate of stale rolls. He never brought up what she had said to him at the parade.

They talked about his police work, about her love of anything purple—grapes, lilacs, beautiful amethysts that were her birthstone and were said to help a person be brave.

He finishes the last piece of bacon. "How's Maya getting along?"

"Much better," Leila says, uttering the standard response. She catches Charlie checking his watch again.

"I've got some things to do. I'm on a short leash these days."

Leila looks at the empty plate. She pulls her hair loosely through her fingers. She watches him get up. Leila can feel the ember glowing on her chest. "It was a really good year," she whispers.

"There'll be more to come, Lei. You deserve it. Say, you hear anything from that old boyfriend of Melanie's?"

"Thank God he moved to Ohio. I think he called her a few years ago from jail. I believe that's what she told me, but I couldn't say for sure."

"I'll check on him. What about Lion?"

"What about Lion?" Leila puts the apron down and runs her fingers under the faucet. She keeps her back to him, splashing hot water over the frying pan, the coppery oil running lattice-like across the black surface. With a palm full of soap, she makes it disappear. Charlie is patiently waiting so he can say good-bye without feeling guilty. Leila rinses the pan slowly, turns off the water, and dries her hands. He feels strange, knowing her kitchen, where she keeps the cups and plates, and the drawer that holds all the broken china tea cups that she can't quite bring herself to throw away.

"I should probably talk to Lion, too," he says.

"I think he's probably gone looking for her."

"I wouldn't advise that. Not that he'd listen anyway." He closes his steno notepad and slips it into his pocket. "Like I said, she'll probably show up. A missing person's report should get things moving. You call me again if you want to. But I've got a feeling you should just sit tight. The best thing I'll say is that people have habits. I'd wager she'll be back on her own." Charlie is fighting with himself over not being truthful with her. Maybe the schmuck with the truck has shown up. Charlie sees a whole line of trucks in Melanie's future. He knows about the Florence Nightingale syndrome, an affliction in which young girls are so compelled by their new maternal instincts that they'll cling to the first loser who walks through the door with a danger sign on his forehead. Charlie calls this a train wreck waiting to happen. No matter how smart these girls are, they'll believe the rescue a worthy cause, even if it means losing themselves.

The fact he's an expert on the habits of girls is the irony of the century, since, at times, he's been both the schmuck and the knight in shining armor. It gives him an odd perspective, one that, he tells himself, only helps him do his job better. He can get right into the minds of both boys and girls. If Charlie had had a daughter, he'd have started early talking to her about it. Maybe he'd drive her by a wreck. Though some folks might find it harsh, he believes it would teach her in an instant what it took some a lifetime to experience.

The saving grace is that some girls learn. They'll grow wise to their own hearts' meanderings. They'll spot a train wreck miles away and they'll run in the opposite direction. They'll find good men to marry and go on to live good lives. But others will spend their lives compelled by the rescue. These women will become the forever disappointed, so much that sometimes it will hurt to look them in the eye. As he does to Leila, now.

As Charlie turns to leave, he reaches out and takes Leila's hand. "Lei, I never meant to lead you on."

She pulls her hand away. "Just go," Leila tells him, her eyes welling up.

"Those three days that we had," says Charlie. "They were the best of my life."

"I said, get out," Leila tells him. But she doesn't turn away when Charlie leans in and kisses her lightly on the lips. "Please," Leila whispers, rubbing her hand over her lips. "Don't do this to me."

"You know, I still think about you," he says, before he walks out the front door. Leila closes the door, leaving Charlie on the front stoop. He gets in his car and drives away, the sound of Melanie's son's crying echoing in the distance as he spots the last of the white stones still littering some of the lawns. Most people have them bagged in their trash by now. A few have used them to adorn their gardens. Some folks have taken them back to the water. When Charlie is halfway back to the police station, he realizes he has left his gun on Leila's kitchen table.

VICTOR ELLIS IS HIDING in Leila's kitchen pantry, the dog bites on his thigh and shoulder bleeding through the bandages. He has been listening to the sound of a baby crying, a baby that he has just discovered is his grandson, a cry now burned into his memory. And he has been listening to Leila's conversation with Charlie Cooke, which has filled Victor with hate. So Charlie Cooke had been the one to fool around with Leila, the goddamn secret that they all kept from him. Victor had screwed up his family to begin with, but this bastard had contributed to it, too. Now Victor will not let anything get in his way again. He has been away too long. This is *his* family. *His* time. *His* need for truth. *His* redemption.

He will make it right with Leila. He will make it right with Melanie and Maya and they will all be a family again as they were meant to be. He hears Leila's footsteps on the stairs and then the baby stops crying. Then the sound of rushing water in the shower. Victor sits down at the kitchen table as he has done for the last two nights, reclaiming his place as the king of his home. Last night he ate some leftover Chinese egg rolls for dinner, took some money from Leila and left to bring Melanie food, which she hardly ate. Old Sally stayed far away from him the whole time and that was all right. He never liked that dog anyway.

Right now, as he sits at the head of the table, he is going over and over that last fight with Leila on the night that the boy died. But it wasn't the burnt bread that had made him angry, that had driven him to drink a full bottle of whiskey. It was Luke. His presence, a reminder of Leila's infidelity, of everything Victor was not and would never be. He was never even close to approaching what that child possessed, that element of lightness. No, Victor was always chained by something. He had thought for years that it was Leila. But it wasn't Leila, and it wasn't the whiskey, and it wasn't the girls, and maybe it wasn't even Luke. It was something else, something deep inside him, made him more animal than human, a person operating on an instinct so strong, it left him with no free will. Remember why the dog was chained up, he thinks, rubbing his bandages.

He gets up and walks through the house, touching everything in Leila's glass cabinet. Once it was his gun cabinet, but not anymore. Now, it is a shrine to Luke. It holds antique frames with pictures of the girls and Luke, a silver baby spoon with Luke's name engraved on it, a yellow paper airplane, a purple scarf, a book about flying, and a glass bowl full of Luke's coveted dimes. When Victor was a child, after his father left for work he used to walk through the house and touch everything in the gun cabinet. He would pick up the guns and look at them, and rub their barrels with his thumb, as though waiting to be transformed. Once Victor began shooting birds for sport, he began to smell just like his father. The scent still follows Victor back from the fields, clings to his skin and his clothing for days. He can smell it now, filling Leila's house, a house that was once his. He wonders if Old Sally can smell it, too, and if that is why she is whining at the door, trying to get out.

There, in the kitchen, he finishes the bottle of whiskey from his pocket and is about to leave to find Maya. His car is hidden under one of the huge willows on a side road. That is when he notices Charlie's gun case on the table. A 40-caliber pistol: shiny, black, and small. Victor picks it up. Seconds later, he hears the front door open and Charlie is calling Leila's name, walking toward the kitchen. Suddenly, Charlie is standing right in front of Victor, open-mouthed. Charlie lunges for his gun.

Instinct is a thing to be feared. Victor, in some part of his mind, knows he is not like other people, that he possesses an absence of free will. Victor hadn't planned to do what he does next. He has only shot to kill once before. But the way Charlie Cooke is looking at him, with that disgusted strangling stare. The old skunk took Leila away from him. It is animal instinct. Victor protecting his territory.

Victor lifts the gun and points it at Charlie. He pulls the trigger and shoots Charlie right between the eyes. Blood splatters across Victor's shirt, across the tile floor, and the organza curtains. The smell of gunpowder fills the air. The black fur on Old Sally's back is now drenched in red.

Charlie, still standing, stares at him for a moment, a look of understanding crosses his face as blood runs from his ears and down his neck.

Charlie falls back, a dimpled hole between his eyes. His arms flail and he staggers back, once, twice. His legs collapse. Then there is only the soft thud of Charlie's body spilling onto the floor, his mouth still slightly open. Victor watches Charlie's right hand open and close. Charlie's legs are moving back and forth as though he were still trying to run, smearing blood in a fan across the tile.

For a second, Victor stands there, paralyzed by the image. In his mind, he is remembering a pregnant doe he shot eighteen years ago, who took a bullet in the back of the neck, right between the shoulders, but kept running, splattering the air with blood. She had run almost fifty feet with her left side completely lame before she fell on the ice. It is all still fresh in his mind. Victor had stood there, shaking, as the doe lunged for him a final time, pushed the air from her lungs, flopping like a clown. From then on, Victor no longer wanted the hunt to end in death. He wanted only a regeneration of life. To make a creature's spirit rise up from its wounds, just as his own spirit had to so many times.

The day he killed the doe was the same day Leila had gone into labor with a premature Luke, who was not supposed to be born for another two months. It wasn't until six months later that Victor noticed the small birthmark between the baby's shoulder blades in the exact spot where the doe had been shot. That is when he knew the child would be his downfall.

Victor, dazed, steps over Charlie's body.

He makes himself leave the house now. He slips out the door, through the overwhelming scent of lilacs, and into Charlie Cooke's car, which is still running, the keys still in the ignition. He must get back to Melanie. She will be hungry. Although he has always feared moving water, Victor will make himself stay with her on the island for yet another night. When it gets dark he will walk to the shore of Squaw Island and stare out at the rippling waves in sheer defiance, trying to absorb the independence of moving water, just the way he had stood on the shoreline of the Shongos' property twelve years ago, watching his three children sail off in a small boat, when only two of them would return.

20

GRANT DRIVES LEILA'S CAR back from Two Bears' Cave alone.

Grant finally falls asleep around dawn. He is dreaming that he and Luke are floating over the treetops and into the whirling winds, following a trail of white stones to a place shrouded in sooty darkness where he can hear the lapping waves. Below, he sees Melanie lying on a pile of hot coals. A flurry of little blue lights hovers above her chest. Grant wakes up sweating.

There's knocking on the window. Someone is calling his name.

He stumbles out of bed, thinking it is Echo. He blinks hard before his mind registers the face. "What are you doing here?"

"Hi. I'm sorry. I need to talk to you. I know it's early," Susanna says. Her smile is sobering. "Can I come inside?"

Susanna's ivory skin is as plain as her eyes are wild, dark. Her hair is cut to the chin, with chopped bangs that stop above her eyebrows. She's wearing an orange silk blouse with black pants and black heels. Slung over one shoulder is a black suede jacket. A purse that has Gucci all over it has replaced her worn blue knapsack. She's probably lost those few extra pounds she was always struggling with. He can't even believe she's standing here.

Grant still has dirt on his face. He glances at the lake. The water is calm, smooth as slate and just as cool. "Jesus. No," he manages to say from behind the screen. "I'll come out."

He has rehearsed a million things to say to Susanna, all with varying degrees of anger, sadness, insult, but now as he looks at her, he's filled with distant fascination. She's like a foreign country he visited a long time ago, once overwhelmed by the mystique. But now, something is missing.

"Okay, well. Have it your way," she says. He catches a glimpse of the black Lexus through the screen.

"I tried to call, but obviously, you have no cell phone and I'm not sure what the deal is with this place." She explains how she tried to find his phone number. It was listed but the phone wasn't working. She tries to make a joke, to laugh it off, but he can't feel an ounce of humor in the air. She has picked up on his feeling, eyeing him distantly as she takes some papers out of a bag.

"I've started doing photography again," she tells him. "You always encouraged me in that way. I've taken a few really beautiful pictures. And I'm working at a gallery. Selling my work and other people's," she says, embarrassed. "But they give me studio space. Can we please sit?" She waves her arms at the wicker chairs, and smiles weakly.

He tries to find some compassion or connection in it all. But he is so exhausted and generally agitated that all he can give her is a nod. As he's opening the door, he's wishing it were Echo standing here. Einstein scoots by him, brazen.

"That is one huge dog."

"What time is it?" asks Grant, pulling his chair out.

"I don't know. Do you have somewhere to be?" Susanna pulls the wicker chair far away from the wall, and neatly smoothes her pants before sitting down. "Well, how are you?"

"Fantastic," Grant says, falling into the other chair.

"Good. Well, you look like a little kid, like you've been at camp or something," she says, folding her hands on the small table between them. "I mean, that's a good thing, you've got some color in your face," she continues. "But all those mosquito bites."

"What?"

"On your arms."

This is all so civilized it makes him want to yell.

Einstein gets up from his place on the grass and stretches his hind legs.

Susanna eyes Einstein nervously. The wolf trots across the porch and flops down across the top step as though to prevent anyone from leaving. Grant gives him the nod, and Einstein licks his front paws and moves over. "I have been wondering how you are." Susanna clears her throat, rubbing her chest with her palm. Then she sits up. "Do you have some tea? Anything to drink? Oh never mind," she says, becoming impatient with his distance. "Your hair's quite long. I always liked it out of the braid."

"Susanna," Grant says. "What are you doing here?"

"Well, as luck would have it, we have an offer on our house."

"I didn't know we—"

"I had to make arrangements, Grant. Things happened quickly. You didn't expect me to just let the place sit there and rot. After all the work you, we, put into it, it's worth a good deal of money. I know that was never important to you, but it was my mother's house and she's not well, and—"

"Love the Lexus," he says.

"Thanks," she whispers.

"Let me see the papers." He pushes his hair back behind his ears.

"Oh, that sun," Susanna says, standing up. She walks across the porch. He listens to her heels clicking across the wood. "I've been picturing this view for a long time. God, it feels good to be back here. The herons. Look at them. Look!" she says, stretching out her arms.

For a moment, Grant can remember what had attracted him most, that sense of little girl excitement. He allows himself to appreciate the quality without having it move him. He leans back, satisfied. Progress.

"There's three of them. God, I'd love to photograph them again," says Susanna.

He glances over the sale papers. "Can you leave these with me? I want to look them over and I'm exhausted. Seeing double, practically. I'll mail them back to you or I can drop them off somewhere. Whatever you want."

"Well, I was hoping, it's just, I really need them now," she tells him, putting on her coat. A warm wind has begun to blow off the water but it hardly touches her hair. She sits back a moment, gazing at what looks to be a huge beaver looping in and out of the water.

"What difference is a few days going to make?" he asks, rubbing his eyes.

Einstein whimpers and runs down to the dock, barking at the water. Grant whistles and he comes bounding across the porch. Grant runs his hands across the animal's fur. Einstein begins to relax, settles down, laying his chin over Grant's bare foot.

"The market's tight and the buyer's a little anxious," Susanna continues. "These things are very time sensitive." She rummages through her purse, and pulls out a small mirror. As though Grant weren't a stranger now, she fixes her lipstick. She looks up at him.

A gust of wind blows a piece of paper from the stack. Grant chases it down the stairs, grabs it. Thoughts of Echo are pulling at the edges of his mind. He rifles through the papers. "No Realtor? How's that work? How are you doing this from Syracuse?"

"Well," Susanna hesitates. "I'm not exactly living with my mother. I'm sort of, you know, back and forth." She slips a gold beaded bracelet off her wrist, and then back on. He notices her bright red nails. She'd never been the type for nail polish. And a few other things have changed, now that he's really noticing. She's wearing a pearl choker he doesn't recognize and her lips are lined with a dark red liner. She hadn't been one for lipstick, either. Said it ruined too much of her clothing. He once knew the most intimate details about her.

Grant reads the name out loud. "Buyer, Dr. Owen Bergen. Why's that name familiar to me?"

Susanna smiles nervously, clears her throat. "You met him. He was one of our fertility specialists. He had the alternative medicine practice. You remember, don't you? In that old mill they made into an office building?"

"Yeah, he wanted you to eat bee's wax."

"Bee pollen." She tightens the belt of her jacket.

"What's going on?" Grant asks.

"Nothing, Grant, why?"

"Susanna, don't treat me like a fool," he says.

"Look, if you can't do this now, then I'll come back. It's fine;

I can wait a few more days. I don't mind coming back. I always liked the drive." She reaches for the papers. He puts his hand on hers.

Grant stares at the large diamond ring that sits where her wedding ring had been only months before. "I didn't want to tell you this now." She looks at the papers when she says this, as though she were reading words from a script. The words fall off her lips but register no emotion as she explains how she and the good doctor met accidentally in the post office six months ago.

"And, you're marrying him."

She moves her purse from one side of her chair to the other. "It's not what you think. It's been over a year since you and I split. The divorce is almost final. . . . I—I know how this must look, but really. What we had, Grant. We could both do better, you know?"

"Jesus, what the hell did you marry me for?"

Susanna takes a packet of Kleenex from her purse. She dabs at her mascara. "I felt a need, I suppose, to try. I loved you. Even though I knew you didn't love me. I know you don't want to hear this. I'm no cakewalk, I know that. But I'm sorry for us both. For the whole thing."

"For the whole thing, you talk about it like it was a bad meal in a restaurant. Four years of my goddamn life."

"I knew you'd react this way. . . . I have no right to ask for anything. Look, I could have done things better. But I refuse to curl up and die, Grant. I want to have my life; I want to have a baby. Anything I could have done better, I would have done. I only regret the end. Just the end." Tears slip from her eyes, which she catches carefully in a tissue held under her chin. "I never had your heart, did I? You were never mine." Grant thinks he sees the feeling in her eyes. He recalls the miscarriages, the images of his children leaving this world. Perhaps he did not love her enough.

"Keep all of it. Everything. Where do I sign?" he asks.

"You'll find someone better," she whispers. "You're easy to love, Grant. But you're a difficult person to be in love with."

Rifling through the papers, he looks up.

Echo has ridden her old bike all the way to Bare Hill, pedaling furiously, determined to tell Grant who he is and how she feels. She needs him to come to the store with her and talk to Joseph. When she reaches the edge of his property, she sees a woman sitting on the porch across from Grant, her long legs neatly crossed, her dark bob haircut perfectly manicured.

Grant is holding her hand.

The sight knocks the wind out of Echo. A small cry escapes from her lips. At that moment, Grant sees her. She quickly turns around and speeds off, even though she can hardly see through her tearing eyes, telling herself she is too late, and that Grant Shongo is not running after her.

21

MAYA ELLIS HAS SPENT the last several years living in a place other than her mother's house. This wasn't at all what she had imagined for her life when she was just a little girl of eight, arms outstretched, jumping across from her own bed to her sister's, soaring back and forth across as though she could fly. She had once imagined that she and Melanie were princesses and that Luke was a prince. Luke. Three children had been a triangle, holding each other together. Now when she remembers him, her mind shuts down. *Don't think about the past. You know what can happen when you think about it.* As long as Maya is alone, she can control what she thinks about, what she hears and what she sees. White cement walls. A wooden bed, not much bigger than the one she had as a child. A small bureau on which to keep her tiara, which she stares at for hours. The only future she thinks about is tomorrow, what she will have to eat, and what scheduled activities she is going to do. There is a wonderful predictability in this. Each morning she has group therapy, where she says only enough to pacify the therapist, phrases like *facing my fears* and *trust in myself.* Tuesday and Thursday nights there are movies in the main hall. A dancer from a local college comes every Wednesday to teach ballet. Art therapy is offered each morning to those who can be trusted with paint. She knows she is lucky that Dr. Shongo pulled some strings to get her into Cheever, whether her mother appreciated it or not. She knows the ins and outs of this place, how to get what she wants from Sebastian the orderly, who sneaks her sticks of gum and brings her perfume on occasion. Most of the time she eats only morsels of food at mealtimes, only enough to satisfy the counselors in the small dining hall. She likes how not eating numbs her mind. She doesn't like to feel anymore. Everyone knows what happens when she has to feel. Her body and mind simply cannot handle it. Something happens that is very bad. *Post-traumatic catatonia.* The rigid stance that overtakes her limbs. The trance-like state that captures her mind. It's her mind protecting her, the doctors have explained. Still, she doesn't like it. She's safer like this, in control, aware but numb enough. Terrible things happen when she has to feel.

She is so thin that her bones actually hurt when she is in her chair, sitting like this in her room. Sometimes she imagines the chair is an old canoe. Sometimes she dreams of sitting in that canoe, and everyone wonders why she is rocking herself back and forth like the waves. She could spend hours staring at the same spot on the wall. Sometimes when she wants something, she lets the orderly kiss her and she imagines her mouth is metal. She imagines her lips are steel and her tongue is silver so she feels nothing. She can exist this way, without a desire to leave much of the time.

"Maya, you have a visitor."

She grabs her robe and slippers. She is walking down the hall to the visitation room, expecting to see Melanie or her mother. As soon as she turns the corner, she sees him sitting there. Her stomach lurches. The tips of her fingers begin to tingle. It is happening again. The blackness siphoning her mind. *No,* she thinks. *Feel the floor under your feet. Notice the temperature in the hallway. Look at the color in his eyes. Stay in control of your thoughts.* Somehow she gets from here to there, to the table by the window where he is sitting. She has not seen her father in all these years. He has that same smell, the scent of dried blood, which she thinks of whenever she sees birds. He still has greasy hair, but now it has turned from black to gray, and a stubbly gray beard. His blue eyes are bloodshot, and the creases in his face make him look like he has been sleeping for days. His black jacket is rumpled, as though he has slept in it. She listens to him speaking, aware that the muscles in her legs are tightening, of the rigidity that is crawling up her legs, inch by inch. Her heart skips a beat as she grips the edge of the table, listening, wondering if she'll be able to stand up or to run.

He wants to take her to a place where Melanie is so they can all be together. "Don't you want to come with me?" he asks, sitting there. She can hear him tapping his black boot against the leg of the table. She is trembling. The feeling is overwhelming. In her silent terror, she has pissed herself; she is certain of it, can feel the urine running down her leg. The sight of her father is bringing it all back. He smells like death. His eyes are shadows. She is afraid. She knows this is bad. The orderlies notice the puddle on the floor beneath her and take her back to her room. As she stands in her shower, steam rising off of her clothing and burning her skin, she thinks of her sister. Her father. Danger. That much of the past she remembers. She needs to find her mother. She knows she has no choice but to leave.

When she pays Sebastian in silver kisses to let her out of Cheever for a few hours, to sneak her out the back kitchen door and cover for her by saying she is in her room sleeping off a cold, she tries not to think of the future, of how the catatonia could grab her halfway there. She could become like a statue in the middle of a forest and die before they even notice her missing. Still, she must go to the only person who has ever made her safe. To her mother.

Outside. Rain. She has feared the outside world for so long. But she must find her mother. Maya is running through the forest, raindrops that feel like a million needles striking her face, remembering what happened all those years ago, her father screaming at her mother about burnt bread, Luke and Melanie running out that night after the dog, running through the woods, running away from him. As she tears through the trees, the brambles catching in her hair and ripping her dress, she feels Luke behind her, running, too. She can hear his footsteps catching up with her, faster and faster, his feet slapping terror back into the earth. Her fear fills the sky like huge gray wings pushing down on her body, sparking everywhere as she looks to the right, then the left. The wind is spinning in the waves, just as it did on the last night she lost Luke. As she runs right into the sky, she believes she is getting closer, her skin wet with sparks that have begun to buzz around her. All she can do is run, run, run, until blood feels like it is coming out of her ears. She can hear the birds' wings flapping like words spoken too fast. Everywhere she goes there is blood rushing inside her arms and into her fingers, there are so many smells, everyone makes too many words, and she sees too many lights and now, her father's smell is everywhere. And then, she thinks of her father's orange hunting hat, hidden away in a box in her closet.

At that moment, the sky floor opens up above her, and the muscles in her legs seize up, and when she trips and falls, her knees crush like ice cubes under her father's fists. When she gets up she sees white-tailed deer everywhere darting into the tall trees, leaving trails of falling stars. She forces her legs to recover and follows the deer, running faster than the rain chasing her. And everything is moving in the panic. Where is her house? If she cried, no one could hear her. The quiet is spilling out of her ears, and here, no one will find her. She had promised not to tell anyone when Victor hit Luke. She should have told. Why hadn't she known it would all turn out bad? Her feet are like rocks. She tries to imagine herself a deer, running with such fluidity of movement. If she can just reach her house. If she can just run faster. If she can just find her mother before her mind goes into a trance and her body freezes.

Maya is out of breath. She reaches the door to her house, which is walled off by the lilac tree. Her eyes follow its path, cascading over the rooftop, falling to the ground and lying in front of the door as though warding her away. Maya steps over it, rushes into the house without knocking. Her mother's car is in the driveway.

There in the kitchen, she sucks in her breath. Charlie Cooke is lying in a puddle of blood. Blood is spattered everywhere. Old Sally is covered with it. The dog runs over to Maya, her tail wagging, leaving smeared blood across Maya's bare legs. Maya watches the blood around Charlie's body dripping down the slope of the kitchen floor. Maya stands there, steeped in it. She looks down, realizing that the soles of her sneakers are bloody. It is happening all over again. Death. Sadness. Despair. Her body is gripped by it. The smell of blood is her father's scent. Memories of the past flood her mind. Stunned, she walks out into the backyard and sits down next to Luke's tombstone, the leaves and fallen lilac petals surrounding it. With her eyes, she traces Luke's name. It has been years since she has been this close to him, close enough to touch him. She hardly feels her limbs as she becomes engulfed in terror turned inward. She can scarcely breathe as her body rapidly turns cold and her limbs seize up. She is now a statue. A glassy haze covers her eyes; she is blind. Her thoughts have disappeared.

When she hears the scream coming from inside, somehow her mind and memory ignite. The sound of her mother's scream echoes through the clouds, just as it did when Leila was told of Luke's death. Maya knows that her mother has found Charlie's body.

Leila rushes outside, throwing up in the bushes. When she gets up, she grabs the phone from the hallway and calls 911. Then she notices Maya sitting by the tombstone. Leila opens her arms, a sign that Maya is really here. Maya wants her mother but she is encased in steel. She can't move. She remembers the psychologist's words: *Focus inward. Find the* me *inside yourself. Hold on to it. Don't let it go.* Maya is struggling, forcing her mind to hold on to the part of her that is the *me,* to climb up and out of the abyss, but the *me* darts in and out, disappears like a small animal. And then she is breaking into bits of light, slipping down into the immeasurable darkness. The *me* resurfaces and disappears, resurfaces and disappears. *Watch yourself on a movie screen. Describe what you see: You are a girl sitting by a grave. There is soft grass beneath you. A white stone under your fingers. There is wind on your face. Don't try to stop the movie or worry about what happens. If you can describe it, you get distance and can separate from it.* She tries harder than she has ever tried in her life, feeling her will returning. She is breaking through steel. Slowly, she feels the *me* and holds on to it until it is separate from the statue that is her body. Her mind-space and the dimension of time re-emerge. She holds on and directs her thoughts. *Smell the lilacs. There are blackbirds chirping above in the branches. See the woman staring at you. She is your mother. Her eyes are blue. The sky is blue.* The ego and its boundaries reappear. She feels a bathing glow surrounding her, tingling in her limbs. She experiences her body as warm and alive again. She is back.

Maya meets Leila's gaze. They stare at each other for a moment and then the girl trapped inside the metal statue breaks free. Maya rushes into her mother's arms.

22

NO ONE IS AT Grant Shongo's cabin when Echo returns there. There is only the scent of perfume lingering in the air. Echo's fingers brush the arm of the wicker chair on the porch, stopping where Susanna's fingers rested. Echo had ridden home through the fields to check on Joseph. When she arrived and broke down, she had surprised herself. She had Clarisse's words in her mind, couldn't push them out no matter what else she tried to focus on. Words about regret. She thought of Joseph and his story about Two Bears. After making sure Joseph was okay, asleep, Echo had headed back to Grant's. For the first time in her life, she had gone back to what she feared, back into something that made her feel vulnerable and afraid. She had forced herself, spurred on by the voices of those who had never given themselves a chance, those who had made bad choices. Or no choices at all.

Now she takes a seat in the wicker chair. As though asserting her very right to the air, Echo inhales deeply. If nothing else, she will tell Grant about his father, convince Joseph to come with her, and then drive back to Boston. Her eyes are tired. Even the trees look exhausted, their branches falling toward the ground. Echo falls asleep. Her sleep is full of thoughts of a woman with hair so shiny it looks like glass.

She awakens to the chug of Grant's muffler. The old Fleetwood pulls up and he gets out, haggard. His hair is tousled, his beige sweater torn across the shoulder. His jeans are caked with mud.

"Jesus Christ, I've been looking everywhere for you," he says, dragging his feet up the steps. What are you doing out here? It's cold."

"Hunting wabbits," Echo says, pulling her coat tightly around her.

He smiles weakly and sits down in the chair next to her. "I'm glad you're okay."

She thinks of Joseph. "I'm pretty far from okay," she says.

But so is Grant. She notices he has a hollowed-out look, his cheeks, moist, cavernous, his chest sunken beneath his fisherman's sweater. He leans over and kisses her on the top of her head. "I know why you ran. It wasn't what you thought." He tells her he'd gone looking for her. That he'd chased Echo through the fields but he couldn't catch up with her. "I stopped by the Feed and Grain but no one answered the door. I figured you were all asleep. But here you are."

Echo gets up. "Did you ask Susanna to stay?"

He reaches out to take her hand. "Are you serious? Christ, you're freezing." He blows on her fingers, rubbing them in his hands.

Echo gently pulls away from him. He sits back, surprised.

"She was on her way to Rochester," he says, taking a stick of basswood from under the table. He positions it between his knees, and grabs a knife from a box under the table. "She sold the house. Needed my John Hancock. That's all it was. I just signed away my old life."

Echo sighs, looks out at the trees. "I hate caring so much for you."

He is not at all the person he thinks he is. He is so much more. She knows she must tell him now, before they say anything else. But looking at him, she feels terrible. He hasn't slept in more than twenty-four hours. She should leave him alone. She's not sure he can handle what she has to tell him.

He begins to slick the blade over the stick in careful strokes. A spiral of shavings crawls up from the end of the stick. "Apparently I'm a difficult person to be in love with."

"Look, I just wanted to talk to you. I don't want anything from you," she says. "I'm going back to Boston tonight." She hasn't felt this much emotion in years. And she knows she isn't as strong as she was at seventeen.

He puts his carving down and sits back. "Don't do this," he says, his green eyes piercing her. "You're willing to walk away again?"

"What am I walking away from?"

He stares at her, shakes his head.

"Tell me," she says. She is so practiced at endings, and he, so practiced at holding on. When the wind picks up, Echo watches a few wood shavings cartwheel down the steps. Her mind is so full of thoughts, she could fill the entire lake with them. One thing Grant has never been is a liar. But the manicured glamour of Susanna is a revelation. How could he still want Echo, in all of her scattered ways? Her coins fall out of her pockets almost daily. She loses her Jeep in parking lots, even when she's made a mental note. Up until Echo was almost ten, she screamed whenever someone tried to cut her hair. She still hates it. And the feel of long manicured nails that keep the world from her touch. She's just not that sort of person. The sort of person Susanna is, at least.

He looks at her. "You don't get it, do you? I kept hoping your Jeep was going to come barreling through the trees. Then I saw you. I went after you, Echo."

"She's beautiful, Grant, really," Echo says, her voice dropping off. "She's perfect."

"I think you're perfect."

She shakes her head. Her neck is moist, the hairs at the base of her neck curling up. He reaches over to touch her cheek. Echo glances at the tips of the blue spruce. Ragged patches of sky pass above them, and then slowly merge into an innocuous yellow haze. It reminds her of Joseph's eyes. It reminds her she is running out of time.

Under the blearing sun, she inhales the sweet scent of pine, and the soft burn of a dying bonfire, but she can't tell if it's coming from up shore, or from the earth simmering below her feet.

The energy between them swirls all around. He looks down at his dirt-stained hands. "I was going to carve you something. Had this dream the other night about carving something for you."

"How about her name in my arm?" She smiles, holds out her arm.

"You show no mercy," he says.

She laughs. "Sorry."

"I had always imagined what I would do when I saw her. What I would say. A marriage becomes a living thing. My instinct has always been to help things grow. Not to let things die. But I couldn't keep it alive. For the last year I've felt like it was the biggest failure of my life." He puts down the wood and knife.

"What about now?"

"I think I failed Lion and Melanie," he says, his face somber, his eyes distant. A mayfly buzzes around his head and he waves it away with his hand.

"Listen to me," she says, taking his face in her hands. "I've never met anyone who tries to help people the way you do. You don't fail anyone."

"I failed you," he says, resolute.

She feels raw, able to feel the scrape of his gaze, the burn of smoldering coals in her lungs. She wants to dive into water so black it makes even the boats disappear, just to feel their sting on her skin. "I'm still here, aren't I?" she asks, defiantly.

"I don't know if you are," he says, looking out at the lake, which is a smooth jade stone now. He turns to her. "Are you?"

She takes a deep breath, ready to tell Grant all that she has come here to say.

Then he gets up and walks away, toward the shoreline. She is about to call him back but she stops, watching as he dips his hands into the crystal water and splashes the water over his face. A nearby heron shakes the water from its wings and utters several squawks. Grant motions slowly toward the bird, calmly, quietly. It steps away, then advances and repeats the dance, refusing his proposal.

When he walks back to Echo his face is pallid. His eyes are cold, having absorbed all the cold in the lake.

"You ripped me open once," he says, standing in front of her, arms crossed.

She looks down. "I never wanted to do anything like that."

He won't avert his eyes even though he is struggling with himself to maintain the connection with her. "What you did was more than I was prepared for."

"Grant, I was seventeen years old."

He shakes his head. "You threw me away. You lied to me."

"I was protecting myself."

"How do I know you won't do that again? How can I trust you?"

"It's all different now. Everything has changed," she whispers, turning away, even though she is not sure that he has heard her, or that he is even trying. How could she have thought that they would just pick up where they had left off? That there wouldn't be any scars. That there would be nothing insurmountable. That he would forgive her.

Grant picks up the stick and chucks it into the canopy. A swell of blackbirds erupts into the air. "Lets go for a walk."

"Now?" she asks.

"I just want you next to me. Will you come with me?" He is too tired to sleep, he says. He wants to stay connected to everything. That's how he had felt about his marriage: If he left, everything would crumble. He couldn't separate the marriage from the house itself. That's why he stayed there, sleeping on the bare mattress for over a year. Now he tells her he's afraid that if he goes inside the cabin and closes the door, everything will disintegrate. "You understand what I mean?" he asks.

She nods, and follows him down the steps and across the lawn. Her heart is racing. She finally gets up the nerve to say it. "You can't save everyone, Grant. Do you know you get that from your father? I need to tell you something. Then you'll understand."

He stops and stares at her. "What are you talking about?"

She takes a deep breath. "Your father wasn't who you think, or he was more than you think he was. All his coldness toward you, the way he made you feel so badly about what you could do, about who you were. It wasn't you, Grant." Suddenly it is all spilling out of her. She tells him Joseph's story about Two Bears, and as she speaks, she watches a shadow cross his eyes. He is beginning to sweat, the water beading up on his upper lip. He listens, rakes his fingers through his hair, and then she watches his hands ball into fists. His face is flushed, and he looks angrier than she has ever seen him. But she continues because she knows she may never have this chance again. "He was trying to protect you."

"From what?"

"From being like him. From failing. From turning your back on who you are and what you can do. From being a secret."

"Jesus," Grant says, looking at his hands as though they were foreign objects. "And Joseph never told me, all these years."

"Joseph made a promise to keep it from you. To protect you. But when I told him how I felt about you—"

"What did you tell him?" he asks defiantly.

She looks away, her eyes welling up suddenly. "That I loved you. That I always have. Joseph told me for your sake. But mostly he told me for mine. He said he could see that not knowing was hurting you. It scared your father, seeing the ability in you. You reminded him of what he'd lost, or maybe what he wished he still had faith in. He didn't want the medicine or the ability to fail you, too."

"This is complete bullshit," says Grant, the waves of anger rising up inside of him. He wonders what he could have done with the knowledge all of these years. How his life might have been different. What about Susanna's miscarriages? Could he have changed the course of their lives? Could he have done something?

"You know you can help more than just birds," says Echo.

He recalls one evening after dinner when he was eight. He had been climbing one of the willows when he heard the loud *wick wick wick* of a young northern flicker that had fallen onto the roof. He climbed up and let the bird watch him through its hazy eyes, its tail feathers stuck out, oily, wet. Its light-purple-spotted chest pumped in and out as Grant edged toward it. Finally, he was so close he could see the tilings on the curved beak, the yellow undersides of the wings. Its feet were light on his finger as he cupped the body. Grant braced himself against a branch and climbed down, the bird resting in his shirt pocket.

"What's that you've got?" his father suddenly called from below. Grant panicked, felt the wings flap impatiently against his chest. He tried to quiet the creature as he climbed down. "Nothing, Dad," he answered. "Show me," his father demanded. Grant reluctantly opened his hands in the grass. The bird shook out its feathers, limped a few steps as though dazed, and then flew away. Grant watched it until the sick feeling in his stomach disappeared.

His father watched it, too. "How many times that happened?" his father wanted to know. "How many!"

"I just helped him a little. Nothing happened," Grant had whispered, paling under his father's stare.

"Don't play around with me, son. You tell me right now."

Grant admitted he had helped five or six birds.

"Whatever you think you can do, you can't. You hear me? This isn't meant for you," Dr. Shongo warned. "This is the last time. You understand? Don't ever let me catch you doing that again. Not to a bird. Not to a person. Never again." He put his hand on Grant's head and then walked him toward the house. "And don't ever talk about this to your mother."

"Thirty-three years of silence and now this?" asks Grant. "No. It's too goddamn late."

"It's not too late, Grant."

He walks away as it all comes back to him, the sound of his father pacing all those nights after losing his mother. Didn't Grant know the feeling of not being able to save someone whom he loved? He would have understood it when he was younger. He would have forgiven his father if only his father had given him the chance.

He closes his eyes, kneels, and runs his hands across the grass. He grabs a handful of dirt and lets it fall through his fingers. It is as though he is absorbing the knowledge.

Grant looks up at the regal pines, survivors that hold the wisdom of wood, knowing that they can never be burnt down entirely, that certain minerals in the wood refused to unite with air. This meant that even if you burn a village down you can never really make it disappear.

He turns around and faces her. "You can't change me, Echo. You never could. I'm still the same screwed-up guy you knew when you were seventeen." He is thinking about how his father wanted to change him, how Susanna did, and now even Echo. He has spent years beating himself up for what everyone else wanted him to be.

Echo stares at him, surprised. "I don't want you to change you."

"You want me to wear my heart on my sleeve and bleed all over the place like I used to?"

"No, I—"

"You should go back to Boston."

Stunned, she feels like she has been punched in the gut. "I am trying to help you. Finally, I can help you. The hiding, the carvings, the birds. Everything doesn't need to be hidden anymore, don't you see that?"

She closes her eyes, letting the tears fall. She can't catch her breath. She feels like she is struggling to the surface of the water, the moment just before coming up for air, when she can hear the rumble of the water underneath and the sound of the birds above, even though their voices are muffled.

"Come with me." He takes her hand. They cut across the street and take an old backyard path that curls into the deep part of a wooded area, one they both remember well. His gaze is tense on the russet sky where the trees become bloody at dusk and stain the hills a deep red, moments before the sun fully sets. They walk over a trail covered with moss and pine needles, stepping over scattered bones, gun locks, and pieces of brass kettles. They pass a hollowed-out tree that once hid gun barrels. Above, the oak leaves turn a shade of vermillion, as if drawing blood from the earth.

They make their way into smoky blue forgotten vineyards where broken trellises sag among the weeds, dwarfed by the oak and hickory. Branches are filling out. Lavender buds are flowering. Newly formed shoots from the vines protrude above the grass. In the distance, Echo notices broken posts along the hillside, some overtaken with branches. She can almost make out the purple clusters of wild grapes beginning to bloom, the vines shooting off in spirals. The air is heavy and sweet. They walk until they're standing at the edge of the marsh. Cattails rise among the reeds. There are red-winged blackbirds flitting in and out.

Grant thinks about his dreams, flying with Luke, about the fact that the boy seems to be pushing him toward something. He thinks about his broken window. About glass shattering the night sky. About the soot tracks in his living room, whether they've reappeared. About a hybrid wolf sitting in the middle of the highway, still as a statue, as though something led him to that exact spot for that exact moment.

He feels confused, angry, and bitter about what this knowledge could have meant for him, how this could have saved him years of self-doubt, years of feeling rejected, years of hiding, and feeling as though he was not a whole person. Maybe he had always known. It had always haunted him in some way, causing him to sneak around, carrying out his healings in secret, his father's scolding him for it but never providing a reason, which caused him to make up his own reasons: that his father hated him, that his father believed Grant was not good enough, that this ability meant there was something wrong with him. And then his inability to help his mother, something he just now realizes that he and his father had probably shared. Could they have consoled each other? Maybe their relationship was too far-gone at that point. And yet it brings Grant some shred of consolation: he understands now his connection to the ancestors, to the earth here. The connection to his father, and to his father's sense of failure. A legacy that his father had passed down to him.

"I could always heal the birds," he admits, focusing on the burst of blackbirds erupting from the trees in front of him. He watches them, and imagines they are carrying away years of self-doubt.

Echo takes his hand. "Joseph says that birds are the only creatures that have blind faith. That is why they are able to fly."

IT'S ALL WHIRLING AROUND Echo now—the acrid scent of elephant-eared weeds, the brassy sound of Stephen's words on the phone when she'd said good-bye, the feel of Grant's sandpaper skin against her cheek. And although she wants to run away from him, she can't quite let go of the back of his shirt.

"I'm sorry I got angry at you," he says. "You're the only one I could have heard this from. The only one I ever listened to."

He grips her hand tighter. They are in step. He stops to pinch off a piece of a plant as though suddenly someone is directing him. "Something I might need," he says, putting it in his pocket. He kneels and places a rock there. She waits, watching him. And when he gets up, she drops her hand near his and lets his fingers find hers again.

Just then she looks up. Something catches her eye, a flash of red in the cattail swamp. "Look at that red-wing up there. Did you see that? It just drew a circle in the air?"

"Where?"

"There," she says, pointing toward a nearby oak.

He follows the line of her fingers. The small dark bird with the red painted wings slices through the air again. It finally settles on a low branch.

"That's as close as I get to magic," she remarks.

"Not true." He lets his lips touch hers. He kisses both her cheeks, then brushes her hair out of the way, and kisses her neck. He squeezes her hand. She feels herself falling into him. She lifts off his sweater. Echo unbuttons her white gauze shirt. "Don't run away again," he says.

"I swear I won't," she says. He slips her shirt off one shoulder.

She takes his hand, places it underneath the soft fabric and over her breast. She is braless, unabashed. Not a little girl. A woman. Unafraid. How had it all circled back to this exact moment? After fifteen years apart. After the last time they saw each other, the first time they made love. She remembers unhooking her bra and standing before him, letting him see her in all of her vulnerability. How brave I was, she thinks. How dangerous. But now, all the time and distance no longer matter. He is here, with warm skin pressed against her. The same man she has loved for half of her lifetime. His fingers are warm as they brush her nipples and circle her breasts. "Echo," he says. And he kneels and he begins tasting her skin with his mouth, moving over and over her stomach, then pulling down her jeans and letting them hold her at the knees as he places his hand between her legs, parts her thighs, and begins to kiss her there. "Let me," he says, and she relaxes. There are colors swirling in the air all around them, all passion and anger, pinks and oranges and swirls of gold. She closes her eyes and breathes deeply as the waves of energy overtake her. Then he pulls her down, and moves her on top of his body, holding his hands on her hips, moving them back and forth, faster and faster. He is swollen hard inside her, and she takes him with every ounce of strength she has. Their lovemaking is not gentle. Rather, forceful and unfamiliar as though demanding an answer neither of them can give. She opens her eyes as he finishes inside her and moans, as though all the questions of the last several years have drifted to the surface and are scattered like the pine needles now circulating underneath what is left of their bodies.

ON THE WAY BACK to Grant's cabin, it begins to rain. Grant grabs Echo's hand and they run as fast as they can until they get to the porch. They fling open the door. Out of breath, flushed, they look around. Something inside has changed. There is a hum of frenetic energy, they can feel it. The temperature inside is too warm, almost hot, for such a cool time of day. The basement door is hanging wide open even though Grant had bolted it shut from the outside. One straight line of soot prints has reappeared, darker than before, leading from the basement door to the living-room window.

Echo grabs Grant's hand. "What is going on?" She hooks her arm through his, afraid. Clearly, he is not. "You know who did this, don't you?" she asks.

He closes the door to the basement, bolting it shut. "I know," he says, leaning against it. *It's time for you to leave, Luke,* he thinks, just as Leila Ellis's car is racing up his driveway.

23

HUGE THUNDEROUS STORMS WRACK the sky. Lightning flashes for miles across the black lake. It is raining again, a needling rain so sharp it can turn skin bright red, or roil the water, causing the waves to wrestle a paddle from the hands of a young girl as it did on the last night Luke Ellis was alive.

The rain beats down on the large black umbrella that Lion is holding over Maya and Leila, who are all huddled together on Grant's porch, their faces wet, arms around each other's waists. Maya is clutching her mother's coat as the sound of the muffled rain becomes deafening. When Grant opens the door, Leila is the first to look up at him from under the dark umbrella, her face streaked with mascara, her eyes red with sadness. Her body is ricocheting sobs from the car ride here. There is a dead body in her kitchen, that of a man whom she once loved. A good man, despite his faults. She has dried blood on her hands. There is blood in her kitchen, on her dog. Blood has streaked the kitchen walls, the very same kitchen where Charlie once ate meals she had cooked for him when she was trying to make him feel like the king of the family. It is her fault. It is her fault that she chose Victor all those years ago and now he is back to make her pay for her mistake. She can't escape it, this trail of tragedy streaming from her one bad choice. She pictures Charlie's body lying there in all that blood. Alone. So alone. And Maya finding him. She shudders, clutching baby Lucas to her breast underneath her long tan raincoat, his lips just peeking out. As Grant ushers them inside, Leila looks sadly at her daughter, choking back the tears. Maya is soaked in a red dress, her blond hair stuck to her face, her cheeks flushed as she clutches one end of Leila's coat, a gesture not of an adult but of a child. Maya is holding on to her so tightly, as though to anchor her for fear that she will drift away.

"Christ, you're all soaked," says Grant. "Come in, come in. What's happened?"

Leila hands the baby to Echo. "May I wash my hands?" Leila asks, holding up her bloodstained hands. Then she breaks down in tears and tells Grant about finding Charlie in all that blood. "My daughter has blood on her shoes," Leila says, gesturing at Maya, who looks down at her bloodstained sneakers as though she hadn't noticed them before. "I think Charlie's dead," Leila blurts out. Leila excuses herself and rushes into the bathroom to splash water on her face and wash her hands. Choking sobs are coming from the bathroom. Maya stands there silently, biting her nails. No one knows that she has blood on her shins underneath her dress. Leila returns a moment later, still tearing up, just as Lion is telling Grant and Echo what happened to Charlie, and that Victor has Melanie on Squaw Island.

"He's a goddamn murderer," Lion is saying. "Charlie's dead and Melanie's next. We are out of fucking time. I took his gun. I'm taking it with me," he says, removing the bloody gun from his pocket. He wipes off Charlie's blood with his shirt. "We've got to get her back now," Lion tells Grant, and then looks quickly at Leila. "You stay here at the cabin."

"No. She's my daughter. I want to come. I'm not afraid of him," says Leila, suddenly. "Do you hear me, I will never again be afraid of that man!"

"Leila, please stay with the baby and Maya," says Echo, leading Leila to the couch, where she sits, trembling. Maya looks away just then, making a dangerous wish, trying to pretend she is disappearing, that she is anywhere else but here with these strangers, with blood on her legs that no one can see, standing in a cabin that she once played in with her sister and her dead brother, a place she hasn't seen in years. She has not left Cheever in months, and she hasn't been in a house other than her mother's in a very long time, and now her mother is falling apart as Maya stares at the angry lake, imagining the feeling of the canoe, that rocking motion overtaking her, and the coldness of the waves numbing her hands and feet. She finds herself aching for the protective loneliness of her room at Cheever. All this unwanted activity. All this blood. And thoughts of Charlie's body keep flitting in and out of her head, each time, the sensation of cold steel biting at her legs and her hands.

"I'm waiting in the car," Maya says to her mother.

"It's safe here, Maya, really, and my dog will protect you," says Grant, waving at the sliding glass door at Einstein, who is standing on the porch, soaked, barking to high heaven.

"It's a wolf, not a dog," says Maya, noticing the soot prints on the carpeting. Her eyes follow the prints across the room to the basement door, which is open. Only Maya knows what this means. She folds her arms defiantly, not believing Grant. Not believing anything that anyone tells her. This much she has learned in her life. "I'll wait in the car. No one can stop me," she announces.

Grant and Lion grab the old canoe that hangs on the wall in the garage. Why had his father kept it all these years? Why hadn't it ever bothered Grant before? Who would keep something like this, a memory of a tragedy? Who else but someone who wanted to be reminded of his failings each and every day. Together, he and Lion drag the canoe, the spiderwebs, and layers of dust falling off of it as they push the canoe across the white septaria that have washed up on the shoreline. "My God, this thunder," says Echo, as she steps into the canoe. The wind is picking up, rifling the branches of the Diamond Trees.

"Get in!" Grant tells Lion. The wind is whipping up little tornados across the tinfoil lake. Lion is eyeing the water nastily, trying to communicate his hatred. If this is the last time he ever looks at the lake, it won't be soon enough.

"Shit, I can't," Lion is saying. "The fucking water."

"Get in the boat!" Grant yells but Lion won't budge. He is trembling, standing with his feet a few inches in water, and he can hardly breathe. Lion's shoes are sinking into the mud. He feels like he's already falling into the dark water. He knows that when he drowns he won't see a thing. All that darkness, swallowing him up, flooding his nostrils, his throat, until he passes out. He can already feel his lungs bursting, his cells exploding.

Now tiny lights scrape the surface of the lake. *Flying Heads. They used to only come out at night. Not anymore.* Lion is staring at the water, trying to make a deal with the lake. Melanie once mentioned something about those trees on Grant's property spreading out diamonds across the water, filling it with lights.

Echo holds out her hand to him. Her eyes are clear and encouraging. There is something about her that feels safe and true. Lion takes her hand and climbs into the canoe. He's got a gun slung in his pocket, and clumsily drops two knives onto the floor of the canoe. When Grant gets in, Lion hands him a knife. This time Grant doesn't argue.

Squaw Island shimmers in the distance. It reappears from the haze, and then vanishes in the sweep of rain and peaking waves. Grant is paddling furiously through the storm, wrestling the waves as the boat sails north toward the island. The canoe lurches from side to side. At one point it tips and freezing water splashes up, numbing Echo's hands and feet. Lion watches the wind twisting in the trees, dropping branches over the water like little toothpicks. The rain clouds look like huge gray wolves running across the sky.

Grant is forcing the paddle into the water, trying to steer as the island gets closer. Now Lion's eyes are straining, searching desperately through the fog, but the water and sky are black.

Lion leans over, shouting to Grant. "I can't picture her face!"

"Just keep it together!" calls Grant.

"Almost there!" cries Echo. "Try to hold on!"

As Lion watches the sky, he thinks about when Lucas was born, how Melanie had reached for the baby before he was out of her body, and how she cried when they'd whisked him away, before Lion even had a chance to touch him. *Matrina, Matrina, Matrina,* he whispers to himself, just as he did that night Melanie led him to the dock on City Pier and then abandoned him for the water. He had watched her dive in, angry and thrilled at the same time, as she kicked at the silvery fish that'd arc remarkably close, their tails caught in the moonlight. That night, listening to the crickets, she'd dried off and cuddled up next to him on the dock just in time to see a singular snowy owl sneaking out to admire its own reflection in the water, its white feathers shuddering in the moonlight. It was the first time he'd heard Melanie sing, just some tune that she had running through her head, and this had made it easier for him to swallow his fear. He knew he was crazy enough to risk his life for her. As Lion held Melanie on the sunset dock, he lost all sense of boundaries as the sky reached down and the waves looped up, and the earth slipped underneath, all at once.

Moonlight gathers in the leaves. Gulls circle above the roof. When Melanie is this close, she can almost reach into the center of her memory. Water. Miles and miles of beautiful water.

A voice is calling. She must remind herself to breathe. A man kneels, his knees pressing on her arms. His scent is so strong, she can taste it. He smells of everything wounded, just as he always had. He removes her blindfold and stares at her. "Look at me," he tells her. "Your mother lied to me just like all of you lied to me."

Was Charlie Cooke the only one Leila had an affair with or were there others? Victor wants to know.

The winds are wrestling with the waves. Melanie hears the voices of all those ancestors rising in a shrieking chorus. Or is it the birds? Gray wolves are darting in and around her body. She can feel Luke nearby, watches the little blue lights circling at her feet, then three little lights forming triangles on the ceiling and then, more spinning, circling down again, surrounding her. She stares at the dusty yellow dirge of her father's eyes when he tries to move her. Victor unties her. Her wrists are bleeding. He tries to pull her up but she can hardly stand.

"I have a boat," he is saying. "Stand up."

Melanie hears the moan escaping from deep inside her. A static sound, cut by the burn in her throat. He tries to get her to stand, but she falls. She has hardly eaten in five days.

As the canoe approaches the shoreline, the small Boy Scout cabin can be seen through the trees. The branches look menacing, as though trying to hide the broken concrete walls and tin corrugated roof so rusted with holes that tree branches have burrowed through it as though it was part of the earth already. Far off to the left, under a shell of willow leaves, an old motorboat is anchored near the shore, bobbing in the waves. As Grant guides his canoe toward the island, it scrapes the rocks and Grant jumps out into the frozen water, stabs his paddle into the mud, and pulls the canoe to shore as he slugs through the large white stones that are moving up and down in the waves. He helps Echo out of the canoe and then Lion grabs his arm, and without hesitation, Lion, too, jumps out of the canoe, his eyes fixed on the cabin, his heart pounding. He turns to Grant. "That's all I needed you for. Stay here and wait. I'm going in for her alone."

"Don't be a hero, Lion," says Echo, shivering.

"Wait," Grant says, eyeing the boy's face, noticing the steely glare, the hint of adrenaline making his eyes wide and glassy.

Lion is so lit up with rage right now, Grant is worried he could kill.

The rain is coming stronger now, slicing through the water. Echo is standing on the shore listening to the thunder, letting the flinty rain cut at her skin, vowing not to be afraid, and watching the lightning illuminate the golden snake slithering across the dark water. She reaches down and picks up a large white stone. Septaria of all sizes litter the muddy sand around the building. Their white glow is unearthly, making the island look as though it was a planet, or floating on a mountain of clouds.

Grant runs after Lion as he pushes his way into the old cabin and is hit by a shock of putrid air, the stench so rancid he can hardly breathe. Rain spills through the roof, flooding the dirt floor. Unopened boxes of cereal litter the area, along with an old coffee thermos. Inside there is nothing but bare gray concrete walls, the smell of mold, what looks to be an old steel sink hedged against the wall with a rusted faucet. There is no glass in the window above the sink. Instead, branches that have broken into it are growing through the building, biting through the walls, slowly breaking it into bits. Then, in the center of the room, a small mattress. Sprawled across it, Victor and Melanie are lying in a puddle of moonlight. Victor has his arms wrapped around Melanie, whose eyes are closed. Melanie lies across Victor's lap in a soiled brown dress, her hands and face bone white. Grant sees the look of surprise on Victor's face. Victor pulls Melanie's small body against his chest, clinging to her.

"You goddamn sonofabitch!" yells Lion.

"Go away!" Victor yells, pointing his gun. Melanie's limp arm falls across his leg. "Don't move. Don't come any closer," says Victor.

"Get the fuck off her!" Lion yells.

Victor stands up, aiming his gun at them. "I was going to bring her home. All I wanted was the truth about Luke. But I found out for myself." Lion takes a step closer and Victor points the gun at Lion. "All I ever wanted was my family. But the things that that little boy could do. The birds. Fixing the birds. He was a freak. He wasn't mine. Do you know how many fucking times she cheated? Charlie Cooke. I showed him. I had to come back for my family. All I ever wanted was my wife and my girls, and to know the truth about the kid's father. Leila wouldn't tell. Tell me, goddamn it. Say it! It was Charlie Cooke, wasn't it?" he shouts at Melanie.

Melanie's eyes flutter open. "Please, Dad. Let me go. I have a son."

A hush falls over the room, but for the rain. "Luke wasn't my son," Victor sobs, shouting at Grant, his soiled T-shirt wet with sweat. "If he was mine, none of this would have happened!" he cries. "I followed those kids that night. I could see the canoe. I stood in the rain, watching. I could have saved him. If he were mine I would have. Did I hate him? I did. I hated him!" Victor yells.

Melanie crawls away from Victor, trying to stand.

"You fucking bastard!" Lion breathes. He rushes at Victor, grabbing Victor's leg in the tussle.

Victor breaks free, holding his gun. He points it at Lion. As the rain thunders down on the tin roof, Lion freezes, staring at Victor with disbelief as though he has already been shot. Victor raises the gun. In the split second that the gun goes off, Melanie lunges at Victor. Lion falls back, and Melanie's body sinks to the floor. Victor drops the gun.

Standing between the two bodies, Victor keeps looking back and forth, first at Melanie, then at Lion. When Lion moans and starts to get up, Victor reaches for the ground to try and retrieve the gun that has flown out of his hands. That is when Grant Shongo feels the kick of action inside himself. And it all feels so natural, the hot metal blade under his thumb, the wooden handle. Grant pulls out his knife and just as he has always feared, it sinks easily into Victor's body. He pulls the knife out and drops it, watching Victor's body crumple onto the floor.

Lion rushes over to Melanie, staring at the bullet wound and the seeping blood. He tries to lift Melanie's head. He kisses her face.

For a moment, Echo and Grant lock eyes. Then Echo's gaze falls to Melanie's pale face.

"She needs a hospital," he says.

"No. There's no time," Echo whispers. "Melanie. She's the one you have to save."

"I can't," he tells Echo.

"I can help you," she says. "Look at me. I will help you."

He stares into her eyes, noticing that same warmth and clarity, feeling her hand on his shoulder, calming him, just as it always had. It all unravels in his mind. Melanie. Victor. And Luke, his dead brother, who has been coming to him all this time, just for this very moment, a spirit who was caught here because his loved ones would not let go—who remained because he could not leave until his sister was safe.

LION WILLIAMS ALWAYS KNEW he'd end up okay, no matter what life threw at him. Even when he found himself in the middle of the Rodney King riots, a crowd of people dodging tear gas, and heavy shots of water spraying in his face. Even after he had his teeth kicked in, and one of his arms sliced open, and someone scraped him off the pavement and carried him to the back of the Chinese restaurant while the rest of Los Angeles was being flung into police trucks, he knew he'd wind up okay. It's that guardian angel, Matrina, which somehow always got him through. But as he holds his dying wife in his arms, he can't touch the feeling.

He's crying terrible sounds. They keep coming out of his mouth. All the pain he's had to take in his life was nothing compared to this. Melanie is like a paper doll. He can wrap his entire hand around one of her bruised arms. He stares at the welts under her eyes. Tears stream down his face. *Matrina,* he thinks. *Where are you, Matrina*?

Lion hugs the body. She is becoming cold. He will not let go of the body. He keeps rubbing her hands, blowing on them like she's just come in from a snowstorm. He touches her swollen lips.

Echo touches Grant's shoulder. "Do something now. You have to try."

Then Lion looks up at Grant, a glint of hope in his eyes.

Grant's face feels hot, the back of his neck warm. He stares out at the foggy coast and the resilient Diamond Trees that light up the black water as if they were stars lighting the night sky. He nods to Lion, motions for him to move away.

Lion gently puts Melanie down. Grant kneels beside her.

He holds his palm an inch over her body, trying to stay calm. The pulse is faint. The energy cycling through her veins is frantic. Her heart is working too hard. She can't take much more of this. "Dying," he whispers, looking at his hands. He is losing her just like his father lost the girl. The story of his lineage is repeating. Maybe if a man doesn't learn, the Creator turns his progeny to ash. Maybe that is the way the spirits work.

"Keep trying," Echo cries, offering him strength, certainty.

Grant has to reach inside himself. Overcome the past, let go of his father. The rain is pouring now, thunder striking the sky. Memories of his father are flooding back. All of the birds. All of the hiding he has done for so many years. He is afraid of losing Melanie. The girl is innocent, paying for the sins of his own father. She deserves better. He knows he must try again.

"Lion, hold her like this, under her neck, just this way. Talk to her. She can hear you."

Lion is trying, but he can't speak. Grant whispers a prayer. His father's words come back to him. Words about the ancestors, words that he'd forgotten long ago. He whispers to them. He tries to listen to what they have to tell him. She will bring healing, just as he will, to those spirits who have passed on, and to those that are waiting to cross over. Grant is a bridge. And so is she. Each person is a bridge, is what they mean to say.

He can hear Lion's low cries, but can't make out the words.

Grant focuses on Melanie again. He works on the resuscitation points. He presses down on Melanie's left little finger, the first entry to the heart, and then to the points under her arms, then back to her finger. He tells Lion to keep doing this. The moonlight gliding in through the roof encircles them like a protective fence, but Melanie's pulse is still weak. Grant can feel the heat pouring from her heart, faster and faster. He can see the waves of guilt spilling from her chest, rushing out of her body. All those years of self-hatred, pushing down on her like heavy rocks. But she is fighting.

"Mel," says Lion, tears streaming down his face. "What's happening?" Grant can feel her soul trying to wrestle itself from the flesh as her body seizes. Outside, tendrils of moonlight drift through the trees as the waves reach toward the sky.

Closing his eyes, he imagines he is standing on the top of Bare Hill, letting the wind whip his face, feeling alive. Feeling in touch with himself. He tries to connect with her soul. He needs to know whether it is time for her to go. He looks at Lion, unsure.

"No. Don't fucking look at me like that," says Lion.

"Tell her it wasn't her fault. Just do it," says Grant.

Lion leans over Melanie's face, whispers to her. "It wasn't your fault. Luke wasn't your fault. You didn't do anything, Mel. We need you here."

"Keep talking," Grant says. "She's still here. Tell her about Lucas. She'll fight for him."

"Lucas needs you. I'm gonna buy us a house," Lion says, cradling her, kissing the backs of her hands. "A new house with a big kitchen and a big bedroom for Lucas. Lucas, Mel. He is the reason you're here, remember, that's what you said?" He is telling her about the time when she painted snowflakes across Lucas's bedroom when she was so pregnant she could hardly walk. Her eyes were so blue. She was so lit up, so beautiful without an ounce of makeup. Lion's thinking of her crummy overalls and his big purple undershirt, how by the time Melanie was finished she had white paint covering her face and arms. He had stepped in some of the paint and walked across the room. "Do you remember how you turned my big old shoe prints into white snowflakes all across the floor?"

The little blue light above the heart is fading. "I'm losing her," Grant whispers. *I couldn't save my mother. My three babies. I can't save Melanie.*

Echo rushes over, kneels next to him. She cradles Melanie's head in her hands. Melanie's face looks like that of a china doll, the white skin, and the long lashes. Echo wipes the hair away from Melanie's eyes and rubs her face, trying to bring back warmth. "Don't think this way, Grant. Listen to me. Keep trying."

There's too much in the air swirling around Grant. It feels like rocks piled up on his chest. Light burns his eyes. He can't focus. Melanie's body is a shell in his hands, the heartbeat irregular, and the cells all contracting in an uneven way. He tries to calm her nervous system, but she's fading. *I can't block everything out*. And then: *I can't do this.*

Then Grant can hear voices whispering all around him, praying. He can feel the dousing wind on his chest, moistening the air as a black bird dives through the broken window and settles on the rafters above them. Melanie's heart is gun-metal cold. *Reach,* he hears a voice praying above him. For thirty-three years he has tumbled over the fields of his family's lore like a branch in the wind, watching seedlings drop into the sweet grass, the softness of their fall, a whisper of all they know about the fallen snow. Yet still they rise and reach as he has done, over and over. Now there is a voice in the air saying *Reach. Reach.* He hasn't yet lived with this kind of knowing. He thinks of flying with Luke near the water's bed, the colors around them flowing into red and gold. He imagines painting the surface of everything he sees with his own colors. He is more than a mirror of his father. He lets go of what he knows. There is a voice nearby, saying *Risk. Risk.*

He closes his eyes, focuses inward, locating the beat of his own heart. He centers himself in the hazy air. He is standing in the cool mist, the smell of mud and trees all around him. This is where he must stay. He lets his mind blacken until there is nothing but silence. He must let go of everything, all those fears, and all those worries. He must let go of his father. In order to let his strength come through, to do what he is meant for, he must let go of the man who gave him the gift.

Reach, he tells her. Grant begins again at Melanie's right shoulder, and then moves toward the narrower part of the heart. He calms the fibrillating muscle. Then he directs the pulsing energy through the blood so that it caresses the valves. Light washes the arteries, the valve that controls blood flow from the left ventricle to the aorta. Grant fills one chamber with a light, and then the other as the blood begins to flow smoothly. Both sides of the heart relax and fill, then contract and empty. He works on the aortic valve, flooding light through their leaflets as they open to let out blood. Grant focuses on them in their perfection, gently massaging the heart muscle with the light, focuses on the node that starts each heartbeat, setting the pace, until it's regular.

"Melanie. It is not your time to go," Grant says. He opens his hand and drops the bullet into the dirt. Then a bolt of lightning strikes the island.

Echo glances out at the shore, at the silhouette of a man tossing a wedge of light across the water.

Grant whispers. "Father."

* * *

NO SKY. HEAVY FEET drumming against the floor. Women reach for the shadows. They are tearing pieces of Melanie to offer to the night skies. They hold each other in a circle with Melanie in the center, the keeper of their grief. They are wailing the names of their loved ones, those that were massacred in the fires all those years ago, when their homes were desecrated and only some escaped. Melanie can feel their wet black hair on her skin as they force her to breathe life into their mouths, to take grief from their hands. Voices plunder her body. Melanie is wind-blind.

Melanie's heart is fraying into threads of light, and then she is lifted into the skies. She can see Lion and Grant and Echo beneath her, calling to her. But she is lifted higher. She calls her own name to her reflection in the lake, which she now sees below her. Her dress is caught like a kite in the branches of the Diamond Trees.

The water dripping from her lips. A red dress. A dress that fills up the whole sky. The waves flood over Luke's face. Shifting prisms of emerald glass become liquid. Luke clings to the round stones sliding toward the surface of the water.

Melanie dives in, comes up holding the debris in her hands. Strands of yellow hair, wings. He becomes a small bird. The sinuous chord of her heart snaps; her heart unweaves. The bird takes off, its wings expanding in light.

There is someone else now nearing the lake's edge. Words, like feathers, fall across Melanie's face, tickling her neck.

From where she is, way up here, resting on a mountain of clouds, Melanie sees Joseph O'Connell standing on one side of the silver river.

24

WHEN CLARISSE MELLON DRIVES to the Feed & Grain to check on Joseph, she doesn't think about what excuses she'll make. She has driven through the rain, fearlessly, barely able to see the road. Now she is knocking on the door. When no one answers, she lets herself into his house. She calls to him. No answer. She lets herself in and finds Joseph sitting in his kitchen, as lost and pale as she has ever seen him. "You've come for me?" he asks when he sees her. He tries to get up.

"For you," she tells him just before he collapses.

Joseph O'Connell has never had a spiritual dream in his life. He fancies himself more of a chronicler of sorts. An observer mostly. He knows Grant Shongo has been a healer since he was a child. But Grant has yet to realize that everything comes with some sacrifice. Pain is a gift. Joseph's been up all night with it. Now it's turning to fire in his head. He doesn't want anyone, especially Echo, to find him like this, dying here in the kitchen without dignity. There will be no hospitals for him. No doctors. Nature must take its course. One side of his body is numb, immovable. He stares up at Clarisse.

He can't make it.

The floor is rising up under him. He is ready, ready. He feels the cold floor against his cheek. Then, a blinding light and floating. He can hear birds twittering beneath him and above him, circling in graceful arcs. More limber now than he's been in decades, he climbs up near the ceiling, notices the spider webs billowing into the corners. Underneath the fibrous white cloud, he looks down and he sees his body lying on the floor, the left arm bent strangely backward.

Joseph is blinded by a buoyant yellow light that wants to cradle him. Distant voices and faces he hasn't seen in years. Echo's mother is standing on the periphery of the lake, her dress, pink, the color of hope, and her hair spun into coils of auburn light. She has the clearest brown eyes, just like her daughter. Echo's father is a hazy figure in the distance. Joseph reaches out. They're so welcoming. It's so warm here. It has been so long since he was this warm.

And then, nearing closer, Rose. She is walking along City Pier, laughing as she feeds the ducks day-old bread. There is so much joy and so much love that Joseph doesn't know how much he can stand before he shatters.

Something pulls him back. Drums. No. A heartbeat. Faint at first, then louder. He can hear the soft cries in the crystal-clear trees. He walks toward the voice. She is farther off, not in the direction of the light but in another direction where there is a mountain just like Kilimanjaro. He is climbing quickly, effortlessly. At the top, he finds Melanie's body wrapped in clouds that drape themselves over the tips of the trees. He kneels, whispers a hello. They can hear each other's thoughts.

Melanie is showing him a trail of forsythia, the golden flowers like fists in the air. She is dancing among the colors, the swirls of white and gold now mixing into the distance. Melanie is naming flowers by touch. There is jewelweed, and chicory, the bluest, its opening a long time coming, like words whispered through the stems. There is one she will not pick, the rarest yellow lily grown wild with petals much bigger than those in Leila's garden. Then a butterfly.

Melanie promises only to touch lightly, only with her thumb, a butterfly wing before letting it fly.

She scans the field. She wants to name a flower after Luke. She looks for one that has no name.

Joseph tells her to go back, it is not her time. He kisses her hand and turns away.

On the other side of the river, Luke is beckoning him from the rocks. Joseph walks toward him, stepping across the mercurial rippling water.

In the kitchen of the Feed & Grain, Clarisse Mellon is kneeling over Joseph's body. She knows that the only man she has ever loved is dead. Still she is holding his hand. And she will do what she had come to do.

"I'll always love you," she whispers, pressing her cheek against his hand.

25

LUCAS?" MELANIE WHISPERS. SUNLIGHT streams in through the windows, filling the baskets of flowers with light. A balloon from the mayor of Canandaigua hovers on the ceiling above Lion's head. There are cards with teddy bears and roses taped to the windowsill.

"Open your eyes," Lion says. He can hardly keep his own open.

"Where have you been?" she asks.

He hands her a glass of water and holds it under her mouth as she sips. The IV is burning her hand.

Lion moves his face closer. "I'm here."

"My baby," Melanie says, letting her lips lightly brush his. Her throat feels like it is filled with sand. "Where's Lucas?"

"Your mom took him home a while ago. She should be back soon," he says, laying his head on her chest. He smoothes the sheet over her stomach. "We missed you so much."

"Joseph is dead," Melanie says.

Lion glances at the nurse. He takes Melanie's hand. "Shh, just rest."

"I saw him." She starts to cry. "And I saw Luke."

Lion rubs her arm. "You need rest."

She reaches for his hand. "Lion, I need to tell you the truth. I'm afraid you won't forgive me."

He kisses her hand. "I already forgave you for everything you ever did and everything you will ever do."

Tears are streaming down her cheeks as she looks at him. Sunlight dissolves into the sheets and the room turns dusky. Melanie's eyes become pale, and he worries that she'll drift off again.

"I almost died just like I did when I was nine. I won't lie to you. I didn't want to come back. Not at first. I thought of you and the baby, and I knew I had to." She turns her head away from him. "I almost died twice," she whispers. "I came back both times."

He squeezes her hand, feeling the cold metal of the bed rail under his arm. He tells himself it's okay, but right now his body aches with such a profound sense of emotion he doesn't know that he'll ever recover. His legs weaken underneath him and he has to steady himself to keep from falling. He can finally close his eyes.

As Melanie watches Lion fall asleep, she remembers their first meeting. It had been Luke that had led her right to Lion. She has always known it.

That night three years ago, her car had almost hit one of those wild turkeys. She had swerved to avoid the kill and her car spun right into the parking lot of St. Mary's Church. She had run inside to use the phone and walked right into a Narcotics Anonymous meeting. It was fate, for she would have never gone willingly. As soon as she entered the room, she saw Lion. Her eyes locked on his. He was sitting at one end of the circle in his shiny black leather, dreadlocks falling across his wide eyes. The people in the room were transfixed as he spoke in his deep voice telling all he knew about patience. The room was warm. His talk was low and generous, every so often sparked by an animated movement. Lion was captivating. He said he knew he'd never kick the habit as long as he stayed in California. She was trying to get up the nerve to approach him after the meeting, but she knew she looked like a sad case, with an odd crew cut that made her look like a militant Nazi nymph.

Barely alive, brittle and thin, she stood trembling in the crowd of people over-sugaring cups of coffee and talking of God. How lucky she was that Lion had approached her. He liked her haircut, he said. He told her it was his three-year anniversary of abstinence from pot and alcohol. He asked her to help him celebrate at his favorite restaurant, the International House of Pancakes. He wouldn't let her pay for the coffee and three stacks of banana waffles. Instead he asked her to listen to him. Addiction was simple: Fear plus attraction, he said. It made sense. She hadn't been able to take her eyes off him. Soon, the conversation turned to her. She told him about the night she'd found herself kneeling in the rain on Interstate 90 after Eddie pushed her from his truck, and how she felt no pain, but she knew she should have, because her knees were bleeding on the wet gravel. She had yelled across the night, groping for the pills he had tossed out the window. Sergeant Charlie Cooke had showed up then. He appeared from out of nowhere, she remembered.

She told Lion about this because he may as well know how pathetic and horrible she was. When he didn't flinch, she told him about the brother she once loved, and how the lake had split open one night when she was nine and all of them had fallen into its darkness. She never told anyone that it was her fault before, that it had been her idea to take the canoe out, and that it had been her stupidity to stand up in the boat to wave at a giant. She waited for Lion to tell her she was horrible and that he had to leave. Lion did get up, but only to put his jacket around her shoulders and then sit back down.

They sat there well into the morning. Lion made her feel gentle with herself, a feeling she had never experienced. The landscape of her life had been softened in one single night. Melanie drove home in the snowfall stunned, replaying Lion's every word. She didn't look in a mirror for a week, afraid she'd scare away the light in her eyes. That is when she knew what love felt like.

Now as she looks at him sleeping by her bed, she knows it all happened as it was supposed to. He and their baby would forever be her reason to go on. When Leila rushes into the room with Lucas in her arms, Melanie smiles and reaches for him. "My sweet baby," she says, as Leila places Lucas in her arms.

NO ONE NEAR THE Shongos' cabin notices the fire when it begins to burn. It is September and the scent of burning leaves is common. Not even Grant gives it any thought, for he is out on his morning run, his feet padding the soft pine as he cuts across the trails and into the forest on Bare Hill, Einstein running alongside of him. The birds are silent. Not even the trees register the movement, though if they could talk, they'd tell you that there are as many shades of fire as sadness. Coal produces a dim glow. Oil and wood give forth heat with a flame. Fire feeds on oxygen, creating its searing touch.

In the house down the shore, a woman spills a glass of wine and laughs. A golden retriever sitting on a dock near Sunnyside suddenly twitches its nose, just having caught wind of the fire. On Squaw Island, a group of boys have spotted the smoke just before they see a large snake rise out of the water. They swim back toward the dock so fast they feel like their lungs will explode.

The willows arch over the Shongos' cabin, while boxes of wooden statues hiss and blister in the backyard, where Grant put them just a few minutes before he left for his morning run.

Now standing at the summit, Grant's eyes glimpse the smoke writhing at the foot of Bare Hill, and he's already begun to run, his heart pounding hard. An electrical fire or something else? He runs down the muddy trail past the locust trees. By the time he reaches his gravel driveway, smoke is pouring from the backyard. He notices that there are tracks in the sand, all across the shoreline leading into and out of the water.

Under the water, the bass gather at the sound of sirens, and the whirling engine of motorboats sound like thunder. A heron lifts up from across the lake, watching Grant. Smoke corners sparrows behind the trees, miles away. Grant calls out to the spirits, who have begun this fire and who will end it when all has turned to ash. He bows his head as flames thrash the air. He says good-bye to Luke as he grabs an old pail half hidden under the willow leaves and fills it with lake water, which he will throw after the fire has died down. He is going to begin anew. Not with his father's gift. But with his own.

26

AS HARD AS PEOPLE pray for something to happen in Canandaigua, they pray harder for things to return to normal. On the Saturday before Labor Day, everyone is waiting for the first flare at the summit of Bare Hill. It's the annual Festival of Lights, the end-of-the-summer rite, a modern-day celebration of the beauty of the lake and all that she gives, based on a Seneca custom of thanksgiving, a gesture of gratitude and for good luck in hunting and fishing. The Seneca used to light festival fires on Bare Hill and around the lake. Up until 1880, some Seneca had still gone to Bare Hill, where they burned sacred tobacco on a rock.

Standing at the summit provides the best view of the Ring of Fire. When standing back from the lake's edge and looking from one end of the lake to the other, it is possible to see the white glow of the fires and the chain of tiny red flares circling the lake for about forty-four miles.

Most people live on the lakefront year round, more so on the northern end, near the city of Canandaigua. Though she has her moods, no one blames the lake for their mistakes. The truth is, things here tend to get out of control. This attracts people, and it also changes them.

On this Saturday afternoon, it's a blistering hot Indian summer day. A perfect day for a parade or a picnic on the beach or a day to visit graves. The sky is so clear you could drink it right up, thinks Clarisse Mellon, who is sitting near Joseph O'Connell's grave, just as she's done each Sunday since Echo and Grant came to live with her while the Feed & Grain was undergoing construction. Religiously, Clarisse leaves a handful of cookies and some fresh-baked banana bread for the birds that seem to flock to Joseph's tombstone. Joseph O'Connell was her one true love, and though he never knew, she's certain he loved her, too. Maybe not like his Rose, but in a way that was meant just for her. Some things aren't meant to come to pass. Not everything is meant to happen. Some things should stay as they are, just like that, full of possibility. It's wanting them that gives you something to hope for, a reason to get up in the morning and put on a fancy dress.

Like clockwork, Clarisse will say a prayer and fill Joseph in on a bit of friendly gossip. As she talks, red-winged blackbirds and orioles will flutter in, occasionally, scattering the seeds of cattails across the dirt. All the while, Echo will watch from her Jeep just a few feet away, holding a book in her lap, while Grant sits next to her, one arm slung over her shoulders.

Each time Clarisse glances back, she sees them talking, their heads held close, the small carving of two wooden herons hanging from the rearview mirror, the carving that Lion Williams dropped off a couple of months ago. Lion said he was meant to finish what Grant had started; something about herons living in pairs and now they both had what they always wanted. Lion said that it still wasn't enough to repay Grant anyway. Even helping to clear out the coal bin in the basement wasn't nearly enough, he said. But it was a start.

A few months ago, after Clarisse gently relocated her new litter of kittens from their post outside the guestroom door, Echo told Clarisse she wasn't sure how she was going to be able to move on without Joseph. She told her, what good's a spirit when it can't hold you in its arms? She had asked Clarisse what right she had to any happiness, knowing that Joseph had suffered. Clarisse had to set Echo straight. Now that Echo was going to be a mother, she had to rid her mind of that kind of thinking. Echo had thanked Clarisse and said she felt indebted to her for the fact that Joseph was not alone in his final moments, that at least Clarisse was with him. Echo could take comfort in that, just as Clarisse had done, in the mornings following his death when her tears formed upon waking.

Clarisse can tell a thing like pregnancy in a woman's face just as easily as she knows the names of her eleven cats. There's Ella Fitzgerald, and Oliver. Well, the rest will come to her. At seventy-eight, Clarisse has finally gotten the family she always wanted. Stranger things have happened.

Just as they've done every Sunday, Grant, Echo, and Clarisse leave the graveyard and drive out to a picnic spot on Bare Hill. Now they are standing near the edge of the path. Grant Shongo's face doesn't register a hint of regret. He is staring down at the Diamond Trees, which still stand tall, unscathed by the fire, their leaves flickering at the sky. Clarisse will be glad when the snow comes and covers the lake. It needs time to recover, to sleep. She takes a deep breath, dizzy. It must be the air, she thinks, noticing that strange movement in the branches of the Diamond Trees. Or somebody jumping on that one branch, the way it is moving like that, up and down, even though there is no wind.

Clarisse watches Echo and Grant walk arm in arm back through the tall buffalo grass. Soon the girl will see that there's as much truth in happiness as there is in suffering. Echo's daughter will know this better than anyone; that will be her purpose. Echo has said she knows she will have a girl. She just keeps dreaming of a little girl with dark skin, green eyes, and curly hair, laughing and dancing in the sunlight.

The day lilies with their thick glassy leaves are in full blossom when Echo and Grant reach the marsh, Clarisse following behind. The petals curl toward the light. Then they pass right by the wild peonies, with their pure white layers of tissue-paper petals. What makes them bloom? The ants are drawn to them because of the sugar. They crawl inside and this helps force the petals to open.

Near the cattails, Clarisse calls out that she's going to stop here, as the ground is damp and mud is getting in her shoes. She spreads out a blanket and sits down.

Everyone has advice as to what to do. But nothing has to be decided in a hurry. Take it all in. Don't make any decisions yet, Clarisse has told Echo in her best motherly tone. The girl could sell the Feed & Grain after the remodel or keep it and turn it into a restaurant or a gift shop, or it could stay just how it is, an old-fashioned local grocery store, the kind that's rare in America these days. Echo and Grant could run it and Clarisse could help, or she could just watch the baby, whatever they decide. There are so many choices now. She knew her life was starting over when Echo returned to Canandaigua. She had the surest feeling. Whatever they decide, Clarisse is content to make herself useful. Hopefully the remodel will take a long time and Echo and Grant will want to stay with her for a while, even after Grant's cabin is cleaned out and updated, and all that horrible yellow shag rug has been pulled up. She, herself, had tried to get out all the soot marks but they refused to disappear. For now at least, Echo needs a mother. If she's lucky, she'll become the roots for people who don't have any of their own. And then she'll no longer be alone.

Clarisse watches Echo sift through a flock of Queen Anne's lace. The little purple spot in the center of each spray of white petals is the crown over the heart, she has told Clarisse. She'll search for the one missing its center. When she finds it, she'll save it in a book for Melanie.

Clarisse and Echo and Melanie are not so different. They all loved Joseph.

How wonderful to feel it, Clarisse thinks, her hair loose, the wind spinning it into tangles like it hasn't done in fifty years.

PEOPLE AROUND HERE SAY the same stories in your life are repeated over and over until you learn the lesson. Echo has always missed the chance to say good-bye. These days, her eyes are blurry with tears. Her doctor says she's emotional because of the hormones, yet she doesn't mind it because tears are what connect her to Joseph. She can't yet stand on Joseph's grave, even with Grant taking her hand. She can't see much else in front of her at all lately, except being with Grant and being a good mother. There is solace here that she has never known, such a strong sense of peace when he holds her for hours and lets her bury her face into his chest as they lie under the old crazy quilt in Clarisse's guest room, Echo examining the fabrics of a lifetime as Grant watches the moonlight change from orange to ash and back.

Each morning the life growing inside her sends her spilling onto the bathroom floor, wrenching her body apart from itself. Grant holds her hair back and then dabs her face with a cool washcloth. Each night after they say good night to Clarisse,

Grant rubs lotion on her stomach and talks in a quiet voice to the little girl. They both talk to her from here.

Eat, sleep, and walk. These things she will do for her daughter.

Now standing under the feathered sky, Grant lets go of her hand. Echo's dress makes a swishing sound as she moves through the reeds. She knows she is safe with him watching her just a few feet away. She whispers to the little girl and tells her about her grandfather. She tells the child that Joseph will be her guardian angel. Then she tells her all about Grant, because he never will. She knows her daughter will be tall just like him. Maybe the girl will have two front teeth that almost touch, and though she'll hate this when she's younger, she'll eventually grow to love it just that way because she can whistle through them.

Echo will tell the child all about freckles.

But she won't say a thing about the birds. They'll have to wait and see.

She looks around. She needs to make sure the two people she loves are still there. In the distance, Clarisse is stretching her stocking feet out on the blanket.

Up ahead, Grant is leaning against the tree, his arms folded against his blue T-shirt. His face is bright, his smile filling up the sky. Sometimes when she looks at him, Echo's heart swells and she feels so much love, she thinks she won't be able to stand it a minute longer. And then she reminds herself she can. That this is the good stuff. Happiness is just as hard to get used to as anything else.

In the same year, Echo will become daughter and mother and a wife. How amazing that everything can change so quickly.

Ahead, a kingfisher with a bent wing flies past her before settling on a cattail. Echo looks down. Her fingers are delicately brushing the edge of the Queen Anne's lace. Is this the one she's been looking for, the one with no center?

Her fingers reach to pull it up from its roots. But instead, she lets go. Everything contains the possibility of change, yet with that has to come trust. It's a deal that the earth makes with the sky. It's a level of trust that is present all the time. It's in the way the earth lets go of the sun each evening and the moon each dawn. Not pushing them away, just quietly trusting they will be back.

Echo turns toward the scent of bonfires weaving across the water. Sooner or later she must grow wise with the time she has, savoring the minutes like gifts, like the words of a precious book that has been lent to her, or a child. To find the right country is the greatest gift. To realize it as the one that has always felt like home is even greater, as Joseph once said. She is certain she has found it.

She walks back toward Clarisse and Grant, who have both been patiently waiting for her for a very long time.

AT THE HARVEST PARADE, an end-of-summer tradition that marks the beginning of the Ring of Fire festivities, a crowd is funneling onto Main Street. Standing in a float adorned with six-foot papier mâché ears of corn, a young Harvest Queen with a spiral perm is waving to the crowd. Just this morning Georgia Petrograss, who has just quit her job at Kelley's Bar, got a belly-button ring, though she knows her mother will ground her for life when she sees it. Georgia is standing up, dancing lightly to the drumbeat of the Buffalo Creek Dancers. On the sidewalk, Lion's got Lucas on his shoulders as he follows Melanie toward the stage. As the dancers shake their rattling instruments, Lion bounces Lucas up and down, which Lucas loves. He peels with laughter, gripping onto Lion's dreadlocks and pulling them so excruciatingly hard that Lion's eyes tear. Standing to the right of the stage, an old man in a feather headdress hits the drum strapped to his side. As he calls out his song, a dozen dancers in brightly colored dress weave in and out of a circle, their eyes holding ground. The chain of bells around their knees jingles with every stomp of their fringed moccasins. Four women flash by, lifting baskets into the air, an homage to the corn god. "I never want to see another corn dog again," says Melanie, holding her stomach. She's wearing a purple bikini top and army pants rolled up to the thigh.

"Then you'd better learn to cook, sweetie," Leila says, tugging down her long T-shirt that Melanie made for her, which says, MY CHILDREN WENT TO CALIFORNIA AND ALL I GOT IS THIS SHITTY T-SHIRT.

"There aren't any corn dogs in Long Beach," says Lion.

"Oh no?" Leila asks.

"They're all off chasing corn cats," Lion says, and laughs.

"Ick," says Melanie.

"Ick," says Lucas.

They find the car and drive down the hill toward the beach and park a few feet back from the water. Every time Lion glances at Leila she looks as though she's about to cry. She reaches her hand into the cooler and pulls out five peanut-butter sandwiches. But she can't hide her tears, and she starts crying into the plates. Melanie puts Lucas in his stroller and then gets up and puts her arms around Leila. She thinks Leila is crying because of Maya choosing to go back to Cheever, and because they're moving away, but that's only part of it.

Getting Melanie back has replaced the space for grief. But only for a time. The grief still seeps out when Leila is caught unawares. It can feel overwhelming when Leila actually lets herself stop and think about all that happened within a short span of a few days. And yet it wasn't just a few days. If she traces it all back, it was, in fact, a lifetime of mistakes. And it rattles her, how years of mistakes can catch up with a person in a span of a few hours. How lives can be lost, suddenly, without warning. She had only been trying for love, trying all these years, for she was a person who thought she needed love to survive. Had she been different, had she not needed it so badly or been that sort of person, her whole life might have been different. But she was that sort of person. As long as she'd been able to breathe, she'd been ruled by it. Love of a man. Love of her children. She had no way of knowing that a blizzard would bring her love, that it would later almost cost Charlie Cooke his life, right there in her house when she was only upstairs trying to wash the scent of sadness from her skin. Charlie Cooke nearly died in a pool of blood in her kitchen, after telling her only minutes before that he still thought about her. He had left her with a bit of foolish hope, just as he always had. It would have been harder if he had said that he loved her. And she is grateful to him that he never said it, even though for years she prayed she would hear those words from his lips. That was the only thing she ever wanted to hear.

And finally, Victor, now in prison, another casualty of the battle that was her heart. But it was his battle, too, and they had both been caught up in it. At least her daughters were not casualties. Not any longer. Her daughters are her greatest accomplishment. Both survivors, showing her the way. Maya is starting to work on her studies. Melanie is strong. Stronger than Leila had ever been. For this, Leila is grateful. She is grateful to Victor for if it weren't for his terror, Leila wouldn't have needed Ben Shongo. And without that need, Luke would not have been born.

At one time, she had three children, and she told them often that they were a triangle, the strongest shape. And though one was missing, the other two had proven they were strong in their own right. Perhaps a triangle was not the strongest shape. Perhaps each person was her own perfectly balanced shape.

Now, to compound the loss, Lion and Melanie are moving to California. Lion once told her that the water was his curse. That when he moved again, he'd use a map and draw a circle with a compass. He'd figure out a place that was at least a day's drive from any sort of water at all. He'd always believed that getting away from California would solve all his problems, but now he says he knows better, that he wants to face the things that have made him run. He and Melanie won't live in Compton, where he grew up. Instead, he wants to live in Long Beach, right on the water. And Melanie is going to apply to film school at the University of Southern California. They'll only be twenty minutes from Los Angeles when she gets her big break.

"Hey!" Lion calls, standing in the water up to his knees. "No hands!"

Melanie shakes her head and looks at Leila. "Luckiest day of my pitiful life, meeting that guy."

This is Leila's biggest joy, taking care of her grandson, enjoying her daughter and her son-in-law. It is official as of last week. Melanie and Lion stood at the courthouse and exchanged sterling silver bands made by a friend in town. "Redeem this dress," Leila had said, handing over her wedding dress. So Melanie dyed it purple in the bathtub, even though Leila wasn't sure if this would exorcise the bad luck. Melanie said she wasn't scared of anything now after what she'd been through. Well, there's still no arguing with Melanie. She wanted a purple wedding dress and that's what she got. She wore a headband with little silk purple flowers, the blond tufts of hair framing her face. She looked absolutely lovely, Leila thought. She wished

Maya could have been there, but the girl was in good hands at Cheever. After what she saw, they decided it would be best for her if she stayed where she felt safe. But Maya told Leila that she wants to move back home soon. It is something to work toward. Something they would do together.

Every few days, Lion comes by with his rake. He insists on raking the grave under the lilac tree himself. Out of respect for Luke, and in gratitude for keeping Melanie alive. That is what Melanie says.

All Leila ever wanted to be was a mother, and maybe that was part of the problem. But at her age, she's becoming an entrepreneur. Hearing Clarisse talk has given her confidence. Leila's about to re-enter the work force. She'll be opening a daycare service. So far she's already got three children signed up and two on the waiting list. What she's really waiting for though is her first trip to California.

"You're gonna be great," Melanie tells Leila, putting Lucas in his stroller.

"You think so?"

"Definitely," says Melanie, with a quizzical smile.

Staring at her daughter, Leila actually believes her. "So are you."

"Well, I'm not getting fake boobs when I get to California," says Melanie, pulling down one strap in order to see her sunburn line. "I think I'm changing my mind about filmmaking."

"You promised you'd try," says Leila. "You said you had a lot of stories to tell."

"I guess. I've died twice. I must really want to be here."

Leila looks at her daughter with her spiky hair and her bird tattoo. "Well, California may surprise you. You may find you like it."

Melanie smiles. "Doubtful."

"I'd bet on it, sweetie."

"What if I hate it there?"

"Then come home."

Leila's already got her plane ticket out to Long Beach for Thanksgiving. By then, Lion has said that the heat won't be quite so suffocating. He's told Leila that even in the heart of the city, the grocery stores are like open-air markets, and you know there's about a million different languages buzzing around. It all sounds so exotic to Leila. She has lived her entire adult life in Canandaigua, in the house where Charlie was almost murdered.

"Well, I guess I can tell you. We're not moving right away," says Melanie, suddenly.

"What do you mean?" asks Leila.

"We need to save money before we go anywhere. And I really want Lucas to know his grandmother."

"Sweetie, don't stay here for me."

Melanie holds up her hand. "Stop. Don't even try to talk me out of it. Lion and I made our decision last night. We're staying one more year."

Don't keep a man in Canandaigua if he doesn't want to stay, thinks Leila, remembering Victor. "Well, only if that is what you both want."

"Lion wants what I want," says Melanie, as though she has read Leila's mind. As Leila sits back in her beach chair, her body shrouded in a long T-shirt, she lets out a sigh. She picks up the pieces of sandwich crust Lucas is throwing into the dirt, and remembers how Luke liked to have his sandwich crust cut off before eating it. She feels a tinge of regret as she stares out at the water, thinking of Charlie, who miraculously survived the shooting, his skull being so hard that the bullet split in two when it hit and exited near the ears. Now he is holed up in a rehab hospital nearby, enduring a painful and slow comeback, Candice never leaving his side, she hears.

The good part is that some feelings die. And it's the bad part, too. Ben Shongo had been a shoulder to cry on that went too far. It was complicated between them. But she never loved him like she loved Charlie. She had ended it with Ben after a short time because he was married. But he kept coming back. And it was then that she knew that he was as lost as she was. He once offered to leave Emily. But Leila had turned him down. Then, when Luke was born, they were inextricably linked. Ben made her promise to call him whenever Luke had the slightest asthma attack. Leila wouldn't take his money or his love, but at least she agreed to accept his help.

Melanie yells from the water, jarring Leila's thoughts. Leila watches her. She's looking for a smooth flat gray stone that's good for skipping. Triangular shapes are the best, she's always believed. She finds one, positions it sideways and flicks her wrist, sending the stone skidding across the skin of the water just as Leila taught her. It dusts the surface, skipping just once.

Melanie comes running back. "Mom, why don't you try? You can still skip stones the best, I bet."

"I couldn't, sweetie. Knowing me I'd probably throw out my back."

"C'mon," Melanie urges, drying off. "See, Lucas wants you to." Lucas wants out of his stroller. Melanie takes his hands and stands him up on the blanket. He bounces at the knees, and then walks on his tiptoes, like a ballet dancer.

"Do it, Mom. Please?" Melanie says.

Leila gets up, smoothing the long T-shirt over her thighs. She smiles at Lion and rolls up her pants. "Well, okay," she says. "Sure, I'll try it."

Leila wades out into the water, the first time she has touched the lake since Luke's death. She hesitates partway out and then stops, startled by its icy waves biting at her shins. She looks down, the water is clear enough to see the smooth rocks below. Leila picks up a flat gray rock and wipes it off with the edge of her shirt. She leans back, and then tosses it sideways into the water. It sails farther than Melanie's did, past the nearby dock. She turns to leave the water and then suddenly the flat stone comes skipping out of the lake, skipping back to her.

Leila is staring out at the hazy image hovering above the water. It first appears as a cloud that begins to move forward and spin, faster and faster, changing shape as it forms the image of a child. The sun is glazing the lake with pink and yellow hues, illuminating the glowing figure of the little boy who emerges out of the haze, his blond hair spun in sunlit curls. Leila gasps as a flood of tears falls across her face. For one crystal moment, he captures her eyes and smiles. He reaches down and scoops up a handful of water and throws it into the air, tossing his head back in laughter as he lets the water shower over him. When he was a baby learning to swim, she would play with him like this to teach him that the water was a safe place.

She is remembering it all, his joyful games, his dimes, the way his paper airplanes went spinning into the air. His obsession with flying.

He reaches one hand out to her just as he used to do when he was sick and he wanted her to know he would be okay. Leila knows she cannot touch him, but she reaches her own hand out to let him know she understands.

And then, he retreats into the haze and vanishes.

The lake is empty now, its waters still, calm. He is gone. She feels it in her bones, and the feeling of longing she has lived with for so long is replaced by a sense of peace. Leila knows Luke will always be with her. She thinks of a small snow angel that appeared early one morning on the lawn, and the branch of the lilac tree waving back and forth even though there was no wind. She stands there, hand on her heart, allowing herself to finally let him go.

Later, when Lion and Melanie are roasting marshmallows under the darkening sky and the ring of fire spreads around the lake, containing it in one glowing circle of light, Leila gets up and wades farther out into the cold water. She is not afraid of the future anymore.

Under her feet, she feels the slip of smooth white stones. She's up to her waist now, but she's plowing through the cold pockets in the water. The evening sky has erupted in a spray of stars. Leila has decided that each star is really an ancestor. She doesn't have to try hard to find hers because they already know who she is and so she always looks exactly at the right one. She turns around and looks at her family. Melanie waves, her face bathed in the fire's glow. Then Leila drops way down into the water, holding her breath, letting her T-shirt billow around her. She opens her eyes. She cannot see a thing below, let alone the face in front of her. Certainly not the silver tomahawk that Two Bears buried on Squaw Island and then years later unearthed on a rainy night in order to return the spirits to the lake before he, himself, passed on.

But when Leila looks up there are little white diamonds and red stars floating on the surface of the water. She wonders how many flares it would take to circle the ocean. Probably one for every person in the world. She tries to imagine the sky so packed with stars that they spill out. All those little white and red lights scattered across the beautiful water. One for every person, living and not.

FROM

ILIE RUBY

AND

AVON A

Writing *The Language of Trees*

I wrote this book over the course of a few years. I researched, wrote and rewrote, as good writers do. I produced a few versions. Okay, I had six versions to be exact. Six 400-page piles of paper sitting in my office on my desk. I carted these versions around with me from office to office during a nomadic time in my life. I felt overwhelmed that I had created so much *paper.* I started writing poetry and painting to take my mind off of these six pink elephants in my office. My painting career began to take off a bit. I just couldn't write anything new. Books become your *babies.* I had to make sure that my book was taken care of, but after a while, I stopped letting anyone read it.

One day, a friend from my writing program at the University of Southern California, announced that she would be visiting from Manhattan and that she wanted to see my new house. (I had just moved, *again.* I had denied her several requests to read my book. She had begged me countless times.) I may have mentioned to her at some point, during a confessional moment between two writers, about my six versions and my inability to choose one. But on the day of her visit, innocently enough, she showed up with a housewarming present—a beautiful vase—and without thinking, I showed her my office, in particular, I wanted her to see the peach-colored walls and my new walnut floors.

When I flung open the door I knew I was in trouble. There, sitting in plain sight, were six manuscripts on top of my packing boxes.

"Is that the book?" she asked me, excitedly, a wild look in her eyes.

I was in shock. "Yes, but—"

Things spiraled out of control from there.

My friend grabbed a manuscript, *Version 3,* to be exact, and tore out of my house with it under her arm, me following, calling her back. She jumped into her car, waved goodbye, and drove out of the driveway, gone with my book, back to New York City with me standing there, outside on my lawn, feeling bereft.

She called me two weeks later. "You stole my book," I said.

"Ilie, this is a beautiful story and it needs to be published. Get it to your agent right away."

I went through the manuscript word by word. It felt exactly right. At that point I realized that all these manuscripts were very much the same, with the exception of a few descriptions here and there. With a sense of relief, I finalized some minor changes and sent it promptly to my agent.

Q&A with Ilie Ruby

The setting of this story is very strong. Did you set out to make it that way?

I grew up in Rochester, New York, and spent my summers in my family's rented cottages on Canandaigua Lake, the birthplace of the Seneca Nation of Indians. Having always been fascinated by nature and the spiritual realm, I have become very attuned to *place*. The gorgeous setting of Canandaigua combined with the Native American folklore, in effect, created a setting that was irresistible, and in the book, became a character in and of itself. This sense of place was very important for me in creating the story, and before I knew it, the *place* became a force that propelled characters into action. Whenever I think of Canandaigua, what stands out most in my mind is an image of huge magnificent willows all around the lake, which of course, inspired the title of the book. I remember walking a dirt road with my younger sister, hand in hand, to our favorite destination point—a little country store where they sold penny candy and rock candy, which in the book became O'Connell's Feed & Grain. I remember stopping to eat sweet peas by the side of the road. I am also a visual artist and have a love of poetry which I am told gives my prose a "painterly" quality. Many parts of this book began as poems about places I have been. In the writing of this story, some of these poems just stood out in my mind and became the fibers I used to weave this story together.

Do you believe in ghosts and the spiritual realm?

I have to give credit to writer Alice Sebold of *The Lovely Bones* for this answer, which I heard during one of her readings. She said something about having a raging optimism about the existence of an afterlife. I do, too. I like the idea that the spirits of people live on and that there is a greater purpose to our lives. Perhaps it is not so much a belief in ghosts but a raging desire to believe in something more. As a child I felt this way. I was always fascinated with folklore and the ghost stories people told. One of the cottages my family rented on Canandaigua Lake was said to have been built on an Indian burial ground. This was likely just fiction. We won't ever know if it was the case for sure, but it sure gave us children a lot of fodder for ghost stories each night around the campfire. The cottage next door was owned by a woman who had thirteen cats. She inspired the character of Clarisse Mellon. She talked often about the history of the place, and told us that someone had died in our cottage long ago, and that the spirit was still in the house. I remember being unafraid of this "ghost." It actually made the place more fascinating to me.

How did you learn about the Seneca Nation of Indians?

You can't live in Canandaigua and not know about Ganondagan and the Seneca Nation of Indians. My family attended festivals and tours there every summer for years. When researching the backstory for this book, I visited the site again. It was interesting to see it from an adult perspective and learn about the issues facing the Seneca, as well as begin to separate fact from fiction. However, there are many versions of the folklore and stories and how this played out around the area where this book takes place.

Why are so many of the male characters so "motherly"?

When first writing this book, in many workshops and writers' groups, it never failed that a man would ask me why most of my male characters were so darn good and nurturing. I had many long discussions with these inquisitors and told them that I could only speak from my own experience. Everything I learned about mothering I learned from the warm and nurturing men I've known throughout my life. For me, the idea of "motherlessness" will always be compelling. The character of Joseph was inspired by a dear friend of mine, Jim, who actually studied in Africa to be a priest, and later met his wife while climbing Mount Kilimanjaro. Though he left the priesthood, he was one of the most sensitive and wise people I have ever known. In many ways he was like a father to me, and his belief in the power of the human spirit was unshakable.

What's with all the hands-on healing and talk about beliefs?
I have always been fascinated with the idea of healers and healing. Growing up, a chronic illness plagued someone close to me and I always wanted to help. I have met many talented people who are capable of amazing things, and I see this fascination only growing over time. Also, I like the idea of a spirit caught between worlds, and am interested in the power of belief. I was a teacher in Los Angeles after the Rodney King race riots of 1992, where I learned that children become what you tell them they are. In *The Language of Trees*, Joseph says, "You ever see a tree that's dying, it's nothing but a bunch of dried-out branches? You can talk to this tree, tell it all about how its leaves are growing green and healthy. Then you sit back and watch how it changes." This statement embodies one of my philosophies in life. In other words, people grow into their beliefs about themselves, and if things don't go right on the first try, well, as you well know by now, I am a firm believer in second chances.

Some History and Folklore

Ganondagan

Located ten miles north of the city of Canandaigua in Victor, New York, Ganondagan State Historic Site claims 611 acres of sacred lands. Dedicated to the education and preservation of Seneca history and culture, the site holds yearly festivals and tours. Along with workshops and lectures, there is a replica bark longhouse that has been constructed in order to mark the site of the French raid of 1687, the spot where 150 longhouses once stood and were decimated in a battle over fur trade. Visitors are welcome any time of year, but summer and fall are the most popular.

To find out more about Ganondagan, please visit their Web site at www.ganonda gan.org.

Facts and Legends

The name Canandaigua comes from the Seneca word *Kanandarque,* which means the "Chosen Spot." The area surrounds the deep and narrow lake, where two sacred hills—South Hill and Bare Hill—stand near the south end. According to legend, the Seneca Nation of Indians was born in a gorge near Clark's Gully, a deeply cut ravine lined with lacy ferns that creep out of the layered shale walls at the foot of South Hill, which rises 1,100 feet above the lake. The gully is little known and unmarked but for the pine, beech, and maple branches that capture the sunlight. The Seneca call South Hill *Nundawao*, where their ancestors emerged, giving birth to a world far more mystical. The Seneca refer to themselves as *Onondowaga*, "people of the great hill." It is said that Canandaigua Lake and the other Finger Lakes were formed when the Creator placed his hand on the earth designating this as the chosen place to live. The region became known as the Finger Lakes, and Canandaigua, in Western New York, was the "little finger."

The legend of Bare Hill is widely known. This 865-foot hill marks the place where a little boy in a Seneca village raised a pet serpent that grew to a monstrous size, eventually devouring all the men and women there. When the young boy shot the serpent with an arrow, it wriggled and writhed down the path in a death struggle, wearing away all the vegetation. As it fell to the shore, it spit out the heads of its victims into the lake. Folks say the large smooth white stones found in the lake today are the skulls of the Seneca people. Geologists call these stones *septaria*.

For years, nothing grew on Bare Hill, not a single tree, bush, or blade of grass. Today, though the snake's path is still clear, the summit is so thick with brush the lake can hardly be seen. A flurry of wildflowers appears in autumn: goldenrod, asters, sweet pea, Queen Anne's lace, daisy fleabane.

The Canandaigua snake monster is another legend, and may well be linked to the Seneca legend of the serpent. Years ago, a steamboat captain was rumored to carry a shotgun on board whenever he sailed Canandaigua. The arcade manager at Roseland Amusement Park told the local newspaper that the snake's head looked like a huge pickle barrel. Then there were countless others who saw it, but never spoke of what they'd seen.

The Seneca

The Seneca Nation is part of the Iroquois Confederacy. Legend has it that several hundred years ago, a Huron prophet sailed across Lake Ontario in a white stone canoe spreading his message of peace to five warring tribes—Seneca, Cayuga, Onondaga, Oneida, and Mohawk—uniting them all under one roof. They became known as the *Haudenosaunee*, or Iroquois. The Seneca, a matriarchal society, were the Keepers of the Western Door, and the Confederacy chose the white pine as its symbol because its needles grow in bunches of five to represent the five tribes. Later, the Tuscarora joined them. They placed the eagle on top of the pine symbol because it could see farthest and yell the loudest. If anyone tried to disturb the great law of peace they'd be warned by its screaming.

Book Group Questions

1. The idea of being "orphaned" and the concept of *rootedness* are themes in this book. Echo talks about her fear of not being tethered to the world and to her life. What are the things that "tether" a person to his or her life? How important do you think rootedness is? Is it created by family ties, or are there other ways to create it? What other characters in the story have similar feelings?

2. How important is setting in this story? The Indian folklore and the history of Canandaigua contribute to the sense of place, almost making the lake become a character in and of itself. How does this affect the mood of the story, and what effect, if any, does the lake have on the people who live there?

3. Joseph says that sometimes you have to tell a dying tree that its leaves are growing and see how it changes. Some might call this lying. What are your thoughts on this? In what ways and to whom does Joseph demonstrate his theory?

4. In the beginning of the book, Echo believes that wishes are dangerous things. Why might she believe this? Do you think that by the end of the story, she still believes this?

5. The theme of second chances is central to this book. Who is given a second chance in the story and how?

6. Echo pushed Grant away when she was seventeen. Why did she do this? How did her past affect her actions and how did time and experience convince her to try again with him? Why does Grant give her a second chance?

7. In the story, many characters, both living and not, return to their past before they can move on. Do you think it is always necessary to go back in order to move on?

8. Leila says that people in a family develop personality traits to compensate for each other. She says Melanie became impulsive because Leila had been so passive. What other characters in the book do you think became who they are to "balance out" their family members?

9. Much has been written about children who are forced to "parent" their parents during times of family hardship. As the primary caretaker of Leila after Luke's death and as the one who dealt with her alcoholic father, Melanie suffered, according to Leila. How do you think this role affected Melanie in both positive and negative ways?

10. Many characters in this book exhibit "magical thinking" or superstitious behavior. For example, Leila believes that if a person wants anything bad enough it is possible to turn the wish into a memory through the repetition of thought, sometimes to the point of no longer wanting it at all. Why might she feel this way? Why do you think certain people develop these ways of thinking? What are some examples of this in the book?

11. While Luke is alive, what is it about Luke that Victor fears the most? When Luke is sleeping in the car after being lost in the woods, the author writes: "The child possessed

so peaceful a presence that it made Victor hurt." What is meant by this?

12. Many characters in the story are lonely or afraid to be alone. This, in turn, causes them to make choices that may not be in their best interests. What are some examples of this?

13. Some of the characters in the book view Emily Shongo as strong. Others view her as weak. What is your opinion? Do you agree that waiting and patience are a life's work?

14. As the "wisdom keeper" in the story, Joseph makes the following statements to Echo: people on earth can do more for each other than spirits can; birds see the world as perfection—that is the reason they can fly; when you're older and look at your life, you can see that everything happened as it was supposed to. Which statement do you agree with the most? How might each of these statements help a person?

15. What does Charlie mean when he says to Leila, "I wasn't a lot of places that I should have been?" Do you think he is referring to being with Candice or being with Leila?

16. Charlie talks about how the Florence Nightingale syndrome ruins the lives of young girls. Do you think many young girls possess this quality? If so, what might cause young girls to feel that they need to fulfill this role? How did it affect Melanie?

17. By not telling Grant about his abilities, was Ben Shongo really protecting Grant from failure, as Joseph says? What would you have advised Ben Shongo to tell Grant?

18. In the story, there is a place between life and death where spirits cross paths, as happens at the end of the book, when Luke, Melanie, and Joseph say their final good-byes. Do you believe in a place such as this?

19. Clarisse says, "Not everything is meant to happen. Some things should stay as they are, just like that, full of possibility. It's wanting them that gives you something to hope for, a reason to get up in the morning and put on a fancy dress." Do you agree?

20. Both Clarisse and Leila say they were ruined by love. Do you agree?